Winter in the
Summer Garden

Winter in the Summer Garden

Natasha Templeton

The acronyms for Soviet institutions mentioned in the novel

NKVD — Soviet security service (1934–43), responsible for all regular and secret police work, security, prisons and concentration camps. The NKVD was the most powerful organ in the Soviet state and the main tool in Stalin's political purges. Other acronyms for the institution were Cheka (1917–22), GPU (1922–34), NKGB (1943–46), MVD (1946–53) and KGB (after Stalin's death). The dreaded names of the successive security chiefs over the years were Dzerzhinsky, Yagoda, Yezhov and Beria.

NEP — New Economic Policy, practised by the new Soviet government during the years of reconstruction, after the devastation of the revolution and civil war. By allowing private enterprise to operate inside the socialist economy, this policy helped to restore the shattered society. In 1928, however, Stalin introduced the first Five Year Plan; all elements of the private economy were abolished and all the privateers, the NEP men, were purged.

ZAGS — the Soviet Registry of Births, Deaths and Marriages, the only institution where marriage ceremonies could be legally performed.

A VINTAGE BOOK
published by
Random House New Zealand
18 Poland Road, Glenfield, Auckland, New Zealand

First published 1999
Reprinted 1999 (twice), 2000

© 1999 Natasha Templeton

The moral rights of the author have been asserted

ISBN 1 86941 369 5

Cover illustration: Debe Mansfield
Printed in Malaysia

For my mother;
For my daughter,
with love

Note on Anna Akhmatova (1888–1966)

On 28 September 1941 the poet Anna Akhmatova addressed the women of Leningrad in a radio broadcast:

> My dear fellow citizens, mothers, wives and sisters of Leningrad. It's more than a month now since the enemy has been inflicting wounds on our city, threatening to capture it. The enemy threatens the city of Peter, the city of Lenin, the city of Pushkin, Dostoyevsky and Blok, a city of great culture and endeavour, with death and disgrace. Like all Leningraders, I can't bear to think of the enemy trampling my city under foot. My entire life has been bound up with Leningrad — in Leningrad I became a poet. Leningrad has been the breath of my poems.
>
> Like all of you today, I firmly believe that Leningrad will never belong to the Fascists. This belief grows even stronger when I see how simply and courageously Leningrad women defend the city, and maintain its everyday human existence.
>
> Our descendants will honour all the mothers of this war, but especially the Leningrad women, who kept watch on the roof during bombardments, ready to protect the city from incendiaries with a boathook and tongs; the volunteer giving first aid to the wounded amidst the debris of burning buildings.
>
> No, a city that has raised such women, can't be defeated. And we, the citizens of Leningrad, enduring these desperate days, know that this land of ours and all its people support us. We feel their concern, care and affection. We are grateful to them, and promise that our courage will not fail . . .

Anna Akhmatova is the most celebrated voice in twentieth-century Russian poetry, and the best loved. Her work is a commentary on the events of her time. She is a witness and chronicler of her people's suffering. In one of her poems in the cycle, *A Wreath for the Dead*, she wrote:

> Only my voice like a flute
> Will sing at your silent funeral feast.

Akhmatova herself shared every step of the cruel history of her contemporaries. In her poem 'De Profundis', she wrote: 'My generation has tasted little honey'. They endured two world wars, the revolution, and the terror of the genocidal purges under Stalin. Like most women of her generation, Akhmatova lost members of her family to the firing squad and prison. In one of the poems from *Requiem* (1935–1940), she wrote:

> This woman is sick,
> This woman is alone.
> Her husband dead, her son in prison.
> Pray for me.

With all those women, Akhmatova stood under the 'red blind wall' waiting for news of her son's fate. And it was there that she promised her fellow sufferers, her sisters, to tell the whole world about their agony.

Akhmatova remained in her beloved Leningrad during the early months of the blockade. An unwilling evacuee, she was flown out with the composer Dmitry Shostakovich and other well-known musicians and artists to the safety of Central Asia. We think of Shostakovich's Seventh Symphony as the requiem for Leningrad, yet it is Akhmatova's poetry that even more poignantly mourns the destruction of that city and its population in the siege.

The poems throughout this novel are all from Akhmatova's published works. The poetry translations are by Nina Templeton O'Leary in collaboration with the novel's author.

The Summer Garden

I want to see the roses in that singular garden,
Framed by the loveliest railing in the world.

Where the statues remember my youth,
And I remember them under the flooded Neva.

In the fragrant stillness among the regal lindens,
I imagine the creaking masts of the ships.

And the swan sails on through the centuries,
Marvelling at the beauty of its double.

And in a deathly sleep rest thousands of footsteps
Of enemies and friends, friends and enemies.

And the pageant of shadows is endless,
From the granite vase to the palace doors.

There my white nights are whispering
About an exalted and secret passion.

And all is lustrous with pearl and jasper
But the source of the light is a mystery.

Anna Akhmatova, 1959

Prologue: Leningrad 1991

Nadezhda is back at the beginning. From the land of the southern lights she has returned to the aurora borealis in Leningrad. It all began here in the Summer Garden, in this park planted by a manic tsar. In these linden trees she heard a crazed voice screaming about the German invasion. The shells came next, the siege and the famine. Then her refugee life began. The flight across time zones and frontiers. Following the retreating Wehrmacht, west into the broken heart of Germany. And later still, after the war, a ship carried her eastward across the ocean to islands floating on the horizon. Aotearoa, fished out of the Pacific swell by Maui, a god of the Polynesian pantheon. That last landfall had become her home.

'Really, Nadezhda? It's unbelievable! You mean you haven't been back!' Her colleagues made it sound like a crime. Their disapproval implied that everyone had visited the new Russia; everyone, that is, except Nadezhda. They recited the achievements of the Gorbachev revolution.

'Glasnost and perestroika have opened the country. Russia is set on a new course. Market economy, nuclear disarmament, privatisation of the land, dismantling of monoliths, freedom of the press, restructuring of institutions. You name it, and it's all underway. Naturally, the Russians can't accomplish everything overnight. But the will is there. There's leadership and determination. It's all happening, or about to happen, mark our words . . .'

Nadezhda has been marking their words, and avoiding arguments. She couldn't confess how terrified she was of going back to that place; even if the Cold War was over, the Berlin Wall had tumbled down, and frontiers had opened into the former satellites of Eastern

Europe. Just now at the Leningrad airport, as she handed over her foreign passport, the expert eyes of the security guard probed into her hidden thoughts. The colour of those eyes matched the ice-blue band on the KGB cap.

Nadezhda has come to Russia armed with an academic brief: to finish her book on the life of the Leningrad poet Anna Akhmatova. When she has done her research, she will return to her real life in New Zealand, her teaching and her husband. As she walks along the streets and stops in front of the houses where the poet lived, she quotes Akhmatova's poems. These are a surer guide to Leningrad than her own memories:

> I want to see the roses in that singular garden,
> Framed by the loveliest railing in the world;
> Where the statues remember my youth,
> And I remember them under the flooded Neva.

Revisiting the past is a solitary journey. Ghosts must be faced alone. How can you tell what might rise to the surface when, from the stingy remembrance, you summon your own discarded self? She has been collecting particles of her childhood, small brittle shells washed up on the beach by the morning tide. She has been trying to breathe the spirit back into them. Forgotten feelings, though, don't respond to a kiss of life. Sometimes, she isn't even sure that the child she is coaxing out of the dark has ever existed. Nadya may be only a fictional character. Nothing of that child remains in the pulse of the woman. Caught in their separate frames, these two are continents and cultures apart. Nadezhda doesn't expect to find a living soul of those who had been part of her life here; not even an echo to guide her back to Leningrad, which has remained mute since the days of the siege. She wonders whether it was fear of the past or fear of pain that has kept her so long from this place.

Leningrad: the sound of the name swells in her imagination. The nine black letters on the airport wall draw her instantly into a magnetic field. Leningrad is the birthplace of her mother. She has family graves in this city. Most important, though, she shared in Leningrad's agony and survived. She didn't die of famine with half of Leningrad's population in the first killer winter of the siege. And since she had a walk-on part in that macabre charade, she is entitled to some gesture of recognition. Surely, a decoration should be bestowed on survivors of a great catastrophe.

On family photographs she has brought back with her, the city is called St Petersburg, and the imperial crest is etched on the back of the cardboard oblongs. The name of this only European among the Russian cities is printed in two alphabets, Cyrillic and Roman, side by side. Yes, she thinks, from the day it was founded, St Petersburg, like me, has been torn between east and west. Mother spoke of her native city variously as Petersburg, Petrograd or Leningrad, depending on the era of her life she happened to be describing; but it was the granite essence of the city, not its volatile identity, that imprinted itself on my mind.

Nadezhda's own identity had changed with each migration; more often than the name of this city where she is walking now on a white night, touching the scars of time. The lustreless light has bleached the pastels of the buildings. Bridges and monuments seem insubstantial, mere shadows of solid objects. She too feels unreal, almost unearthly. There are few people about, except one or two wanderers, like herself, and an occasional native insomniac with a spectral face. She knows that this is a city of doubles. She has seen faces in the street that could have been her own. What is she doing here on a night as long and as light as day?

She knows this city by heart, remembers its monuments from infancy, has forever admired its beauty on photographs, has been returning to old St Petersburg in the poems of Pushkin and Akhmatova, and on the pages of Dostoyevsky's novels. For years Nadezhda has been teaching the poetry and prose that celebrate this haunted capital. Now, standing on the Neva embankment, she wants to impress on the glassy river that her knowledge of the city and its dark history is proof of citizenship. Perhaps she seeks to convince the very stones and the water of this nacreous city that she belongs here.

Leningrad 1941

In the Summer Garden

Early morning in the Summer Garden is peaceful. The mildest breeze may rush in from the Neva, ruffle the crowns of the lindens and then flit away as capriciously as it had arisen. On the gravel path, sparrows have started a raucous war dance. They have ambushed an intruder and are defending their domain. A large solitary bird, the Siberian crow surveys the attack gloomily, caws in protest and, with a heavy beat of wings, takes off into the green unoccupied space. For a while all is silent again. Soon, when the Sunday crowds arrive to occupy the park, children's voices will invade this quiet corner. At present an old woman in black sits there on a park bench, reading a book. A little girl beside her comforts the agitated sparrows with breadcrumbs from a paper bag; small, dark and scrawny, the child resembles the fledglings of the flock.

After a reluctant spring, June weather has finally settled in Leningrad, but the morning air under the linden trees is still fresh and the old woman wraps herself in a shawl. The park is her haven from the noisy living she must endure at home. As so often these days, her mind reaches back to an extinguished civilisation and she will start reminiscing aloud, offering her young companion treasures retrieved from the past. The child has been on some of these journeys before, yet each rediscovery weaves a new spell. As she listens, she will scan the network of wrinkles and memorise a map of old age.

Yes, Nadya, says the grandmother in the singsong of the accomplished storyteller, in my time Sunday was God's day. We kept it holy and spent it in a seemly manner, in church. On the eve of a feast day we always went to confession. The grandmother pauses, and drops her voice to deepen the mood she is setting. When she was young, she loved the mournful chants of evensong, the hush at the end of the service, as the candles melted away and the golden faces of the saints faded into shadows and mystery. You knelt before an icon, and as you waited to confess you gathered up your sins. When you were called, you bowed your head and approached the black cassock. What if he sent you away unforgiven? But the priest covered your head with his embroidered stole, and in the hot darkness of the tent you smelled the garlic on his breath. Go in peace! The priest's voice was heavy with all the sins he had collected from the imperilled souls in his care; whereas you were now pure and weightless, radiant with grace. The old woman crosses herself: Lord have mercy on us. Then she withdraws into a cell of private thoughts, where no one is allowed to follow. Nadya waits outside for her grandmother to return and to continue.

At the liturgy on Sunday you received the gift of the holy eucharist. You stood with all the other worshippers. The choir was a host of angels; their voices melted your soul, sent your spirit soaring into the cupola. The royal gates stood open. The clergy stepped out clad in their gold and silver vestments. But even a talent for storytelling can't express the exaltation of faith, the tenderness she once felt for all of God's creation. In later years all this vanished, the beauty with the ardour. The cathedrals were closed or, like the great St Isaac's, had become museums of atheism. Churches had been turned into workshops or clubs. The lovely St Eugenia, their neighbourhood parish church, was now a student hostel; the hospice and the convent beside it were communal apartments. Her mind drifts back to the god-fearing merchant home, where she grew up, where everyone predicted that she, a handsome girl with a fine dowry, would make a good match. But she had been headstrong, foolish in her choice of husband. She rejected her local suitors, and married a stranger.

She rummages in the dusty storeroom of memories; in the darkness she identifies each recollection by touch, and plucks out another remote, yet sharp, unforgettable moment of her life. 'I was just thinking how the century began . . .' she sighs. 'The war against Japan was followed by the first rumble of revolution. The priest Gapon led a crowd of chanting people to the Winter Palace to see the tsar. They cried out to him, "Batyushka!" But the tsar refused to come out to them. He sent out the Cossacks on their horses to disperse the marchers. Many were trampled to death.' She was in St Petersburg at the time. Her marriage to Yevgeny Shubin and the city would always remain welded together, because her husband was as forbidding as Peter's capital. The children must have a good education, he said, and so her sons and daughters lived in this cold city with their father, while she lived in Yaroslavl and managed the family store. The old house she had inherited from her father had draughty rooms, the floorboards creaked and votive lamps blinked under the holy images. The faces of her ancestors, dark like the icons, glowered from the walls. She couldn't have imagined then that one day she would look as old as those portraits. Her windows opened on the Volga. In the mornings, mist drifted over the water and at sunset the river would be sealed with eighteen-carat gold. Seasons flowed by on the Volga, years drifted past. The revolution came and crushed like an eggshell the solid world she had known. She shouldn't talk so frankly to her grandchild, she thinks. Life is even more dangerous today.

'Good morning, Anna Pavlovna,' says a young mother, holding on to a small protesting hand. The old woman in black may be an identity in the park, but just now she is immersed in the warm current of recollection, and she won't be seduced by the call of the present. A regal nod should discourage anyone from stopping for a chat. 'Where was I?' she turns to Nadya, who is too young to guide her grandmother through the labyrinth. 'Ah, yes, in 1917. That was a terrible year. There was the first revolution in February, and a provisional government with Kerensky at its head. Then another revolution in October — the Bolshevik one. The following year the civil war began.' Civil wars are the worst, she reminds herself sadly. When brother is murdering brother, there's no pity left for anyone else. She looks at Nadya, the latest offspring of revolutions. Like most, an unbaptised heathen, raised on propaganda. What lies in store for her youngest grandchild?

Nadya is swinging her brown legs to the rhythm of a song she has picked up from the state radio. At first she hums the tune and then quietly begins to sing the words.

> Higher and higher and higher,
> We send our birds flying.
> And each propeller echoes
> The vastness of our land.

Anna Pavlovna presses the child's bare knee, 'Not now, Nadya.' Smudged and scratched, the child's skin looks newly created against the parchment of her own hand, stained with liver spots. 'Let's enjoy the Lord's peace.' Bozhyi mir also means God's universe. Nadya falls silent. She remembers that Babushka hates new songs: she likes the old ones about a snowstorm sweeping the street, or a coachman dying in the empty steppes. Whereas Nadya sings anything. Nadya has music in her blood, so her mother has told her. She was born with everyone singing, celebrating, drinking champagne in the first minutes of a brand-new year. And even before she could speak, Nadya sang tunes perfectly, says her mother, who lives in the Caucasus Mountains, at the bottom of the map of Russia. Nadya mostly thinks of her mother in the evenings and cries herself to sleep.

Nadya's given name is Nadezhda, but only her grandmother, when she is displeased, calls her that. The name of a patron saint, she says, should not be trivialised. The Russian language, however, is rich in diminutives, and Nadya answers to Nadyenka (her mother's endearment) or Nadyusha (the name her aunts and uncles keep for her in Leningrad.) Her sister Vera, who is three bossy years older and who has been claiming all kinds of privileges since she started school, rudely calls her Nadka; while poor Nadya is not even allowed to boast that she knows the alphabet better than any schoolgirl. Adults talk smugly about keeping your light under a bushel, and they don't seem to notice how often Vera pinches her younger sister under the table and pulls her hair.

Tsar Peter's Shrine

'Let's go and see the statues,' Nadya proposes. They take turns deciding what to do on Sundays in the Summer Garden. It's democratic, says Babushka, but she often appropriates an extra turn. Last time they were here, because the morning was overcast and river damp is bad for rheumatism, they had to go to the Summer Palace. Again. Whatever the weather, Nadya wants to stay outdoors. Her legs itch to carry her to all her favourite spots in the park. So many, she can't decide in which direction to run first. She loves the pond and the great marble vase standing guard at the top gate. At the river end there's the cast-iron railing that protects the gardens from the Neva. She has been told it's the most beautiful railing in the whole world. The River Neva beyond the railing is not to be trusted. Once a century it pounces on the city and destroys everything in its rage. If you ask her, Babushka will recite from memory the poem about the bronze horseman galloping down the street and across the squares of Petersburg in the great flood of 1824.

There was another disastrous flood exactly a century later, when Nadya's mother was a girl. On the Nevsky the wooden cobbles lifted and floated out to sea. Coffins were washed up in cemeteries. Sofya told her daughters how she ran across the bridge and up the Nevsky, as the furious river rushed behind her, licked at her heels and spilled into the basements of houses. Sofya's story of the flood is embellished with new details in each telling.

Nadya likes the tsar's Summer Palace from the outside. She wonders, though, why it bears this grand name. It's so tiny compared with the Winter Palace, whose pale green facade stretches forever along the embankment. Peter's summer residence, Babushka says, is just a house where the tsar could pretend to be an ordinary citizen. Nadya knows too well the cramped rooms; she could describe each picture on the Delft tiles of the stoves. In the kitchen the empress herself cooked dinner for the tsar and his friends, who sat and smoked in the dining room. Nadya has been here so often that there are no more surprises left to be discovered. Babushka brings her here whenever the weather is uncertain, which in this city it frequently is. Leningrad is a cold sore weeping on the lip of the Neva.

Here in Tsar Peter's shrine you have to wear felt slippers over your shoes so that you shuffle along like a cripple. The wardens here are more ancient than Babushka, and they regard children as potential vandals. Suspicious eyes follow Nadya from room to room, as though she were a terrorist disguised as a child. Last time she was not even permitted to press her nose against the glass cabinet displaying the tsar's collection of curios: shrunken heads, two-headed deformities and wonderful monstrosities preserved in glass jars. The wardens lifted their faded eyebrows, rolled their eyes and shook accusing heads: a grandmother should supervise her charge better than that. Such horrors were unwholesome viewing for the impressionable young. This poor child (they indicated Nadya) was bound to have nightmares and wake up screaming.

In the tsar's bedroom Nadya trails her fingers along the silky tassels of the bed hanging, and observes audibly that the bed is far too short for the giant tsar. How did his fat wife, she wonders, manage to fit in beside him? When they hear Nadya's precocious opinions, the guardians of Peter's historical reputation hiss, 'Nekulturno!'

In the royal assembly of Nadya's imagination the true empress is her grandmother. Tall, majestic in a dark dress, her wiry hair the colour of the pewter candlesticks on the tsar's dining table, Anna Pavlovna reigns over the vassal households of her sons and daughters. She is indulgent with Nadya, and sometimes she even smiles at the childish liberties of her youngest grandchild, but her imperious grip on the rest of the family never slackens; from her adult children she demands and receives old-fashioned homage. When Nadya was born, Babushka had already installed herself as a permanent member of Alexei and Sofya's household in Pyatigorsk. When sister Vera was born (a few years before Nadya herself appeared), Anna Pavlovna made the long journey from the north to the Caucasus Mountains in the south of Russia to get Vera baptised. That's how she explains it to Nadya.

Anna Pavlovna is more truthful with herself as she looks back on that mellow slice of life. How having triumphed in her effort to impart Christian grace to the young family, she decided to settle with them. That was it. She didn't ask them if they wanted her; she simply stayed with Alexei and Sofya. Pyatigorsk, where they lived, was a spa town famous for its mineral springs. The local narzan was recommended for all manner of infirmities to which ageing bodies might be prone. The continental climate of the Caucasus and the health-giving waters she drank regularly at her chosen kiosk eased Anna Pavlovna's rheumatic aches. To be fair, though, having been brought up in the stoical tradition, she hardly ever complained.

There were other attractions tempting her to remain in the south. Alexei's apartment was spacious, luxurious even, and on closer inspection Sofya seemed a malleable daughter-in-law. That was in the beginning. A more delicate imperative, Anna Pavlovna knew, was that for the time being she had exhausted the hospitality of other filial households, especially that of Alexandra, her eldest daughter in Leningrad. In any case, Alexei, her youngest, was the favourite son. Unlike her other children, he didn't stand in awe of her. His irreverent humour amused her; she even allowed herself to laugh at his jokes. But then she struck trouble. It was her fault, she had to admit it to herself later. She had always been driven by her stubborn instinct rather than good sense. She couldn't help setting her own rules in the young household. When she didn't get her own way, when Sofya rejected her advice, Anna Pavlovna made her disapproval known. Her attempt to reform her daughter-in-law, however, had been a mistake. Alexei was familiar with his mother's iron will, which made an easy target for his teasing, but Sofya couldn't live with the ominous silences. Alexei sided with Sofya. One morning at breakfast, he put a train ticket to Leningrad in front of his mother. 'You'll be happier with Alexandra,' he said.

Anna Pavlovna had never before faced such naked insubordination. This was rebellion. Needing God to witness the ingratitude of her children, she went out looking for an open church. Hopeless. The Soviet state had closed them all. She had to capitulate and returned home that evening with an olive branch. From then on she kept her views about housekeeping to herself.

Anna Pavlovna had brought with her to the Caucasus all her valuables: a trunkful of pre-revolutionary finery that had survived the years of barter, and a few remaining pieces of jewellery, craftily sewn into the lining of her most-worn everyday jacket and in the waistband of her house-skirt. Unpacking the four suits in English worsted and two fur coats, she gave the fox fur to Sofya. The last time Anna Pavlovna wore the special-occasions corset with her tailored suit was at Vera's christening, a solemn rite conducted in secret. The ancient priest nearly dropped the baby in his poor palsied hands. Even without the help of whalebone, Anna Pavlovna always carried herself with a proud posture; she taught Nadya to hold her head high in what she called the Shubin way. Alas, Nadya remained a heathen. By the time she was born, all the priests had been deported to Siberian camps, or shot, and the churches had been desecrated. Anna Pavlovna's own precious family icons were hidden in the attic.

Between the Past and the Future

In later years Sofya remembered a great deal about her mother-in-law, but she couldn't satisfy Nadya's curiosity. She had few answers to Nadya's many questions about her grandmother. Yes, she was remarkable; Alexei used to call her a cabinet minister. But as to the year of her birth? Well, she must have been around seventy at the time of Vera's christening. No, she must have been older than that but she still wore a corset. Anna Pavlovna had always seemed a very old woman to Sofya, who had no experience of the process of ageing, whose own parents had died young. As she grew older, Sofya sometimes forgot her age and pouted prettily like a young girl, though the expression no longer suited her tired face.

In the photographs of that Gogol Street era, it's Vera who always clings to her mother. With their ringlets and eyes of a lost angel, these two look alike. Nadya watches the world from her grandmother's arms. There's a group of the kommunalka mothers and their children taken in the yard. A coterie of subjects with cropped hair and peasant faces surround Empress Anna Pavlovna with Princess Nadya in her lap. These two faces are dark, solemn, Byzantine.

'When was Babushka married?' asked Nadya. Again, Sofya couldn't answer. She knew that Anna Pavlovna had raised six children. The eldest, Pavel, was killed in the First World War. The next son, Vladimir, died of a broken heart, because his mother forbade him to marry the woman he loved. Anyway, that's how the family legend went. Alexei was a late child, an afterthought. There were also three older daughters.

As for grandfather Shubin, unsmiling in his silver oval, he was with a Petersburg merchant firm and died of the revolution. This seemed a ubiquitous cause of death at the time, which could describe anything from perishing through famine to vanishing without trace; or, like Sofya's parents, dying *from the Spanish flu that raged all over the globe after the war.*

Nadya's quest for the truth went on stubbornly. 'But Mama, you must know more. You and Babushka lived together for years.'

'Oh, Nadyenka, you ask too many questions. Must you know everything?' How could Sofya explain to her curious child that she and Anna Pavlovna had lived uneasily, in a state of diplomatic truce? Their bond was Alexei; all else caused disagreement. Sofya refused to call her mother-in-law Mother; she addressed her formally by name and patronymic. In later years, when she was mourning the loss of the family, when she was fleeing from Russia, a refugee, alone with her children, Sofya regretted most of all her war with the old matriarch. 'I used to buy sweets for you children, but I never offered any to Anna Pavlovna. Yet, I knew very well how she adored sweets.'

She tried to distract Nadya from her obsessive questioning. 'Do you remember our first apartment in Gogol Street? That's where you were born, at home.' How could any of them forget Number 20? Its imposing yellow facade, and the solid gate opening into the cobbled courtyard. At the back of the house, and perpendicular to it, stretched the black wing. Once it would have been the servants' quarters, the kitchen and storerooms; now it was a genuine Soviet communal apartment.

The Shubins had a separate grand apartment in the main residence. Outside the windows chestnut trees blossomed and shed their leaves with the changing seasons. They could see the eternal snow on the mountain peaks. 'That was before the purges, when your father had an important government post.' And all the privileges that went with it. 'When they arrested him' — that was the second, the final arrest — 'we were evicted.'

Sofya, Anna Pavlovna and the little girls were moved into the dingiest room in the black wing. Their new window looked out on a corner of an abandoned herb garden, a wild tangle of weeds with a few clumps of self-sown tobacco. In the dark summer night the nicotianas glowed white-hot like stars. Their spicy scent filtered into the room, and clung to Sofya's hair until morning.

Wings of Steel

Back in the gardens, summer heat has vaporised the clouds, the sky is a glaze of blue, and Babushka has decreed that it's ice-cream weather. We're going to buy the most giant morozhenoye. Thin cries of excitement beckon them towards the kiosk, and there is the striped awning behind the tree trunks playing hide-and-seek with the white sideflaps. A swarm of Sunday-best children are buzzing around the ice-cream vendor, who dispenses the frozen nectar with the competence of Solomon and the precision of a pharmacist. The woman is dressed in hygienic overalls, and a white pilotka is perched on top of her permed head. The pilot's cap reminds Nadya of her unfinished Air Force song, and she takes it up again as she waits her turn.

> Stalin gave us
> Steel arms for wings,
> And a throbbing motor
> For a heart.

People are staring at the little girl who is so boldly singing about Stalin. Alarmed to hear that splendid, that awesome name uttered without due deference, though in a sweet little voice. In times like these, you can't be too careful. It's dangerous even to be seen close to this kind of sacrilege. Why doesn't the old woman hush the child?

Anna Pavlovna tugs at the back of Nadya's collar, and instantly regrets her action. Oh, let them think what they please. Why should she reprimand her grandchild in public? She defies the critics silently: Yes, look at my Nadya. Her knees bear the scars of rash enthusiasms. Even now, as she sings, she's picking at a drying scab. Compare her with your pudding-faced darlings who cling to your skirts, grizzle and pout. Your little girls with satin butterfly bows in their hair, and little boys scrubbed too clean to run about. My Nadya is as free as a bird, proclaims Anna Pavlovna in silent triumph.

The children at the ice-cream kiosk are unaware of this fleeting tension that has unsettled the adults. Deciding on the ice-cream you want is a more than serious matter. You have only one chance to pick the best, the most delicious of all. No, thanks, you don't want the one you had last Sunday. Yes, it was nice, but today you want a different kind; like that one over there, which the boy with the big ears is licking. Such a blissful look on his face.

Nadya balances on tiptoe, a baby stork stretching its neck out of the nest. 'I'm going to have a chocolate bomb,' she announces in a confidential whisper. In the queue it pays to be secretive, in case other children hear you and decide to have the same, and then there mightn't be any left when your turn comes. But she's lucky, chocolate-coated bombs are not in vogue this Sunday. The woman in the pilotka hands Nadya her bomb: dark-brown, snow-tipped, sweating tiny beads of moisture over the chocolate surface. Nadya clutches the stick with longing fingers, and begins to lick it. Around her mothers are admonishing their young: 'Don't drop it. Watch your dress. Let me hold it for you . . .'

Nadya's grandmother doesn't have to remind her of such obvious things. She says instead how proud she is of Nadya's accomplishments. What other four-year-old can tie her shoelaces so competently, and climb the six flights of stairs to their apartment, with no adult helping her? Can you imagine a girl as independent as Nadya dropping her ice-cream? Dizzily content, Nadya hums the obsessive tune, while the icy sweetness burns her lips, and her frozen tongue can't shape the words about Stalin's steel wings.

'Good, is it?'

'Mm,' Nadya moans. 'But what about you, Babushka? Have one too.'

'Not today.'

'Then have a lick of mine. Please. There's plenty for us both!'

Anna Pavlovna admires the generous impulses of her grandchild, but gives a definitive shake of the head. 'No, thanks, ice-cream is not good for old people like me.'

How can her grandmother refuse this mouth-numbing pleasure? As she reflects on the peculiarities of adults, Nadya is seriously considering the next angle of attack on the chocolate bomb. It's a problem of pure physics, where to take the first balancing bite. In the meantime, Anna Pavlovna is steering her absorbed grandchild away from the crowd. Steadily, past 'Grandpa' Krylov's monument, where lessons always go on, as children swing on the chain and parents eagerly recite the fables carved around the bronze plinth.

'Look, Petya, there's the Wolf and the Lamb! We know the words of that fable, don't we?' A mother starts declaiming, 'On a hot day a lamb was drinking at a brook; but as ill luck would have it, a hungry wolf chanced to be passing by . . .'

'Tanya, Tanya, do you remember the one about the dragonfly and the ant? "The darling dragonfly sang all summer long, but in an eye-blink winter came. Crushed by an evil fate, she crawls to the ant's house: Cousin, help me . . ."'

No fables for Nadya. Her eyes are fixed on white flashes of marble at the end of the path. These are her statues. Around them linden trees bow and whisper like old women at evensong.

The Fate of the Grande Armée

On grey Leningrad mornings Aunt Alexandra carried Nadya to the china cabinet and waited for her to choose a cup she wanted to drink from at breakfast. Nadya's fingers brushed the fine edges of the china shells, traced the delicate patterns shining through the translucent bulges. Every morning aunt and niece played their special game. Nadya's hand would reach out to the high forbidden shelf, and her aunt cried out in mock alarm, 'Not the Napoleon cups, Nadyusha!' Aunt Alexandra had a soft hesitant voice; she even looked frightened, as if Nadya had already dropped one of those precious pieces of china on the parquet, and they were witnessing the ultimate disaster of the Napoleon set shattered in hundreds of tiny shards.

The aunt's accomplished acting delighted the child; she would have liked a second run, but knew she would have to wait till the next morning. Nadya clapped her hands and laughed, 'I was only joking.' And her aunt concluded the game with an expression of exaggerated relief: she was so glad, said the nervous half-smile, because for a moment she had almost believed Nadya.

Aunt Alexandra did not have to act anxiety; all she had to do was to remain her usual fearful self. A worried woman with a thin face, she looked like an unfinished sketch of her regal mother. They were the same height but Alexandra apologetically hunched her shoulders. Nor had the daughter inherited her mother's fine complexion and thick hair. When Anna Pavlovna unpinned her hair in the evening, its shiny chainmail covered her back and shoulders. In her mother's presence, Alexandra forgot that she was a perfectly competent woman in her forties with her own grown-up daughter. She hesitated over words and deferred to Anna Pavlovna's opinion.

But then, they nodded sadly behind her back, poor Alexandra has had problems with her nerves for many years.

In any case, Nadya would never have asked for one of the Napoleon cups, although admiring their history and beauty was a daily observance. The 1812 commemorative set, finely crafted in the imperial china factory, had been a Voskresensky family heirloom for several generations. Uncle Dmitry Voskresensky, Alexandra's husband, wore a brown uniform, with the engineer's insignia on his collar.

It was a full set, twelve cups and saucers, accompanied by a rotund coffee pot, cream jug and sugar bowl. Gold-rimmed, the cups were deep, deep blue on the outside and snow white inside. Each piece of china was decorated with a different picture framed in a gold medallion. Nadya had been told the story of 1812 many times, knew how Napoleon's Grande Armée had marched into Russia and we-the-Russians set fire to Moscow to drive the French out. It all sounded brave and glorious, but aunt and niece were forever disturbed by what they saw in the miniatures framed by the gold ovals. On the coffee pot Moscow was in flames, and Napoleon, his hand tucked into a grey lapel, the tricorn jammed low over his frowning brow, gazed at the ancient Kremlin towers black against the burning sky. If you looked long enough at the emperor's face, you saw his expression change from pride to regret. Nadya couldn't forgive him the sack of Moscow, but she was moved by the sadness of Napoleon's rout. In the ovals, hand-painted horses lay in snowdrifts, their frozen legs pointing to the sky. French cuirassiers, their blue coats ragged, huddled against the Russian blizzard. Our brave peasants pitchforked them, our brave soldiers in their dark green coats shot them. We-the-Russians were forever victorious, and they-the-French forever perished. As they paid their daily homage to Napoleon's tragedy, Nadya and her aunt always found some new detail on the china set, and a fresh patch of untilled compassion in their hearts.

'Good morning, comrade Emperor,' Nadya whispered, embarrassed that she should be feeling sorry for a foreign invader, and hid her face in the folds of Alexandra's neck. Her fingers stroked the aunt's straight hair. With a playful tenderness Nadya was trying to compensate for her aunt's failings. Alexandra did not have Anna

Pavlovna's good looks, nor her majestic bearing, yet her skin was softer. Small for her age, Nadya sat lightly astride her aunt's hip. She planted butterfly kisses on the scrubbed cheek, and inhaled the clean smell. Her aunt and soap were faithful companions; Alexandra washed her hands all day long.

'Well, Nadyusha, what have you chosen this morning?' Alexandra had the kindest voice in the family, even kinder than Nadya's mother's, if such sacrilege could ever be spoken aloud.

'The birds.' Nadya pointed to the yellow cup with green and orange plumed parrots. To fetch the cup from the shelf, Alexandra loosened their embrace and set Nadya down. Her movements were deliberate, but her hands were shaky, and she didn't trust them. With the history lesson behind them, they could now drink tea and eat fresh bulochki, with butter and cherry jam, baked each morning in the bulochnaya on the ground floor. The warm smell of breadrolls wafted up to their open window, and with it the sounds of summer. Down in the street trams clattered and squealed on the lines. Children played noisy games in the square. The large apartment building they lived in stood on a windy corner; the locals called it 'the house of the seven winds'.

The Voskresenskys shared the apartment with four other families. Aunt Alexandra, with Uncle Dmitry and their daughter Nina, had two rooms next to the kitchen. The wide corridor was the children's meeting place; here they played among abandoned pieces of furniture, too bulky for the crowded rooms. The old mahogany wardrobe and chest of drawers were splendid hiding places. As Babushka pointed out, two rooms were a luxury in these hard times, when most families were lucky enough to have one room to themselves. Babushka, who had inspected all the Shubin households on her extended visits, had the experience and the moral authority to make comparisons, and she also felt obliged to count unappreciated blessings. At least Anna Pavlovna's criticism was even-handed: she grumbled against each member of her family in turn. Since she had made her own permanent home in the Caucasus, with Alexei and Sofya, she left them out of her commentary.

Aunt Alexandra, who never contradicted, would mutter behind the matriarch's back, 'Mother had a house in Yaroslavl so large that the regional Soviet commandeered it for their offices. And there she goes on about our luxury living.'

Grandmother and aunt agreed on one thing — Nadya's bedtime. The child had to be tucked in by seven. In the summer it never got dark. Leningrad days went on and on, eventually fading into a white night. The late sun streamed into the window as Nadya said her prayers. Grandmother had taught her to pray, but Aunt Alexandra supervised the nightly devotion. The Shubins were heirs to an established religious tradition. Neither the revolution nor its offspring, the atheistic state, could shake their belief in the importance of prayer. They also knew how to conceal religious observances from their neighbours, and hid their family icons, some of which were disguised as old paintings in ornate frames. All this was achieved with a subtlety worthy of their ancestors, the canny Volga traders. But, to their lasting regret, Anna Pavlovna and Alexandra had to throw away the silver votive lamps, which used to burn day and night under the icons in the houses of merchants.

The child's bedtime and the prayers were in Alexandra's domain. Nadya would begin her detailed litany with her father, who was in Siberia, though she didn't know the name of the town. She had a feeling that he was not expected back immediately, but didn't ask. This silence around Alexei's fate was a tighly drawn curtain, a door permanently locked, not a subject discussed in front of the children. Next Nadya prayed for her mother, alone in Pyatigorsk, working at her job, while Babushka and Nadya (oh, yes, and Vera, of course) were 'having a summer holiday in Leningrad'. Thoughts of her Mama brought on instant sadness: she missed her most in the evenings. Later, when they left her alone in the room, Nadya would weep.

'Ask the Lord to bless your sister Vera,' prompted Aunt Alexandra.

'Lord, bless my sister,' who was probably still up, having a lively time with their cousins, who were older and never went to bed. Then came prayers for Babushka. Her aunt had said once that Babushka surely had a special relationship with God, though it was hard to believe that even the Almighty would feel at ease with Anna Pavlovna Shubina. Blessings were invoked on the Voskresenskys, in order of seniority: Uncle Dmitry, Aunt Alexandra and then Nina.

'Shall I pray for Slava too?' she asked. And although her aunt looked flustered and tried to hurry her through the rest of the prayers, Nadya did include Nina's friend Slava, who had promised to teach Nadya to swim. Finally she prayed for her Aunt Katya (Mama's sister) and their whole family: Uncle Misha, and Ada and Kira, the musical cousins. Those lucky things who stayed up all night together with her sister Vera.

'Sleep tight, Nadyusha.' The aunt made a sign of the cross over the child and kissed her forehead. Her lips were hastily replaced with a hand: 'Your skin is hot. Are you feeling well?' Aunt Alexandra always panicked over people's health. She decided that the blanket could come off on such a warm night, and folded it down. 'Sleep, my little one. Sweet dreams.'

'Babushka said we're going to the Summer Garden tomorrow,' Nadya offered generously: 'Let's all go together, you and Uncle Dmitry and Nina and Slava. It'll be another lovely summer day . . .'

'We'll see. Morning is wiser than the evening.' Her aunt spoke in proverbs, like grandmother. She stroked the child's bare arms, brown against the white sheet.

'Oh, please, don't pull the curtain,' Nadya's white enamelled cot stood by the window; if only she would wake up in the white night and see the world touched up with fairy-tale silver. Now the brass knobs on her cot held reflections of the room, objects bloated into distorted shapes. Her cot was a cage. Nadya was a wild creature caught behind bars. 'Please, let me go,' she begged the invisible keeper. 'I promise to grant you three wishes . . .' Furniture around her was shaping fantasies. The stack of pillows was an Egyptian pyramid in the Nile kingdom of Alexandra's double bed. In the corner of the dining room, Nina, a kidnapped princess, was imprisoned behind a partition. Actually it was Babushka, the guest, who occupied Nina's bed now. Nina slept on the sofa; she didn't mind it at all, she said, it was an adventure.

The mammoth wardrobe winked at Nadya across the room; its oval mirrors always caught her misdeeds in triplicate. She had no strength left to turn her uncle's desk and her aunt's dressing table into mysterious objects, but the intricate tapestry of the chaise longue flickered before her sleepy eyes like a magic carpet flying above the vast Russian plain, along unending rivers to the mountains of Caucasus, where her mother waited for her. 'Mama,' she cried out, 'I want Mama.'

The Secret Shame of Dmitry Voskresensky

> He liked three things in this life,
> The singing at Vespers, white peacocks,
> And threadbare maps of America.
> Didn't like it when children cried,
> Didn't like tea with raspberry jam,
> Or female hysterics.
> . . . And I was his wife.
>
> From the book *Evening*, 1910

In the main room, they were drinking tea under the tasselled apricot lampshade, its circle of light holding the three adults in a rosy embrace. Anna Pavlovna and Dmitry Voskresensky, her son-in-law, preferred tea glasses fitted into silver holders; Alexandra drank out of one of her precious china cups. Even though she was married to a Voskresensky, she observed the old custom, which decreed that tea in a glass was for men. By virtue of her seniority, Anna Pavlovna could have a glass or a cup, whichever she chose. Alexandra clung to the Shubin commandments: she feared God and honoured her parents.

Anna Pavlovna looked across the table at her daughter and, as so often, thought how little Alexandra resembled either of the parents. Her looks were a feeble imitation of her mother's, and she had none of her father's cold calculation. Anna Pavlovna loved her daughter, naturally, but she couldn't overlook Alexandra's faults. Her hysteria was a kind of feeble-mindedness. All that hand-washing and those obsessive terrors of hers. Anna Pavlovna traced with her little finger the silver filigree of the glass-holder and thought how lucky Alexandra had been in her marriage. She would never really understand why Dmitry remained devoted to his anxious wife. But then, he was a decent person, a kind one, a man of the old intelligentsia.'

Alexandra was now worrying about Nadya. 'The child prays for Alexei every night, but she never asks about him. That's not healthy.'

When she disapproved, Anna Pavlovna had a special way of looking down her Byzantine nose. 'Sofya wanted to tell the girls the truth but I was adamant that we should not.' She slammed the negative with the palm of her hand on the tea table. This emphatic gesture implied that her daughter-in-law was not a sensible person either. 'Anyway, I ask you, whose truth? Sofya's truth or . . .' Even an empress had to drop her voice to a whisper for the fearsome name — Stalin's. She looked into Alexandra's face. 'And what can you tell Nadya? That her father is an enemy of the people? Or would you like to explain to her what it means to be a victim of the purges?' Anna Pavlovna noticed Dmitry's nervous expression, and stared back at him defiantly.

'The least said the better,' he said mildly. A lecturer in the School for Army Engineers, Dmitry was not dogmatic in his domestic circle. As a rule, he listened carefully, and was uncritical in family discussions. Now he looked worried. Was he uneasy about the way Anna Pavlovna spoke, or what she would say next? His bald head was sweating with tension.

'Dear Lord, will they ever release poor Alexei?' sighed Alexandra. The fate of her brother tormented her all the more because her own husband had been spared when so many people had perished in the mass arrests all over the country. When the military purge got under way, they rounded up most of the officers, including Dmitry. Oh, how she prayed, how she prayed! And the Mother of God brought Dmitry back after a month in the Kresty. Even the name of that prison was sinister: an echo of the crucifixion, of Golgotha, a place of the doomed and the dead. After Dmitry's release from the prison, she had felt crucified. Even now she was tormented by guilt and gratitude. Emotions were clearly charted on Alexandra's tragic face.

Dmitry frowned. He knew very well where such conversations led, to tears and valerian drops. Although she was not aware of it, his wife's thin fingers were drumming a nervous tattoo. He covered her hand firmly with his own; the beat stopped. Alexandra raised her eyes to him. 'There must be hope.' He spoke only to her loyal eyes, forcing a note of conviction into his voice, but to him the words tasted and sounded flat.

Anna Pavlovna was puzzled by the scene she had just witnessed. She couldn't fathom her daughter's excessive anxiety, nor Dmitry's efforts to stop the conversation. Everybody was fearful these days for their own life, for family members who were in prison, but Alexandra behaved as though her troubles were greater than most. For heaven's sake, she still had her husband, unlike poor Sofya, who was without Alexei. To remind Alexandra of her blessings, she began talking about Sofya's hardships in Pyatigorsk, the long hours she worked at her job.

'She's grateful to have the job. She tries to please, works harder than anyone else. Do you know how many employers turned her down when she was looking for work? They'd demand her labour book for the past year, and as soon as they saw that she'd been in prison, they were no longer interested in her diploma . . . Yes, that's what happened to all the wives of enemies of the people.'

Dmitry was now resigned to this disastrous conversation. Wherever you turned you had to cross a minefield. He should be training sappers, not engineers. These days, manoeuvring, knowing how to detect and defuse landmines in daily life was more important than building bridges and fortifications. There were alarming rumours about, though it was difficult to trace their source. That's how he had to report three days ago: 'Source unknown.' The thought of his last visit to that dreaded building made him feel unclean, as if he had surfaced from a sewer. The stench and the shame clung to him as he walked past the bland facade on his way to work. Every day. Once a month he entered, a criminal creeping in late at night. Walking up the stairs, hoping never to meet anyone he knew, he knocked on the blind door and inside Shamokhin greeted him. 'We know everything, citizen Voskresensky. You're not our only informant.'

He suspected that, like him, some of his colleagues might have been forced to inform, but this realisation was of little comfort. He was tormented just then by recent arrests. Safronov had been taken at work, he thought, and Belkin. Had this been his doing? He was not going to think about that, not now. He forced his obedient mind to switch to military matters — the whispered war rumours he'd been hearing. All of them in uniform understood that the threat was real. 'Hitler's gathered a massive force on our western frontier. While our own defences are still unfinished. Our famous Stalin line is deep in the interior. In places a hundred kilometres away from the Brest border.' He knew all this, he had been on the planning team for its construction. Even at the time, he was uneasy about its positioning, its distance from the western frontier. Since then Poland had been divided between the Soviet Union and Germany and their border had been shifted even farther west to Brest. He smiled unhappily, 'Our German allies!', and felt a mad urge to yell at the confident matriarch, tell her that war might break out any moment. Instead, he scratched his head as he always did when he was agitated. His sparse greying hair was cropped military fashion, so short that it made him look bald, and older than his forty-five years. He took a grip on himself and asked politely, 'When did you last hear from Alexei?'

'We received his letter on the eighth of March,' his mother-in-law answered in her lilting voice. 'He thanked us for the parcel, especially for the padded jacket we had made for him. Sofya and I quilted it by hand. His valenki had worn out and he was pleased with the new pair of felt boots we sent him.'

Alexandra responded with a small sad laugh. 'How amazing that you should receive his letter on the eighth of March, his birthday. A present for you both on Women's Day!'

'There was no such nonsense as a women's day when Alexei was born.' Anna Pavlovna was severe; she did not encourage interruptions. 'Alexei's been ill, though the sentence about that was scratched out. Censored. Well, you know how weak his lungs are. He suffers badly from the cold. He says the winter temperatures had been so low that his brain cells were frozen.'

Alexandra brought out some home-made jam to comfort them all or to celebrate her brother's resilient humour. She passed the jar round the table. 'You must try this one, Mother; wild strawberries. Last summer Nina and I spent a whole day berrying in Rybatskoye. Wouldn't it be nice to go out together one Sunday, the whole family, and pick berries for next winter? Mushrooms too. How I love mushroom hunting, don't you, Mother?'

Anna Pavlovna took a spoonful of jam and nodded, 'Yes, it's

good.' Could it be Alexandra's cooking that nourished her husband's devotion? she asked herself. Examining her pale daughter, she decided to voice an irritation that had bothered her all evening. She did not approve of her granddaughter going out with that Slava Lukyanov and couldn't resist reminding Alexandra and Dmitry of her feelings. 'Nina is late again.'

'She's with her classmates celebrating the end of exams,' said Dmitry. 'I thought we all knew that.' Even though Dmitry could not protect his wife from her mother's criticism, he would not allow attacks on his only child. 'Nina's twenty-three, Anna Pavlovna. A fourth-year student! Next year she'll qualify as a doctor. We can't dictate to her, interfere in her personal life.'

Anna Pavlovna was ready for battle, 'And who'll be responsible for her life, if her parents won't interfere?'

'Just the other day, Dmitry was telling me about his own graduation.' Alexandra was bravely changing the subject, deflecting her mother's irritation from Nina. 'Has he ever told you how they walked all night, across bridges, along the river, singing, reciting poetry outside Pushkin's house?'

Dmitry's face grew brighter, lost its haunted look. Wonderful days! How well he remembered them. But two months after the graduation, he and his fellow students were called up. He couldn't bear to think about his friends dying in the Masurian swamps. 'Come, think of something cheerful!' he ordered himself. How he recited Pushkin on the Fontanka, in front of the house where the poet had lived and died with a duel bullet in his gut. An agonising death. How gloomy his thoughts were tonight!

In the bedroom the child called out in her sleep, 'Mama, I want Mama!'

Alexandra dropped the jam spoon. 'Poor little thing. When I kissed her goodnight, her forehead was burning.'

Anna Pavlovna pushed back her chair, stood up and straightened her back. 'I'll go to her.' She walked into the shadow of the doorway, and they heard a softer voice comforting the child, 'There, there, Nadya, it was only a dream.'

Talking to the Statues

In the Summer Garden, Nadya played and Anna Pavlovna sat reading on the green bench; she could still read without glasses, though she had to hold the book at arm's length. Nadya, who had recently mastered her alphabet, could spell out the gold letters tooled on the leather cover of deepest blue: W-A-R-A-N-D-P-E-A-C-E.

When she read, Anna Pavlovna's eyes did not lift from the page. Her concentration could be a nuisance if Nadya needed an audience for one of her games. But, on the other hand, Babushka never forgot anything. She could remember the titles and names of all the authors she had read; she knew long poems by heart. When she recited Lermontov or Pushkin in her Volga voice, you could listen to the magic all day.

Nadya's playmates on the block were never taken to the Summer Garden. These deprived children from the house of the seven winds, who companionably called her Nadka, didn't even know what they missed. They, poor things, played ordinary games of tag and hopscotch; sometimes, the boys played war and, as a special favour, allowed the girls to be nurses. But here in the Summer Garden Nadya's imagination was let out of the cage. Her favourite game was talking to the statues. She had perfected the technique and strictly followed the rules she had invented herself. Nadya had started playing this game as a little child in her home town, Pyatigorsk, with the statue of Lermontov, the poet, who had met his violent end in a duel on a neighbouring mountainside.

Nadya and the poet Lermontov held intimate conversations. He was like the prince of the fairy tale, with jewelled eyes. She was his eyes and ears, his messenger, his little swallow who reported to him everything that went on around. She spoke to him in a silent language, without moving her lips. Cautiously, because no one could be trusted with the secret game; especially not her sister Vera, who would have trumpeted it about, and destroyed the magic. The sad poet and now the classical statues in the Summer Garden spoke to Nadya with their marble lips sealed.

Nadya hated Saturn's bloodthirsty activity; she begged him to spare his children. Greedily devouring one of his poor little boys, the god only grunted in reply. She would not confide her distress to Babushka, who was condescending about marble idols. The atheistic legislation of the state had spared Nadya the torments of a Christian conscience and admitted an egalitarian spirit into her pantheon, in which Christ and Saturn enjoyed equal status.

Since her grandmother was a suspect source of Greek and Roman mythology, Nadya had to draw on the expertise of her cousin Nina, who was willing but rarely available. Nina, a medical student, was in love with a fellow student. He was a champion swimmer, had red hair and a triumphant name: Slava meant glory. Babushka did not approve of Slava. Aloud, she said that Nina was too young to be seriously involved, that she had her life ahead of her, but privately, she muttered that Slava was the incarnation of the red devil. In Babushka's spectrum of politics and religion the colour red didn't have welcome associations.

On her occasional walks with the two students, Nadya gained an insight not only into the gods of antiquity but also into the nature of love. Freed from the company of their peers, away from the crowded family apartment, Nina and Slava were frolicking lambs in the green meadows of the Summer Garden; like ten-year-olds, they chased each other down the geometrical avenues. Slava pursued the ticklish Nina until she collapsed, helpless, in a fit of giggles, and he would revive her with slow restorative kisses. Whenever they thought Nadya was absorbed in her statues, they kissed behind tree trunks, embraced in the uncut grass. Nadya tactfully pretended not to see them, while she developed an acute perception of passion. She dwelt thoughtfully on the naked gods and goddesses: the sleeping Eros and his adoring Psyche looked remarkably like Slava and Nina.

With Babushka there were other compensations. First of all,

their visits to the Summer Garden were regular. Only the most inclement weather kept them at home, and even then their walk would not be cancelled, only postponed. Raised in the iron discipline of her generation, Anna Pavlovna did not neglect promises and obligations. She was also a treasure trove of poems and a living dictionary of quotations. As particular in her memorising as in her social obligations, Anna Pavlovna had once, for her own enjoyment, learnt whole chapters by heart. This very morning she recited *Russian Women*, a long poem about the wives of Decembrists, who followed their husbands to the salt mines of Siberia. She muttered that it was apt for the present times.

The old woman with her proud back and the humming-bird child, so like her in colouring and expression, walked among the legion of marble busts and statues.

'There's a hundred of them,' Nadya quoted her radiant cousin, 'almost.' Anna Pavlovna let that pass. She did not openly disapprove of Nadya's obsession with classical antiquity, but she wished her older granddaughter, Nina, who should have more sense, would stop filling the child's head with legends of the Greek and Roman deities. Graphic details of lascivious and bloodthirsty activities may have been appropriate knowledge for medical students, she conceded, but hardly for an imaginative child. Yet she said nothing for the time being. No, she must not inhibit the younger generation, she reminded herself. Her memory of the unfortunate clash with Alexei, when she tried to instil her values in her daughter-in-law, were still painful. That episode had taught her a late-life lesson; she has become more cautious with all her children. She lifted her head from Tolstoy, whom she was rereading, and glanced in the direction of Nadya's secretive game. What incantations was the child muttering? Then she adjusted herself comfortably on the park bench and returned to the novel.

Nadya was devoted to her sculptures. They were her familiars, her friends. Some she adored, others she feared. Two-faced Janus on the bank of Swan Ditch frightened her. He was the patron of her birth month, the god of all beginnings, Nina had said, and especially of war. One of his masks was kind and the other was evil. In later years she would think of the sinister presence of Janus in the Summer

Garden as prophetic. Even now, on this warm June day, Janus was deception incarnate. She ran to greet Nox, her favourite statue. And there they were, the Roman goddess and the Russian child looking at each other. Nadya threw her arms around the marble woman. Swathed in her mantle of stars, the beautiful Night rested her enigmatic smile on her young friend's scabby knees.

The Moment War Began

De profundis . . . My generation
Tasted little honey. And now
Only the wind whistles in the distance,
The only song it sings — a requiem for the dead.
Our hours were numbered,
Our task not completed.
We were just a breath away
From the longed-for watershed,
From the apex of the ultimate spring,
From the violent flowering.
Two wars, my generation,
Illumined our terrifying path.

From the cycle *A Wreath for the Dead*, 1944

For the rest of time I will remember the moment war began, thinks Nadezhda. The silence of summer broken by a harsh explosion of static, high above their heads, where the black loudspeaker lurked in the linden branches. A crackle of cicadas rubbing their magnetic wings or an insistent warning from the stratosphere. And as the ancient tocsin in the brain rang its alarm, the pulse of life began to beat faster.

All over Leningrad, in all the cities and villages of the Soviet Union, public loudspeakers hissed day and night. Like poisonous blooms, they glinted in the greenery, clung above the tram stops, hung on the walls of city buildings. These black funnels blared announcements and broadcast martial songs. They harangued citizens in communal apartments. This is your public radio. It's here to fill your lives with cheerful slogans, to proclaim party messages, to tinkle excerpts from Swan Lake, and sing rousing songs, which stick like cobwebs to your protesting, saturated brain.

Anna Pavlovna felt unwell. A pain in her sternum like indigestion was an old sensation of well-rehearsed fear. 'Nadya,' she called out, and wondered why she was doing this. The child did not need her protection. It was she, the adult, who just then wanted the closeness of another human being to reassure and comfort her. She didn't attempt to explain why she had torn Nadya away from her game; she herself couldn't quite understand her panic. She was superstitious, always had been, though not a neurotic creature like her daughter. Those noises above her head shattered the peace of her parkland, brought back a memory of another day, hot and still. But when and why? The air around her was now saturated with menace. A thin voice trickling from the loudspeaker was dripping poisonous syllables, which all at once made sense to her.

'Attention, attention, citizens of the Soviet Union, today at four o'clock in the morning German troops, without declaring war, attacked our country, launching assaults on our frontier at many points, and dropping bombs on our cities . . .'

'Why is Molotov speaking? How significant was this?' In her confusion, Anna Pavlovna was searching for logic. 'Stalin himself should be making this announcement and not his foreign minister. Surely, the Great Father of the Peoples himself should be telling the nation what a terrible catastrophe had just befallen their country.'

Anna Pavlovna remembered the day when the First World War broke out. She looked down at Nadya's face, so tranquil. If only she could spirit the child away this very moment, protect her from the horror of war she knew was approaching. She clamped her hands over Nadya's ears, as if to shield her a little longer from those pitiless words. 'Mother of God,' she began to pray, releasing the child and clasping her hands in a painful knot, 'save the child from war and pestilence.'

Nadya, who only listened to songs on the radio, was not paying much attention to the speech. But adult alarm was contagious. Looking up into her grandmother's face, she saw tears running down the channels of the wrinkles, rolling over the promontory of the chin into the darkness of the dress. She watched the progress of those tears, as the martial clusters of words exploded around her, until they began to take shape: Savage-attack-fascist-rulers-ours-is-the-righteous-cause-the-enemy-shall-be-destroyed . . . She was too young to understand what it meant for a people to be at war, but she sensed that something terrible was happening. The simple world she had known was growing more complex and dangerous with each passing minute. She watched her grandmother slumped on the wooden seat. For a moment this broken old woman seemed a stranger. Nadya would always remember this metamorphosis of proud imperial majesty into a rag doll.

Patches of polished blue were glinting through the linden dome. On the airwaves the voice went on, crunching like sand under her sandals. Sparrows and shadows and dappled spots of sunlight were dancing on the path. Nadya was stacking these images in her heart, storing them for later. She would carry them across Russia, into the scarred cities of Europe, and finally bring them, like a dowry, to a distant land.

The chocolate bomb was melting in her hand; sticky rivulets ran down her wrist and gathered into a small brown pool in the crook of her elbow. She licked it up, unhurriedly. There was nothing else she could do, except go on eating her ice-cream. Anna Pavlovna rose to her feet. Her face was once again a Byzantine icon, dark with age and worship. Deep eyes, grieving mouth, the image of Our Lady of many sorrows. She must have imagined that she was there alone, because she was thinking aloud. But then, perhaps, she may have wanted Nadya to hear her unbearable presentiment.

'Four wars,' she lamented, 'I've lived through four wars. Wars bring only destruction and grief. My brother went down with the fleet at Tsushima. I lost my firstborn in the Great War. My husband died of the Civil War. And I watched the young marching to their death in Finland. Too many wars for one lifetime. And what have I done to deserve yet another trial in my old age? I won't live to see the end of this war.' She stood in the middle of the path. Straight as a tree trunk. Inscrutable. Dignified. She was again Empress Anna. She addressed Nadya now, as she would an adult, with her full and formal given names. 'Nadezhda Alexeyevna, it's war. We must be with our family.'

Flight from the Summer Garden

> To live — you need freedom.
> To die — you need your own bed.
> The road to the graveyard,
> Muffled with straw.
>
> 'The Day War with Finland Began', November 1939

Holding Nadya's hand, Anna Pavlovna made her way to the gates at a pre-war pace. She couldn't have walked any faster had she tried. People hurried past them to reach home, to reach any place where they would find reassurance, information. Colliding with strangers in the crowd, they called out. 'The Germans are bombing our cities.' 'Has anyone heard which cities?' A woman cried, 'I have a sister in Minsk.' In front of Nadya, a man was saying: 'I wish Stalin would speak to us.' Another asked in a frightened whisper, 'Do you think he's alive?' Stunned by the events, or indifferent, an old couple remained sitting on the park bench.

Anna Pavlovna and Nadya had to wait on a crowded tram stop for a long time. Around them were families who had been spending their day off in the park, buying balloons for the children, eating ice-creams, reciting Krylov fables at the monument. Now they stood about in tense clusters, men talking about the war, tearful women swapping fears and the children, silenced by panic, listening to the gloomy predictions of wartime shortages to come. Across the street, a growing queue was gathering at the food store. At a militia station nearby, reservists were reporting for duty. Down the Nevsky, a platoon of students was marching to enlist. And on Ostrovsky Square, at the foot of the bronze Catherine, old men, like her obsequious courtiers, waited for a repeat of the war broadcast. They stood around gazing upwards into the trees, as if expecting Molotov's little moon face with its glinting spectacles to pop out of the loudspeaker in the foliage.

Teeming with people, the streets resembled a May Day parade. Only there were no banners or colourful costumes; neither were there any marching ranks or thunderous hurrahs. The crowds today were congregating for comfort. They wanted explanations. How could our ally, Hitler, have dealt such an underhand blow to us, the Soviet Union? Treachery made war even more appalling. Disaster yawned, inevitable, unstoppable.

Anna Pavlovna's trip home took half the afternoon. They could have walked the distance more quickly, even at her snail's pace. For a long time they could not get on the overcrowded trams. When they finally managed to squeeze in, the tram crawled along jammed streets. Their tram driver was dreamy; he waited at each stop much longer than was needed, to hear the latest reports.

'Any developments? What's the news?' he questioned all the new passengers, as they pushed their way into the packed car. A cheeky young voice called back from the anonymity of the swarming tram stop, 'Just the same old bullshit as before.'

'Who was that?' No one had caught sight of the miscreant.

'What did he say?' Nobody wanted to quote what had been said.

'We're bound to run out of food supplies,' spoke a worried voice.

'Surely not in a place like Leningrad,' a confident woman replied. 'In the provincial towns, maybe, but not in the capital cities.'

'Moscow is the capital!' someone grumbled. 'We've been a provincial city for over twenty years . . .'

'There's already a rush on the shops. Look at the queues out there.'

'The queues at the sberkassy are even longer.'

'Naturally. People want to get out their savings.'

A man in uniform sounded buoyant. 'We're mobilising. The collection points were opened half an hour after the declaration of hostilities. See the banners over there, that's one of our stations.' Everyone turned to look at the freshly pasted posters on the walls of buildings.

The tram crawled past apartment houses. On this hot afternoon the windows were thrown open into people's lives. Nadya saw a silent film, and wondered what all these actors were saying to one another. A girl with a braid down her back, her bare arms raised above her head, was putting up black curtains. 'Those are blackout curtains,' a passenger instructed Nadya. In another frame a man and a woman were caught standing very still, holding hands, looking at each other, trying to memorise each other's features. From a courtyard archway a crocodile of small boys came marching out into the street.

'Look, Babushka, they're going to war,' cried Nadya and began a song she had learnt from Slava, the Red Devil.

> Clouds loom over the city;
> A promise of storm's in the air.
> A young fellow comes walking
> From the Narva gate.
> Oh, what a long, long road it is!
> Come out to me, my sweetheart,
> We'll say goodbye to each other,
> Maybe, it's forever.

'Please don't, Nadyenka!' Babushka pleaded softly. And the way she had changed from the formal Nadezhda to a caressing Nadyenka was even more frightening than Molotov's announcement, even sadder than her tears on the green bench.

Aunt Alexandra opened the door. Her eyes and nose were swollen and red. She had washed her face, but her voice was still full of tears. 'Oh, Mother, you're home at last, thank God. I've been frantic with worry. What a terrible, terrible day!'

Since Anna Pavlovna prided herself on her punctuality, Alexandra must have been imagining all kinds of accidents. Dmitry, she lamented, had already reported for duty. Nina and Slava had rushed off to the institute. They wanted to donate blood straightaway. But she had no idea what they were doing there so long. It was bad enough to hear that war had begun, but it was even worse to have your family away from home and, above all, not to know what rash commitments the young might be making without your consent. She wondered tearfully if Nina might be enlisting.

'Oh, and we've got guests,' she remembered. 'Katya has been here since one o'clock, waiting to talk to you about the girls. She says we must send them back to Sofya in the Caucasus. You're the only person who can travel with them. I said to her I wasn't sure you were up to it.' Alexandra's nervous chatter was a symptom of a state of high distress.

There was no sign of dinner. Aunt Katya, her daughters and Nadya's sister Vera were sitting round the empty table, waiting for Anna Pavlovna to enter the room, hoping for advice from a wise old woman who had been through so many crises in her life. Across the room Vera gave her sister a superior seven-year-old smirk. The musical cousins, Ada and Kira, greeted Nadya with their mother's friendly smile. Both had Aunt Katya's grey eyes, fringed with very dark lashes, and identical brown pigtails. Aunt Katya had jumped up from her chair and was squeezing Nadya against her full bosom. Her arms were soft and her skin had a fresh scent like bread. 'Nadyusha,' cried this impulsive aunt, tickling Nadya's cheek with the dark moustache that grew on her upper lip. 'Don't worry, don't be frightened, my little one, you'll soon be home. We'll get you back to your Mama in no time.'

Aunt Katya

>People's ordinary lives
>Were changed violently.
>This was not a city sound,
>This was not a country sound.
>It most resembled, like a brother,
>A distant growl of thunder . . .
>As the sound expanded and grew,
>My anxious senses wouldn't believe
>That it casually carried destruction
>To my child.
>
>'The First Long-range Firing on Leningrad', 1941

In their orphaned childhood, Katya had been a mother to Sofya, her younger and only sibling. Now she lavished the same maternal concern on Sofya's daughters. At the outbreak of war, Katya's first thought was not for the fate of Russia but how to return Sofya's children and to relieve her sister's appalling anxiety.

Katya did not hear the first broadcast of Molotov's announcement, because the girls were playing and, while they practised, the loudspeaker was disconnected. Music came first in the Karpovs' daily routine; it was a serious infringement of house rules to interrupt practice. Going over a difficult passage, the girls were at a critical point where the violin comes in again. Suddenly their father burst into the room, red-faced, and puffing from the run up the stairs. That in itself was alarming, because Misha Karpov was no longer the athlete he used to be; he climbed stairs at a more thoughtful pace these days. His outburst was another surprise: the jovial, easy-going Misha was not given to noisy melodrama. Yet there he was now waving his arms and shouting, 'Turn on the radio, hurry, turn it on. It's war!'

An emergency of this magnitude instantly stopped the piano and the violin. Kira carried a chair to the loudspeaker, and Ada, the taller climbed up to turn it back on.

'Attention, attention, citizens of the Soviet Union. Today at four o'clock in the morning, German troops, without declaring war, attacked our country, launching assaults on our frontiers at many points, and dropping bombs on our cities. The responsibility for this savage attack against the Soviet Union rests completely and entirely with the German fascist rulers. Ours is a righteous cause. The enemy shall be destroyed. Victory shall be ours!'

Katya, looking around, was shocked by Misha's boyish eagerness and the animated faces of her daughters, while she herself was overwhelmed by the news. Why, Misha and the girls were actually excited by the war. Her family's dizzy response appalled her, brought home to her the capricious nature of disasters. Her body felt terribly heavy, her legs were too weak to support her weight; she sat down on the sofa.

'Sofya!' she remembered next. Alone, far away in the Caucasus, her sister must also be listening to these ominous words, agonising about Vera and Nadya. She would send a telegram to Sofya, immediately, and tell her not to worry: she would make sure the girls were safely delivered back to her. Katya's spirit was resilient; she was already recovering from the first blow, and translating resolutions into action. Yes, of course, she planned, Anna Pavlovna will take the girls to their mother. The Caucasus was now the old lady's home as well. But what if it's like the other war? Katya thought of her experience of war in 1914. It was summer then too and the trains were mobbed by panic-stricken travellers trying to get home. An hour from now, all of Russia might be on the move. Such a catastrophe would paralyse the telegraph network all over the country; the main centres might cope, but certainly not the provinces. The telegraph office had been Katya's first job, when she was raising Sofya. Now her mind conjured up desperate messages getting lost in the clogged wires, failing to reach their destination. And it's only beginning, it's the first day of the war. She shivered, as if one of the river fogs were taking over the summer day. These are just the blossoms, she murmured. The berries are still to come.

When she was agitated, Katya's sallow face flushed, her eyes filled with tears and she absolutely, but absolutely, had to talk the problem through with Misha. She wanted a man's rational view on what this war would really mean to their family here in Leningrad, and advice on the best way of getting Sofya's daughters to the Caucasus.

Misha, however, shied away from expressing opinions; instinct urged him to avoid domestic conflict at all cost. In his experience, all problems were eventually solved, whether you took action or simply allowed things to follow their natural course. The less energy you expended on worrying, the more pleasant life could be. And Misha loved life. He admired his wife's determination, was proud of the musical achievements of his daughters and appeased his formidable older sisters; he enjoyed work, adored sport and worshipped his football team. At thirty-nine, Mikhail Lvovich Karpov, as he was known at work, was still Mishka the goalie to his football mates. All of them had by now retired from the field, but remained forever loyal supporters. On the day war broke out, he was looking forward to an afternoon at the stadium where his team was about to avenge itself on the cocky Muscovites. In an earlier contest the Moscow team beat Leningrad hollow. Misha's football mates decreed that this, naturally, had been a fluke. Now those Muscovite skites would get their comeuppance, a taste of the real Leningrad; Misha's team was about to thrash them. Misha himself was such an ardent football supporter, that his mates called him Mishka, the aching heart. Like a native of some Pacific island, he would have willingly trodden on hot coals for his favourite players. 'Oh God, please, please, make us win' — he only prayed before an important match.

Molotov's broadcast had not changed Misha's Sunday plans but it had delayed his departure for the stadium. Katya caught him in a moment of indecision; he was contemplating the inconvenience, the monumental injustice, of war breaking out on the day of the most important match of the season. He was aware that his disappointment was selfish, but he couldn't help feeling that Katya, of all people, should spare him her worries until he had sorted out the football calamity.

'Katya, my love, not just now, please.' The corners of his mouth drooped and he wore his guilty look which, he knew, wasn't convincing. She expected more from him. But what was he to do? The game had to go on, even if the Germans had attacked the Soviet Union. And, in any case, had he not warned his wife and his sisters that Hitler was up to no good, couldn't be trusted? Sure enough, here were the Nazis crashing into Russia.

'I'll just find out if the match is on or off.' He tried to placate Katya. 'One foot here, one foot there, and I'll be back in a jiffy! Cross my heart, Katyusha. I'll just check what's happening.' There was all the time in the word to send a telegram to Sofya and put Anna Pavlovna on the train, he assured her.

'Wait, Misha,' she protested, but he was already waving to her from the corridor. A last winning smile, and the lock clicked decisively as he backed out of the front door.

She ran after him and called down the stairwell, 'Misha, listen, I'm going over to Alexandra. Please, come after the game. Will you?' His reply was swallowed up by distance lengthening between them. As he ran across the yard, Misha muttered, 'Aie-aie, what a shit I am . . . My poor Katya.' The day around him was perfect for a football match.

The Grand Piano

Only this morning Katya had been making plans for the summer. It was the start of the holidays and she hadn't yet done anything about renting a dacha. If they hurried they might still find something on the coast, but she must remind Misha to get on to it. The alternative was another disciplined summer at Murzinka with Misha's sisters.

'And that won't be easy,' she sighed. She meant both difficulties — the girls' mounting mutiny against the aunts, and Misha's unkept promises. Her irrepressible husband was not a man of initiative. But she couldn't make demands on him the way his sisters did. 'Mishka, the tap in the bathroom needs fixing,' ordered Maneka, and Lika would be complaining that he had not yet shifted the wardrobe in her room. Poor Misha was the only male in the extended Karpov family so everyone relied on his muscles.

Katya's annoyance with her sisters-in-law was fleeting; she didn't hold grudges and her good sense always prevailed. Why shouldn't Maneka and Lika expect help from their brother? They were much older; they had been like mothers to Misha, and had raised him in the hard years. And that couldn't have been easy in a family besieged from all sides by the new order. Their apartment had been requisitioned by the house committee and, when they were eventually allowed back, much of their beautiful mahogany furniture had already been chopped up for firewood, looted or damaged. But the Karpov sisters did get their revenge: their brother turned out a perfect proletarian.

It amused Katya to think of her husband dashing the conventions in a family of doctors and musicians. Misha dropped out of school, took up the accordion and joined the Union of Communist Youth as soon as he was old enough to be admitted into the ranks of the Komsomol. His baritone voice was always in demand at the factory club. Misha's proletarian vigour got them back into their old family apartment, or at least a quarter of it. Some of their looted furniture was returned. Thank goodness, the piano survived unscathed. Almost. The two deep scratches on its lid were honourable scars, a reminder of the revolution.

'The war, the war,' Katya remembered. And the piano tuner was coming this week. Even in the midst of a catastrophe, how could she forget the needs of the grand piano next door, when her whole life revolved around it. The hours of daily practice, the tedious complaints from the neighbours. At least, now in the summer, windows were wide open and music could blend with the Leningrad street noise. War or no war, Katya said to herself fiercely, the girls' music must come first. She was certain that music was their professional future. Last year Kira came first in the Tchaikovsky competitions. 'How would war affect the girls' training?' she sighed. But, even in her troubled reverie, Katya did not stop counting: 'Ada, Ada, go back to the fifth bar. It's an adagio you're playing, not a rondo! Kira, give her a lead-in . . .'

In the next room the piano and the violin paused momentarily. She heard the girls' soft voices, conferring, then the sinuous fiddle resumed, and the piano chords came in again. In the kitchen, Katya continued tapping time with the sonata, and drying the lunch dishes. She knew by heart the pieces her daughters practised.

The room where the girls were playing was the largest in their quartered apartment; in the days of old St Petersburg, it used to be the Karpovs' drawing room. In these days of communal living, it was Misha Karpov's allocated living space. Katya and Misha's bedroom was behind a Chinese silk screen at one end, the girls' beds at the other end, behind another screen. The centre of the room was for music practice.

Very occasionally, this former salon reverted to its original purpose, when Misha's sisters, Maneka and Lika, gathered their friends for an evening of music and poetry. There had been two more Karpov sisters, but they had fled abroad, and no one mentioned their names. On these solemn occasions, the girls were expected to perform, and even Misha dared not refuse Maneka's command. He would wedge himself obediently in the curve of the grand and sing with true feeling from *Die Winterreise*.

The beautiful Karpov grand piano still stood in its pre-revolutionary pride of place, between the two tall windows, and claimed more attention than any other member of the extended household. It was regularly tuned, and covered up against chills of early autumn when the wind brought in a clammy fog from the Gulf of Finland. Like Katya's own parents, the Karpov family were natives of Peter's city and knew instinctively how to protect themselves against the wretchedness of its climate.

When Maneka and Lika were growing up in their father's urbane home, famous pianists and composers played at the musical soirées in this salon. These days the piano was treasured not only as a fine old instrument but for its dazzling past associations. 'Remember, Scriabin remarking on its beautiful tone . . . And Rubinstein's playing,' sighed Maneka and Lika. They took the musical talent of their own nieces for granted; the girls simply continued in the rich musical tradition of the Karpov clan.

Not Katya. She marvelled at her daughters' musicianship, was awed by their talent, and humbly acknowledged that it was a Karpov family gift. Katya considered herself a musical illiterate; she neither played an instrument nor could sing. She was forever amazed by her confident supervision of the girls' daily practice, and her own understanding of the music they played. She humbly thought of herself as an efficient human metronome.

From an early age, Ada and Kira had been singled out as gifted musicians and admitted to the special school at the conservatorium. From then on Katya's motherhood was focused on monitoring music practice, caring for instruments, taking the girls to rehearsals, waiting outside examination rooms, talking to music teachers, encouraging her daughters, cajoling, comforting, and rejoicing in their successes. Ada, at thirteen, was a promising pianist. Her teachers praised her dedication. Yes, she certainly has that, thought Katya, for a moment isolating the piano part in the sonata that the two girls were now rehearsing.

Tapping her foot and drying the dishes, Katya was now listening to both instruments. As so often, her younger daughter's playing touched some melancholy echo in Katya's heart. There it was again, that moving lyrical phrase. How could someone so young convey so much emotion? This kind of depth was never plumbed in Ada's accomplished piano playing.

Kira had some quality that set her apart. Her phrasing was not as perfect as her sister's, the swings of her mood often made her playing uneven, but when she was performing on stage, this round-faced ten-year old wove a magical spell. Just then, as the girls resumed their interrupted movement, Kira's violin began to sing. It was a good instrument, but only a student's fiddle, and yet Kira could coax from it this poignant tone. Katya's eyes began to itch with the salt of tears and a chill crossed her shoulder blades. In her modest way, she never quite trusted her own perceptions. Did Kira's playing touch her maternal pride or was it really her daughter's gift? When Kira won at the Children's Olympiad last winter the judges praised her playing as outstanding. How was a mother to cope with predictions of a brilliant career? How to keep Kira's feet firmly planted on the ground? After the competition, Katya took her excited daughter home to bed; and the next morning she was tapping time and shouting through the wall: 'Go over it again, Kira! You've missed B flat.'

Everyone Has a Talent

Sisterly loyalty encouraged Katya to look for musical talent in Sofya's daughters and she discovered that the little one had true pitch. 'We should start Nadyenka on the piano straightaway . . .' she wrote to Sofya in the Caucasus. But Sofya was tone deaf ('An elephant must have trodden on your ear,' Katya teased her sister) and she hadn't done anything about it. Now, living with the Voskresenskys, Nadya wasn't getting any musical training either. They had no piano. Alexandra and Dmitry did not go to concerts, and didn't even play gramophone records. Alexandra had disconnected the public radio system because the speeches of the stakhanovites made her angry, and now not a musical note was to be heard in their apartment. Yet Nadya was singing all the time. Where did she pick up the tunes, wondered Katya, and the words of all the songs she sings? A tug on the sleeve interrupted her thoughts. Vera had quietly entered the kitchen: 'Aunt Katya, aren't we going to the Voskresenskys? You said we were going to see Nadya.'

Katya was instantly moved by such sisterly affection. 'Yes, of course, Vera.' She gave her niece one of her motherly hugs. 'We'll go as soon as the girls finish their practice.'

'Kira,' she called,' you've missed a whole bar,' and shook her head in annoyance. 'If they don't concentrate,' she confided in Vera, 'they're not coming with us!' Then she smiled at her own severity. 'But they'll get it right, you'll see.'

'Look what I've made!' The girl showed her aunt the doll's dress she had been sewing.

'That's beautiful. Such neat sewing, like a machine stitch. You're a clever girl, Vera.' Katya's delight and praise were genuine. Vera's lack of interest in music made it difficult to fit her into the pattern of the girls' life. It was not easy inventing amusements for an unmusical child in a family wrapped in musical activity. Ada and Kira played four hours a day and even longer before examinations or performances. At their school music came first; work in other subjects was peripheral.

Vera was placid and easily occupied. She sewed complicated outfits for her dolls, who had arrived with her from Pyatigorsk, and played house under the grand piano, while her cousins practised.

Katya took Vera shopping. They walked down Ligovsky Prospekt to the different shops and sometimes stood in a queue. In the Leningrad manner, they would buy only what they needed for each meal. Perishable food couldn't be stored in their communal kitchen. For the soup, Katya would buy beef bones, one onion, one carrot, a bunch of parsley and some potatoes. She might see fresh veal. 'We'll have noodles with the stroganoff,' she would instruct the housewifely little Vera. 'Now let's get some sour cream for the veal. And we'll have some berries for dessert. If we can't find fresh ones, I'll make you a jelly out of sugared cranberries. You do like my kissel, don't you, Verochka?' Vera loved her aunt's kissel. This fair rosy child was so like Sofya that she made Katya yearn for her sister.

'And bread. We mustn't forget the bread.' A meal was not a meal without it. Katya would go into the bread shop. Ah! You could stand forever in a bulochnaya, breathing the warmth of fresh baking. There were different shapes and varieties. The crust could be knobbly, crunchy, or smooth, or flecked with poppy seed. Every kind of bread! Black bread or fine rye peklevanny or the pale sitny, or caraway bread, and there was a lovely loaf called doctor's bread. And the many kinds of bulochki.

'Seven of peklevanny.' Katya bought bread in slices, or by the loaf. 'Half of that warm sitny, please.' And she always bought Vera a sweet bulochka as well. And along the Ligovsly Prospekt, Vera would help her aunt with the shopping bag, empty on the way out and bulging on the home journey. Poor Kira and Ada missed the shopping fun and the sweet bun, practising their pieces and learning theory. Talking about the end of year exams, they often sounded obscure.

'Andrei's failed his Russian literature.'

'Who cares about silly old literature! He's got straight fives in all his music. That's what matters,' Kira said.

Generations and Customs

When Katya took all three girls out, people looked at them and smiled. She herself delighted in their appearance. Three girls walked out of the doors of 82 Ligovskaya, and crossed the yard in a neat crocodile file behind Katya. Ada, already taller than her mother, then Kira, tossing her head and swinging defiant pigtails and, behind them, Vera trying to keep in step with her older cousins, complaining that the others were walking too fast, that it was too cold or too hot. Her protests and her pouting lips, so like Sofya's.

Three girls in their red and white polka-dot summer dresses. Katya bought all four cousins identical dresses last summer when they went on their Ukrainian holiday. Since then the girls had grown taller, and just the other day Katya had let the hems down. White socks, red shoes with a strap across the instep and a dear little mother-of-pearl button. Three round faces. Two sets of brown pigtails, and one fair head. With her rotund figure, Katya was a mother duck taking her brood for an outing.

'It would have been nice if the girls had Sofya's profile, and not my potato nose,' Katya observed, with her usual self-deprecation. Misha disagreed; she had a real Russian nose, he declared, and it was charming. Katya didn't trust Misha's taste in noses (besides, he was a clumsy flatterer). It didn't matter, anyway, what their noses were like, as long as the girls were good musicians.

Three girls walked along carrying two music cases, a violin and one doll. 'Must you always bring the doll, Vera? It makes you look like a baby.'

But Vera clutched the doll more tightly. From excessive affection, Irochka was rather bedraggled, but she was a talisman from home. She had travelled with Vera all the way across Russia.

'Let her be,' Katya cautioned her impatient daughters. The doll, she said, needed a walk just as much as everyone else. At the tram stop they chatted away as only little girls will, about everything and nothing. They saw things no one else might have noticed. They laughed at their own private jokes. 'Let's play the game of "Who– where–when–what did he say–what did she say–what was the verdict of the world . . ."'

Listening to them, Katya wondered if she had ever been as carefree as that. She caught a vivid glimpse of her own Petersburg childhood, so compelling that for a moment it washed away the sights and sounds around her. In place of her daughters, she saw herself and her sister, the two Meier girls, walking in old St Petersburg with their stately mother. 'Bozhe moi,' she sighed. The traffic on the Nevsky is quite different; she can see horse-drawn trams and cabbies with their sad-looking nags. Their mother is wearing a close-fitting jacket and a grey hat with a wide brim. Grey kid gloves, very smooth, clasping her reticule. She is a tall, good-looking woman. People turn to look at her. They are going to the Admiralty to attend a very special ceremony at which their father, a civilian, is to be honoured with an officer's rank and uniform in His Imperial Majesty's Navy.

'How do you like your Papa's uniform?' Did her mother really have a lovely voice or did Katya and Sofya invent all her perfections in their orphan years? Was she as tall, beautiful, kind and clever as they described her to each other?

Katya has the photograph taken on the day of the investiture, her parents standing side by side. Yes, she was taller. Their father, Nikolai Nikolayevich Meier, looks a stocky man, splendid in a naval jacket, gold braid, epaulettes and shiny buttons. His beard and moustache fashionably trimmed like the tsar's. At His Majesty's pleasure. At His Majesty's service. A great honour bestowed by His Majesty. The Workshop for Navigational Instruments, where father is chief engineer, had been founded by Tsar Peter, and was his favourite workshop; the tsar had worked in it himself. And did they know (Father took general knowledge seriously) that the first ship built in the imperial dockyards was called *Nadezhda*? Is that why

Sofya named her daughter Nadya . . . Nadezhda? Hope.

In later years, Sofya, the bolder sister, applied to the university as a daughter of the proletariat. The Workshop, she claimed, made their father 'a worker', one of the toilers, a proletarian. That's how you survived in the new revolutionary society: if you could get away with it, you rewrote your past, fictionalised your family history, made yourself politically acceptable.

Katya remembers their father at breakfast time, formal in his collar and tie, apologising to Mama for his appearance if he entered the dining room in his shirtsleeves. And she compared him with her own husband Misha, who never wore a tie, not even when he sang Schubert's lieder. Misha had taken to the great social experiment like a duck to water.

Generations passed, with their customs and values. She no longer knew anyone from her parents' circle. They had all died or fled abroad or perished in the dark ages of the revolution. Was there anything left of her childhood Russia, except beautiful memories and this, her marvellous city? At least Petersburg-Petrograd-Leningrad was still here. It had belonged to her parents, now it was hers as long as she lived, and later it will belong to her daughters, and their children after them. What about her own generation? Would they, Katya and Misha, Sofya and Alexei, be forgotten? Would the memory of the terror they had suffered also vanish without a trace? Perhaps it would slide back into the history books of future generations, stealthily, like the Finnish fog.

Misha Karpov in Uniform

> They parted from the girls with dignity.
> They gave a hasty kiss to mother.
> They dressed up in new uniforms
> And went off to play at soldiers.
>
> From 'The Wind of War', 1943

Her husband's army uniform appalled Katya. Drab and shapeless, the ill-fitting tunic was too small for Misha's wide shoulders. He kept shrugging them as if to free himself from a trap. His hair under the forage cap had been cropped very short. His ears stuck out ridiculously, seemed to have grown larger. Misha's open Russian face begged, 'Please, don't examine me too closely, I feel a clown in this silly outfit,' but his eyes spoke to Katya alone; the girls must not guess at the embarrassment hidden under this display of soldierhood. Far from being disappointed, the three girls were impressed by Misha's manliness. Awed and coy in turns, they were too excited to catch his discomfort or Katya's anxiety.

'Papa,' Kira shrieked, 'you look like a film actor! Let me try on your cap.' She snatched the khaki cap and marched round the room, chanting, 'I'm going to join the army, I want to go and fight!'

'Uncle Misha, where's your rifle?' Vera wanted to know. Stroking the shiny leather belt, clutching at the skirt of his tunic, she clung to this uncle, who stood in for a father whom Vera had not seen in three years.

Katya watched her husband wistfully, memorising each small detail of his body, the good-natured smile. In uniform, going to war. These may be their last hours together, she thought. Reporting tomorrow, he'll be sent to a unit. Where, when, will she hear from him? She couldn't let him go into the terrible dangers of battle, couldn't bear to think of soldiers killing one another.

The war had caught them all in its web. In the past few days, since the nightmare began, they had all been overwhelmed by the force and speed of the invasion. From the cryptic bulletins they heard on the air and read in the papers, it appeared that the Germans were advancing along a broad front, and that the whole western flank of this immense country of theirs was under attack. Heavy battles were reported around Minsk and Germans were moving into Estonia. When you looked at your map, and everyone in Leningrad was following the course of the war with a map, it became clear that two spearheads were converging on the city. On the Karelian Isthmus, just above Leningrad, the Finns were closing in on their old frontier. Katya had a fleeting memory of a summer they spent in Karelia, when she was a little girl. Even then the Finns hated the Russians. She remembered how their Finnish neighbours stopped their wedding music when they saw the Russian children next door dancing. The Russo-Finnish War two winters back hadn't improved relations between them. Now the Finns were allies of the Germans.

Children of Revolution

Now nobody will listen to songs.
The days we feared are here.
The world is no longer a miracle.
Be silent, my last song, don't break my heart.
Not long ago, as free as a swallow,
You made your morning flight.
Today you're a hungry beggar woman,
No door will open to your voice.

1917

Katya was fifteen and Sofya twelve when they were orphaned. Two young girls, who used to recite homework to their mother and went with their father on botany walks in the Finnish woods, were left alone in the midst of winter and revolution. The civil war was about to begin.

Their father died on the day of the big snowstorm. Trams were not running, and Sofya walked to see him at the Navy hospital. Later, when the sisters sifted through their pain for grains of comfort, neither could remember why Sofya was alone that afternoon, why Katya was not with her. They had always gone to visit their father together. Whiteness shrouded every landmark beyond a few paces. Snow blew into Sofya's face. An icy crust stuck to her eyelashes and blinded her even more. Flying icicles stung her skin. Frozen strands of hair broke loose from the woollen bonnet and scratched her cheeks. She tried to brush them away, but her fingers had gone rigid inside the double mittens; even the felt boots she wore did not protect her toes from the terrible cold. Her legs ached from the struggle of lifting those heavy valenki out of the snowbanks. Wrapped up in a fur-lined coat, with her mother's Orenburg shawl tied over it on a cross, Sofya's body was steaming. She was so slow, making no progress as she scaled those mountains of snow and balanced on icy ridges. Since the footpath had vanished she followed the wrought-iron railing of the embankment; it was her only guide. And as she fought through the blizzard, Sofya was aware that this elemental force was magnificent; admired the perfect precision with which the hoarfrost had trimmed the metal design of the railing.

She was so tired from battling the snowstorm on the embankment, she wanted the comfort of her father's arms, needed his smile to revive her. When they had seen him the day before, his skin was waxen and his voice weak. With the moustache and beard shaven off, his naked face no longer resembled the tsar's. His hair had turned white when his wife died, and now he looked an old man. He was only thirty-eight, the sisters recalled later when they were grieving. He had given them a letter — it was a power of attorney, he explained. Just a precaution, to protect their property; you never knew in these difficult times. The document, witnessed and signed, certified that they were his rightful heirs and owners of the apartment and all its contents. There were no debts or mortgages. He had worked honestly all his life, he said, and had paid for everything that he owned.

'Don't, Papa, don't talk like that,' they beseeched him, fearful and sad.

'Just in case.' He stroked their hair, Katya's dark head and Sofya's fair one. Foolish creatures, did they really imagine he would die and leave them alone in the world? Wasn't life without Mama hard enough? He had not completed an itemised inventory, he explained to Katya. The most valuable things were on his list, Mama's jewellery, the silver, the furs, the rugs and, of course, Shishkin's forest painting. It was a sensible thing to do. He wanted them to start learning how to take care of things. His hands trembled as he pressed the folded paper into theirs. He was dying. They knew. They sensed it. Surely, that was what the document meant. They tried not to weep at his bedside, not to upset him with their grief. Neither could they stay with him. They ran out into the street, and were disconsolate all the way home.

An endless walk across an alien planet that once used to be their city. Two young girls alone in the midst of civil disorder, in a society that had lost its way. The sisters kept cautiously to the kerb. Streets were unlit; buildings were dark along the Nevsky. The once bright and busy shopping arcades of Gostiny Dvor were deserted. There was talk of muggings. Gangs of dedicated proletarians, people said, roamed the city, hunting the bourgeois.

'Remember, Mama once saw a policeman being lynched.'

'We mustn't talk about frightening things.' Katya spoke like a parent. But how could you stop the terrors that came to your mind? They had to be said aloud, exorcised by reassurance.

It was warm inside the hospital. Sofya felt drowsy, and for a moment forgot what to do next. Oh, yes, she must take off her coat. Here they still had a cloakroom and an attendant; the old veteran took her coat and gave her a shiny brass token. She clutched the lucky number twelve, her own age, and walked down the corridor. Her fingers and toes hurt her as they began to thaw; the warm air was as painful as the frost outside.

She should have known that her father was dead as soon as she saw his stripped bed, should have guessed from the silence in the ward as she entered. His fellow patients were sailors who greeted the sisters with clumsy jokes. 'Never fear, girls, your dad will soon be well enough to dance at your wedding! As good as new.' Now they watched Sofya slyly, pretending she wasn't there. She stopped beside the empty bed, and stood stroking the grey mattress ticking with her frozen fingertips.

An elderly sailor limped up to her and put his hand on her shoulder. 'Your daddy's gone, died just a short while ago. He waited for you, but he couldn't hold on. When death came for him, he had to go.' His peasant crooning was a lullaby for an abandoned child. A gift of consolation, his voice thawed her senses, unlocked grief. Sofya wept, with her face in her arms, leaning against the white tiles of a ceiling-high stove.

Their mother's funeral six months earlier had been on a wet afternoon in July. A crowd of friends and cousins attended. The sisters recalled their father's dazed face, and their own discomfort at being the chief mourners. Katya held Nikolai's elbow and, in a whisper, reminded him to leave the roses with Mama. Their father, that unblemished authority of their childhood, was a wooden puppet. A tug of a string, and he dropped the bouquet into the grave — crimson blooms on a white coffin. To cauterise the pain that would not subside, the sisters continued to talk about their parents' death in a strangely impersonal tone, as if observing changes in social mores which had occurred in the months between their two losses.

The funeral service for Nikolai Nikolayevich Meier was held in the parish church of Mary Magdalen and he was buried beside his wife in the Marininsky cemetery on the Okhta bank of the river. But at this second funeral there were hardly any mourners. Outside was an apple-crisp January day. The blizzard had swept the world clean. The fresh snow was deep and sparkling in the sunlight. All this brightness hurt the eyes. Inside, the church was an ice chamber; a shaft of coloured light from the window beamed into the open coffin. The sisters didn't recognise their father's dead face, and could not weep. They felt their tear ducts had frozen as solidly as his profile.

It was warmer at the graveside. The pine box slid into the trench; rock-hard clumps of clay clattered on the lid. The huddle of mourners hurried away to warm themselves with some acorn coffee at the wake. They nodded sadly that God would take care of the orphans, and ate every crust of bread in the house. Just then someone reported that potatoes were expected at the grocer's on Novocherkassky. In a rush to get to the store while the supply lasted, the guests borrowed blankets and a toboggan. They did not return the toboggan, precious because it was essential for survival in a snowbound city. The next morning, the newly appointed chairman of the house committee knocked on the Meiers' door. Their apartment, he informed them, was needed for two proletarian families. The girls could apply to share living space in someone else's apartment, or move to another building.

Sofya was furious after he had gone. 'Stupid, pompous creature.' But Katya was too sad for anger. 'We've become socially undesirable.' It was a betrayal of all that had been stable in their life; she felt this keenly. Best to go somewhere else, she proposed. In the days that followed, new and old tenants tramped through their rooms, buying for a pittance all those much-loved pieces the sisters had grown up with. 'How much are you asking for the dining room table and chairs, and that dresser?' Katya answered so softly they could barely hear — 'Whatever you can give us.' Around the corner, Sofya wept angry tears. 'That was Mama's lovely walnut dresser.'

The sisters loaded the few possessions they had kept on the second toboggan, and handed the keys to the chairman. Their last glimpse of home life was their mother's porcelain soup tureen, which used to grace the walnut dresser, sitting in the middle of the dining room parquet. Years later, the sisters still felt the sadness of their broken childhood; they could not forgive their parents for abandoning them in the midst of a disintegrating society. The pain of rejection festered, refused to heal. They comforted each other that most families they knew had suffered losses. After all, they were children of the Russian revolution. Perhaps the lives of their generation were meant to be as cataclysmic as the revolution itself.

The Street of Jewelled Memories

> Through the prison gates,
> Through the swamps behind Okhta,
> Along an untrodden path,
> Across an unmown meadow,
> Through the night cordon,
> Sheltered by the Easter bells,
> Uninvited,
> Unbetrothed,
> Come share my supper.
>
> 'Incantation', from the manuscript *Out of the Prison Gates*, 1935

Katya remembered when the new Okhta bridge was finished, the bridge of Peter the First. The Workshop was shifted from the Admiralty to the Okhta bank and the family also moved across the river. Okhta had an unhurried suburban air about it. Hidden in a wild garden, their new home was in a side street, five minutes from their father's work in Novocherkassky Prospekt, named after the regiment stationed there in their red-brick barracks. Neighbours called on Augusta Semyonovna; they were mostly officers' wives of the regiment.

For Sofya, who was very young when they moved to Okhta, that childhood home was full of jewelled memories. Here mother had taught her the first prayers and poems. All the beautiful moments happened here. Could all this be simply nostalgia?

'Do you remember how I used to recite Lermontov?' she asked her sister.

'Oh, yes, always the little actress. I was quite jealous of you!'

'I'm sorry, I must have been a show-off.' Sofya tried to sound modest, though she was quite sure that everyone admired her charm.

Katya smiled and kept her thoughts to herself as was her wont. Sofya might be vague about her juvenile performances, but she still liked to be the centre of attention. Then she prompted her sister's memory. 'You used to stand on a chair and recite:

> What is he searching for in that distant land,
> What has he abandoned in his own country?'

Mother's birthday. Gathered round the damask-decked, crystal-laden, silver-laid table are Sofya's admirers: there's Mama's dearest friend, Aunt Olya, whose lace-covered bosom heaves when she laughs; there's Papa's younger brother, Victor; and other guests, whose faces and names have been forgotten. But both sisters remember the tiny cakes from Fillipov's patisserie, petits-fours shaped like fruits, a plate of them in the centre of the tea table. At the end of her recital, Sofya is invited to choose her favourite strawberry cake.

Remember Uncle Victor? He always wore his student cap. An eternal student, like Petya Trofimov in *The Cherry Orchard*. They saw him for the last time at their father's funeral. Sofya's nurse and playmate, he vanished in the revolution.

Sofya remembers riding high on Victor's shoulders in the garden. Spring. Everything is budding, bursting into leaf. Victor, the racehorse who has been galloping up and down the path, neighs and stops: 'Let's pick a willow branch for your Mama.' They keep galloping up and down the path, until the willow branch has lost all its fluffy catkins. 'Don't cry, little princess,' he comforts Sofya, 'we'll get a better one.'

'I sometimes think Victor was in love with Mama,' Katya says in her thoughtful way. Her insight is sharper than Sofya's.

'Remember the tsar's oak tree? Yes, the brass plate said: "Planted by Peter the First." It was just inside the railing of the officers' club. Huge and gnarled, wasn't it?' In the winter, the soldiers of the regiment built a wooden hill for tobogganing. And made a skating rink. Children skated in the afternoon, but in the evening there was music and coloured lights for the parents. Their mother loved skating. 'Wasn't she lovely in her fox hat? Her face like a rose, and those deep grey eyes. She always took the fur muff to keep her hands warm. The muff was like a Persian cat.'

And when their mother dressed up for the theatre, she put on a long velvet cape, fur-lined. Her hair, piled up high, made her even taller. She always wore her long double-strand of pearls. Real? Absolutely. Everything she wore was real! And the snake's-head bracelet with the sapphire eyes. But she only wore her jewellery when she went out; at home she always wore the gold bracelets.

'It was Papa's first gift.'

'I didn't know that.'

'Oh, I thought you did.'

'She was first engaged to Uncle Vladimir, wasn't she?'

'Yes, the eldest brother. Then she had a change of heart and married the younger.'

'While Papa was still a student.'

'Yes, and Grandfather never forgave them?'

'Nor did Uncle Vladimir.'

'I remember Mama saying how shy she and Papa were when they were first married. They slept in separate rooms.'

'She was quite frank for those days, wasn't she?'

'You couldn't avoid a husband nowadays, living in one room as we do!'

Their music teacher offered them a room in her apartment — 'You can move in with me.' They pulled their toboggan to her house. 'You poor things!' Tearfully, Lydia Mikhailovna hugged both girls. She couldn't give them music lessons for free, but she was sure they would work out some kind of payment. Housework, perhaps? A bit of dusting?

The upravdom had warned Lydia Mikhailovna that her living space would be reduced. (This awful new jargon! A month ago he was simply chairman of the house committee.) Any day, strangers could have been moved into her apartment. You never knew with these people. Apart from the bedroom, she had the drawing room with the grand. Inviting the Meier girls to move in was a stroke of genius. That would spike the proletarians! Be careful, it won't do to gloat. The girls could move into the drawing room. She only used it for teaching. God knows, there were precious few pupils left. 'It's a bit chilly, but you'll be comfortable,' she told them. She could put the screen across, so the pupils wouldn't see the bed. 'It'll be more aesthetic!'

They moved in behind the aesthetic screen. The few belongings they brought with them were stored under the bed they shared. Lydia Mikhailovna fixed a shelf for their cooking utensils in the communal kitchen. 'You can always find a bit of space on the range. We're lucky here, we've still got some firewood in the shed. Under lock and key!'

Food was even more scarce than firewood. The art of cooking was simplified: a few potatoes or a handful of groats thrown into the pot, and the soup was ready. Sometimes carrots or cabbage appeared, and there would be a rush on the shops. The bread ration could be collected when bread was available. It wasn't a famine, as their music teacher complained, but the daily struggle to survive never ceased. They shared the bathroom with all the other tenants. Hot water was now a rare luxury; the public baths were mostly closed.

In the Public Baths

That city, I've loved since childhood,
Appeared to me today
In its December stillness
As my squandered inheritance.

1929

On winter evenings they went to the baths with their mother. It was always frosty. Wide-open stars watched from their dark universe. Tall banks of snow spilled over the kerb. The building of the banya was full of lights and steam. You left your clothes in the lockers; Mother tied a metal number tag on her wrist. Shivering in the chill, shy in your nakedness, you walked quickly into the doors of the baths and the sheltering curtain of steam. Mother found an empty wooden bench and the serious ceremony of steaming would begin. You sat down on the warm slats, surrounded by soap, loofah and zinc basins with ringing handles. Other bathers were swallowed up by the steam cloud, invisible as you were yourself. Your body burned from the roughness of the loofah. The zinc shaiiki were filled with hot water, as hot as you could stand, and poured over you, until you gasped and cried that you were going to float away in the soapy flood.

Muffled in woollen shawls, feet snug in the felt boots, they drove home in a horse cab, the snow squeaking under the sledge runners, and the sky above them sprinkled with stars. At home they drank tea, and waited for Katya's long hair to dry before bedtime. 'Never go to bed with wet hair, unless you want to catch your death from a chill.' Katya lost her braids later when she had typhus. She lay in the Botkin hospital, too ill to have visitors; not even Sofya. At school they were nervous. There was a lot of sickness around, better not spread it. The form teacher told Sofya to stay at home until her sister was well again. At home, the music teacher was just as afraid of infection: she had her pupils to think of. Sofya stayed away. She walked in the street or in the hospital garden, waiting for news. When it was too cold outside, she would creep into the warm corridor. In the evening she let herself into the apartment, very quietly, and found her bed in the dark. In the grey light of the morning, the open music on the piano made her think of letters people wrote before they died, and she wondered if the music pages were a message from Katya. She would suddenly feel utterly convinced that Katya had deserted her as her parents had before; that her sister had died, but the truth had been hidden from her. At the hospital they called her in one day and told her that Katya was out of danger; the crisis had passed. Sofya's carapace cracked then; she hid in the cloakroom and sobbed.

Katya came home in a knitted bonnet. She pulled it down to her eyebrows to hide the shaved head. Little blue veins throbbed under her transparent skin.

Sofya was late from school the next day and took off her hat. She had her hair cropped short like a boy's.

'Oh, dearest, how could you do this to yourself,' Katya lamented. 'Now we both look like little orphan girls from an institution.' When they were small, they watched the girls from a nearby orphanage going out in their grey capes. 'God protect the orphan children,' their mother used to say.

While Katya was in hospital, someone had broken into their suitcase. Three silver spoons were missing, as well as Sofya's baptismal cross. Checking their possessions, Katya was bitter. 'No, God doesn't protect the orphans.'

Lydia Mikhailovna was appalled at the sisters' carelessness. 'You should have asked me to look after it for you. This is, after all, a communal apartment . . . All kinds of people walk in and out.'

Their mother's best friend, Aunt Olya, who had been such an admirer of Sofya's recitation, kept their box of valuables in her safekeeping. When the sisters asked for it back, most of the jewellery was gone.

'The pearls are missing,' Katya said to Aunt Olya. 'And Mama's bracelets.'

Sofya was dying of embarrassment: 'Katya, please don't . . .' But her sister was learning not to shrink from responsibility.

'You're not suggesting that I took your mother's jewellery,' Aunt Olya sounded tearful. She was offended, shattered, by such a suggestion. 'The box hasn't been touched! It's exactly as it was when you brought it. You had the key to the box all the time it was here. All I did was to keep it safe it for you, as a special favour.' Aunt Olya's large bosom heaved with emotion. 'These are terrible times,' she moaned, expecting a tiny bit of gratitude from the daughters of her best friend. She dabbed her eyes with the lace edge of her handkerchief.

On the way home Katya turned furiously on her younger sister. 'You might have supported me, Sofya. You know as well as I do that Aunt Olya is a thief. She did take those things. Didn't you see how she kept pulling the shawl round her throat, hiding our mother's locket inside her blouse. Oh, Sofya, Sofya, we really are alone in the world. God doesn't protect orphans . . .'

A Deserted House

The Sentence

Today, so many tasks . . .
I should annihilate memory,
I should turn my soul to stone,
I should learn to live anew.
No, that's not it . . .
This hot rustling summer
Is a feast outside my window.
For a long time I have dreamt
Of a bright day and this deserted house.

'Summer 1939', from *Requiem* (1935–1940)

Sofya was at the washtub when she heard Molotov's announcement. 'I don't believe it, I don't believe it,' she thought. Her hands gripped the edge of the washboard, but her mind kept on working, tugging at questions for which she had no answers. Why? What had she done to deserve more misery? As she listened to the wheezing voice, she thought she heard a whine of fear in its emasculated pitch, and felt the bile of hatred rising and choking her. 'The miserable little toad sounds scared. Good. I hope the Nazis squash you all under their tank tracks.'

Vengefulness had a strong, satisfying taste. No one could mend her own broken life, but she would accept all her misfortunes, if only Stalin might be punished; if he and his blue-capped henchmen were made to pay that for all the tears and suffering they have caused. And for all the dead. No, not even Hitler could be as monstrous as Stalin. The violence of her thoughts shook her like a fever. You dared not even dream about things like that, and here she was making death threats, almost shouting them like a hallelujah.

Sofya stood over the tin tub, still as a statue of a woman with red hands and a tired face, her breathing uneven as the violence subsided. Then she resumed rubbing the wet pillowcase on the washboard so fiercely that the wooden ribs scraped her knuckles. The commissar went on with his dreary rhetoric but she no longer heard the droning voice.

'What if . . .' She drew in a rapid breath, and gagged on the acrid smell of the laundry soap. 'But what if there's a miracle, if this war brings Alexei back from prison?' The surge of hope was sudden and strong. She not only felt her spirit rising, but her body was floating in waves of joy and longing. She could see Alexei crossing the yard, his boots clicking on the cobbles, walking on the squeaky floorboards of the corridor. His arms were around her now and he was saying in that slow teasing tone of his, 'I'm home for good. So much for your worries, my heart.' He was real to her. She saw the hungry hollows on his face, she even smelled the stench of prison on his clothes. She tasted the salt of her own tears on his lips.

'Oh, my love.' She felt faint with tenderness and pity. 'I can tell you've been ill. You're so thin.' And that stubble on his poor face. They don't allow him to shave, and he is so fastidious. Heat bucketfuls of water and fill the tin tub to the brim. Scrub him gently, massage every muscle of this poor body. 'All those bruises, my love!' Then make up the bed with clean sheets. Let him sleep. There's too much light in the room. Draw the curtains. There, he can sleep like a child. 'Like a child . . .' Repeated aloud, the thought of her children tore her out of her husband's embrace. Her husband was still in Siberia. Russia was at war and her children were in Leningrad.

For the past two months, since she had put Anna Pavlovna and the two girls on the train north, Sofya had been in a dreamlike state, pacing through the routine of her daily life, feeling truly alive only when she was thinking of her children and her sister Katya in Leningrad. She imagined hour by hour what they were doing: having breakfast, going for a walk, falling asleep. At first she followed the travellers on their train journey, which she had done herself many times. She could recite the railway route like a well-memorised geography lesson: from the southernmost corner of Russia you travelled to Moscow, then another night's journey took you to Peter's city on the Gulf of Finland. In the past her husband would put her on the train and send her across the plains of Russia to see Katya in Leningrad.

Two months ago she settled her family in their compartment, helped to stow the food basket, kissed the children for the tenth time. Vera looked sleepy and yawned. Nadyenka was frowning as the train started. She saw Anna Pavlovna make a secretive sign of the cross, and mouth behind the glass, 'Nu, s Bogom.'

Sofya repeated, 'Yes, with God's blessing.' The little girls flattened their noses against the windowpane and, as the carriage and the platform stretched farther apart, they were blowing kisses in her direction, just as Sofya had done in the past when she was leaving Alexei behind. She ran along the platform, waving and wiping away farewell tears.

Going home on the tram, she saw them getting ready for bed. The bunks pulled down, the window blind lowered. On her own trips she could never sleep on that first night. She sat up in her bunk as the train shuddered on the rails, clattered over crossings, and sighed to a halt at a junction in the middle of nowhere, in the black loneliness of the southern steppes. The lights of those tiny railway stations would finger their way along the edges of the blind, and through a crack she would spy the bustling platform, passengers rushing with their suitcases and bundles, carrying sleepy children. Tears, embraces and last-minute reminders. Invisible, in the cave of her bunk, she imagined their lives.

The steppes were Cossack country, Sofya was thinking now at her washtub, imagining the vast grassland prairie she had crossed many times. Not so long ago a warrior people grazed herds of horses there, raised crops in the rich soil and sent their sons to serve the tsar. But the revolution and the civil war wiped out their way of life. Some Cossacks took up the tsarist cause and fled abroad; others stayed at home to be rounded up in the kulak hunts, or mopped up later in the collectivisation. And just in case any trace of dissent remained, the Father of the People ordered a famine. The whole southern region, that granary of Russia, was sealed off. At gunpoint, the bread-growers gave up their seed grain and were left to starve. Yes, Sofya thought bitterly, it was the surest way to root out opposition, to force the kolkhoz culture on Cossackland. And the southern seed grain, as everyone knew, was sold to the West as surplus. Proof of an abundance in the new Soviet state; another milestone on the path of socialist success.

On her annual pilgrimage to Leningrad, the pampered Sofya of those years hardly noticed what was going on around her on the land. Her mind was on fashionable shoes, her husband's promotion and the delights awaiting her in her native city. On the first night in Leningrad, she and her sister Katya would talk till dawn. On the second night, they would go to a play at the Mariinsky Theatre. And all day long she would catch the reflections of Leningrad in the polished surface of the river.

Rostov-on-the-Don

Quiet flows the quiet Don.
A yellow moon comes into a home.

Comes in with his hat cocked,
The yellow moon sees a shadow.

This woman is sick,
This woman is alone,

Her husband dead, her son in prison.
Pray for me.

From *Requiem* (1935–1940)

At the time of the southern famine, Alexei and Sofya were living on the very edge of the steppes, in Rostov-on-the-Don and, like everyone around them, they were blind to the agony in the countryside. They even argued that radical change was essential in order to achieve a true communist utopia. How much did they really know? How willingly did they allow themselves to be deceived? Now, Sofya squirmed with shame when she recollected her pious excuses at the time. She was not heartless, though. How could anyone have remained indifferent when they saw beggars rounded up by the militia in the street. She gave alms to starving women from the villages, who held up their skeletal babies to passers-by. There were gangs of besprizornye who had escaped from the famine cordon. These children of the streets had evolved a subculture of urban crime: they spoke their own patois, even had music of their own. Sofya and her comfortable friends sang the salty little songs of the besprizornye, danced the foxtrot to the catchy tune of Yablochko:

> Where are you rolling, my little apple?
> You'll drop into my mouth,
> And that'll be the end of you.

Those cynical little gangsters knew the truth about the great social experiment, yet no one else seemed to learn from their songs; or from the hollow-eyed starvelings; or from the kulak round-ups. Even before the famine began, thousands of families had been deported to Siberia to die in the virgin lands. No one paid heed to these signs; nor were they alarmed by the ruthlessness of the methods used to exterminate whole social groups. There was no indignation at the time, no protest, not even fear. Fear set in later.

'But Alexei did protest.' She was grateful for this forgiving reminder. He spoke up at a party meeting; he asked if such hardships could justify a social objective, however great it was. Hardly a case of dissent — he merely gave his view in a discussion — but it was noted, and quoted to him at the time of his arrest. Poor Alexei, his argument was not even against the monstrous machine, which he must have already begun to suspect and fear; he was making an ideological point. They shouted him down. When he came home that night from the meeting, he made a joke of it, 'Now I'll have a black mark in my party record. My colleagues branded me a Trotskyite.' Sofya had a vague sense of unease, which she quickly dismissed as she did any other unpleasantness in life. In those halcyon years she despised fears for personal safety. They were taking part in the most exciting socialist experiment ever and, to retain that membership, they had abandoned their childhood beliefs and all the values and traditions of the old civilisation.

When you arrived in Rostov in the morning, the quiet waters of the Don flashed you an intimate welcome. Sofya knew the city well. She spent her early years of marriage in that southern metropolis. Alexei was posted there to work in the Party Control Commission. The head of his branch was Tolmachev, a brilliant theoretician. They compiled the history of the party. That was before Stalin declared himself the party's chief historian and started churning out his own volumes.

From the brooding northern city, the newly-weds came to the open-hearted south. The city they had left behind was no longer even the capital; Moscow and the Kremlin were the heart of the Soviet empire and, a year after Lenin's death, Petrograd had been renamed Leningrad, although everyone kept forgetting the new name. To its natives, it was as always Peter. It was her own city, and Sofya missed it.

They arrived in Rostov in June, an eventful month in Sofya's life: a month of joys and tragedies. She was married in June. Their first child was born on a hot June midnight a year later in Rostov. Dinochka died on her third birthday. Alexei was arrested in June. And now, on 22 June 1941, war has broken out.

Back in their first southern summer, Rostov-on-the-Don was a lively place, so colourful it dazzled you. Alexei and Sofya arrived with one suitcase between them. They were given a room in a green and shady street. Virginia creeper climbed up the walls of the old mansion. In the luxury of its bourgeois past the house would have been occupied by wealthy families, each taking up its own spacious floor with a grand entrance from the street, and a tradesmen's door at the back. Now it was a proletarian kommunalka. Even during their orphan years, when she and her sister moved from room to room, Sofya had never witnessed such overcrowding as she now met in Rostov. The house was bulging with tenants. In their apartment, seven families shared six rooms and a kitchen. One married couple slept in the bathroom, and had to vacate it on bath nights. The Shubins had a room with a parquet floor, a moulded plaster ceiling and glass doors opening on to a balcony. The balustrade reminded Sofya of the wrought-iron railing on the bridges and embankments in Leningrad. How she missed her grey granite city, where each canal traced its own metal signature. At the time of their departure from Leningrad, lilacs were just about to bloom. Here in Rostov the horse-chestnut candles had finished flowering and a film of summer dust had settled on the octave-wide leaves.

Their room was not large. An iron bedstead (from a hospital or a prison cell, they joked) was one of the pieces of furniture they had inherited; the other was a three-door wardrobe of Karelian birch, left behind because of its size. It was too wide and tall for the door and the stairs. They wondered how it had been brought into the room in the first place. Alexei took one of the wardrobe doors off the hinges and put it on the metal frame of the bed. 'Our bridal bed,' laughed the young builders of Soviet Russia, proud to be free of old-fashioned inhibitions. 'Can you imagine, my parents were too shy to sleep in the same room!' These two had tossed aside bourgeois traditions and prejudice. What did Alexandra Kollontai say about sex? It's like a glass of water: have it when you're thirsty. Since there was no mattress, they padded the board with their linen. In the night, as the stacked linen shifted, they sank on the boards.

Sofya was allocated cooking space in the communal kitchen. She had part of the windowsill, just wide enough for her primus burner. They bought the primus with Alexei's first pay, and the nineteen-year-old Sofya began her housekeeping. Alexei left for work and she went to the market; she walked a lot in that slovenly southern city. Rostov, in those days, was marked with scars from the civil war: pitted facades, burnt-out buildings. As in other parts of the country, people here were out of work and in need. Crippled war veterans sold matches on the pavement. Watch out for pickpockets, her new neighbours warned her. In the marketplace Sofya clutched her purse close to her chest, and kept a suspicious eye on her shopping bag. Oh, the cornucopia of Rostov markets! The glut of wares spread before her seemed unreal. At the vegetable stalls peasant women set out their produce in fancy patterns. Tomatoes sat in pyramids of five, red and rotund; bunches of spring onions were watered in a bucket. The potatoes were scrubbed and stacked up in mounds. Bouquets of radishes bloomed scarlet against dark-green cucumbers. Poultry and meat stalls were hung with chickens and chunks of lamb. A kerchiefed owner would be plucking a fowl and praising her superior goods. At the fish stall, fresh catch from the River Don splashed in a basin. Farm butter sweated on grape leaves, pots of sour cream crowded on the counter of the dairy stall.

After the hungry years, Sofya and Alexei feasted on the lavish produce of the southern steppes. Sofya loved sour cream on warm crusty bread. With Volga blood in his veins, Alexei couldn't eat enough fresh fish. Their dining table was inside the monster wardrobe. They sat there cross-legged, with a picnic spread between them. On

Sundays they treated themselves to dinner at the party club. The tables were set under the trees. After the scarlet Ukrainian borshch they had kotlety with aubergine sauce. The river lapped at the bottom of the garden. On these summer evenings they went exploring. After the day's heat the city around them rested in the cool air. The scent of jasmine and children's voices drifted over the stone walls. Darkness fell much more quickly in the south.

In Leningrad, they reminded each other, it was now the season of white nights; you could read outdoors at midnight. Twilight blanched the river and tinted the city monochrome. Only at dawn would the walls of the palaces, like chameleons, restore their colours. The parks would be green again, and the first sun of the morning would ignite the gold leaf on the dome of St Isaac's. Nature never forgave the tsar for disturbing the melancholy of the Finnish marshes, Sofya mused; the beauty of Leningrad would always be austere. Here, at the other end of the country, Rostov was nature's darling, flushed with gaudy colours and exotic sights. Indolent blooms spilled over the garden walls. In the street you felt the closeness of Trans-Caucasia. You'd see a mountain tribesman, with a waist as slender as a girl's. Arrogant Chechens sold silver-tooled horse gear. Kalmyks had shaven heads, wore embroidered skull caps and spied on life through their narrow eyes. Armenians and Georgians lived here in large and prosperous communities. There was a Persian enclave in their street. Yet neither the fragrances in the evening air, nor the riotous Rostov markets, nor the southern languor could dispel Sofya's homesickness. She knew, of course she knew, the wretchedness of its climate, yet she longed for her dream city. She pined for the moody northern summers, where one day stifling heat would descend into the stone canyons of the streets, and the next day a chilly mist poured in from the Gulf of Finland.

Strolling arm in arm with Alexei through the soft darkness, Sofya yielded to the southern allure, but when she was alone in the daytime, a desperate longing took hold of her. Alexei worked a long week; Sofya yawned through interminable and identical days. When she heard a whistle in the distance, she wanted to run to the station and jump on a Leningrad train.

Alexei worried about her — 'We must find you something to

do.' But there were no jobs to be had in Rostov. It was the time of the NEP. All over the country, profiteers flaunted forgotten luxuries, while most of the Russians, hungry and unemployed, were still scrambling out of the rubble left by the civil war.

One evening she was waiting for him at the street corner and saw him, in the dusk, leaping off the moving tram. 'Eureka,' he called out to her, 'I've found a job for you!'

Rostov-on-the-Don,
14 August 1925

Darling Katya,

You can't imagine what Alexei has found for me. Can you see your sister as a theatre director? They've set up a theatre group at the party club and invited me to take charge, in effect, to run the whole project. Naturally, they can't pay me. It's a contribution to people's culture — a voluntary one. But they've offered me all kinds of blandishments: a free pass for dinners at the cafeteria, complimentaries to all the shows in town, films, theatres, concerts. This is not considered a perk, but an educational involvement to keep me in touch with the state of the arts. What a pity they can't send me to Leningrad twice a year to see all the new plays, and to spend some time with you. Oh, how I miss you, Katyusha. In my dreams I visit you often. I get off the train at the Nikolayevsky Station, look for you in the crowd, and feel terribly disappointed that you are not there to meet me. I start walking to you on the Ligovka. I arrive at the Karpov apartment, and there you are waiting for me at the door, laughing and crying and hugging me. And we set off immediately down the Nevsky to the Admiralty and to St Isaac's, then to the Hermitage, and across the Palace Bridge to Vassilyevky Island . . . It's all so splendid in my dreams! Thank goodness, I don't dream as often now, or at least, I don't moan about my dreams to Alexei as much as I used to.

As I've described to you before, the first month in the south was the most tedious time in my whole life. I thought I'd die of boredom. Can you see me as a contented little housewife, shopping in the market, and spending hours over the smelly primus burner to make Alexei's favourite soup? Well, thank goodness that's over. I've grown new wings and I'm flying again. We have a group of amateurs keen to rehearse after work; every night if necessary. We're working on *A Son of the Soviets*. It's a two-act play about workers. A really contemporary piece. The club secretary and I have discussed plans for future productions. He said to me that, with my experience, I could choose whatever I liked. Quite a compliment, don't you think? They call me here the Leningrad actress. The title doesn't embarrass me. Anyone who has seen as many plays as you and I have, must have some idea what theatre is about . . .

Now, the most important question, how is it between you and Misha Karpov? You were so miserly with your news of him in your last letter. Don't you like him any more? You know my opinion. I would prefer a different type of man for you. But you've already told me that Misha is a wonderful person, and that a kind heart is a greater asset than high ambitions and film-star looks. I've got to accept that, but at least tell me a bit more. Tell me too if you are still typing and taking shorthand at your old job on Malaya Nevka? I've often wished here that I had your secretarial skills.

We've bought a sofa and a table. Our room is beginning to look like home. Oh, yes, we also bought a crêpe de Chine dress length for me, and I've found a wonderful dressmaker. Just wait, when you come to visit, you won't recognise me. You'll be met by the best-dressed woman in Rostov. Lots and lots and lots of love,

Sofya x x x

Katya in Rostov

The following spring Katya came to Rostov. Sofya spotted her at the other end of the platform, and thought how plain her sister looked. If it were not for Katya's politeness and her soft voice, no one would notice the dark-haired girl. She was thinner and even more quiet than usual. Alexei noticed a new expression in Katya's face; she looked serene and happy, he thought: 'Yes, a quiet happiness. It shines in her eyes.' Sofya was too excited to notice anything. She chattered across the raucous rattle of the tram all the way home.

'Have I told you that we're going to spend August in Tuapse? Just think, we'll be swimming in the Black Sea . . . Oh, yes, I wanted to ask you about the Voskresenskys. How are they? Did you see Alexandra before you left? And how are your fat landladies — as maternal as ever, and as matronly? And what about Misha? I'm dying to hear about your romance.'

Alexei tried to signal to his wife that this might be a delicate subject, but Sofya didn't care for hints, ignored the meaning of his glance and kept on with her questions, not waiting for replies.

Katya didn't even try to interrupt her sister's monologue. As always, Sofya was inviting everyone around to admire her charming appearance and vivacious manner. Even though she remained seated, Sofya had taken the stage and was performing to an audience. She was attracting the attention of the other passengers. Everyone was listening to those intimate questions about the family, about Misha . . . Katya dropped her eyes. 'So silly and cruel,' she thought. 'The Karpov sisters, so carelessly dismissed, are my dear friends. Yes, they're fat and motherly, but they have been my support.' In the lonely months after Sofya's marriage, their concern for Katya's welfare had grown into a mission. And they were delighted that Misha, their proletarian younger brother, had at last shown some good sense. Katya was a girl from a good family. The Karpov sisters were from the old Petersburg intelligentsia, and quietly snobbish about it.

At home, Sofya threw the glass doors open on to the balcony where the white chestnut branches reached in through the iron bars of the railing. The sisters sat down on the sofa, in opposite corners, with their knees drawn up as they used to in their childhood. More slowly than her impulsive sister, Katya began to talk. When they were children, the younger provoked battles, the older made peace. Now that they were women, the sisters had grown closer, more harmonious in their views. Sofya waited for the right moment to surprise Katya with news of her pregnancy. Katya had to tell her sister that Misha Karpov had proposed on the day of her departure, and she had accepted.

She had been packing her suitcase when he came in to say goodbye. Leaning inside the doorway, barring her escape, or his own, the jovial Misha appeared uneasy and unhappy. 'I wish you weren't going away,' he said.

Katya finished folding her dressing gown, and looked up at her suitor gravely through thick lashes. 'It's ages since I've seen my sister.'

Surprised at this unexpected misery, Misha was silent. He had never told Katya about his feelings, because it had not occurred to him that she might want to hear his declaration. Looking at her now, he realised that this girl, who was mechanically folding her dressing gown for the third time, was the dearest person in the world. Nothing else mattered; all he wanted was to keep Katya beside him in Leningrad. He thought suddenly, 'If she snaps the suitcase shut, I won't be able to tell her.' His resolution was melting and, with it, hope of keeping her. He reached out to Katya across the vast continent of the bed, across the half-packed suitcase, and heard a voice that was not his own: 'Couldn't we get married, or something? Then we'll be always together.' He stepped around the corner of the bed and pressed her tightly to his chest. He wished his heart wouldn't thump so noisily; it sounded like a factory machine. Although he didn't understand why Katya was crying, her weeping distressed him. Her tears were more painful than the knee cartilage he had damaged in his last soccer match.

'Oh, Katyusha!' The whole room was invited to witness Sofya's delight. 'Alexei,' she called to her husband, who was trying not to intrude on the sisters' confidences. He was setting the table for the feast they had prepared to celebrate Katya's arrival. He put out glasses and laid the cutlery in a neat pattern, although he knew that Sofya would swap everything around to establish her own order. He didn't really mind; it amused him to see her superior domesticity.

'Katya and Misha are getting married,' Sofya cried and threw her happy arms around her sister, then around her husband's neck. 'Let's drink to your marriage.'

Alexei poured sparkling wine into brand-new glasses and handed them to the sisters. 'To Katya and Misha,' he proposed. All three took a deep gulp of wine. After that first mouthful, Alexei bowed to Sofya and raised his glass again. 'To my wife and our daughter.'

'Oh, Alexei,' Sofya protested with playful exasperation. She shielded her stomach with both hands and smiled to herself, to a dream. 'He's convinced the baby is a girl.'

'I thought so.' Katya laughed quietly and embraced her sister. Then she sat back into the corner of the sofa and waited for the resolution of the Shubins' domestic ceremony. She had never seen anything like it before. Here was a courtship dance of two beautifully plumed creatures. Both were adept at it, confident; both enjoyed the intricacy of the steps, and the mutual erotic arousal.

Alexei scooped up his wife from the sofa and carried her to the table.

'Oh, you've got it all wrong,' Sofya pouted prettily. 'Let me down. I'll do it again.' He laughed and held her tighter; she struggled and pretended to be angry. Then he released her, and she began changing round the cutlery and moving the glasses.

'Sofya's playfulness doesn't suit her,' thought Katya, lying on the sofa behind a folding screen that night. The sheets were smooth and the pillow soft. Outside the uncurtained window a conspiratorial street light winked at her through the branches of white blossom. 'I'm never going to play games with Misha,' Katya promised herself as she fell asleep.

Letters from Rostov

Rostov-on-the-Don,
15 January 1927

Dearest Katya,

Dinochka is six months old today and we are still amazed at the miracle of her. Now honestly, could you have imagined your restless sister as a mother? And Alexei — a father? That tireless builder of a new society, that's what I call him when he arrives home from work after midnight, and pulls me out of bed because he can't bear to eat supper alone. So he wraps me in the yellow eiderdown, sits me on the sofa, and threatens that if I dare fall asleep while he tells me about the ever-thrilling activities at the office, he'll put me out on the frozen balcony. Your niece sleeps like an angel through all such dramatic episodes. I keep peeping at her every few minutes. I can't resist it. She's just so beautiful when she's asleep; when she's awake she smiles.

Remember, you wished me a daughter with our mother's good looks? As you can see from the photograph, Dinochka doesn't look like Mama, she's the image of Alexei, except for her hair; it's fair like mine. She has Alexei's dark eyes and eyebrows, his nice mouth and chin. She even has his big ears! Poor child. Though I think she may have Mama's long fingers and beautiful narrow feet. I suppose all mothers adore their firstborn, but I really think she is prettier than any other child in our street. Everyone stops to admire her when I take her for walks. And I feel ridiculously proud.

I used to be impatient before Dinochka was born. I marvelled at your kindness, and thought that some women were naturally maternal, while others, like me, were not. But not any longer. With my small daughter I have all the patience in the universe.

Yesterday was our father's anniversary. I kept thinking all day how you cared for him those last five months of his life, after Mama died and he was grieving for her. It was you, Katya, who kept the household together. Oh, Katya, do you remember how he wept all night in his room? All those hours he sat at her grave, and we used to beg him to come home, to have some food and rest. It still breaks my heart when I think of it. I hope never to see such pain and loneliness again. What sad thoughts your pessimist sister is indulging in on this sparkling winter morning. Winter has truly settled in now; the snow is deep and crisp, and the days are wonderfully sunny. We take Dinochka out on her little toboggan. We built a snow baba for her last Sunday. She watched us so seriously while we rolled the huge snowball, decorated baba's face with carrot and bits of coal and put a broomstick in her arms. Neighbourhood children gathered around us. Then Dinochka began to laugh and wave to them from her winter wrappings.

Sometimes I think that all people do these days is produce new Soviet citizens. Two more babies born in our apartment; the neighbourhood is full of prams. Alexei says we are really making a new society.

With many, many, many kisses, x x x x x x

Your Sofya

Rostov-on-the-Don,
29 July 1927

Darling Katya,

I knew you would disapprove, even before I received your letter. But what am I to do if my restless nature drives me out of the house and into the workplace? Now, Alexei doesn't share your view; he agrees with my decision to finish my studies and have a really useful diploma. To tell you the truth, I wasn't that keen on the economics course, but he said economic planning and management were the most useful skills for our future. Comrade Patriot that he is! I tease him and remind him of his patriotic school years: how he played truant, and followed the street riots. He told me once how he joined the mob looting Becker's piano shop; he said he enjoyed smashing up grand pianos. He and his friends also helped to toss tea-chests out of the Vysotsky Tea Company's windows. His parents got wind of his patriotic activities, and there was a terrible row. They never trusted him after that. Have I ever told you that, when Alexei joined the Red Army, his father stopped speaking to him altogether? And then he died while Alexei was serving with the Army in Central Asia. I know Alexei can't forgive himself for the rift, and especially for not being with his father at the end. He's convinced he broke his father's heart when he defected from family traditions. Just as well his father never found out that Alexei had joined the party. It's strange how often I think of our parents' generation these days, as if I need to understand them better, now that I have a child of my own.

The past keeps turning up at every corner, especially in my thoughts. The other day I was sitting in a lecture on Marxist-Leninist theory and suddenly remembered: it's the 23rd, the day Mama died nine years ago. Everything around me seemed strange: the voice of the lecturer sounded so strident. I looked at the portraits of Marx, Lenin and Stalin as though I had never seen them in my life. It really was an extraordinary sense of alienation. I felt upset that our parents' world was still being bashed and violated; that we're forced to spit and trample on it at every step; not allowed to praise its finer qualities: kindness, intelligence, decency and good manners. But this anti-social mood passed quickly, thank goodness. I switched back to the lecture on the dictatorship of the proletariat, but that topic had a sting to it I'd rather not have noticed. It reminded me of the lynched policeman, lying on the Palace Bridge, the large red stain surrounding him. I thought of the proletarians looting our home, offering us a few worthless roubles for Mama's dining room furniture; they probably used her lovely chairs for firewood. Ah, well, it's all in the past. We're building a different future for our children. If you, darling Katya, would only join me in the ranks of socialist motherhood!

Last, but most important, we've got a nanny for Dinochka. Her name is Marya Fyodorovna Khaustova, and it's love at first sight: she and Dinochka adore each other. I can't imagine how I ever managed without her. She cooks, she cleans and she looks after Dinochka when I'm at lectures. But when I'm home — Dinochka is MINE! I send Nyanya Marya off to the market.

With love and kisses,

Sofya

Rostov-on-the-Don,
14 November 1927

Darling Katya,

Being with you day after day, evening after evening. Waking up at night to hear your little snores. (Yes, you do snore! Don't ever try to deny it, I've got witnesses!) The joy of your visit followed by the sadness of your departure. I wanted to howl and run after the tail lights of the express which took you back north; wanted to pull you back with my own hands. Thank you for the wonderful birthday present. What a feast of poetry. I've been looking for Akhmatova in all the bookshops here for ages, and couldn't find a single volume. And you've managed to find the four books. Oh miracle of miracles! All of them early editions, and so exquisitely bound and printed. As soon as your parcel arrived I went into seclusion. I lay on the sofa and let Akhmatova's poems wash over me like summer rain. What a wonderful, wonderful poet. Aren't we fortunate to live in her century, and to share Leningrad, the city we all love, with her?

> But I'll remember the talk,
> The smoky noon, Sunday
> In the grey, tall house
> At the sea gates of the Neva.

Poet talks to poet! I love this poem to Alexander Blok. And the poem where she grieves in southern exile. That's how I felt at first in Rostov.

> Everything is taken: strength and love.
> The body thrown into an unloved city
> Cannot rejoice in the sun. The blood
> In me has gone quite cold.

It's as if Akhmatova writes about me in the poem about farewells.

> We're no good at saying goodbye —
> We keep wandering shoulder to shoulder.
> Already night draws in.
> You are pensive, I am silent.
>
> We might walk into a church and see
> A funeral, baptism, a marriage.
> Without looking at each other, we leave . . .
> Why are our lives so different?

Alexei and I wandered in the snow just like Akhmtova's lovers. After our interminable farewells in the cold, Alexei got pneumonia. That's when the doctor warned him that he would be safer in the south with his weak lungs, and Alexei accepted the job in Rostov, this unloved city where I shrink from the sun. Well, there's not much sun here now in November. It may not be as dismal as our Leningrad autumn, but the slush is just as miserable and, if anything, the mud is deeper. So when everyone arrived for my birthday supper, the corridor was full of galoshes. The gramophone was playing my favourite foxtrots, and the table was set with Nyanya Màrya's special dishes. Her southern cooking is out of this world. She has taught me how to marinade fish and how to make a real Rostov borshch. We bottled vegetables last autumn. Now we have jars of purple aubergines, red tomatoes, yellow capsicums and white salted mushrooms decorating the top of our monster wardrobe. For my birthday table she made a delicious cabbage pie (just like Mama used to make it) as well as a Napoleon gateau, which I adore.

At first we all danced. (We had moved Dinochka to our neighbours for the evening, with her cot, and her potty.) For once my new shoes didn't pinch. Yes, I know exactly what you'll be thinking, that I should buy my shoes half a size larger. However, I've solved the problem: Nyanya Marya stretched my new shoes for me. They cost the earth, but I was lucky to get them at all; imported shoes get snapped up before they even reach the shelves. Just imagine, Nyanya Marya walking about in our communal kitchen, wearing the most fashionable shoes. Though I must tell you she's an unlikely nyanya; she's young, very good-looking and well educated. I think she comes from the Cossacks; she doesn't talk about her family. Anyway, last night I put my shoes on, and they fitted me like a glove. Softest leather. Bronze colour. Beautiful.

After dancing we all sat down to supper. There were cries of delight at the sight of the spread, toasts and congratulations, and later Lyova Shatov sang the birthday aria from *Eugene Onegin*, specially adapted for the occasion of my birthday: 'Brillez, brillez, belle Sofya.' With his seductive baritone, he should have trained for the opera instead of engineering, but nowadays everyone is an engineer. Whenever I hear Lyova, I think of your Misha singing Schubert songs. And speaking of musical people, you know my friend Anya Olenich? You've met her here: she's the small dark girl with big, big eyes. Well, her husband Mitya Ivanov has had a letter from his mother. She is married to the conductor Nikolai Andreyevich Malko; he's conducting in Germany and America. Mitya is not happy about this correspondence with overseas. He doesn't want any unpleasantness. But he can't stop his mother from writing to him, can he?

And apropos of unpleasantness. I didn't want to write about this, but it's been on my mind a lot, and you know I can't keep anything from you. A few weeks ago Alexei came home depressed. I can always tell when he's hiding something. Well, at their party meeting there had been a discussion on the restructuring of agriculture. Alexei voiced his doubts about collectivisation. He said the plan was too rigid. You needed the support and goodwill of the rural population, as much as of the factory labour, in order to achieve a truly socialist economy. And his friend Lyova Shatov supported him, of course.

Well! They were shouted down, accused of Trotskyite views and censured by the comrades. Now they'll have a reprimand formally recorded in their party dossiers. One of the comrades got so vicious, he demanded their expulsion. But the others soothed him down. Someone even suggested they shouldn't be allowed to attend the 7 November celebrations. But that too, thank goodness, was dismissed.

It all seems to have blown over. Oh, Katyusha, I can't tell you how worried I've been.

At my birthday, to my relief, there were no political discussions, only gypsy songs, and lots of dancing, which I adore. Alexei had brought some fabulous records from his last Moscow trip.

I was so pleased to read about you and Misha leading your sedate married life in the Karpov apartment. Oh, you lucky creatures, you've seen *The Bedbug*. I still dream of Meyerhold's staging of *Masquerade*. Whatever he directs, be it a Mayakovsky play or a nineteenth-century classic, his productions are supreme. Don't you agree? He's just so inventive, so avant garde. What I miss here is great theatre. And, by the way, my own theatrical contribution here has fallen by the wayside after Dinochka's birth. So when I think of you and Misha going to the Mariinsky, I turn green with envy. But most of all, I miss you, Katya, your company and the sight of our lovely city.

With love and kisses,

Sofya

Rostov-on-the-Don,
8 March 1928

Katya, my clever darling sister!

You're pregnant. That's the best news I've had for ages. Your letter arrived yesterday, but I decided not to tell Alexei until this morning, and give him an extra birthday present. Well, that baby of yours will have a wonderful time deciding whether to arrive on the 7th November holiday or a week later on my birthday. And I refuse to speculate what you'll have. (In the softest whisper, I predict it's going to be a boy, and you'll call him Nikolai, after Papa. I haven't written this, and you haven't read it.) I'm sending all Dinochka's baby clothes to you straightaway, so that you can start clucking like a little hen. As I've told you, I don't want any more babies. Dinochka is an angel, but one is quite enough for me. We haven't been able to get a larger apartment. This room is crowded with cot and toys, potty and pushchair. I couldn't cope with more than one child, anyway.

My job in the Lesprom is fascinating. Thank goodness, I'm not the only greenhorn in the team. My mentor is Tarakhovsky, the Chief Economist himself; it's like talking to God. He drills us like soldiers, forces us to work till we grovel for a rest; he is such a wonderful teacher. Thanks to him, I'm beginning to understand the economics of the forestry industry. It's my turn to visit you this year. I was going to ask Alexei to let me go to Leningrad in August, but I think I'd better wait till November, and come with Dinochka to see your baby.

With love and jubilation,

Sofya

Rostov-on-the-Don,
6 January 1929

Darling Katya,

I've been home for two weeks, and I still can't get you and our lovely Leningrad out of my mind. Such is the irony of life, that when I'm with you, I miss Alexei, and when I'm back in Rostov, I pine for you and Leningrad. This visit I really felt as though I had returned to the city of our youth. A strange sensation, when we both are married women with children of our own.

I suppose what transported me back was the grey time of the year. The city was as stark and cold as in the days of the revolution. No magical reflections of palaces in the river this time. But it was so lovely when I was with you in the Ligovka apartment, in your domestic oasis. You suit motherhood more than anyone I know. You're so kind, so calm. And little Ada reflects your serenity; she lies in her basket like a doll. How sweet of your sisters-in-law to track down the Karpov family cot so little Ada can sleep in the same cot as her father, and his sisters before him.

I keep going over images from my visit like photographs. Which reminds me, I'd like you to take Ada to the studio for a portrait, and send me one soon. It was wonderful that the four of us were together with our little daughters in Leningrad, even if it was just for two days. Pure chance that Alexei's trip to Moscow coincided with the end of my visit. It's the first time Alexei and I have been together in Leningrad since the summer we got married. Your Misha wasn't on the scene then.

I often take out that first photo of you and me with Alexei. We look so young, which I suppose we were then. I was nineteen and you were twenty-two. Now I can't wait to see the photo of the four of us. Only I wish we had taken the babies along with us to the studio.

Travelling with Alexei was bliss. A train journey with a small child is so much easier when there are two of you. Dinochka was very lively. She even managed to throw one of her new shoes out of the window somewhere near Kharkov. A silly man opened the window, and she very cleverly pushed the shoe through the crack.

Oh, Katya, I'm so happy that you've got to know Dinochka. She's no longer a baby, but a real person. And she does look like Alexei, doesn't she? You know what Nyanya Marya says: a girl who looks like her father is born lucky, she'll have a long and happy life. I can't wait to see who Ada will resemble. At the moment she's her own adorable baby self. She'll be very different at our next meeting. And I simply can't wait for Dinochka to start talking.

x x x x x x x Sofya

Rostov-on-the-Don,
24 March 1929

Darling Katya,

These are strange times. Dreadful things are happening on the land. Here in Rostov, the stalls at the marketplace are overflowing with the first spring greens and fresh eggs, but out on the land, people are disappearing. No one talks about it or, if we do, then very cautiously. We don't know what to make of it. Alexei is moody and jumpy. He leaves early, comes home late, and doesn't encourage any questions from me. In my own job, I'm pretty isolated from developments in the countryside since we deal with orders for industrial plant.

There are unscheduled trains moving through Rostov, full of kulaks and their families. They are being deported. No one knows where. The recent decree says that anyone helping the kulaks will be arrested and deported as well. And in the meantime, villages are depopulated, houses are empty, cattle abandoned. I know all this from my Nyanya Marya; her parents have been deported, and she is beside herself, but neither of us dares talk to Alexei about it because he's in a black mood. Who could have thought that collectivisation would turn against the sort of farmers who were the mainstay of agriculture? At least, I believed that the new collectives would make the countryside a wonderful place for all the peasants, that all would co-operate, each help the others. But if you exile the successful ones like Nyanya Marya's family, who will be left to do the work in the village? And if the law punishes those who give the unfortunate a helping hand, or a piece of bread, for heaven's sake . . . Well, what's left then of our traditional compassion, of our Russian soul?

I've written all this down, and suddenly I feel frightened. What if somebody reads our letters? Maybe I won't even send this. Oh, rubbish, who can be bothered with women's gossip. Anyway, what's wrong with being concerned about human beings? Russian people have always prided themselves on having a conscience.

12 April (continuing) I felt too nervous to post this letter; it has been in the desk drawer all this time. I really must send it. And I must tell you what's happening here in the streets of Rostov. I saw a woman begging, with two small children. I stopped to give her all I had on me. She looked up, and her eyes were red-rimmed, hollow. I asked her where she came from? She said, 'From hell.' No emotion! At the time of the round-up, she was away from her stanitsa. Her family has been deported to Siberia. She was desperate to find shelter for her children. Could I help her? I wanted to help. But what would happen to us if I helped a kulak?

I left her in the street with her children, and said I would come back for her. At home, I told Nyanya Marya, and we decided to take her in, whatever the risk. We both went back for her, but she wasn't there. She must have been picked up by the militia. I still feel awful about it. I did abandon a human being in terrible need.

The city is full of petty crime. The besprizornye are everywhere. There's a constant hunt for them, but they have a keen nose for danger and strong legs; few of them get caught. I saw a handbag snatch just beside me on the tram stop. A very small boy, only about seven, but so expert at it. He just melted into the crowd. We had some besprizornye hiding in a woodshed, in the next courtyard; and no one even knew they were there, until they were arrested. I saw them being taken to the militia van. Two young boys and a girl, no older than eleven or twelve. They were snarling like wild creatures. Poor things. Though I must say I'd hate to be attacked by a gang of them in a dark street.

And to make it even more scary there are all sorts of epidemics sweeping the town. They say, because of hunger and dislocation in the countryside, a lot of infectious illness has been brought into the city. Although I try to keep Dinochka away from other children in the park, she demands company. What can I do! Oh, Katya, she is so lovely, with those big brown eyes and fair curls. And always so serious. It's not that she lacks a sense of fun, not at all. She can be very playful. But she sometimes has the look of a sad adult.

Your loving sister,

Sofya

Rostov-on-the-Don,
10 July 1929

Dearest Katya,

You left yesterday, and I don't know how I'll cope without you. If anything my pain is sharper, my grief is deeper — it's bottomless. Neither of us sleeps much. I hear Alexei gagging his groans as he pads quietly up and down the room at night, but as soon as he hears me awake, he pretends to be the stronger one.

Oh God, what have we done to be punished like this? In the past I used to ask myself the reverse: how did we deserve a pretty, clever little girl? And now she's dead. Why, Katya, why? Isn't there some kind of explanation, why a child should be taken away? A child you love so much, and miss so much.

You came immediately, as I knew you would, and while you were with me I probably didn't thank you, didn't tell you what your presence meant to me. You left your own baby and rushed to comfort me. And now you are going to spend three uncomfortable nights on the journey home.

I must have told you a hundred times, but I can't stop thinking how sweet Dinochka was, even when the fever was burning her up. Her hair turned dark from sweat; she looked like an angel painted by an Italian master. Why did she have to die? Other children came down with measles in the epidemic. Some, like her, had scarlet fever as well. Yet all seemed to have recovered except my Dinochka. I suppose diphtheria was the last straw. My poor little daughter — she couldn't cope with all three infections.

There is nothing of hers left. The toys and clothes you didn't take home with you, have gone to other people. The room is empty, as if a bright little girl never lived here; never chatted, sang, played with her toys and gave us heart failure when she tried to climb the balcony railing. The last wrench was letting Nyanya Marya go; she went to my friend Anya Olenich. You met her here, remember? Her little boy is eighteen months old.

I'm going back to work next week. We'll both work hard, and try to find some meaning in our life. Oh, Katya, it's so bleak here.

Your sister Sofya

The Peaks of Mount Elbrus

Nadya wasn't meant to be born. Her parents already had a substitute for their much-mourned firstborn. Sofya and Alexei's second daughter, Vera, was born in the same Rostov clinic several years after Dinochka's death. And now, just as life had settled into a comfortable path, Sofya was pregnant again. Unplanned. It was a nuisance. Alexei's star was rising in the managerial hierarchy. Sofya had a job she enjoyed and, with the arrival of Anna Pavlovna, who had secretly baptised little Vera, the child and the household were in capable hands. Indeed, Sofya was almost forced to cleave to her career, because her mother-in-law's imperious ways made it difficult for her to stay at home.

Alexei was now regional director of the wine industry in the Northern Caucasus. About the time of Vera's birth, the head office of the southern region was transferred from Rostov to Pyatigorsk, the spa town in the foothills of the mountain ranges. Sofya was glad to leave Rostov, that unloved city with its sad memories, for a new start in a smaller and prettier town. She liked Pyatigorsk from the moment she saw it on a spring day when the snow was melting on the slopes of the great mountains. The five peaks didn't doff their caps: the snow glittered on the tops throughout the long hot summer. Pyatigorsk lay at the foot of Mount Mashuk, which seemed a hill beside the other giants. The sleepy town sprawled on the slope all the way down to the fast-flowing Podkumok. The houses were white, the roofs matched the green of the gardens. The chains of the Great Caucasus were strung on the neck between the two seas, the Black and the Caspian, cutting off the southern plains of Russia from the mysterious face of Asia Minor.

'What a gypsy move that was,' Sofya told Nadya in later years. 'Vera was a baby. Anna Pavlovna came to visit, and then stayed on, settled in permanently. The apartment went with the job. We had two rooms. Marvellous rooms — huge, high ceilings. A small corridor-room between them — that's where Babushka slept. It was her own corner. I thought it was like a monastic cell. We shared the bathroom and kitchen with one other family. You entered through the grand entrance and walked up the wide stone staircase to the top landing, which we had to ourselves. The stairs were a wonderful playroom for Vera and her little friends. They used to swing on the coats hanging on the top. Once Vera fell headfirst into a pot of soup below. Thank heavens, it had already cooled down.'

After each expedition into one of the golden moments of the past, Sofya would fall silent, locked in her private vision of the pretty wife of a party executive, luxuriating in flattery, fine wines and imported shoes. The petted Sofya of those days accepted compliments as her due, as genuine admiration. It was lovely, though, while it lasted, she would sigh to herself and then go on with her story.

'There was an army of poplars marching up Gogol Street, burnished bronze each September. Outside our own windows, just as in Rostov, we had chestnut trees. Their creamy candles lit up in May. Wherever you turned the five snowy peaks smiled at you in the sunlight. Beshtau was like an ice cone, the moody Kazbek was mostly hidden in a cloud and the two peaks of Elbrus were so lovely . . .'

'But what about me?' Nadya couldn't wait to be let into this seductive picture, in which sister Vera had already taken up far too much space.

'You came later. You were a treasure from the moment you uttered your first cry. But, you do know, you weren't really meant to be born.'

'We don't need another child,' said Sofya, and booked herself in for an abortion. The clinic was on the upper slope of Mount Mashuk, where all the sanatoria and clinics were housed in the summer palaces of the pre-revolutionary rich. Early on a summer evening, Sofya and Alexei were strolling up the hill to the clinic. The air was warm and still. Daylight had faded in the valley below, but the mountain peaks above them were rose-petal pink in the last of the sun.

Sofya walked in a pleasant dream. 'You know, I feel almost in love with this place. It's so peaceful here.' She had accepted this quiet town into her favour, as she never had Rostov. Everything here charmed her. Yes, she mused, she could easily live here for a few more years, though she couldn't remain here forever, she added quickly. She couldn't be disloyal to her lovely northern city. Some time later they must move back to Leningrad. She wanted to be close to Katya, the theatres, the river. The years she had missed might be reflected in its lustrous flow. Sofya leaned her head just below Alexei's dependable shoulder, as far as she could reach. He was her protector, her lover who indulged all her whims. She felt cherished and spoilt by him, as if she was still a girl. His passion flattered her more than it excited her own desire. But that was how she wanted it to go on, forever. 'The place where you live isn't everything . . .' Her tone implied that, if she wished, she could be sensible. After all, there were more important things in life than accidents of geography.

Alexei made a vague sound of assent. He felt no need to contradict his wife; he was content living in the south. Besides, he had a lot on his mind. The aftermath of Kirov's death was worrying. His murder, and the purge of the party members that followed, mainly in Leningrad, should be old history by now. But there was another purge under way. Only this one was advancing on a much wider front. More than just ominous rumblings: front-page articles appeared more frequently in *Pravda*, denouncing various groups of sabotage or treason. Engineers working on great construction projects were accused first. The top military had been arrested, tried and shot. The country was suddenly seething with wreckers and spies. Vigilance, cried the press, ranting against those cunning enemies of the people, who were lurking in every nook and cranny of Soviet life. Not even the party was sacrosanct. He had just heard that his former colleagues in the Rostov commissariat had been rounded up. The news depressed him. He had a feeling that a searchlight was scanning the field, and any moment the beam might catch him in its glare. He shivered.

Sofya looked up at him in surprise. 'Are you cold?'

'I've become a real southerner. Even a summer evening feels too cool for my thin blood.' Alexei was not wont to brood. All he had to do now was to squash those oppressive thoughts. A few moments later, he felt himself restored to a state of well-being. That was better. He took a deep breath of the mellow air, and tightened his arm around Sofya's shoulders. Her upturned face, damp from the climb, was close to his. The odour of her sweat made him giddy. What if he picked her up and carried her into the shrubbery over there? He needed to feel her warmth, wanted to caress her until she welcomed him. 'I want you,' he whispered into her ear, and scanned the neighbourhood for a quiet place. The bushes he had selected for their tryst a few moments ago turned out to be in the centre of a commune. Children were playing nearby; he caught sight of two fat women gossiping across the fence, watching them and other couples, lovers looking for privacy. Not one of those men could possibly be as desperate as he was, he thought. He drew Sofya behind a tree to kiss her. His hands, those determined explorers of her flesh, found her breasts. Now that she was pregnant, her nipples were more sensitive to his touch. She sighed as she joined him in the kiss, and guided his hand under the floating fabric of her skirt.

A few years ago in Rostov, while Dinochka was still alive, he told Sofya that he would gladly trade the rest of his life for just ten years of happiness. Superstitious like all women, Sofya cupped his mouth with her hand, and cried, 'Don't ever ever say it again, Alexei, you mustn't joke about such things.' Well, he still felt astonishingly happy with Sofya. Even the frightening rumours around them could not infect his joy, not even the ache for the lost child. Yet here they were on their way to terminate an inconvenient pregnancy. They had been over most of the arguments for and against another child; they had made their decision. None of their friends had large families. Wives had their own careers. They had been brought up to quote that, unlike previous generations, Soviet women had the freedom to take part in the construction of their socialist future. He himself believed this, even if he continued to joke with other men that a woman's place was at home with the children.

Yes, but childbirth was so distressing. Even now, he couldn't bear thinking of Sofya's agony with Dinochka; she'd had an easier time with Vera. Suddenly, he had a clear recollection of his first child, just born, crinkled, red-stained, screaming and punching the world with her tiny fists. And his sense of wonder at the sight of this small human that he and Sofya had created with their bodies. In all his life, filled with goals and achievements, nothing had moved him as profoundly as the mystery of his child's birth.

And what about the fistful of gristle, blood and tissue about to be scraped out of Sofya's body? If they allowed it to grow, it would be a child, like the others. Was he changing his mind, going back on their decision? 'Sofya,' he held her tighter. Tenderly he repeated, 'Sofya?'

'Mmm?' she pressed her body closer to his.

'Sofya,' he repeated her name tenderly, 'let's keep the baby.' His voice was pleading with her not to be upset.

Sofya looked up at him, her face astonished, 'How strange!' she said. 'That's exactly what I've been thinking. I was looking at the mountains, at Elbrus with its two pinnacles, and I thought, how nice it would be to have two children.'

He had often laughed at her muddled arguments; her feminine logic was beyond him, he complained. Now it delighted him. It seemed the most sensible observation she had ever made. He wanted to jump and sing like a boy. 'We are going to have another child! Perhaps, a son. We'll name him Nikolai, after Sofya's father.' He looked at his wife's profile, soft in the falling dusk. Her smile was a mystery he didn't want to invade. She was so small, so unbelievably, inexpressibly dear. 'Ah, my little one.' He loved her warmth inside his embrace.

Nadezhda Means Hope

On New Year's Eve the Shubins had a party. Just a few close friends, they decided; they were going to have a good time while they could. The baby wasn't due for another week. Soon enough they would start the next round of nappies and wake-up calls. Alexei and Sofya raised glasses; their secret toast was to a son. Sofya had been feeling irritable and tired. Her feet were swollen, she complained before the party. Her shoes pinched and there was no Nyanya Marya around to stretch them for her. As for Sofya's figure, she was so much larger with this baby than she had been with the other two. In fact, she felt quite ugly tonight.

Sofya's labour started without warning in the middle of the tango. 'Jealousy . . .' she was humming, even though she knew she sounded flat. Who cares. And then a sudden stab of pain made her cry out. She felt herself doubling over, slipping down, hanging limp like a doll in Alexei's arms. He carried her to a chair. She breathed more easily as the pain passed. 'Don't stop. Tell them not to stop dancing.' Another sharp twist followed swiftly on the heels of the first. Sofya gasped, 'This baby insists on arriving in the middle of a party. How unfair.' After the contraction, she waved to her friends from the door of the bedroom. The guests obediently put on another dance record. Alexei had gone for the midwife. And in the first minutes of the New Year, after a short labour, Sofya gave birth to another daughter. 'That was a good decision last summer,' she smiled at her husband. 'Yes, the two peaks of Elbrus,' he whispered back.

The baby's urgent arrival did not spoil the party; indeed, it made it the most memorable New Year celebration any of their friends ever had. Only the midwife felt cheated. The baby's rushed appearance robbed her of the soothing ministration which she took pride. She definitely did not approve of the noisy party next door. The father, too, was a nuisance, hovering in the room instead of waiting quietly somewhere out of sight until the women's business was completed.

'She's got a cowl,' the midwife announced proudly, as if she herself had arranged for the special feature.

'What's a cowl?' asked the ignorant young mother, who should have been limp with exhaustion, but instead was looking indecently perky.

'A cowl is the amniotic sack. Some babies are born wearing it like a shirt. There's an old saying that children born in a "little shirt" are lucky.'

'A child born auspiciously,' added Anna Pavlovna.

Sofya was sitting up against the pillows, her face bright, her eyes very blue. The afterbirth had come away like a charm and the baby's face beside her on the pillow was not at all red and scrawny. 'I want some champagne,' she ordered and stretched out her bare arms, as if showing off their smoothness, and the charm of her full breasts under the sheer nightdress. She felt her power over the whole world. Alexei handed her the champagne, sat down on the edge of the bed and stroked the creamy loveliness of those arms. Oblivious of others, they kissed, shared the champagne and kissed again. The midwife turned away, thinking peevishly, 'These new women are indecorous, indecent. And the husbands are just as bad.'

'Well,' Alexei couldn't turn the delight on his face into a more sober expression, 'now let's be serious. We haven't got a Nikolai Alexeievich, you've given me an Alexeievna. What shall we name her?'

Sofya purred like a much-stroked kitten. 'Poor Alexei, your last hope of a son gone. Yes, hope — Nadezhda. Let's call her Nadezhda. Nadyenka. Nadya. Nadyusha.' She burst into laughter at the large collection of endearments for such a diminutive creature. The champagne had gone straight to her head. She tried to keep her eyes open but her eyelids were heavy with fatigue. Sofya reached out her hand to Alexei's face; light as butterfly wings, her fingertips stroked his hair, brushed his cheeks, fluttered across his lips. On the pillow beside her, the baby was a chrysalis. She bent down and kissed the small dusky face. 'My little Nadya,' she murmured, as she fell asleep.

Lying beside her mother, bound tightly in a white swaddling blanket, Nadya raised her lids and looked into her father's identical eyes.

The Land of Women

(*The Second*)

There was no such thing as a rosy childhood . . .
Freckles and teddybears and toys
And kind aunts, frightening uncles and
Friends made of river pebbles.
From the beginning I felt like
Someone else's dream or delirium
Or a reflection in a stranger's mirror.

From 'Northern Elegies', July 1955

Nadezhda could not remember her father; she grew up without him. After the purges of '37 and '38, there were few fathers left; most of them were in Siberia. In those years Russia must have seemed a land of women. It was women who worked on construction sites, who stood forever in queues, who waited outside prisons for news of their men. That's why, in the first years of her life, Nadya knew mostly women. In the Caucasus her mother and grandmother cared for her. In Leningrad, later, her aunts joined the band of her protectors. This women's kingdom included her medical cousin, Nina, and the musical cousins, Ada and Kira.

Vera was always around describing, in that supercilious tone of the older child, what their father had been like. Nadya wasn't sure if there was anything she actually remembered about him. Tucked away in a secret little box, she treasured a tiny collection of images: the echo of a voice, a laugh, a fleeting expression. What she knew of her father had come from her mother's stories and family photographs. A face that was an unlined twin of Anna Pavlovna's: Nadya's eyes and a mouth that Vera had also inherited. There was a picture of the young Alexei, taken one summer in the twenties, with a fashionably shaved head. Another photo showed a smiling executive among his colleagues, confident, successful. There was also the sick Alexei. Nadya studied all these different faces until they blended into an image as familiar as a poem learnt by heart. As intimate as if she had just said goodbye to a real father on the stairs. Yet, in moments of anguish, she would cry out to Vera, her sister and her rival, that she didn't even know what their father looked like. The ultimate truth was that she couldn't accept being fatherless, and that there could be no substitute for her loss. Sometimes, she hated that lost father. She wanted to kick and scratch him, scream at him for having allowed himself to be removed from her life.

Between Past and Future

Later, in the middle of the war, after Leningrad, when their refugee journey began, Nadya would ask the questions and Sofya would talk. What else was there to do but talk, as they retreated with the Wehrmacht, west across occupied Russia? They would stop in provincial towns for weeks, sometimes for months, until the gunfire caught up with them, and then they would start fleeing again, to the next peaceful haven, or so the place would seem to them after the terrors of the war zone. Through endless nights, squatting on their bundles, they waited for trains in draughty railway stations.

Refugee life was an existence suspended between countries and cultures, between a rich past and an empty future. Your possessions were what you could carry. Your most guarded treasures were your children and your memories, which you now shared with your children. As the three of them travelled from Russia into the heart of Europe, through bombed-out cities, burnt villages, past skeletons of noble cathedrals and romantic palaces, past dead hospitals and empty schools, a mother would compose colourful wreaths of her life to comfort her young daughters.

(i)

'Your father and I met at a youth rally in Leningrad: in an ocean of young faces, students, workers, school children. It was the Day of Youth, the 1st of September, and all of them had been ordered to parade. The organisers were strict. In the morning you had to report at your meeting point, then you marched with your own group.' The unpunctual Sofya was running late, terrified she would miss her group. That would have meant a black mark in her komsomol card; there was already her suspect social origin. 'We all had to work hard to prove our loyalty to the state.'

They marched in ranks down the Nevsky, waving banners and singing Red Army songs. 'Songs of the Stalin years were written much later.' *They gathered on the square in front of the Winter Palace to listen to speeches. One after another, party luminaries paid tribute to their wonderful new society. The young were the new wave, children of the Peasants and Workers, citizens of a Radiant Future. They would prove to the rest of the world that in the Soviet Union the vision of Marx and Lenin had been realised: here they had a benign dictatorship of the proletariat.*

It was their second big rally that year. In the summer when Lenin died they were brought together for a wake. 'And we did grieve.' *They wept for the father of the first communist state; for the man who had made the revolution. They idolised Lenin, said Sofya. Besides, they all wanted to believe in the promised future.* 'There was so much hardship around us, hunger and chaos behind us, that it was balm to believe and to belong.'

It was a long day on the square. They sat on the warm stone paving, listened and talked among themselves. Next to Sofya's group was another collective. One of them, a dark young man, made amusing comments about the speakers. Someone said that his name was Alexei Shubin. Too sure of himself, Sofya thought; he's smiling to show off his teeth — nice teeth. He was older, had been in the army, and was now studying and working, as all of them did in those days. And that might have been the end of it, if she hadn't met him again, a week later. He came to the youth club, where she was the cultural organiser. She put on plays, took groups of young railway workers on Sunday tours of palaces and museums. Her charges were young lads from the provinces, speechless at the splendour of this formerly imperial city. Sofya loved guiding them, showing off her Petrograd.

Alexei came to invite members of Sofya's club to pay a fraternal visit to the industrial plant nearby, where he worked. They were putting on their first play, and they needed an experienced audience. She went to see The Red Dawn. *Like so many of those komsomol theatricals, the play was about the bad old days and the glorious victory of the workers. The actors suffered from stage fright and forgot their lines. The curtain wouldn't rise, and in the end it collapsed on top of the stagehands. Alexei Shubin, the star of the show, was a grizzled railway man, exploited by capitalists.* 'I've lost my arm because of those bloodsuckers!' *he tried to enunciate through the Maxim Gorky moustache, which muffled his lines. As the tsarist Okhrana came pounding on the door, Alexei flapped his empty sleeve and shouted,* 'Brothers, fellow workers, hold *fast! Don't give in to the demands of the bourgeois bosses. Our solidarity will vanquish them . . .'* The revolutionary rhetoric was too ardent for the moustache — it was coming unstuck. At that point the 'lost' arm shot out of Alexei's tunic to save the sliding cotton wool on his upper lip.

(ii)

How vast these squares are,
How steep and resonant the bridges!
Above us the shelter of night
Heavy, starless and peaceful.

And we two are mortals
Marking the fresh snow.
Isn't it miraculous that today
We share the hour before parting?

From 'The White Flock', 1917

A man and a woman are wandering through the snowdrifts. The brave new world is unfriendly to lovers on a winter night. They have been walking up and down the Ligovka, probably for hours. They stop in the gateway of No. 82, where Sofya lives, to hug each other warm, but a homebound tenant startles them, so they take flight like birds and set off into a white nowhere lost in whirling snow.

'I'm freezing. Let's walk faster,' says Alexei to the Orenburg shawl. Inside the woolly cocoon is Sofya, snugly wrapped up in her padded coat, shod in felt boots. He can see the slits of her eyes with frosted eyelashes. They walk all the way to Znamenskaya, where he lives, and stop in his gateway. Oh, those wonderful Leningrad gateways that take you from the impersonal street to the intimate world of your fellow tenants. The yard is a square (green or white, depending on the season) walled in by four stone blocks. Doorways are marked with staircase numbers; some of the numberplates are missing. The tenants are no longer listed on the board at the porter's window, as they once were. The porters, too, are gone for good. The city gateways are shelters for children's games and babushkas' gossip in the daytime; in the night they are a haven for lovers. But drunks can also get stranded in a gateway, and leave behind the stench of vomit and urine.

Alexei lives with the Voskresenskys. 'See, on the ground floor, that's our window.' He argues with his brother-in-law about politics, and Alexandra gets upset. Why can't Dmitry concede that the old order must be swept clean away, before they can build a new society? The family suspects that Alexei is in love. 'When can they meet you?' he asks the white Orenburg shawl.

Sofya is evasive. 'Soon,' she murmurs. Two lovers alone on a planet. Cold, uninhabited, the planet is spinning in a white universe. How hard it is to say goodbye. Even if it's only for a night; even if they'll see each other again tomorrow.

'What are you thinking, my love?'

'If only we had a place where we could be warm and alone.'

'Going out tonight?' Alexandra asks her brother at dinner. Supplies in the shops have been improving; meat in their soup is a welcome change from pulses and cabbage.

'Yes, there's the new Charlie Chaplin film.'

Alexandra takes stock of how thin he looks; his face is pale from lack of sleep and an excess of emotion. The family had a terrible scare a few weeks ago, when his revolver went off in the middle of the night. They ran to him. 'He's shot himself!' Alexandra moaned. 'His girlfriend must have left him and he's taken his own life . . .' They found him sitting in bed, dazed and quite alive. The loaded army revolver he had stored under the mattress had gone off accidentally, he explained.

'But you could've killed yourself,' wept the tender-hearted Alexandra, so relieved to see him alive that she couldn't scold him for his stupidity. Dmitry took away the revolver. 'Think of it, keeping a loaded weapon!'

The Voskresenskys had already seen Hard Times but they wanted to catch a glimpse of Sofya, and went to see it a second time. The girl hardly reached Alexei's shoulder. Fair hair. Blue dress with a lace collar. 'Her mother's . . .' Alexandra decided, and her heart melted. Things like that could only be inherited these days. 'The girl is from a good family.' 'And very pretty,' said Dmitry.

'Uncle Alexei,' Nina was running off to school the next morning, 'Mama and Papa saw your girl last night at the cinema. They said she's very nice. Can't I see her too, please?'

Sofya came at Easter. The Neva was on the move, and even at a distance from the river you could hear the explosions of cracking icefloes, like shellfire. A sharp wind from the gulf swept the mackerel sky and chilled the capital. Alexandra had baked a tall kulich. Nina brought out her watercolours to decorate the red Easter eggs with the symbol of resurrection. She gave one to Sofya. 'I made this blue and gold one specially for you.' She was still shy with Sofya.

All this took Sofya back to the abandoned traditions of her childhood; she had not sat at an Easter table since her mother had died. Now she was reminded of the Easter vigil, candlelights shivering in the cold night, and then at last the church doors were thrown open and the great joy of Resurrection burst out with the jubilant voice of the choir: 'Christ has risen . . . Risen indeed!' This unexpected rush of memory moved Sofya to tears but in the Meier family you had been taught not to display your emotion in company.

(iii)

You are free, I am free,
Tomorrow is better than yesterday,
Above the dark waters of the Neva,
Under the cold smile of
Emperor Peter.

'Verses About Petersburg', 1913

Sofya wore her blue dress with the lace collar to the registry; it was the better of the two outfits she owned. In honour of their marriage, Alexei borrowed a tie from Dmitry. It was June and summer had just arrived. The ZAGS office was across the street from the Admiralty, in one of the former palaces. Both Sofya and Katya felt a breath of the past, nostalgia, as if Nikolai Nikolayevich Meier, in his naval uniform, was keeping watch over his daughters from his old Admiralty window.

The celebrant was a square-jowled woman with a martinet's voice. She might have been a commissar in the Civil War. Surveying the small group of relatives with an ideological eye, she decided they were distinctly non-proletarian in origin. The young couple, though, looked sensible. Not like some of her clients who arrived at ZAGS in a drunken stupor, and celebrated the start of their married life with more vodka. She filled out the register and the certificate of civil marriage between Shubin, Alexei Yevgenyevich, aged twenty-four, and Meier, Sofya Nikolayevna, aged nineteen, and signed it with a masterful flourish. Yakovleva, N. P. (The Registrar).

Katya hid her sadness and tried to stifle the panic she felt. Her sister, the only family she had, was leaving to start a new life in Rostov-on-the-Don. She wondered when they would meet again. They might be parting forever. She bit her lip till it bled, and swallowed her tears.

Alexandra Voskresenskaya was also dabbing her eyes, upset by this impoverished marriage rite of the new Soviet society. She grieved because her young brother was not being married in the solemn Russian Orthodox tradition. She and Dmitry were wed in the Znamenskaya church, before the revolution. The Saviour and his saints looked down on their union with a gentle benediction. The jubilant choir sang, 'Isaiah rejoice . . . Isaiah rejoice . . . Isaiah rejoice!'

The Stars of Death

Introduction

> Above us the stars of death.
> Blameless Russia convulsed
> Under the bloodied boots,
> Under the tyres of the Black Marias.

From *Requiem* (1935–1940)

How much grieving does it take to break a human heart? Sofya knew that hers was still intact. There had been moments in the past few years when she thought that she was going mad, yet she continued living, working, loving what she had kept of the real Alexei. The only purpose in her life was her children, loving and protecting them. Now, as before, she went on with the Sunday chores, pushing Molotov's announcement to the very back of her mind, as if she had not heard it. She hung out the washing, as if war had not been declared; swept the floor, as if everything was tediously normal. She searched out every speck of dust in her runt of a room, shook out the rugs savagely in the courtyard. And all the time, inside her, fear beat its frantic wings. Her children were in Leningrad, while she was here in the Caucasus, at the opposite end of Russia, more than two thousand kilometres away.

Anxious huddles of neighbours gathered in the yard, talking about the war. They left her out of their congregations, and she made no move to join in; she had been an outsider too long. There were few she trusted in the Gogol Street kommunalka and none she would want to confide in. Since her husband's arrest, and the resettlement to the far corridor of the annexe, she and Anna Pavlovna had lived the life of pariahs. One morning they discovered that their primus stove had been shifted into the darkest corner of the communal kitchen. Neither of them found the courage to complain. In any case, what would have been the use of protesting. No one would have stood up for the wife and mother of an enemy of the Soviet state. People had turned into packs of wolves hunting down the families of arrested men.

The only ones who understood and had retained some compassion were those who themselves had been visited by the NKVD in the early hours of the morning, had been humiliated or arrested. Oh, those noisily arrogant boots counting the steps, the old floorboards creaking in the corridor and then the muffled sounds of a search, sobs and thuds and curses, that went on till dawn. If there was compassion, it was not expressed; it remained hidden as a silent fellow feeling. Words of comfort could not be spoken aloud.

The first time they took him away, Alexei was thirty-six. 'Bozhe moi, he's been a prisoner four years,' she thought. And now he was older than her parents were when they died. In a complex convergence of images, Sofya remembered Alexei's fortieth birthday, which she and her mother-in-law celebrated without him earlier that year. On 8 March, on International Women's Day, when colleagues gave women flowers at work, and at home in the evening husbands and friends drank toasts to the Great Leader and to the happy new life he had created. To the Soviet womanhood who had new opportunities, respect, freedom from drudgery.

That evening when Sofya arrived from work, Anna Pavlovna was getting the girls ready for bed. As always, the children's needs came first. They went through the nightly routine of bathing in the white enamel basin. 'Face and neck first, hands next, then your bottom.' Nadya protested: 'It's too hot . . .' and Sofya wearily reassured her, 'Nonsense, Nadyenka, just sit in it. And last, feet into the basin.' Sofya wrapped the child in a bath towel and hugged her tightly. Nadya squirmed, laughing inside the cocoon, 'You're squeezing me to death, Mamochka . . .'

Anna Pavlovna carried out Nadya's bath water, and brought the hot kettle from the kitchen for Vera's ablutions, which followed the same sequence: face and neck, don't forget the ears. The older girl insisted on washing her bottom behind the screen; she was discovering modesty.

When the children were in bed, the two women, who hadn't received any chocolates or flowers that day, sat down quietly at the table. Sofya brought out a bottle of red she had kept from the old Vinprom days. She poured the wine into two glasses that had survived from the set she and Alexei bought long ago for Katya's first visit to Rostov. Everything she touched was a reminder of loss, a remnant of a life as it had been once, and would never be again.

Anna Pavlovna raised her glass. 'To Alexei!' She sounded severe, as if she disapproved of her favourite son for being in prison.

'To Alexei,' Sofya echoed and felt the sting of tears. She caught sight of the girls, wide-eyed witnesses watching guardedly from the bed.

'I wish Papa was here,' Vera whispered to her sister. 'He and I used to play games and he told me stories. He took me skiing too.'

Just then Nadya could not reciprocate with any personal memory; she had been too young when her father was arrested.

'Don't be sad,' Vera consoled her sister in a spirit of rare solidarity. 'He'll soon come back, and if you don't remember what Papa looks like, it will be like having a brand-new one.'

After Alexei's arrest, some of Sofya's closest friends stayed away. These new Soviet women, her contemporaries, were suddenly slaves to archaic superstitions, fearing the evil eye. They shunned the afflicted family as though misfortune was contagious. Later, when their own husbands were taken and fed to the insatiable NKVD machine, Sofya's friends came back to weep on her shoulder. And a year from then, Sofya and her friends were arrested as wives of enemies of the people. They all met in the prison cells.

The Pyatigorsk prison was a long way out of town, on the River Podkumok. A shapeless pile, it must have been built as a fortress at the time of the Caucasus wars in the nineteenth century, when the imperial troops stormed the homeland of the mountain tribes to push out Russia's southern frontier. These historic associations were of little interest to Sofya, or to the hundreds of women who came to the Pyatigorsk prison for news of their husbands and sons, and brought them food parcels. They were acquainted with the walls and the waiting room. Only when their own turn came did these women find out what the prison was like inside.

In the cities, in the countryside, that was a time of terror. Black Marias prowled day and night, hunting down the victims. People were taken from home, arrested at work. You were summoned to the director's office where two NKVDists might be waiting for you, invariably two in civilian clothes. Sometimes they stalked you in the street. A car would draw up at the kerb beside you. A tap on the shoulder: 'Citizen, step inside, and don't make a sound.' The marked man was no longer their 'comrade'. As for Alexei, he was arrested in a hospital bed.

A tide of madness swept away reason and decency, kindness and hope. All day truckloads of prisoners were carried from the NKVD centre to the prison buildings out of town. At night, trains left for other less crowded prisons, and the final destination — Siberia. The tram that went past the prison was always crowded. Weary women, their eyes swollen from tears, got off at the prison stop, with parcels and letters for the prisoners. An ocean of common grief, which could not be shared; at least not in the early months of the purges. Each woman guarded her own private hope that her husband's case was unique, that his arrest had been a mistake, that he had been wrongfully accused, and was bound to be released any day.

Whether they shared their hopes and despair, or not, all these women were sisters in misfortune — an old mother wept for her son; a young wife, with a baby at her breast and a toddler hanging to her skirt, was lost without her husband; a peasant woman with hands rough from the harvest; the pampered Sofya, who used to buy imported fashion shoes at the Torgsin. 'Bozhe moi, look at us now!' Sofya entreated a faraway God to witness the agony of her sisters. 'Look at our ravaged faces, at our bodies crippled by grief. How can You allow such suffering?'

Anna Pavlovna, who had spent a lifetime of intimacy with God and his saints, could no longer pray. She went to the market, queued at the shops and cooked nourishing stews for her son. 'He likes green peppers and tomatoes,' she muttered, wrapping the saucepan in a baby's blanket to keep it hot. Sofya took the food to the prison. When the tram was full, she walked the three kilometres alongside the stony bed of the Podkumok. The mountain peaks of the northern range stood in her sight; the white peaks of Elbrus, and Kazbek with his faithful cloud, remained her companions. Surely something desperate was happening to mankind if, on those lovely summer days, under such majestic mountains, lives were being senselessly broken; if a woman was running with a parcel of food towards the prison gates, where guards unwrapped the food, dug their fingers into it, searching for hidden messages, and handed the pot back to her: 'The prisoner refuses to accept this.' Sofya carried the desecrated meal home, and the baby's blanket became soaked with tears, which ran faster than the mountain stream beside her.

Later, when Alexei was arrested a second time, Sofya would bring Nadya with her. Then they would wait for the tram, because the child could not walk the distance that her mother had covered frequently in the previous year. At the prison wall mother and child paced in sight of the windows of the cell block. Sofya hoped that Alexei might look out and recognise his small daughter in his favourite red dress. Or perhaps another prisoner might see the child and say to the others, 'There's a little red dress dancing in the street.' Then Alexei would know immediately it was his daughter.

'Dance, Nadyenka, sing and dance for me,' Sofya begged.

Nadya held out her skirt and danced for her mother. When the child refused to dance, Sofya would scatter coins on the road: 'Pick them up one by one and bring the coins to me . . . one by one.' She didn't know at the time that inside there were wooden shields in front of cell windows. No one could look out, not even the guards. That wisdom came later.

Sofya never took Nadya into the waiting room. The air there was heavy with grief, damp from weeping. She wanted to protect her small daughter from unhappiness just a little longer. Not yet, not yet. The children must not know that their father will never come back. She was stonily certain that Alexei would not be released a second time.

The First Arrest

> They took you at dawn.
> I walked behind as if you were dead.
> The icon candle drowned in wax.
> In the dark room the children wept.
> Your lips — cold as a corpse,
> The sweat of death on your brow.
> I can't forget it.
> Like the Streltsy wives, I'll
> Howl under the Kremlin Towers.
>
> From *Requiem*, 1935

They arrested him at the sanatorium where he was recovering from tuberculosis. He told her about his ordeal later, at home, before he was taken again. The second time was final. In prison he was interrogated night after night; they forced him to stand for hours. Back in the cell, after the interrogations, he was forbidden to lie down in the daytime. He could have his medication, they told him, only if he signed. His charge sheet named him as the leader of a counter-revolutionary group. He was ill, losing his will to live, and he probably would have signed it. But Alexei's charges implicated forty-seven other men. Most of them were strangers, but he recognised some of the names of his former Rostov colleagues. 'I couldn't sign other men's death warrants,' he told Sofya later.

He spent the first three months in a solitary cell. He had no warm clothes. Until he confessed, they said, food parcels from home would be refused, and so would be letters. As his illness grew worse, they started taking him for treatment to the TB clinic in town, once a week.

One evening in a busy street, Sofya met Dr Donskaya, who worked at the TB clinic. The two women knew each other because their daughters went to the same kindergarten, and had been to each other's birthday parties.

'Sofya Nikolayevna,' said Dr Donskaya, 'I've been wanting to see you. I couldn't phone you, you understand. This is not the place, but I must talk to you.' There were people around them. Donskaya was expecting a colleague to join her any minute. They agreed to meet on the tram stop near the park next day. 'By chance, of course, you understand? We both will be catching a tram.' Sofya understood.

They met as arranged, looking like any two women who had not seen each other for a while, and stopped for a casual chat. 'What I'm telling you is dangerous for both of us.' Dr Donskaya's untroubled expression was at odds with the gravity of her message. 'Whatever happens, you mustn't give me away. Your husband is extremely ill. He may not live long. If you want to see him . . .' The doctor kept up the carefree facade. She looked round, as if checking the number of the approaching tram. 'They bring him in on Wednesdays for a pneumothorax. Not that our treatment is of much use under these conditions.' Sofya might see him then. But only a glimpse. Whatever happens, she mustn't utter a word, mustn't appear to know him. 'Don't betray me.' Here was a smiling woman sharing trivial gossip with an acquaintance. The tram arrived, and they waved a cheerful goodbye.

Sofya remained on the tram stop. She tried to think, but her thoughts whirled past her on a merry-go-round. What day of the week was it? she asked herself. Why, it was Tuesday. So tomorrow Alexei will be at the clinic. She will see him tomorrow. She couldn't sleep that night, fearful that his treatment might be cancelled before she saw him.

Sofya was at the clinic early the next morning. She found a seat in a corner of the waiting room, with her back to the window; from her vantage point she would be able to watch both doors. She sat looking down into her lap. If she couldn't will herself to become invisible, she hoped that at least she looked unremarkable. She didn't expect it would happen so soon. A uniformed NKVDist suddenly appeared in the doorway and inspected the room. His suspicious gaze registered the faces of the waiting patients, and lingered on Sofya's. Her heart stopped, 'Oh, God', but his eyes moved on; he wasn't interested in her. She could breathe again. The NKVDist muttered something to the nurse, and left the room.

'Move out of the way,' the nurse commanded. In Sofya's experience, all people in authority spoke in that peremptory voice. 'They're bringing in a dying man.' The patients in the waiting room were docile Soviet people. Even before the nurse finished speaking, they cleared the centre of the room. All except Sofya. She pushed through the crowd and positioned herself outside the doctor's surgery, facing the door into the corridor. Any moment now she'd see Alexei, she thought, and caught sight of three men in the doorway — two guards and Alexei. They held him up by the elbows. He couldn't walk; his shoes scraped the floor. Since she last saw him, her husband had turned into a skeleton; his hair was thin, quite grey. He lifted his head, and she saw death in his face. He must have recognised her. Just for a blink of a second, she thought she saw a spasm of recognition, so harrowing it could have been a spasm of pain. Then his face went blank again. Another moment, and he was gone inside the doctor's surgery, as if she had never seen him. Sofya then moved into a position where she could watch his departure. Time passed. She didn't calculate how long she had been waiting, when they finally brought out his slumped body. She couldn't see the face, only a grey crown of hair. His head had fallen forward on to his chest, a pumpkin lolling on its stalk. Heavy. It rolled from side to side between the sharp shoulder blades. A dying man was dragged back to prison.

Sofya was back the next Wednesday. She no longer had to beg for leave at her workplace. Like other wives of the people's enemies, she had been dismissed from her job. Now there was all the time in the world for vigils. The same two guards brought Alexei in again and as soon as she saw him she could tell that he was much worse. His face seemed to have shrunk, the shoulders and kneebones stuck out at sharp angles. A puppet suspended from a string. Limp. Lifeless. Except for his eyes; distended, despairing, they searched the room for her, found her. He was comforted. His eyelids closed, and the features once more rearranged themselves into a grimace of pain. Sofya felt no joy at the sight of him. As he was carried past her, she prayed. Not to the distant God, who was of no help in their suffering, to this saint, here, to Alexei the martyr; to her husband: 'Don't give up. Hold on a little longer.'

As before, the surgery door remained closed forever. But this time Sofya heard new sounds of agitated voices inside. All at once, the panic spilled outside. One of the guards ran out and returned with the driver of the NKVD car. A few minutes later both ran out again. The agitated nurse was explaining to someone that the patient inside was dying. Sofya listened to the death sentence coldly. 'All this is happening to someone else,' she told herself. 'It doesn't concern me,' but she pushed her way closer to the door.

They carried Alexei on a stretcher. His eyes were closed and the features stuck out sharply; all the flesh had melted away under the wax, set and cold, on his skin. Even if they had ordered her, Sofya couldn't have touched him; her own body had turned as rigid as her mind. A witness at a crucifixion, she watched her dying husband. Perhaps, he was already dead. She thought, 'I must say goodbye to Alexei,' and puzzled what a last farewell in a clinic should be like, as the procession moved down the corridor — out of sight.

She must be with her husband at his dying. Her mind was thawing; she could move her limbs again. She was possessed by a new fearlessness. At the NKVD offices, where the queues were long, and the petitioners were rarely satisfied, Sofya, a woman demented, shamelessly pushed ahead of others, begging and demanding answers. Yes, confirmed an official, prisoner Shubin had been transferred to the hospital wards. Someone else issued a written permission for a visit to her husband. At the hospital, there was another obstacle: they wouldn't admit her. She needed the director's signature on the pass and he was in a meeting. She waited in the corridor, praying to Alexei again, 'Stay alive, stay alive for me.' At last the director came out of his meeting. Sofya's desperate face may have moved him; he signed the pass on the spot. Flying to the wards, Sofya remembered that she had not thanked the man. Spontaneous kindness was such a rare gift.

There was a guard at the prisoner's door. He checked the pass (so slow!) and let her in. Alexei lay propped up high on pillows. His body moved restlessly. His eyes, wide open, stared out the window. He was saying something that made no sense to her. She knew that he was too frail for emotion; even joy had to be fed to him gently, drop by drop. She whispered, 'I'm here,' and took his hand. He didn't turn towards her but, sensing her presence, squeezed her hand. He was talking faster now, as if afraid that she might be gone before he had finished saying what he wanted. 'You wept under my window all night. I heard you. I knew it was you out there . . .'

This was delirium, surely. She had wept many nights at home, but how could the sound of her grief have breached the prison walls? Now Sofya's tears were washing her face, dripping down the neckline of her dress. She needed a handkerchief. But her movement made him agitated, his grip tightened. Staring past her at the square of daylight, he begged, 'Don't go away, don't leave me. They'll take me back to the cell.'

Sofya was oblivious to the lack of privacy. Didn't care that the NKVD guard heard every word they spoke, watched every move. After three months of hell, Sofya was in heaven, holding her husband, talking to him. If this was his last hour, at least she was there to comfort him in his dying. The guard changed. A kindly voice was saying to her, 'You should go home and have some rest. It's past midnight.' She wouldn't leave him. Sometimes she had to step aside to allow the doctor to examine to him, or a nurse give him oxygen. They looked grave. As soon as they were gone she resumed her vigil. Some time during that confusing night a nurse offered to take her to the lavatory. When Sofya stepped into the cubicle, she could barely hold on: her bladder was full to bursting. The rush of her urine sounded like a waterfall. She washed the salt off her face under the cold tap, dried herself with a handkerchief and, feeling much stronger, returned to his bedside. She did not need sleep. As the night passed, she watched the black window turning grey. In the chill of dawn she took shelter under the corner of his blanket.

If there had been any thoughts during that endless night, Sofya couldn't recollect what they might have been the next morning, when the NKVD sergeant gave her permission to take her husband home. He did not need to explain that the dying prisoner was now a nuisance. This was clear to the staff, to the guards, and to Sofya herself. Calm and dry-eyed, she left the bedside to find a car. There might still be some human beings prepared to help, even if it was for a fee. An off-duty driver agreed to carry them home. A nurse helped Sofya to arrange the limp body on the back seat, and the car set out on its careful journey. They had to stop when Alexei couldn't breathe, and opened the doors to give him more air. Sofya observed in numb resignation, 'Here is a body transported on a hearse.' When the car finally stopped in Gogol Street, the driver took off his cap in respect to the dead. Anna Pavlovna came to the door, keening softly.

They were still living in the front apartment then; the eviction came after Alexei's second arrest. The two women carried the body up the flight of stairs. Motionless. So light. But still alive, Sofya knew, as they put him down on the bed. Then he began to cough, to choke; he was in a terrible distress, fighting for air in harsh, painful gasps. Sofya lifted his head from the pillow and cradled it against her breast. The paroxysm subsided. Normal breathing returned. She saw him stroking the yellow quilted eiderdown, slowly, with his parchment fingers. 'Bozhe moi,' he whispered, 'I'm at home,' and he slept.

For His Resurrection

> No, it's not me, another woman is suffering.
> I couldn't be like that, it couldn't have happened to me.
> Spread the shrouds,
> Take away the light.
> Night has come.
>
> From *Requiem*, 1935

She should have allowed him to die at home, as he wanted. He should have died with his mother kneeling before the icons, which she had retrieved from their hiding place for the crisis. The lamp at his bedside cast a martyr's halo round Alexei's head on the pillow. In the next room Nadyenka slept through the nightly panics, and danced in her cot, laughing with the morning sun. Remembering in later years how she had nursed Alexei back to life at the time, Sofya could not forgive herself: she should have let him die in his own bed.

When Alexei's career had been in its zenith, the Shubins were at the centre of a galaxy of friends and followers; now hardly anyone called to ask how he was. Dr Nikolsky, whose surgery was down the road, was one of the loyal few who came to see the sick man. After his daily visit, he talked to Sofya on the stairs. Avoiding her hopeful eyes, he tried to warn her that the patient's new calm was nothing but apathy, exhaustion, to prepare her for Alexei's death. 'He's trying to fight but he hasn't got the strength.' Sofya understood, and from then on secretly began to plan how to die with her husband. She thought constantly of death, even in the street. One day walking in a dream of suicide, she met Dr Donskaya.

'Sofya Nikolayevna,' called a voice she knew but couldn't place.

Sofya looked round, saw the woman who had snatched Alexei from prison, and thought ungratefully, 'Why didn't she let him die in her surgery? Then I could have taken him home dead, and buried him, and we wouldn't have had all this suffering.' She said vaguely, 'Oh, hello. We've run out of milk. I must get some . . . for Nadyenka.'

'How are you?' the doctor examined Sofya's face for symptoms of widowhood, diagnosed that the patient must be still alive, and asked firmly, 'How is Alexei Yevgenyevich?' She could tell that Sofya no longer hoped for a miracle.

Brought back from her destructive reverie, Sofya began to talk to Donskaya about Alexei. About the nights more terrible than the days. How he woke up gasping for breath, drowning.

'What does Dr Nikolsky say?'

'That Alexei can't fight any longer. Though Dr Nikolsky won't say it to my face, I know that Alexei is going to die. I know it.'

'Sofya Nikolayevna, you mustn't despair.' As she said this, Donskaya knew how facile her admonition sounded. She had an idea. Something that might or might not help Alexei, she told Sofya. She had a theory about canine fat being beneficial in cases of terminal disease. Not just any animal fat, no, it had to be specifically dog fat. One of her TB patients was given daily doses of this. The trial proved successful; he made a complete recovery. 'It might be worth a try. It won't harm Alexei, and there's a chance that it might help him.'

Now that her hope had been restored and she had a clear purpose, Sofya became a determined huntress. A dog. She must find a dog to save Alexei's life. The black spaniel down the street was a friendly creature. She often stopped to pat him in the past; now she began to tempt him with irresistible morsels. 'Here, Tuzik. Good boy.' The new, scheming Sofya coaxed the neighbours' pet. After a week of secret blandishments she had won the spaniel's trust. One evening she lured him with a piece of sausage to the other end of Gogol street. She tied Alexei's leather belt to the dog's collar, and took him for a walk. She had already found a man willing to slaughter the dog.

'Tuzik,' she pleaded, leading the dog to the suburb where the butcher lived, 'you won't feel a thing. I'll make sure you won't suffer, and you'll save my Alexei's life.' The spaniel had another mouthful of sausage, wagged his stub of a tail, and willingly followed Sofya. But at the gate of the suburban cottage Tuzik stopped. He sensed danger, and pulled on the leather strap, wound tightly around Sofya's knuckles. She held on. The spaniel now tugged desperately. 'There, there, Tuzik,' she tried to soothe him with more sausage. 'Here boy, have some more.' Instead of the sausage, the spaniel savaged Sofya's hands. The frightened animal fought for his life; he snarled and bit her, but Sofya would not let go of the strap. Finally with a fierce tug, he tore himself free and ran barking and howling in the direction of home. Sofya knocked on the cottage door with her bleeding hands and fell on the front steps.

All that winter they fought for Alexei's life. When he began to revive, they were convinced that it was the dog fat that had saved him. One day a man with a parcel arrived at their door. Anna Pavlovna did not know him, but Sofya recognised the butcher who, at their previous dreadful meeting, bandaged her bleeding hands, when the spaniel Tuzik had broken free. Now he brought them a slab of dog fat: for the patient, he said. It was a miracle, Sofya and Anna Pavlovna kept repeating. One of those inexplicable things. Sometimes both wept, because there was still some kindness left in their dangerous world. The man refused payment for the fat. He mumbled as he left, 'Another time will do.' And soon he was back with more. Anna Pavlovna melted down the yellow lard, and put spoonfuls of it into everything she cooked for her sick son. Alexei ate porridge and soup laced with it, vegetables buttered with it. If he noticed a strange smell, he didn't complain. Perhaps, after months of illness, his taste buds had become blunted.

Dr Nikolsky had not seen such a remarkable recovery in his years of practice. 'I suppose it can be called a miracle,' he agreed, but remained sceptical about the dog fat. He preferred to think, he told Sofya, that recovery was due to the patient's strong constitution. 'Alexei had willed himself to live.'

Yet it could have been Sofya's determination ('I'll never give you up!') that had won him back. A triumph of love over death. Or he may have been spared by his mother's prayers. Anna Pavlovna knelt for hours before the family icon. Sofya slept in the armchair beside his bed. The nights, when she watched him tear his pyjama top open and gasp for air were fewer. Less frequently too did Anna Pavlovna order her daughter-in-law: 'Pray for his soul, Sofya.'

That year the snow came mid-December. Tucked under the white cover, its noises stilled in the snowdrifts, the little town at last fell into a winter slumber. In the Shubin household the two women continued their vigil. They grew accustomed to the silence. For all they knew, the world outside might have suffocated under the weight of the snow. One evening Sofya heard the pulse of a motor outside. Through a slit in the curtains, she saw a black shadow rolling down the street, leaving a pattern of tyre tracks on the fresh powder. As the motor died away, Sofya sighed, relieved that the car had passed their house without stopping. She had just settled into the armchair, when she heard a car door click. Panic was rising, spreading, numbing her limbs. Sofya knew it was the NKVD even before the knock on the front door.

For a moment she remained seated, as if tied down; unable to speak, as if gagged. Then she found the strength to call out softly to her mother-in-law, 'Anna Pavlovna, they've come for Alexei.' Her mobility returned and she went down to let in the nocturnal visitor. The plain Russian face surprised her. She must have been expecting a mask of evil, because she was confused by his benevolent expression. This nondescript civilian couldn't possibly be an NKVDist, who had come to take her husband back to prison. Except for the round steel-framed glasses there was not a single memorable feature in his face. The man's manner was apologetic.

'What a frost tonight. Don't you think you should close the door.' He spoke softly, but the articulated words rang clear in the cold air. And when she had shut out the winter night, the man introduced himself. 'Kozlov,' he said and smiled. 'You look worried, Sofya Nikolayevna. No, I haven't come to take away your husband. I need a signature on a document, that's all. So that the trial can proceed without him.'

She wondered how he knew her name and patronymic, and why he was so impeccably courteous. His manners were those of an old-fashioned professor; he reminded her of another era. But behind the round lenses his unblinking eyes unnerved Sofya. She noticed a row of metal crowns revealed by his careful smile. It struck her then that Kozlov might not be at all benign; she saw in him a large cat, padding on soft paws, playing with his prey, and waiting for the best moment to strike. 'Now, will you take me to Alexei Yevgenyevich? It won't take us long.'

Sofya's face, hands and body would not warm up. She led him through the dining room, through Anna Pavlovna's cubby hole, and opened the door into her husband's sickroom. 'Alexei,' her voice was as frozen now as her body, 'Comrade Kozlov is here to see you.' Kozlov moved her aside and stepped into the bedroom. 'Let's close this door, shall we?' he said. And just before the door was shut in her face, Sofya saw terror in her husband's dilated pupils.

Alexei was alone with Kozlov. Listening to the quiet murmur of a monologue, for a moment Sofya felt reassured. The NKVDist's voice was a purling stream. Alexei remained silent. Anna Pavlovna, who had bent her ear to the keyhole, crossed herself hopefully, 'He seems a civilised kind of man.' In their imagination, they both could see Alexei lying on his high pillows, and the NKVD man, so unexpectedly solicitous, was bending over the patient, gently unfolding his request. This soothing scene was interrupted by Alexei's desperate cry, 'Lies. I won't sign lies.' Choking, fighting for breath. Kozlov's scream, 'Sign, you bastard, or I'll kill you. Shoot you in front of the family.' This was the voice of the NKVD.

The two women looked at each other, helpless. They did not dare to open the door, to say, 'Enough! Get out!' Alexei's tormentor was a member of the State Security, and all of them in this household, all of their fellow citizens in this vast society were prisoners of the state.

The door flew open, and Kozlov ran out past them, down the stairs. The front door slammed shut. Only when they heard the revving motor of the departing car did the two women run into the sickroom. Alexei was unconscious. His breathing was faint, his pulse weak. Anna Pavlovna went down on her knees and began to pray. Sofya slid her feet into felt boots, pulled on her coat, and ran to fetch the doctor. She ran through the darkness, stifling her sobs in her mother's Orenburg shawl.

They Never Give Up

Spring stirred early in the Caucasus and, for the first time in her life, Sofya understood what the poets meant by the awakening in nature. In the northern city of her youth, the change of season was always tainted with melancholy. One day it was warm, the next day spring retreated as the fog rolled in from Finland. Here under the mountain ranges, on the edge of the great fertile plain, spring rushed in with torrents of melting snow and jubilant birdsong. Brown chestnut buds began to swell outside their window, sticky with sap. Each day the sun rose a little earlier into a confident blue. Then, overnight, the slush drained away, and the next morning you left your galoshes at home and stepped out light-footed on the dry cobblestones. Finally, you filled the pockets of your winter coat with mothballs and stored it at the back of the wardrobe. This is when your body became really weightless, and you felt airborne in the street.

'It's our first true spring. It's the best spring of our life.' Sofya's heart sang watching Alexei. He breathed easily now; the night attacks had stopped altogether. The colour in his face was unlike the former feverish brightness, it was a blush of returning desires. In Sofya's imagination, Alexei was gaining weight. 'Darling, you'll soon be a fat man,' she laughed. When it was warm outside, the windows were left open in the afternoon, and Alexei sat in an armchair, greedily breathing in the spring air. They were still nervous of infection, and would not let him hold Nadyenka. The older child, Vera, was in Leningrad. They had sent her away when Alexei first fell ill with tuberculosis. Now Katya wrote that the child was fretting; she had been through just about every childhood infection in the past winter. It was time for Vera to join the family. Sofya wrote back joyfully, 'Soon, soon.'

Sofya had found work again. Anna Pavlovna cooked and kept house. Nadya played in her father's room behind a barricade. She chatted to him in her incomprehensible tongue. She sang to him too, and her ability to hold a tune amazed him. As he grew stronger, he started reading to her. The child sat in her nursery chair, solemnly nodding her head. It seemed to Alexei that his small daughter understood not only the fairy tales he read to her, but everything about their tormented life. He thought that, having lived all winter with the spectre of death, and miraculously recovered, he should be grateful for the gift of a new life. But his happiness was blighted by nightmares. He woke up in the night and waited till dawn for the sound of the Black Maria.

Early in May, Alexei and Sofya went for a walk down Gogol Street. Not as vigorously, perhaps, as they once would have hiked in the mountains or skied across winter fields. Alexei was unsteady on his feet, as if intoxicated by the spring air. Beside him, Sofya tripped so lightly she seemed to be dancing. They walked through a tunnel of trees, and their faces were dappled with sunlight. In the lost months of his life, Alexei had forgotten city noise; the traffic and people tired him out. He was sweating. On the corner, he stopped to wipe his face. 'That'll do for the first outing,' he said.

'Not yet, just a little farther,' cried Sofya. She wanted to take him to the Lermontov Gardens at the end of the street, to admire the panorama of their pretty town spread below. 'You must see Pyatigorsk again,' Sofya pouted. 'You haven't seen it for such a long time.' Now that her husband was back from the dead, her old kittenish playfulness was reviving.

A black car was parked at the entrance to the gardens. Sofya's heart lost the beat of its song. Why should a black car frighten her? She tried to shake off her fear. It was surely the madness of the times they lived in, which made people see ghosts wherever they turned. She can't remain a coward for the rest of her life, can she? But as they passed the car, they both saw a bland face in the open window, and the glint of steel-rimmed spectacles. Alexei's elbow tightened on her arm.

'That's Kozlov,' he said, and sat down, exhausted, on a park bench. His lips were bloodless; beads of sweat came out on his forehead. 'That's Kozlov,' he repeated, 'that's Kozlov,' as if the name was an incantation to ward off evil.

Sofya could find no words to comfort him or herself. It was her fault, she knew. Her wilfulness had brought on this disaster. She had delivered her husband to the NKVD, with her own hands. And now the executioner had witnessed Alexei's resurrection. 'It's my fault. It's my punishment.'

Alexei's voice was as drained of colour as his features. He sounded flat, resigned. 'I didn't want to tell you about Kozlov when he came last winter. Didn't want to frighten you.' In prison, Kozlov had been Alexei's torturer. 'He interrogated me night after night. He put me on the stand. He insulted me, beat me. He threatened to arrest you, Sofya, if I didn't confess. Now he's seen me alive, he'll be back for me. He still wants my signature to wrap up his case. They never give up.'

They are Taking the Wives

Dedication

Before this grief mountains bow down,
The great river refuses to flow,
But the prison locks are strong,
And behind them are the prison cells
And deathly anguish.
The fresh wind blows for someone,
The sunset luxuriates for someone —
We wouldn't know, all prisoners are the same,
Hearing only the hateful grinding of the keys
And the heavy tramp of the guards.

From *Requiem*, March 1940

One of them was in uniform, the other wore civilian clothes. 'Shubina, Sofya Nikolayevna? We've got a search warrant. You're coming with us for questioning.'

Sofya had heard these words twice before and knew they meant arrest. She stepped behind the screen to slip into the dress she had worn the previous day. Blue crêpe de Chine. Silky, slithery, easy to slide over your head, over your body. Worn on that blue day called yesterday. That cloudless yesterday now seemed a historical past, a treasure trove of pleasures. Yesterday she took Nadya for a walk on the slopes of Mashuk. Since Anna Pavlovna insisted on coming with them, they had to walk more slowly; the old woman's hip bothered her. All that happened in one perfect slice of time. So much, yet not enough; she wanted a rerun of yesterday. All these echoes confused her; collisions in her head. A moment ago she couldn't even remember where Vera was. Then it came back to her: Vera was in Leningrad,

'She's safe with my sister, thank goodness! Because here, none of us is safe . . .'

Yesterday was Sunday. Sofya in blue, Nadya in red and a sombre Anna Pavlovna in black, strolled under the old chestnuts in the spa gallery. In the main rotunda they stopped to admire the pretty view of the town, but Sofya really watched Nadya performing one of her little dances on the footpath, singing as always to herself. Sofya suspected that her delight in the child, her maternal pride, might be foolish. But even if she had tried she couldn't have found fault with her dancing daughter. Not a fingerprint of humility in her own heart. Nadya was quicksilver. Other children were dull. That was a plain fact.

On a Sunday all of Pyatigorsk stepped out to promenade on Mount Mashuk. A motley crowd of patients from the sanatoria, families with children, were out walking, eating ice-cream, trailing coloured balloons and, naturally, stopping at the green-domed rotundas for a glass of the narzan. Each rotunda advertised its own unique mineral spring and the sparkling water was served by officious white-coated women, whose unsmiling manner was more telling than words: Drink it up to the last drop. It's meant for your health, not pleasure. Don't you dare enjoy it.

On the climb up Mashuk, you passed the pastel palaces, imagining how grand life must have been here in the past century, when Petersburg came to Pyatigorsk for cures and entertainment. But, really, had anything changed? The white villas spotting the slopes remained the homes of the aristocracy. The only difference was that today's anointed ones represented the proletariat; privilege was now bestowed not by the tsar but by the party. You walked past the poet's cottage, and more history. Exile in a spa town, poetry in a humble shack behind a picket fence. And Anna Pavlovna was instructing you again, 'That's where Lermontov wrote his *Hero of Our Time*.' Ah, but if you escaped, went on climbing higher still to the rocky ledge where the poet died in his duel, you could rest assured that neither your mother-in-law's legs nor her teaching could keep up with you, the swift one, the young one. But such luxurious reflections belonged to yesterday; today you stared into the face of the twentieth century.

Nadya woke up crying. The search went on. They had all the papers in their possession already, thought Sofya. At the time of Alexei's arrest they confiscated his personal files, publications with his articles; they even tore out the book pages he had annotated. They carried away boxes of paper. Now children's books were on the agenda. They were thumbing through *Grimm's Fairy Tales*. She watched the remembered rituals of intimidation — pull the wardrobe out from the wall, sweep everything off the shelves, empty the drawers — and wanted to scream, 'This is madness. Stop, for heaven's sake!' She stood by silently.

Nadya had already forgotten the fear of her awakening, and was taking an interest in the search. One of the men was sifting the photographs; the child joined in the game, and was calling out, 'That's Uncle Misha. Look. That's Aunt Katya. And my Papa's here . . . and there.'

The NKVDist didn't want to play games. He slammed the album shut, and turned to Sofya. 'Hurry up, grazhdanka,' he said very quietly, quite mildly. 'Pack a few things, will you? For a couple of days.' (Wasn't this what they said when they arrested Alexei?) Then, as if ashamed of his unprofessional weakness, he shouted, 'Step it up, Shubina, get a move on. We haven't got all night!'

Called by her surname, Sofya was a prisoner already. Panic made her clumsy: she couldn't tie her shoe; the tooth powder spilled on the floor. She heard her mother-in-law's unfamiliar, croaky voice, 'I'm packing a bag for you,' and watched a pair of wrinkled hands holding out her summer coat. 'Take it. The cell may be cold.' Sofya pulled it on obediently. Accepted the proffered bag, thinking in a sluggish, detached way, 'I can't take this away. It's Nadya's toy suitcase.' Sofya had bought it herself for Nadya's birthday. She had a fleeting vision of her small daughter 'travelling' in a row of upturned chairs, wearing Sofya's blue beret, carrying this small brown case. Nadya stored her most precious possessions in it: her books, her magic charms. Where would she keep them all now? Sofya stood lost in thought, clutching the small suitcase.

'What's in it?'

'Towel, tooth powder, toothbrush, comb, a change of clothes,' Anna Pavlovna ticked off the inventory.

The NKVDist reached for the suspicious case, opened it, checked its contents and snapped the lock shut.

Throughout all this, Sofya stood as if paralysed, on parade, to attention; only her eyes moved. She was a camera filming a take. Two actors, one in mufti, the other in uniform. Then the lens swung to an old woman. Grey skin, grey hair, dead eyes. Then her feelings returned, and she cried out in pain, 'Anna Pavlovna, take good care of Nadyenka. Tell my sister, tell my Katya that I've been arrested . . .'

'No messages!' the NKVDist barked, and tried a forced laugh. 'You'll soon be home. Don't fuss.'

Fear was a fever. Sofya's teeth chattered; her body shook. Everything was out of control. She tried to steady herself on the edge of the table, gripped it with both hands. Sweeping the room with wild, open eyes, she saw her small daughter. 'Nadyenka! I haven't said goodbye to her.' She clutched the child in her arms, crushed her against the breast. Heard two hearts fiercely hammering: 'Nadya's heart's beating and my own heart is breaking.' In her head a mother's voice was warning, 'Don't frighten the child,' while another frantic voice incited: 'Nobody comes back from there. You'll never see her again. Wouldn't it be better to kill your child and kill yourself?' She heard a hysterical voice: 'I'm not leaving my child. She needs her mother.' Madness or delirium?

'Grazhdanka, pull yourself together! Anatoly, bring her some water.' So she was still a 'citizen' (with or without civil rights?) and they had names. Torturers with Christian names. Perhaps they also had wives? Even children of their own? Strangely, the thought that these men were fathers, calmed her. She drank the water, but would not let go of the child's warm body in her arms. Nadya's breath tickled her cheek; felt like a moth or a brushed on kiss.

Man in mufti looks at his watch. Night is still deep in the window. They have to get going. Mufti nods to the uniform. By the book. No fuss. Understood? The uniform nods back: understood. What a sad joke, thought Sofya, catching their silent communication. As if anyone in this house, or any house in the land, would dare to stir while the Black Maria stood parked outside.

'Now, now, grazhdanka, don't get hysterical.' The man in mufti was on the peace path now. 'If you want to take the child with you, that's fine with us. We've got all kinds of facilities for mothers and children. Hurry up then, Babushka, get some things together for the little one.' How kind 'the little one' sounded, almost tender. 'Babushka', on the other hand, came out crude, demeaning. Nobody ever dared to address the empress as granny; this privilege was granted only to her own grandchildren. In the past Anna Pavlovna would have parried such an insult with one of her pointed retorts, but she was no longer her old majestic self. Her proud back was bent over the pile of Nadya's clothes. For the first time in the years Sofya had known her, her mother-in-law resembled a humble old gran.

The mufti man snatched the bundle from the grandmother's hands; the man in uniform reached out to pick up the child.

'No,' Sofya screamed, 'don't touch her!' She couldn't bear those hands touching her baby. But Nadya didn't share her mother's revulsion. She stretched out her arms to the shiny insignia on the NKVD collar.

'You see, she's not afraid of me.' The uniform smiled smugly. 'I'll take her out to the car, while you say goodbye to gran.' This was meant as a special favour, she supposed, a generous gesture from hardened hearts.

The mufti man stayed behind to spy on their farewells. Sofya turned to embrace Anna Pavlovna, but just then the old woman's body began to sag and she slumped heavily on the floor. Sofya heard a thud as the old woman's head struck the edge of the table or the floorboards.

'Anna Pavlovna!' Sofya went down on her knees beside the body, until a hard grip on her arm numbed her compassion. She looked up into a pair of implacable eyes, and begged, 'Please, she needs help.'

'This way, Shubina.' The voice was smooth, cold granite; his head jerked in the direction of the door. She allowed him to lead her out, without another look at the body on the floor. The door clicked shut behind them. They walked through the murk of pre-dawn to a pair of dimmed parking lights. 'Get in!' he whispered. Was it out of consideration to the sleeping neighbours? she wondered. His grip on Sofya's arm bit in harder, as he pushed her into the car.

'I'll have a bruise tomorrow . . . today,' she noted, indifferent to the pain. She strained to see where Nadya was and, still in a slow daze, realised that the child was neither in the back seat with her, nor in front seat with the driver. The man in uniform had also vanished. 'Nadya!' she cried and began to struggle against the mufti man's grip.

'Stupid bitch,' he swore. His hand clamped over her mouth. The skin of the palm was hard and smelt of nicotine. 'You want to wake everybody up, do you? I'll teach you how to behave, you slut.' An expert fist struck her on the cheek. Sofya, who had never been hit before, curled up into a hedgehog ball, shielded her head from further blows and whimpered. Some quirk of vanity from a previous lifetime pulsed though a brief worry that she would look like a battered woman.

The man released her. 'That's better.' He began brushing the sleeve of his jacket. 'The child has gone ahead in the other car,' he reasoned, as if he and Sofya were continuing a casual chat. 'You'll see her when we get there.'

'Where are you taking me?'

'To the NKVD.' The man was almost polite now. He handed her Nadya's blanket, which she had brought with her from home and dropped in the struggle.

Sofya clutched the pale blue piece of cloth to her breast and felt comforted by its washed-out teddy-bear motif, as if it was a link with Nadyenka, a promise that soon they would be reunited. 'I'll wrap her up in the blanket,' she thought, 'and sing her a lullaby. The poor baby hasn't had much sleep, with the search going on.' She felt disembodied. Drowsiness was diluting all earlier sensations. Nothing grieved her any more, nothing hurt. All she had just experienced seemed remote, as if it had happened to someone else; the real Sofya would never have allowed anyone to strike her. Exhausted, and no longer even worried about the safety of her child, Sofya closed her eyes. When she opened them again, the car was slowing down in the gates of the NKVD.

Sofya had been in this building before. She knew the patterns of the cracks on the plaster walls of the waiting room downstairs. She used to come here often when Alexei was first arrested; here she had begged for information, demanded an interview with 'someone in authority'. As the wife of an important manager, a party man, she imagined herself still a person of some consequence. All she needed, she believed then, was to reach some high-ranking man who would check the facts of the case and declare her husband's arrest an absurd misunderstanding. She realised the foolishness of her illusion very quickly. She resumed her visits to the NKVD after Alexei's second arrest, to persuade anyone who would listen that her husband, barely recovered from tuberculosis, was still a very sick man. Would they at least give him his medication? Here it was. She had brought it with her. The reply was always the same, from all ranks, 'Don't worry, we have excellent medical facilities in prison.' Yes, she had seen the result of those excellent facilities last autumn, when Alexei was sent home to die. It was she who had saved her husband's life. With Anna Pavlovna's help, of course, and thanks to the man who killed dogs. 'But I love dogs,' she thought. 'When I was a little girl, we always had a dog.' She rescued one called Boule when he was a puppy. How can you say that you love dogs, when you helped to butcher them for dog fat?

The black car. Kozlov's unblinking steel-framed eyes. The second arrest. And how she learnt about Alexei's sentence from a food parcel receipt; instead of the prisoner's signature he wrote: 'Sentence 10/5.' A faint message in pencil. It didn't make sense. In May he was still at home. And then she understood that he had been sentenced to ten years of prison and five years without civil rights, which meant that he would not return to his family for fifteen years, if he lived that long.

She had found out a lot by then, learnt that the condemned were never allowed meetings with their families. The idea of a prisoner's farewell was some romantic notion from the tsarist past. Yes, she thought, when the Great Father of the People was himself a prisoner in Siberia, he was allowed to study, write letters, receive visitors. Such treatment of prisoners, however, was not a feature of Soviet justice.

When she got home with that scrap of paper saying 'Sentence 10/5,' Sofya knew that she would never see her husband again. The tears would not stop. Anna Pavlovna gave her valerian drops, 'Drink up, you'll feel better,' but Sofya couldn't swallow; her teeth chattered on the rim of the glass. Now she and Nadya were prisoners too. A whole family in prison. Clutching the toy suitcase and the baby blanket tightly, as if afraid that these poor tokens of her once-free existence might be snatched from her hands, she followed a guard down a corridor. She told herself she must block out thoughts of Alexei, of Anna Pavlovna, perhaps dead, on the floor of the deserted room. She knew that the guard was taking her now to Nadya, who had been alone too long. Her trusting little Nadyenka, who chattered fearlessly to adults, and who had allowed a stranger to carry her away. She wished the child had screamed and refused to go with the NKVDist. Oh, she had been remiss; she should have taught her little girls to distrust all strangers.

'Stop!' grumbled the guard. He unlocked a door and pushed Sofya in. The door must have been effectively padded because, from the corridor, one couldn't hear a sound. The room Sofya entered was overflowing with women and noisy voices. A Soviet citizen, Sofya was rarely alone; she was used to communal apartments, packed trams and crowded queues. But this human swarm reminded her of the insect kingdom — a beehive, an anthill, a swarm of locusts. It was just like that, she remembered, in the revolution, when a solid mass of humanity would storm trains at a railway station. The unfortunate were crushed underfoot. Sofya braced herself against the door and found just enough space to stand on the floor.

She grew calmer, and began to recognise some of the women around her: wives of managers, of party officials. She saw an old acquaintance, Shaiira Petrosyan, whose husband had been Alexei's colleague and had also been taken. She tried but couldn't catch Shaiira's eye. The stench of sweat in the room made her gag; loud voices confused her. From all sides came sobs and snatches of conversation. 'They've been arresting wives for a week now,' someone was saying. 'Five taken from our apartment house last night', 'They'll send us to the camps with our husbands', 'My little boy is alone in the apartment', 'Where have they taken my children?'

'Mine too,' Sofya called out to these tormented voices. 'They took away my little girl and told me I would see her in here.'

'There are no children here,' said a quiet voice behind her.

'But where's Nadyenka!' Sofya whispered, appalled by what she had unwittingly done. Instead of leaving Nadya with Babushka, she had insisted on taking the child with her. Sofya heard herself scream.

Cell No. 7

Epilogue 1

I learned how faces fall apart,
How fear hovers beneath the eyelids,
How suffering scores its brutal
Cuneiform curves on the cheek.
How fair hair and dark hair
Suddenly turns grey.
How the smile freezes on submissive lips
And a dry cackle tinkles with fear.
I'm praying not only for myself
But for all those who stood with me
Under the red blind wall.

From *Requiem* (1935–1940)

Moving human cargo was a well-oiled operation. Covered lorries idled in the backyard, spewing out exhaust fumes. The prisoners were packed in, and the convoy drove through the sleeping town, along the river, towards prison. Dawn was a pale rose streak in the eastern sky.

Sofya's lorry was unloaded, and the women were herded into another space, too tight for the number of prisoners. They were now in the hands of prison guards, even more sullen than the NKVDists in town. The female warder with a fat face said coldly, 'Move over here. Search.'

Sofya felt the woman slide her hands over her body, push apart her thighs and thrust her fingers into Sofya's vagina. It was over so quickly, she wasn't sure what had occurred and why. 'You're crazy,' she gasped, and saw the warder wiping her fingers, stained with Sofya's menstrual blood.

'Not allowed.' The warder pointed at the harness that held up the sanitary pad. 'But you can keep the pad.' Sofya's wedding ring was also 'not allowed', and her watch was taken away. There was nothing left that she could use to harm herself. 'Next,' snapped the fat warder.

Sofya was taken down a corridor. A felt runner in the centre muffled the footsteps, but she heard another prisoner walking somewhere close behind her. She turned and caught sight of Shaiira Petrosyan.

'Eyes front.' The growl did not frighten away her instant happiness — she was not alone. Sofya walked on, looking ahead. She had already learnt the first lesson of prison life: to keep mute and not look behind.

'Stop here.' The lock and hinges creaked. She read No. 7 on the door as she was pushed into the prison cell. Shaiira followed her. When the door closed, the two women joined hands for courage. Before them breathed a nightmare of sleep, all the more sinister because the room was deep in shadow. A dim bulb on the ceiling lit up the figures of sleepers on bunks along the walls, and pressed together tightly all over the floor. There may have been seventy or more women sleeping in a space no larger than an ordinary room. The floor was concrete, the window high under the ceiling was boarded up with a wooden shield. No one here would ever see the pink streak of dawn that Sofya had just abandoned outside the prison gates. Women were tossing in their sleep and calling out. One wept. Another hissed for silence. Three black figures were awake, huddled close together in the middle of the cell.

'They're nuns,' Sofya whispered to Shaiira. Like black birds, the nuns were praying in their tiny circle. Their arms rose and fell as they made the sweeping sign of the cross and bowed low in unison. Sofya disliked nuns and monks; a prejudice inherited from her Lutheran father, and reinforced by the anti-religious propaganda of her Soviet youth. She was, after all, a child of her era. As her eyes adjusted to the gloom, Sofya could see that there were two or three bodies inside each narrow bunk. The floor under the bunks was also fully taken up. Women's bodies were pressed tightly together; not for warmth or comfort, she realised, but because the room was too small for that number of sleeping human beings.

The two newcomers were marooned on the tiniest island of floor space. They couldn't possibly lie down, or even sit. If they had tried, they would have landed on top of the sleepers. Elbows and knees were ready to repulse them from one side. On the other side of them stood a wide low tub; the metal lid buckling over its top did not seal off the sour stench of urine. So this was the parasha that everyone had heard about, and they were almost on top of it.

The sleepers kept a small respectful distance from the parasha but, because the tub was either too full or leaking, a dark pool of urine was spreading on the floor around it. Sofya was mesmerised by the scene. She saw a sleeping woman being pushed closer to the puddle; she did not wake up when her body touched the foetid slime.

Shaiira put her hands and her head on Sofya's shoulder. Her eyes closed; her lips moved. Perhaps she was praying. Their backs against the metal door, these two new members of Cell No. 7 stood leaning on each other throughout their first prison night. Dozing, infected by the heavy sleep around them. Like the other prisoners, these two would soon experience a constant craving for sleep, and the torpor this induced. The first of prison tortures was longing for sleep and having it denied.

'Reveille! Podyom!' The ringing of the bell and the warders' voices dragged Sofya out of her sleep to a weary awakening. Where was she? she thought, not recognising her surroundings. How did she get into this bedlam? Around her, women were bobbing up from the bunks and off the floor, collecting their clothes, hurrying to grab a bit of space near the wall to store their possessions. Nobody paid any attention to the new arrivals. The heavy metal door clanged and shuddered behind them and Sofya and Shaiira were pushed aside.

A warder shouted his way into the room: 'Anyone still lying down? You, and you there, waiting for a personal invitation, are you? You'll have a week in the punishment cell, more likely.' The warder was a heavy man, with one of those flat northern Russian faces that you expect to be smiling indulgently at the world. But there was nothing of the good-natured Russian peasant in his snarl. 'Want a taste of the solitary, do you?'

The women he was berating jumped off the bed they were sharing, grabbed the mattress in a practised unison and dragged it towards the door. The warder relented for a few seconds: 'All right, don't push, don't push.' Then he raised his voice again, though it seemed hardly necessary to subdue the cowed women any further, and yelled with his earlier menacing tone: 'Mattresses out! Quick!' From the door he supervised the procession of bearers, who stacked the mattresses against the corridor wall and returned to the cell carrying narrow planks. These were placed on the edge of the wire netting on the beds and some were put flat on the floor.

A low voice spoke at Sofya's elbow: 'We'll be sitting on these planks for the next nineteen hours.' She turned. Beside her stood a flat-chested woman, tying back her hair with an embroidered ribbon. It was the same woman who, in her sleep, had rolled into the overflow from the parasha. The seat of her skirt was stained dark, and all of her childlike presence stank of urine. Sofya nodded thanks and whispered, 'What happens now?'

'You arrived in the night, didn't you?' A pair of lively eyes examined Sofya. 'The warder must have had a heart to let you in without waking us all.' The smelly woman gave Sofya a small twisted smile, 'Nobody here has a heart. When they take one of us for interrogation, they make a point of waking up the whole cell. Quite deliberately, I assure you.' She frowned down at her stained skirt and turned back to Sofya. 'When and why?' she asked mysteriously, but Sofya understood her instantly. The woman's matter-of-fact voice encouraged confidence.

'They've started taking all the wives,' whispered Sofya. She suddenly wanted to tell someone about the horror of the previous night, when all those wives, whose husbands had been arrested before them, were rounded up into a holding cell, crying for the children they had left at home alone.

'Prepare for latrines! Opravka!' commanded the warder, and Sofya's new friend whispered urgently: 'Get into the queue. The first shift gets more time to wash. Quick, come with me. I'm desperate to wash this muck off.' Her shoulders twitched in disgust at her own state. They lined up and waited until a detail of women, whose turn it was to take out the night latrine, shuffled out of the cell, bending under the weight of the tub, careful not to spill any more of its reeking contents.

'Get on with it. Hurry up,' the warder urged them. Along the corridor teams of warders had positioned themselves along the walls to escort their own cells to the latrines.

A low hum of voices was rippling through the prison corridor. 'Quiet. Silence, you bitches!' swore the warders. 'You'll be sent back to your cells.' But not a battalion of warders could stem the flood of women surging along the felt runner in their bursting need to reach the toilets. Besides, it would have been impossible to isolate the culprits; every one of them was muttering something to her neighbour.

The ablutions area was a large washroom. Along one of the walls was a wooden box with six latrine holes in it, and four handbasins were lined up along the opposite wall. The women waited in queues for the lavatory, and for a turn at the cold tap.

Because Sofya was bleeding, she was allowed a little longer to wash out her napkin. The women who followed her at the handbasin did not seem to mind that it had just been used for menstrual blood.

How unbelievable, thought Sofya, that she should be dealing with her monthly guests in front of thirty strangers. Menstruation had been a private and embarrassing affair, from the day when her sister found Sofya weeping in the music teacher's bathroom. Katya taught her how to fold clean rags and tie them on to a little harness, 'It's the monthly thing, the "guests". We all have to live with it. You'll get used to it.' In their orphan years, Katya was the authority on all practical matters. And here was Sofya, in prison where nothing would be private again.

'Keep looking at the walls,' Sofya's guide instructed her, pointing to the crowded graffiti on the latrine walls. 'You won't be able to make anything of it the first time, but when you get used to it, you may find some useful information.'

'Have you had news?' Shaiira asked. The woman with the ribbon shook her head. 'He was shot . . . in '36 . . . after Kirov's murder.'

Her voice remained low and even. 'On our way back to the cell, try to say your name as you pass the cell doors. Someone may hear and pass on that you're here . . . Be careful, though, that they don't jump you, especially near the special corridor. That's where the death cells are. People are kept there, after they've been sentenced. Before they're shot.' A chill gripped both Sofya and Shaiira.

'So were you arrested with other wives?' Sofya asked as they were vacating the latrines to allow in the next impatient group.

'No, I'm here as myself.' Her statement sounded ominous.

Sofya felt much better after the *opravka*. She had also found out that the name of her helpful neighbour was Yelizaveta Ivanovna. The first prison day was beginning to take shape, and there was some comfort in the mundaneness of its routine. Roll call, or rather a head count, came next. 'Sixty-nine with two new arrivals,' reported the cell elder. Tall and grey-haired, she looked like a headmistress. 'One is in the isolator, and three away at interrogation.' The elder had already found a space for the newcomers on the planks where they could rest after the harrowing night. It was Yelizaveta Ivanovna, however, who took upon herself to teach Sofya and Shaiira the rules of prison life.

'They had us sitting on the floor until we asked for wooden planks. We had to explain that it was unhealthy for women to sit on cold concrete all day long. It took some graphic explaining before they understood what we meant by female ailments.'

Breakfast arrived with the familiar clang of the metal door. Warders brought in a bucket of hot water, a basket of bread and a small bowl of lump sugar. The bread and the sugar were tipped out on a blanket spread in the middle of the cell. The hot water was dished out quickly. Half a litre each, 'to last you till evening'.

Everyone had some kind of container or mug. Sofya found the blue and white enamel mug and a matching bowl in her bag. Anna Pavlovna must have guessed, or known, what was needed in prison. She remembered her mother-in-law's trembling hands, and the loud thud of her fall; although home was only a few short hours away, it all seemed like another era.

Shaiira had brought very little with her; she had neither mug nor spoon. She had been in anguish as she packed, leaving three children, one of them a baby, alone in the house. She had already missed two feeds and her breasts were swollen with milk.

Sofya gave the enamel bowl to Shaira, and kept the mug for herself. 'They're one of the children's breakfast sets,' she explained, 'This one is Vera's, and Nadyenka's is red. Alexei bought them for the girls in Moscow on one of his trips.' She had often stirred the semolina porridge in this bowl and urged Vera to eat up so they could see the flowers on the bottom. To drink up, because the flower in the mug wanted to see the sun. Just then, catching sight of the little blue flower in the steam, she had a vision of her daughters' faces: Vera's pretty mouth and fair curls and Nadyenka's dark eyes, so like Alexei's. All the Shubins have these sad, sad eyes, she was thinking.

'Shubina.' The headmistress elder handed Sofya a hunk of bread and a small piece of sugar. Impartial as Solomon, she distributed the daily ration, surrounded by a wall of hungry eyes. She had another prisoner, with her back to the bread, calling out the names. Since the bread hunks were unequal in size, this clearly was the fairest way of dealing. Sofya put the sugar ration into the mug and bit into the crust.

Yelizaveta Ivanovna watched Sofya with a wistful look. 'You're lucky to get the crust, it's supposed to be more nutritious. Besides, you can chew it longer. But don't eat it all at once — it'll have to last you all day. There'll be no more bread till tomorrow.' Sofya didn't take in the significance of the warning but, just in case, she began to chew more slowly, if only to prolong the pleasure. The taste of that bread was quite wonderful; she couldn't remember anything like it. It crossed her mind how Anna Pavlovna would enjoy the irony of prison bread tasting sweet. The memory of her mother-in-law's inert body left lying on the floor made the texture of the bread turn to sawdust on her tongue.

At two o'clock a different pair of warders brought in a bucket of soup for lunch. Balanda, they called it. This watery concoction of oatmeal was spooned up with relish. The same kind of balanda was dished out at seven, together with the evening half-litre of hot water.

In the afternoon they were taken out for a thirty-minute walk in the prison yard. By the time they had been lined up, counted, cautioned and kept waiting at each of the many doors they had to negotiate, the outing lasted only fifteen minutes, if that long. They walked in a concrete square, hemmed in by tall prison blocks with hooded windows. The only ones without shields must have been prison offices; they looked empty. They were ordered to walk Indian file with hands behind their backs and no-talking-unless-you-want-a-taste-of-the-punishment-cell. Shaiira in front kept stumbling; she couldn't keep in a straight line. 'Your friend's not well,' whispered Yelizaveta Ivanovna, who was walking immediately behind Sofya. 'We need Dr Kryukova.' She fell abruptly silent, as one of the warders approached.

On their last lap in the exercise yard, there was a brief commotion: Yelizaveta Ivanovna tripped and fell on her hands and knees. The warder shouted at her; she recovered quickly. In the first doorway, she opened her hand and showed Sofya the reward for her accident. On the palm of her hand lay a green shining sliver of bottle glass.

Shaiira fainted as soon as they got into the cell and all those women who had pushed to get first into the latrine queue, shoved to occupy more space on the sitting planks, were now helping her. The peephole rattled. 'What's going on here? Not allowed to lie down in daytime!'

'She's fainted. She's got a fever,' the women cried. The warder slammed the door shut and retreated. 'We don't get much medical help in prison . . . We've got the best right here in our cell . . . Dr Kryukova is . . . But she's at an interrogation . . . It's the third day since she went . . .'

Shaiira's face was a pale oval against the fan of her black hair and the crimson blanket, on which bread had been shared out that morning. Her breast milk was oozing, dark patches growing on her blouse. She moved her head and moaned.

'Give her a little sip of water . . .'

'Lift up her head . . .'

'What have they done to us all?' keened a plump peasant woman.

'She needs a cool compress on her breasts,' ordered Yelizaveta Ivanovna and wiped Shaiira's forehead. 'Oh, I wish Zina Kryukova were here . . .'

Dr Zina Kryukova

Dr Zina Kryukova returned from the interrogator's half an hour before reveille. Two warders dragged her into the cell and dumped her just inside the heavy door, next to the parasha. Sofya, who had been dozing close by, sat up and watched the still shape on the floor. 'Dead,' was her first thought. 'No movement, she must be dead.' How could they just dump a dead body among the living? Sofya knew straightaway that this was Dr Kryukova, who needed help even more urgently than Shaiira.

The previous evening, when the clock in the prison corridor struck midnight and guards yelled out the welcome order, 'Bedtime', Sofya couldn't go to sleep. Exhausted by nineteen hours of enforced idleness, her fellow prisoners fell down on their mattresses or on the bare concrete and slept, while Sofya, who had thought many times during that endless day that she wouldn't last another hour, that she would collapse any minute, now lay awake for a long time. She knew she needed rest after the harrowing night of her arrest, the loss of her child, the shock of the prison cell. She worried that, in a few hours, the warders would be shouting reveille, another prison day would begin and go on for ever. Oh yes, in these first twenty-four hours she had already learnt the main principles in the catechism of prison survival.

The woman stirred. Sofya reached out for the blue and white mug, poured some of her saved water on a handkerchief and very gently began to wash the bruised face.

'Lies . . . I'm not signing lies,' the woman moaned and licked her cracked lip. These were Alexei's words on the night when Kozlov came to demand his signature. Sofya wanted to weep.

'Hush,' she lifted the woman's head tenderly, 'have a little water.' She cradled the shapeless face in the crook of her arm, a mother feeding sips of water to her sick baby. The battered creature swallowed meekly. Then she moved her head slightly, signalling that she had had enough; she rested for a few minutes, and slowly opened her eyes. Sofya no longer noticed the face disfigured by violence, forgot the woman's bruises, lesions and her monstrously swollen legs. Sofya was drifting on a tide of pure aquamarine, so transparent she felt she could reach the thoughts and regrets submerged on the sea floor. How could anyone harm a human being with such astonishing eyes?

'Thank you,' the woman whispered. The effort to speak hurt her, yet she wanted, needed, to talk. She lay still a few minutes longer, and then tried again. 'He kept me four days and nights . . . with the body-mechanics . . . I counted the shifts.' She grinned crookedly at Sofya, but smiling was even more painful than speech. 'They won't break me . . . They'll kill me . . . but they won't break me.'

'There, there, you mustn't talk.' Sofya continued to rock the broken body of a woman she had never met before, a woman who had survived the conveyor belt treatment.

In prison slang, Sofya and most of her fellow inmates were known as 'kontras'. They were wives of enemies of the people or, like Yelizaveta Ivanovna and Dr Kryukova, political prisoners in their own right. Other cellmates, the non-political prisoners, were called 'urkis'; they were convicted criminals. Women's cells had fewer urkis than the men's. In men's cells the criminals were a sinister presence.

In Cell No. 7, the urki corner was a small hierarchical society. Their leader, Galina, was a Cossack woman, orphaned in the revolution and raised by a street gang in Rostov. She would have been a bespirzornaya in the streets, when the Shubins lived in that city. Sofya could just see this bold creature racing bareback in the southern steppes, or bringing in the harvest as feistily as any man in the Cossack stanitsa. In her parents' world on the River Don, the wilful, big-breasted Galina would have been married young to a Cossack, bred sons for the tsar's regiments and ruled over her own homestead like an ataman. In the Soviet underworld, Galina became another kind of commander.

Sofya had never before loved other women as deeply as she did during her prison months. Isolated from their children and the outside world, kept in the dark about the fate of their husbands, cellmates survived in the strength of their prison sisterhood. Affections in their earlier existence faded beside the intensity of these new loyalties. Sofya fell in love with Zina Kryukova from the moment she was brought back to the cell, after her ninety-six hours' treatment. The Czech woman's life story emerged much later in whispered confessions: how she and her communist idealist husband migrated to the Soviet Union from Prague. How he was arrested and shot. Zina's second husband was a Russian, a heart surgeon in the Kremlin clinic. But even Dr Kryukov's exalted connections and eminence could not save his Czech wife from prison. Zina was charged with espionage for a foreign power.

The background of Sofya's other friend, Yelizaveta Ivanovna, was similar to her own: she also had a husband in prison, and didn't know the fate of her children. Yelizaveta, a research scientist, was accused of conspiracy to poison government leaders. The plot of her case had grown so complex that even its authors, the NKVD, had trouble in pulling its fictional threads together. In the meantime, Yelizaveta sat in Cell No. 7. Having endured only two interrogations, mild ones at that, she was pessimistic about her future, convinced that worse was yet to come.

Yelizaveta Ivanovna was the miracle worker of Cell No. 7: she sewed. She used the piece of green glass she had found in the exercise yard to cut cloth. A needle had been smuggled in by the urki from another cell. Threads were pulled out of a cotton towel. She fashioned a sunfrock from the lining of Sofya's coat. The perfect hand finish on the sarafan was admired later when Sofya wore it 'outside'. But why a sunfrock, they asked? Because it was very hot in the cell, Sofya explained; and the blue crêpe de Chine dress in which she was arrested would not have lasted long in the prison cell. Also because you couldn't help hoping that one day they would release you, and then you'd have a nice dress to wear on your trip home.

How ingenious they all were, Sofya remembered later. If none could match Yelizaveta Ivanovna's needlework, each had some skill she shared with the sisterhood. Zina looked after the sick in No. 7. She helped Shaiira get over the mastitis. With a special massage she could reduce the elephantine swelling of legs after the 'stand'. She made a paste from masticated bread to heal lesions. 'You have to have healthy teeth for it. If there's any decay, the paste won't help. On the contrary, it will infect the wound.' Later Zina lost her perfect teeth in a particularly long and brutal interrogation. After that she finally confessed her many crimes against the Soviet state. 'Before we came here,' she told Sofya, 'my first husband, Vladek, used to dream of your country as the first paradise in human history.' And Sofya, stroking the disfigured face, mourned, 'Oh Zina, why did you agree to follow him to our paradise?'

Natalya Stepanovna, the stern elder of No. 7, was a scholar, who had written textbooks on ancient civilisations, and now offered her fellow inmates lectures on the Egyptian dynasties, the mythology of Ancient Greece and the fall of the Roman Empire. Ancient history needed no political doctoring, she said. In any case, there was no ideological censorship in prison.

When Zina had healed Galina's hands with her bread paste, the Cossack woman began to tell the cell stories of her childhood in the southern steppes. How well her family lived in the stanitsa. The food they ate, the songs they sang, the seasons on the land that lifted your soul. And as Galina spoke about the beauty of a vanished life, which surely must have had its share of ugliness and brutality, she stared down at her fingernails, broken with hot needles by an interrogator who punished her for her Cossack blood.

In prison, all worries and pleasures of their former life outside seemed absurd. How could you ever have complained about discomfort or fatigue, when here in the prison cell you fought perpetual tiredness? The five hours of sleep allowed each night were never enough. You were hungry all the time; you treasured your bread ration like the holy grail. You saved up your water ration to wash your hair, to rinse out your pants and bra, to resuscitate a cellmate after her interrogation. Day and night warders shouted orders and threatened the women with the punishment cell. When Sofya herself returned from the nightmare of the isolator, her friends had saved up their water ration to wash the slime off her body and to launder her clothes. Zina, Yelizaveta and Shaiira coaxed her back into the world of human kindness.

A Woman Alone

> Seventeen months I've been crying,
> Calling you home.
> I threw myself at the executioner's feet,
> My son, my nightmare.
> And I can't tell anymore
> Who is beast, who is man,
> And how soon is the execution?
> There are only dusty flowers,
> The ringing of the censer,
> And footsteps going nowhere.
> While staring me in the face,
> Threatening oblivion,
> Hangs the huge star of death.
>
> From *Requiem*, 1939

Anna Pavlovna came to her senses wondering what had happened to her. Her mind was quite blank. She was lying on the floor. Beyond the walls of her room, the house was echoing with early morning sounds; other tenants were getting up, queuing for the bathroom; pots clattered in the kitchen. The clock on the desk ticked very loudly; time passed. Her body ached, there was a burning pain in her cheek. Yes, she must have grazed it against the table corner when she fell. As her mind began to clear, she remembered the fall, and she groaned, retrieving one by one the events of the previous night. She was alone now. Old and alone. Alexei and Sofya were in prison, and even her grandchild Nadya had been taken away by the NKVD. She had to get up from the floor and start doing something, keep going, stay alive, save her family.

Outside the door lurked the rest of the world, snide and suspicious. Silence greeted her in the kitchen, when she went to put on the kettle. Her fellow tenants in the annexe were a cowardly lot, she thought, lighting the primus. But how else could this gullible herd respond, when all the news stories they had been hearing on the radio and reading in *Pravda* were about enemies of the state. The trial of Bukharin and Rykov, the trial of the engineers in the coal industry, arrests of saboteurs and wreckers all over the country. At work these cowards attended meetings where their colleagues were accused of espionage or counter-revolution. More and more people were being arrested, exiled to the Far East, to the Arctic Circle, wherever the state needed cheap labour to mine minerals, mill forests, dig the White Sea canal; or on the mammoth Bratsk hydro-electric project in Siberia, where Alexei was now.

Ah, the neighbours nodded slyly, there is no smoke without fire. Innocent people don't get arrested, they whispered. Unless, of course, the innocent happens to be you. But you don't allow yourself to think about that sort of thing. Anna Pavlovna took the boiling kettle back to her room and made a pot of tea. She stored the sugar cubes in the old cut-glass container with a silver lock; one of the few heirlooms left from her home in Yaroslavl. What an irony, when you came to think of it that, in her former life of plenty, they used to lock up the sugar, to count the silver spoons. All her training for prudent housekeeping had been a waste of time, a farce. She had always been impatient with fussy customs of the past, even when she was a proud young mistress of her household. Now that the old duties and privileges had been swept away with the family property, only the pulse of life remained; it made you realise what life was about, if not its meaning. She was grateful that she had few possessions, and no attachments; she was free now to grieve for her son, to fight for the release of her daughter-in-law and her grandchild.

After a cup of sweet tea she felt stronger, but was no more certain of where to begin. On a normal Monday, Sofya would have been at work, and she would have taken Nadya to the kindergarten, and gone in search of queues. She would find out at the tail of one queue that soap was available there, and decide whether she could afford the hour and a half. Another might be for children's shoes, and she would stand for a good two hours to buy a pair for Nadya. Then there might be some delicacy that her diminished family had not tasted for months. In the queues there were other old women like her, keeping house, cooking meals, raising children in a family, just as burdened or bereaved.

Her thoughts were as heavy this morning as her heart. She felt that there had been some sinister edge to Sofya's arrest, but her mind was too sluggish to grasp it. The room around her looked as if a storm had swept through it and torn everything apart. Open drawers, clothing and books were strewn on the floor. Her eye fell on the photo album beside the child's cot. Nadya had stood in her cot, helping the NKVDist to identify members of her family in the photographs. The nightmare scene returned to Anna Pavlovna in each terrible detail. She heard Nadya's clear voice, 'That's Papa . . . that's my aunt . . .' Why, she thought, it was as if the child was betraying her family. And just then she realised what had been troubling her, why she had lost heart in the early hours of the morning. It was Nadya, the way they took her away. The NKVDists had two cars last night; she heard one of them drive away as soon as they carried the child outside. What if Nadya was not with Sofya? What if they had taken the child somewhere else? Wherever she is, Anna Pavlovna must find her and bring her home.

Reception Centre for Orphaned Children

On their refugee journey, Sofya talks about the past. Sitting on their suitcase at some railway junction, indistinguishable from the previous one, somewhere in the middle of a countryside traumatised by war. The station room poorly lit, the platform abandoned to the cold of night-time. Waiting with other families, their children and bundles, for a train that might or might not arrive.

'What about the time at the orphanage?' Nadya wants a real-life fairy tale with a happy ending, even though she has heard it many times. Then Sofya's soft murmur carries them far away from the screams of tired babies and the anxious conversations of their fellow refugees.

'They took you away, Nadyenka, wrapped up in our yellow duvet . . . In prison they told me that you were back at home with Babushka, and they told her that you were in prison with me. And this is what we both believed for six months until I was allowed my first parcel from home.'

What a joy that parcel was, she remembers, even though it had been dug over and carelessly tied up again. Anna Pavlovna had wrapped it lovingly but, by the time the warders had finished checking the contents, the sugar cubes were smashed, the piece of pork fat slashed, the bread rusks pulverised. Anna Pavlovna had packed a child's pink pinafore, and in its pocket there were Mishka sweets. (You know, the ones with bear cubs on the wrapping paper: four cubs playing on a fallen tree trunk in the forest.) That was the moment when Sofya realised that the Mishkas were meant for Nadya, they were her favourites; but this could only mean that Nadya was not at home with her grandmother.

There was that story in Pravda how the children from socially unfriendly groups were cared for in special reception centres. She thought at the time that it must be a euphemism for orphanages. Now she wondered if it meant that children of arrested parents were being raised in state institutions; given new names, trained to be loyal Soviet citizens, taught to forget their families. In prison she'd heard rumours that more and more young children were being taken away at the time of the parents' arrest, and used to blackmail prisoners. If you refuse to sign the confession, the interrogator threatened, your family will suffer for it: your wife might be put on the conveyor belt, your children might get lost in a reception centre.

Sofya found the Mishka sweets in Nadya's pinafore, and lost her way. She clutched the pinafore to her breast, and felt her heart beating a staccato message that her child was in an orphanage. An hour earlier Sofya was savouring the smell of her hunk of bread, the closeness of her friends, but now the cell had turned into a wasteland. She was aware that the warder expected her to sign for the parcel, saw the blank line on the docket in front of her eyes, but some primeval cunning guided her hand to scrawl 'Nonadya' instead of her own signature. 'The pinafore,' she begged the warder, 'give it back to her, she'll need it for the child.'

Waiting in a crowd of women grey with grief and fatigue, Anna Pavlovna was handed the pinafore and the receipt. Sofya's message was unmistakable: it confirmed her own suspicion that Nadya must be in a state orphanage. She could hear Sofya's voice pleading with her to rescue Nadya from the state machine that would erase the child's name and memories of her family. 'Save her, Anna Pavlovna, before our Nadyenka is lost forever.' This new demand on her failing strength should have made her despair but, instead, Anna Pavlovna's mind and even her muscles were charged with fresh energy. She felt as resolute as she had been in the days of the Civil War, when she carried her dying husband home to the shores of the Volga. Nadya was her own flesh and blood. She was not going to allow the state to mould her grandchild and change her name. The child must always be Nadezhda Shubina. Wherever she might be, Anna Pavlovna would find Nadya.

'And she did, she did!' cries Nadya, applauding her mother's story.

A Letter from Lenin's Widow

Nadya spent nine months in the orphanage. She remembers stairs leading to a door, a corner room, a cot with high mesh sides. To the right is a window. Above the cot hangs a portrait of a man in a military tunic with dark hair brushed back from a heroic brow, a heavy moustache. Then he might have looked like God. Now she knows it was Stalin. At the end of the windowsill, a glass-fronted bookcase starts; it stretches along the entire wall and reaches up to the ceiling. An army of identical volumes bound in leather line up to attention on the shelves. The surface of the polished glass panels holds the reflection of a child's face. Nadezhda's memory provides her not only with sensations of that alien place but with a photographic image of herself standing in that institutional cot. Crying. She remembers the taste of her grief, even though she can't recollect the smell of the food she wouldn't touch or the shapes of the toys she refused to accept. She also rejected arms that offered to comfort her.

It's daylight in the open window. A tree shakes its red and yellow leaves: 'Look over here . . . Smile.' And in the garden below children's voices are calling out, 'It's mine . . . mine . . . mine!' The child caught in the glass of the bookcase is crying, 'I want Mama!'

Memories and legends are yarns woven into Nadezhda's family tapestry, the woof and warp of her past. Is there a discernible ridge in the weave that she might find with the tips of her fingers, the dividing line between truth and fantasy? Which memories are Nadya's own, and which are a legacy from her mother? The images and dreams she shelters are constantly twisted by the currents of time.

And what corrections has time made to the people she loved, to their features and voices? She wonders if they had been as beautiful and noble as her mother described them, touching up their virtues with her nostalgia. There must have been some ugliness among them, greed and betrayals.

Once Anna Pavlovna knew that Nadya was not with Sofya, she began her search for the missing child. She enquired at every office in town, begged for interviews, wrote letters to every high personage she could think of or who was recommended to her by others. After a suppliant's day of knocking on official doors, she returned to her room in the black wing, put down her shopping bag and took off her coat, in fashion before the revolution. 'Dear God, I'm so tired.' Her own mother always said to her: 'Anna, when you're truly tired, you'll know it. That's when you'll collapse and die. Until that happens, pull yourself together and work.' She went to the kitchen where, as always, conversations ceased. A woman who had lost her entire family was bad luck to have around. Neighbours shifted uneasily while she lit the primus and heated a pot of soup. She took the pot back to her room, and spooned the soup into her mouth, slowly, thoughtfully. Again her own mother's voice: 'Anna, food is a blessing, enjoy every mouthful.' She tried to keep all God's blessings in mind. Oh, how she tried. When she had finished her meal, she pushed the chair close to the bronze lighthouse and, in the green glow of its lampshade, she wrote another letter in her old-fashioned hand. This one was addressed to Lenin's widow, Nadezhda Krupskaya.

Dear Nadezhda Konstantinovna,

You are my last resort. I have tried everyone but no one will help. I am looking for my granddaughter Nadezhda Shubina. She was taken by the NKVD on 20 September and has disappeared.

I have since been told that she is in a Reception Centre but not given its location. Nadya is all I have left of my son's family. Please help me find her.

Yours faithfully,

Anna Shubina

In the months of her search, Anna Pavlovna lost her belief in human kindness. She had met too much indifference and callousness. Why should anyone care what happens to the rest? Anyway, what possible interest could Krupskaya have in a child lost in the maze of state institutions? Even if that child happened to be a namesake, Nadezhda. But Krupskaya must have taken some trouble to trace the child, and to discover the home where Nadya was kept. One day there was a letter, an official notification that the child, known to be Nadezhda Shubina, now resided in Centre No. 56, in Pyatigorsk.

Anna Pavlovna read the letter so many times that it was copied out word for word in her memory. Bozhe moi, to think that, throughout all those desperate months of searching, Nadya had been in the neighbourhood, within reach, yet so thoroughly hidden that it needed Lenin's widow to locate the little girl. Always truthful, Anna Pavlovna blamed herself first, as implacably as she blamed the state. Old fool that she was, why didn't she begin with the local children's homes, here on the slopes of Mount Mashuk? Why had she been so certain that Nadya had been taken to some godforsaken place? She had discounted the obvious, and the most likely. Intuition, experience, wisdom. She had been proud of this old woman who embodied them; the woman who was an illusion, and whose ephemeral virtues had betrayed her. She mourned the loss of that illusory intuition most of all. If only she had gone last winter, spying through the bare branches into the overgrown gardens, she might have found Nadya among the children playing in the snow.

In the night she got up to pray. 'Thank you, Lord, that Nadya has been found.' She crossed herself again and again, and bowed low toward the iconless corner. She knelt on the floorboards until her knee joints grew stiff. They took a long and painful time to unlock. All that night her spirit lurched between hope and terror. 'What if, what if they move the child somewhere else before I get there to collect her?' And the thought of Nadya's final night in the orphanage was more unbearable than the nine months that had just passed.

She thought of Alexei and Sofya in prison, as one remembers the dead, accepting their loss. Months ago, she had wiped the slate, settled old scores, laid family quarrels to rest. She forgave Sofya for bringing sweets for the children, and none for her. 'She knew about my sweet tooth. She hurt me. Deliberately.' These old grievances seemed trivial; she was ashamed of them now. Now that Alexei and Sofya had partaken in the Russian rite of suffering, she had elevated them into the ranks of martyrs; they had become her personal saints. Beautiful like the holy icon images, they would remain forever blameless.

It was still dark, dawn was just about to break, when Anna Pavlovna shuffled into the empty kitchen to pump up the primus and heat the kettle. She desperately needed tea to revive her. The night of fears and prayer had exhausted her. She felt faint as she waited for the water to boil, and had to lean against the kitchen table, grateful that no one else was up, that she still had the kitchen to herself when the water finally began to bubble. She tiptoed down the corridor back to her room and closed the door noiselessly behind her. Making her first cup of tea was a sacrament; she could perform it wearing a blindfold. She threw a pinch of tea leaves into the pot, poured in the hot water and let it draw. In the glass the Krasnodar tea looked like the red amber from Lebanon. Just as she liked it. It was strong and never tasted bitter. Their old supply was almost finished. Where could she get some more? She stirred in an extra cube of sugar. Today she would need a lot of energy.

Your Nadya Knows All the Old Songs

The other tenants were stirring when Anna Pavlovna locked the door of her room. Along the corridor she heard a few voices. There was a separate world behind each of those doors. In each room lived a family: children cried, adults squabbled. Walking across the yard, she thought that her own family had lived in a seemly manner. Such an old-fashioned expression this; no one else said 'seemly' these days. Wearing her dark dress and sensible lace-ups, Anna Pavlovna set out on her mission. First the long trek up the slope of Mount Mashuk where the old mansions had been converted to sanatoria. There she hoped to find Reception Centre No. 56.

The road snaked through the green belt above the town. Although the morning air was cool, the walk uphill had tired her; she had to stop for breath and, when she saw a park bench handy, she sat down for a brief rest. She kept her feelings numb, her mind blank, so that she could focus her will on reaching Nadya. She dared not imagine that some vengeful meteorite careering through the cosmic gloom might crash into her small bright planet.

By midday she had knocked on the doors of several children's homes. In each she went through the same tiring formalities, producing the official papers, sweeping Krupskaya's letter ceremoniously before surprised and then alarmed faces. No, Nadya was not on their roll. No one knew of a child with her particulars. She was not worried that they might be lying, refusing to release the child. The letter in her handbag was a safe conduct through the labyrinth of bureaucracy. But her strength was almost gone; some of it was lost in each encounter. A woman had just mentioned to her another home two blocks away; she did not know much about it, except that it might be for special purposes. Her words drained some more of Anna Pavlovna's courage.

She found it. A large white house hidden behind the thick shrubbery of a neglected garden, from the street it did not look like an institution. Only the number on the gates told Anna Pavlovna this was the place, and the children's voices floating out of the green wilderness. Her disgraced intuition, which had let her down before, now led her to the orphanage. Nadya, it prompted, couldn't be far away. Her legs were buckling under her, yet she continued up the path towards the green front door and rang. No one answered the bell for some time. She waited in the glass porch. At last a woman in a white coat opened the door. She didn't ask what the visitor might want; she waited for the suppliant's explanation.

The last of Anna Pavlovna's strength surged with all that was left of dignity. 'I've come for my granddaughter Nadezhda Shubina.' Her voice betrayed neither her exhaustion nor her renewed doubts; even to herself she sounded imperious. She fished out the document and held it up in front of the unfriendly face. No, she would not let Krupskaya's letter out of her hands to be shown to someone else, she said; she must see the person in charge herself. The woman admitted Anna Pavlovna inside, and left her in a room with bare walls, to fetch someone of greater authority.

From the window Anna Pavlovna had a view of the garden. She saw the children whose voices had brought her in from the street. They were playing on the lawn, building some kind of a tower out of boxes. Boys and girls, alike, in their striped pinafores, their heads shaven. 'Bozhe moi, these little ones already look like prisoners,' she thought, scanning their faces for familiar features. Not one of them resembled her Nadya. Just then, beyond the playground, she spotted a child walking round and round a tree. Alone. Even though the dark hair had been shaved off, how could she have missed the olive skin and the straight Shubin back. The little girl raised her head, and Anna Pavlovna saw Alexei's eyes. 'Nadya.' Her whisper was worshipful as in a prayer. Her breath left a cloudy patch on the glass. Sandpaper dry, her lips would not shape the words: 'Nadya, I've come to take you home.'

'You don't look well. Can I get you a glass of water?' a voice asked softly. Anna Pavlovna had not heard anyone come into the room and now regarded the intruder sternly. Had this cleaner with her mop and bucket been sent to spy on her?

'Thank you.' She accepted the water and regretted her suspicion. How could she be a spy with that Cossack voice of hers? The woman had a kind face and spoke with a lilt of the southern steppes. 'In fact, this woman may have passed through as many chambers of hell, as I have. She may even guess why I'm here.' Anna Pavlovna drank the lukewarm water, and returned the glass. 'Do you see that little girl who's making herself dizzy walking round the tree? She's my granddaughter. I've come . . .' Anna Pavlovna couldn't go on.

The Cossack woman's gaze rested on the child and a smile lifted the corners of her mouth. 'They call her Lydia here, but she won't answer to it. She's a stubborn little thing. She says her name is Nadya.' The Cossack woman's pleasure was spreading all over her face till it reached her eyes. 'You've come for her. I'm glad . . . I'm glad,' she nodded. 'She sings, your Nadya. How that little one can sing. I mop the floors in the wards at night. The children are all asleep, but not our Nadya. She's awake and we sing for each other. Softly, you know. We never wake anyone.' The cleaner straightened her back and held her head high. Perhaps she was remembering all the songs she had taught Nadya in the night.

'Why, this one is a handsome woman, and much younger than she seemed at first glance,' Anna Pavlovna said to herself.

'She knows all the old songs, your Nadya . . .' The cleaner shook her head in wonder at a child who had brought a fresh breath of the steppes into her bleak life. Footsteps were approaching along the corridor. The Cossack woman hunched her shoulders, and went back to mopping the floor.

All Souls Day

Epilogue II

I want to name each one
But they took away the list, I can't find it anywhere.

From their pitiful words, overheard,
I would weave a wide shroud.

I think of them always,
I can't forget them amidst new grief.

And if they gag my tortured mouth,
Through which a hundred million cry,

Then pray for me too
On the eve of All Souls.

From *Requiem*, March 1940

On her return Sofya couldn't talk about her time inside; even if she had dared to confide in her dearest friends, even if she'd still had any friends outside. She had left all her true friends behind in Cell No. 7.

The documents, which she was obliged to sign on release, bound her to perpetual silence. She must not disclose any detail of her prison experience to anyone. She must report monthly at the NKVD. She was forbidden to leave town, to attend public meetings. An endless list of prohibitions. Sofya signed away her civil rights, indifferently. At the time all she hoped for was to walk out of the prison compound, before they changed their minds and marched her back to her cell.

Outside the prison gates August was on heat. Languishing in the sun, indolent in the shade of summer gardens, here was the world she'd thought never to see again. She had forgotten the infinite shades of colours; she was shocked by the bitter green of the grass, and the sheen of sky blue blinded her. Infinite space. The sky was a sea flecked with racing cloudsails. She stood on the tram stop, gorging on the splendour of this recreated world, gasping with an urge to pray her wonder aloud. 'Thank you, for letting me see all this again.' Sofya had begun to pray in prison, renewing the old evening solemnities of infancy. The words of those simple devotions had now grown into a medley of the holy and the secular, a fusion of bedtime prayers and of the poems she used to recite on her mother's birthday, standing high on the dining room chair. She was aware that prayer had been restored to her, not out of prison despair, but through the acts of kindness she had received from her prison sisters.

She boarded the tram. Her fellow passengers avoided each other's eyes on this notorious route between town and prison. If they had chosen to observe, they would have seen a pretty woman, enraptured, smiling in her private bliss. Sofya's hair had begun to curl in prison, as it had in childhood. She was in the blue dress, saved for just such a happy occasion. In the cell she had worn the sarafan made by Yelizaveta. She carried her now-unlined summer coat over her arm. The eyes, which delighted in all the things around her, were bright blue with release.

'Been away on holiday?' the tram conductor asked her. He might have remembered Sofya's face from her many journeys along this route in the past, and not realised the length of her absence. What if she said to him loudly, so that all the other passengers on the tram would hear, 'Yes, on a Stalin holiday for almost a year. My husband is still a guest of the state, sentenced and exiled. I don't know where my children are, and whether my mother-in-law has been evicted from the annexe.' She wondered what would happen if she shouted like this. Would the faces around her slide behind masks? She, of course, would be instantly rearrested for anti-Soviet agitation. Sofya smiled mysteriously: she wouldn't give them the satisfaction. She was still smiling when she left the tram at the corner of Gogol Street. Bozhe moi, how lovely the street looked on a summer afternoon. The footpath was speckled with shade under the great chestnut trees. At the end of that cool tunnel rose the shining summits framed in green. Every little nerve in her body began to jump. She was going home. 'Home!' her blood sang.

Anna Pavlovna heard the door opening and the footsteps, but she didn't look up from the task at the table. She was kneading dough for a cabbage pie. Her new neighbour, Raissa, from the front part of the house, was having a birthday supper, and Anna Pavlovna had offered to bake a real pirog. Raissa was her only friend in the kommunalka; the one person to whom she could talk about the family.

'Come in, Raissa, I won't be a minute.' Anna Pavlovna was pressing the dough deftly with the heel of her hand, rolling it into a ball, slapping it and heeling it again. 'Just about finished with this.' The visitor was too silent behind her and the old woman turned. She stared at Sofya's ghost.

'Anna Pavlovna, it's really me.' Sofya crossed the little room and reached her arms around her mother-in-law. The two women stood locked in their embrace, weeping, mumbling tremulous reassurances neither of them needed to understand. Sofya felt the sharpness of the old woman's shoulders. Fleshless bones, so much frailer than before, she thought. Anna Pavlovna's flour-dusted hands were decorating Sofya's dress with white five-finger prints. They sat down on the sofa. 'I still sleep on this,' said Anna Pavlovna. Just as it used to be when the old woman and the younger one with the two children shared this room. Sofya slept in the big bed with Vera, and Nadya had her cot. Now Sofya was too frightened to ask about her daughter. No, she steeled herself, she had to know.

'Anna Pavlovna, where's Nadyenka?'

'Safe. In Leningrad with Alexandra. I found her and brought her home two months ago, but I couldn't care for her. I'm sorry, Sofya. The child wouldn't stay with Raissa. She needed someone with her all day. She was terrified they would come and take her back to the children's home.'

'Both are in Leningrad, Vera and Nadyenka.' Her voice was very small, as if her vocal chords had just been crushed by disappointment. Nor did her body obey. She slumped against Anna Pavlovna's shoulder, weeping.

That evening, in a clean dressing gown, with a towel turban wound round her wet hair, Sofya was drinking tea with Anna Pavlovna. After a long soak in the tin tub, scrubbing away the last traces of prison, she felt light and cleansed. A piece of Raissa's birthday pie sat in front of Sofya. Such a feast but, after a few mouthfuls, she couldn't swallow any more. She thought of the culinary conversations in Cell No. 7: mouth-watering recipes of favourite dishes, descriptions of what they would choose for their first freedom meal. And here, on her first evening at home, she had no appetite.

So much to tell, yet neither woman knew how to begin a review of the lost months. Anna Pavlovna started with her search for the child. The letters she had written, the doors slammed shut in her face, finally her appeal to Lenin's widow. In the measured voice of a storyteller, she described the little prisoner walking round and round a tree, a shaved head, a striped pinafore. And the Cossack woman who taught Nadya songs of the steppes in the night.

When it was her turn, Sofya hesitated. She couldn't tell her prison tale. Impossible. The horror was too alive, too personal. She had shared her thoughts and tears with her fellow inmates, but she couldn't confide in her mother-in-law. An old resentment she had forgotten in prison was taking hold again. 'For heaven's sake, what's wrong with me? She's Alexei's mother. He loves her.' Anna Pavlovna was an amazing, wonderful woman, who had not spared herself while Sofya was in prison. She'd rescued Nadyenka from the orphanage. But she was also the mother-in-law, whose tutelage had always riled Sofya.

Neither could Sofya talk to anyone else about her prison experience. Not only because of the NKVD threats, but because, in the harsh light of the outside, those hours, weeks, months spent inside, seemed unreal. There was no bridge between the then and the now, no connection, no echoing event she might grasp as a link, a comparison. At times she had an absurd feeling that she had enjoyed greater freedom in the cell than here outside, na volye. She dreamed of her friends in Cell No. 7, and missed them on waking. Prison routine still ruled her day. She woke up at five, waiting to hear the bells and shouts, realised that she was at home and felt almost disappointed.

After that she could not go back to sleep. She lay in the dark, wondering where Zina Kryukova was now. Had she been sent to another prison or into exile? Had Yelizaveta's case been brought together? Was she facing more interrogations, or the firing squad, the rasstrel. And what about the Cossack woman, Galina, the leader of the Urki gang? Later, in the war years, when the Leningrad survivors began to arrive in the Caucasus, she noticed in them the same kind of isolation, an obsession with their own experience. Like famine victims, former prisoners were trapped for months, for years in a warp of their own anxiety.

Anna Pavlovna was hurt by Sofya's secretiveness; her grievance was transparent and legitimate, Sofya agreed, and tried to make amends. In the evenings, which the Shubin women spent together in the little room, a reluctant Sofya would don the storyteller's mantle and force herself to relate some episode from prison life, or draw an occasional character sketch from the community of Cell No. 7. Even impersonal descriptions were not easy.

'We were cut off from the rest of the world,' she would begin. 'When a new person was brought in, especially if she was fresh from outside, the cell wanted to hear all the news. A newcomer was our newspaper. If the prisoner was transferred from another cell, she might bring prison news we had not heard. If from another city, she might tell of arrests in other parts of the country. This is how I met Tukhachevsky's mother-in-law. She spent only a few days in our cell but she had a lot to tell. A woman of the old school, like you, Anna Pavlovna, she told us about the purge of the military command. How families of high-ranking officers had been rounded up, wives, children, in-laws . . . About the executions . . . By then Marshal Tukhachevsky had already been shot.'

Sofya spoke about the nuns, because Anna Pavlovna liked the religious. 'Those poor nuns didn't stay very long in our cell. One day they were called out with their belongings, which meant either a transfer to another cell or to rasstrel. I think it was the latter: they were probably shot. But while the nuns were in the cell they shared everything they had with others. They even gave away most of their bread ration to women who had cramps, because they just couldn't endure hunger. Those nuns prayed for everyone, even for their torturers.'

Some of her other discoveries were beyond description. Like the night she saw two women in their corner bunk, making love. 'What are they doing?' Sofya nudged awake her doctor friend. From then on she kept a sly watch on the woman and her acne-faced companion, who couldn't have been more than sixteen. Whatever their nocturnal activity, that pair of Galina's underlings stayed apart in the daytime. Though, on a few occasions, Sofya intercepted a trusting smile between the two, and a casual touch of their hands.

Neither could she talk about her interrogation. How she was called in the middle of the night, taken out into the cold darkness, put in a car and driven to the NKVD building in town. She followed down long corridors, empty and silent. The doors she passed were closed. She thought she heard raised voices in one of the rooms. Her guard opened a door and told her to wait. The door behind her was padded. She was in a large luxurious office, with a desk by the window and bookcases along the wall. Sofya had been away from books for such a long time that the shelves stacked with glowing leather-bound backs attracted her like a magnet. But even if she had had the courage to walk across and browse, it would have been difficult to read the titles in the shadows. The room was lit only by a desklamp. The green glass shade reminded her of her father's bronze lighthouse on the desk at home. Home, cried her heart, but her mind, distracted by the mysteries of the room, was reaching out to the book titles, unreadable from where she stood across the room. Too far away, she thought. I must move closer to see what authors are read by the KGB.

She recognised Kozlov as soon as he walked in. She had not forgotten his inoffensive looks, nor the voice swearing in Alexei's room that night. Now she was looking again into the hard eyes locked in the steel circles of his spectacles. She would never forget those eyes staring at Alexei from a car window on that perfect, that blighted May afternoon, when her husband went out on his first walk.

'Good evening, Sofya Nikolayevna.' Kozlov's lips shaped a courteous smile. 'You're looking well. Prison has been positively kind to you.'

She must not show her fear. A small terrified feline caught in the circle of his stare, paralysed, she waited mutely for the reptilian coils to tighten and suffocate her. Even if she had needed to save her life with a polite reply, she wouldn't have been able to squeeze out a single syllable.

'I thought it was time for us to have a little chat.' He was settling down behind his desk, adjusting the green shade. 'Please, sit down.'

Like a disciplined schoolgirl, Sofya sat down opposite his desk and saw him tilt the lamp in her direction. The spotlight was his unblinking stare, grown immense. It blinded her. She lost sight of him. He was a voice behind that searing eye. And fighting the fog of panic in her brain, she knew that if Kozlov even threatened to put her on the conveyor belt, she would tell him anything he wanted to hear, straightaway; would agree to sign any document, implicate any friend. Terror was an instant stimulant: she was ready to plead for mercy, confess to the interrogator in advance. 'It's all Alexei's fault.' It seemed so transparently logical that Alexei had brought this trouble, had infected the household with his political disease. If only Sofya had married someone else, she would have been at home now with her children, and not here, not the wife of an enemy, facing a torturer. Then, as abruptly as it had possessed her, the madness ebbed. She came back to her senses, and was appalled at how easy betrayal was.

Kozlov seemed to keep in step with her thoughts, following each twist of her confused mind. 'Don't worry, Sofya Nikolayevna, we won't use any of our methods on you,' he sighed. 'We have all the information we want. Your husband has signed everything. He's already serving his sentence. Quite some distance from here, I must admit.' His voice was tinged with a mocking reassurance. 'But we'd like you to stay with us a little longer, just to remind you that we don't like wives who cover up for their husbands. Don't you know that shielding an enemy of the people is a crime against the Soviet state?'

'My husband is innocent.' Sofya's whisper was barely audible. What a coward she was. She felt as if her body had just been lifted out of the prison parasha, and all the yellow slime was oozing out of the pores of her skin.

'Oh, no, you're deceiving yourself. No one here is innocent.' He shifted the angle of the lamp and she saw his face again, as bland as his voice. 'You know, Sofya Nikolayevna, you too could be sent away for ten years.'

'It's all been a terrible mistake.' Her defence sounded unconvincing even to herself. 'My husband has never . . . I would never plot against the state.'

'Well, if I were you, I'd think that one over carefully. In any case, we are offering you an opportunity to do some serious thinking.' Kozlov's lips stretched into a thin line.

Only when she was out of the interrogator's room, taken to the Black Maria, and driven back to prison, did Sofya remember Nadyenka. She should have begged Kozlov to tell her where her child was but, in her fear, she had forgotten about her daughter. 'What have I done?' she whispered fiercely and banged her forehead against the bars.

As Kozlov had promised, she did get a chance to reflect. Straight from the interrogation she was thrown into a punishment cell, so small that Sofya's body seemed to fill it, to squeeze out the oxygen she needed to survive. She could touch both wet walls at once with her elbows. Sofya pressed her back against the cold metal of the door. They must have found out about her fear of enclosed spaces, or they may have guessed it. Perhaps everyone in the world was claustrophobic? When the lock had clicked, she told herself that this was the end. She could feel the unyielding walls closing in, strangling her; the ceiling coming down like a lid. She had a nightmare once of suffocating in a concrete coffin, and had woken up swimming in sweat. 'Let-me-out!' She banged on the door until her fists were bruised, then bleeding, and she had neither voice nor strength left. She curled up on the damp floor like a worm. Time stopped. When she came to she had no idea whether she had been lying there for minutes or for hours.

Strength began to flood back with the instinct to fight for her life. 'Breathe deeply,' she ordered herself. 'Breathe slowly. Now calm down and look around.' A feeble bulb muzzled by a wire basket dimly lit her tomb. The concrete slabs surrounding her oozed foetid damp. Sofya slid along the slimy floor to suck fresh air from the crack under the cell door.

Life After Prison

Sofya went looking for work. She knew that economic planners, who were always needed in industry, were at present in particularly short supply. Nobody dared to say aloud that the purges had depleted most professions. She went from one director's office to another, with her diploma and references. After all, she had been trained by the legendary Tarakhovsky in Rostov. Each time her diploma was eagerly examined, Tarakhovsky's letter read with a knowing nod of the head. They looked at her workbook. Why the long gap? they asked. Why had she been out of the workforce for over a year? She produced her passport with the NKVD stamp, which explained that citizeness Shubina had been investigated by the Security Organs. Everyone recognised this euphemism for prison.

The smiles of welcome would turn to clumsy retractions: 'Actually, there is no specific job going at this particular moment. Naturally, we'll let you know if and when something turns up. We'll write to you.' Some were hostile and crude: 'We've enough troubles on our hands without hiring ex-prisoners.' People, she discovered, were kinder one to one; in a group they exercised implacable political purity.

At the Myasokombinat, the director looked worried. 'I really don't know what to do. We need someone like you, your kind of experience. But there may be hell to pay.' He avoided Sofya's eyes, chewed on his pencil, and gazed out the window. Sofya began to pack up her diploma. 'Look . . .' The director's frown cut his forehead in two. He stood up, appearing much shorter than he looked sitting behind his desk. A podgy man, he was sweating in his jacket. Sofya decided that he was going to be one of the polite ones;

he'd shake her hand and tell her how sorry he was. 'Look, it's a risk,' his frown relaxed, 'but what the hell. You can start tomorrow at eight.'

The Meat Combine sat a few kilometres out of town, at the tram terminal. On her way to work and returning home, Sofya travelled past the prison. Twice a day she saw the grim wall and the grey blocks beyond, and every time her heart pounded against her ribcage — let-me-out. Her skin was salty with sweat. Her mind fought a host of images, ghosts from her prison past. She heard Zina Kryukova's tender laughter and her groans: I'm-not-signing-lies. She saw Yelizaveta's ribboned crown bent over her stitching, sheltered by the shoulders and the backs of other inmates from the eye of the warder in the spyhole. But most frequently she saw and heard Kozlov: No-one-here-is-innocent. Then came the icy slime of the punishment cell, and the battle for breath.

When the prison panics began to fade, Sofya returned to the cares of everyday Soviet life. Now on her way to work she worried that the tram might be delayed and she would be late for work. She left home earlier, to give herself extra time, and to avoid such an unspeakable disaster. The new law on truancy was an ominous incentive for punctuality: the penalty for unauthorised absence was ten years of hard labour. Even arriving late for work was reported and noted. Sofya became so anxious about this that she often missed seeing the prison buildings altogether. That, at least, was a blessing. At the office she worked hard to demonstrate her reliability as well as her punctuality; to prove how indispensable she was.

On the tram trips, when she was not worrying about being late, or about the figures for the regional plan, she thought about Alexei. This constant anxiety about her husband was by now a chronic condition. Alexei was serving his sentence in Siberia. The parcels they sent to him were often returned with an official note: addressee refuses to accept. And so Anna Pavlovna would patiently repack the parcel, replace the foodstuffs that had gone stale or had been damaged. They sewed the parcel up in a fresh piece of bedlinen and printed on it in indelible purple, 'Krasnoyarsk region, Kansk, c/o Prison Administration, to Shubin, Alexei Yevgenyevich'. Then Sofya took it back to the post office.

Letters were getting through to him. He had permission to receive and reply to one letter a month. Written with a blunt pencil on rough scraps of paper, these monthly letters arrived erratically, but at least they did arrive; they were a thread between them. His handwriting had changed: it was childish now, clumsy, as if he wrote in haste or, perhaps, even lying down. The wording in his letters was stilted, so unlike the warm, funny Alexei who had been her lover. She sensed that he was ill again.

Letter 1. Hello, dearest Sofya. I send you many kisses and wish you all the best. Thank you very much for the photograph. How the girls have grown, especially Vera. It seems strange that such a little girl will be starting school this year. She reminds me of you in your childhood photographs. And Nadya is sweet with her little thinking frown. The children look well, and although you wrote to me that Vera has lost weight I can't see it in the photo. You were probably surprised that I didn't ask you for their photo. But I was afraid that having the children's photo here, and not to see them daily, would make the separation more painful. Anyway, I am happy for them and quite confident, because I know that in our country children are enjoying a happy childhood, such as neither you nor I even imagined in the days of our childhood. Take care of them. Goodbye now. Kisses to you, to Mother and to my little daughters. Your Alexei.

Letter 2. Hello, Sofya, dearest! I'm sending you my best wishes and a thousand kisses. If I could only express on paper my feeling of love, tenderness and closeness. But that's impossible. You are the only friend who has not deserted me in trouble. (You and Mother.) I don't deserve all this. I have your letter of 7/6. None since. Sofya, my dear, I beg you, take good care of yourself and of the children. Kiss them and my Mother. Goodbye for now. I kiss you again. Your Alexei.

Conversations with Dmitry

Sofya was a woman deranged with delight when Vera and Nadya returned from Leningrad. 'Oh, my little ones, let me look at you again.' She laughed and cried, and would not let the children out of her sight. 'You've changed, my darlings. Vera, you've grown taller. And there's nothing of the baby left in Nadyenka. Such serious little faces. Oh, my God, am I really holding my own precious darlings in my arms?' She hugged Dmitry, her brother-in-law, who had brought the children back to her. 'Thank you, thank you, dear Dmitry. You're an angel. And so is my dearest, kindest Alexandra, for letting you come all this way . . .'

Dmitry Voskresensky was using his summer leave for this urgent family mission. He remained ten days in Pyatigorsk, taking a cure like any other summer visitor to a spa resort. An excellent opportunity to build up one's fitness and health, he said, gently dismissive of the praises and gratitude lavished on him extravagantly by Sofya. He drank mineral waters, walked on Mount Mashuk among the steaming, bubbling springs, and even climbed up to the place of Lermontov's duel. In a few days Dmitry's face lost its Leningrad pallor. He said that he felt a new man, and was grateful for this perfect holiday in a spa. Back in Leningrad there was work and more work piling up, waiting for him.

Sofya was not seeing as much of her brother-in-law as she had wanted and hoped. At the Myasokombinat the semi-annual report was about to come out, being checked and rechecked, and this meant long hours at the office for the accountants and planners. She left home early, returned late and, as the days of Dmitry's visit passed, she was irritable. In the evenings she pressed Dmitry to come out walking with her, even though she knew how tired he must be after tramping in the mountains all day long. She had to talk to him, she insisted, and talking was safer out in the open. Since her prison days, Sofya had been fearful of being overheard. In the annexe, there were eyes and ears. Anyone in their community could be an informer. She confided in Dmitry, because there was no one else she could tell about her prison experience. The need to describe it had become an obsession with her since her release; a need deepened by her self-imposed silence. Dmitry was not only a close relative, but a man of the world who would understand, would explain how these terrible events had come about, how their country could possibly endure so much suffering and not crack like a china cup.

But Sofya's conversations with Dmitry did not satisfy her. His bland, cautious replies disappointed her and she was offended by his patronising tone. When she first met Dmitry, this future brother-in-law impressed her as a quiet, yet fair person. You always had to wait for his view, but at least he spoke his mind honestly. (Goodness, that first visit to the Voskresenkys, when she helped Nina to paint Easter eggs, was a lifetime ago!) Sofya sensed that this new judicious Dmitry was reluctant to talk about things political, and especially avoided the subject of the purges. She did not know how to breach the armour of his reserve. At least he had remained the same careful listener; she was grateful for that. As they walked in the black southern night, she began telling him about Kozlov's repeated intrusions into her life: how the interrogator had tormented her dying husband; how Alexei was rearrested, as soon as his health had improved. She talked about Cell No. 7 for the first time, about her prison friends, the urki and the kontriki, but she still could not speak their names aloud to an outsider. What did Dmitry think? she asked. Would the arrests go on or was the madness abating? She wanted reassurance from him; he was another survivor of the purges.

Dmitry did not reply. He sighed wearily. For a while they walked in silence through the summer warmth of the night. Sofya caught the scent of nicotianas, which used to flower under her annexe window, but those plants did not survive her prison winter. There they were: a whole constellation of blooms burning in the darkness. She bent over the low picket fence to smell them. The perfume made her head swim and, feeling faint, she stretched out her hand to steady herself against the fence. She wanted to stay here forever, a lotus-eater drowning in that voluptuous scent.

Dmitry's voice brought her back to the unreality of the life she lived. Had she been following the newspapers? There was a lot of space given to our friendship with Germany these days. His detached, lecturer's voice made her chilly and forlorn. No, she didn't bother much with newspapers, didn't really care about the politics of Germany. 'Is it true then that Stalin is making friends with Hitler?' As she asked this, it occurred to her that he never spoke Stalin's name. How evasive he had become.

A picture of a different man came to her mind. Dmitry had just met Marshal Tukhachevsky, and was saying to Alexandra, happily, across the soup tureen: 'Tukhachevsky is our Red Napoleon. He's good-looking, talented, incredibly charming.' Later Sofya heard how demented with grief Dmitry was when the brilliant 'Red Marshal' was shot. Soon after that Dmitry himself was arrested, as were most of the officers. But he happened to be one of the lucky ones; he was not accused of being a German spy, had not been executed with the others. He was released and given his job back. Sofya had been kept well informed in Cell No. 7. She knew how badly the Red Army was affected in that terrible purge of the military; she'd heard the story that Stalin had destroyed the marshal out of envy. Things like that couldn't have been even thought, let alone spoken aloud, outside prison.

'I met Tukachevsky's mother-in-law in my cell,' Sofya said to Dmitry. 'You worked with him, didn't you? You liked him, he was your hero.' With a sudden cruelty she needed to see his discomfort.

Dmitry looked around nervously and scratched his bald head. His bony figure, so military in its erectness, stooped. In the light of the street lamp she saw his frightened expression, the trickle of sweat on his brow. He made an effort to stretch his thick lips into a smile (or was it an apology?). 'Yes . . . I was on his staff . . . but for a very short time, really. Just on secondment from the academy ...' He spoke so softly that Sofya had to strain to hear some of the words. 'I was only a lecturer, you know, not a career officer.' He fell silent. They walked on.

She thought, 'Oh, Dmitry, you could have asked me about the old lady, about your hero's mother-in-law. Aren't you interested in what she might have told us? Whether the poor woman, whose only guilt was being related to the doomed marshal, had been released or sent to the camps. Is it too much to expect you to weep with me over the senseless destruction of human beings? We both have witnessed it.'

Dmitry looked so distressed that Sofya felt sorry for him. Perhaps it was his pessimism that invited disasters? So unlike her other brother-in-law, the optimistic Misha Karpov, whose only worry in life was that his football team might lose a match. Well, if Dmitry was afraid to talk, she would. If it had to be a monologue, so be it.

'I can't understand how an entire society can submit to terror.' Sofya heard her voice recklessly rising a decibel with each word, but she was past caring about the consequences. 'How did we allow ourselves to be arrested, tortured, convicted for all these absurd crimes! Not just Alexei and me, but everyone: the Army Command, Bukharin and Rykov. And before them Zinoviev and Kamenev. The Shakhty trial. The whole country knew that all these people had been falsely accused, that all these trials were for show, yet none of us uttered a word of protest! What was it, a conspiracy of silence or a silent complicity? Just as no one said anything when the villages in the south were starved into submission in '32. It was all happening on our doorstep . . . Alexei and I were living in Rostov then, and we didn't say a word!'

'Sofya, please, please, keep your voice down.' Dmitry had tears in his voice now. He put out his hand as if to stop her mouth. He seemed to have grown even more stooped during her angry tirade. He muttered brokenly, 'I don't know, my dear. I don't know anything. Maybe terror paralyses decency and courage, reduces a human being to a miserable coward.' In the play of light and shadow, Dmitry's bald head and bony face appeared like a skull. She couldn't read his eyes, sunk into cavernous hollows. His thick lips were set in a grotesque rictus.

After Dmitry left, Sofya began to read foreign reports in the papers. Hitler marched into Poland; that was on August 1st. Three weeks later, Germany and the Soviet Union, having divided Poland between them, signed a mutual non-aggression pact. On September 2nd Britain declared war on Germany and, by the end of 1939, the Soviet Union was at war with its tiny neighbour, Finland.

A Summer Holiday in the Ukraine

The summer after the Finnish War, Sofya received permission from the NKVD to leave Pyatigorsk for a holiday. She persuaded Anna Pavlovna to make her annual pilgrimage to the Leningrad family. Now she was free to join Katya for three weeks in the Ukraine. The sisters had not seen each other more than two years. Since Sofya's release from prison, their correspondence had been chary. Nervous that their intimacy might be losing its spontaneity, both felt the need to spend some quiet time together. Sofya packed her prison sarafan, which her friend Yelizaveta had lovingly finished by hand, and left with her girls for Kiev. Simple to say, three weeks in a Ukrainian peasant house, with young children, demanded some determined planning, and a good deal more luggage.

But Sofya left all the details to Katya; in her own letters she escaped into her old dreaminess: 'It will be such fun living in a real Ukrainian khata. I wonder if it'll have a thatched roof, like something out of Gogol's stories. By the way, I'm bringing a copy of *Evenings on the Farmstead Near Dikanka*. We'll read Gogol aloud. Pushkin's *Poltava*, too, would be in tune with Ukraine. Can you bring a copy? I can't find ours.'

Katya's letters were entirely practical: 'There will be enough beds for all of us — I've checked. But you must bring the bed linen. Don't forget. We won't need much in the way of clothes, just sandals and sarafans. I believe August is the hottest month there. But since we'll be miles from civilisation, we must bring everything for the children. Kira will be practising for the competitions, so, of course, we're bringing her violin and music. You know my girls and their music! Though I'm happy to report Ada will not be bringing the grand piano. She'll be allowed a real holiday . . .'

Travelling from opposite points of the compass, Katya and her girls from Leningrad and Sofya's trio from the Caucasus, the sisters met in Kiev. They clasped each other on the platform and wouldn't let go. Both wept, both couldn't find their handkerchiefs and then, in unison, they had a fit of weepy giggles. Sofya laughed through tears, 'You're so pale.' And Katya, stepping back to examine her sister, declared, 'You're too thin.' The four cousins watched their mothers making a display of themselves. A family performance in public. It was very embarrassing. At least the children didn't have to examine one another; they had all been together recently in Leningrad. Next, Sofya shifted her ardour to her nieces — 'Adochka, Kirochka, you've grown.' She was embracing them, wetting their faces with her tears. 'How you have grown.'

From Kiev, the holidaymakers took a local train to Belaya Tserkov and, as the name described it, there was a pretty whitewashed church in the township. The sisters agreed that it did not appear desecrated or neglected. If the church had been turned into a club or a cinema, there were no posters on the walls to announce its secular denomination. 'Look,' Sofya pointed at an old icon hanging above the doors, 'this may be a working church.' The sisters exchanged looks of surprise.

In Belaya Tserkov they hired a cart to take them to the village, where Katya had rented their house. They travelled along a dusty road, at a pace as somnolent as the stifling afternoon. Fields of tall corn stood as a guard of honour all the way. Above them hung a limpid sky.

Katya sighed. 'That's how I always imagined the Ukraine.' All the cares of their planning and packing for the long journey were melting in the heat of this sunbaked road, vanishing into the white cloud of dust behind their cart. The rhythmic creaking of the wheels rocked the sisters into a drowsy mood. Sofya started reciting Pushkin.

'Mama, where's my music?' Kira's high-pitched scream brought the two mothers back to their responsibilities. Their pleasant musings about literary works set in the Ukrainin countryside were abandoned.

Katya's younger daughter wailed, 'I can't see the music case.' Everyone had been alerted to the drama; no one had seen the music case. How was Kira going to practise for the competitions without the music? She was tearfully sure the music case had been left behind at the station. The cart stopped in the middle of the cornfields. The driver and his horse dozed, as the excitable city folk grew more excited by the minute.

'I asked you again and again before we left the station if you had all your things with you.' Red patches were breaking out all over Katya's face. 'You told me you had everything.'

'Ah-ah,' keened the musical prodigy. She had a fine pair of lungs as well as perfect pitch. 'I thought I had it . . . I thought I saw it . . . I can't practise . . . without my . . . mu . . . sic.' The violinist wept piteously.

'Kira, stop this howling. I can't think. When did you last see it? Now think *where* did you see it last?' Katya's practical nature was taking over; the human metronome was returning to a working beat. 'Think,' she commanded. 'Stand up, I mean, jump off the cart, here, on to the ground, and start thinking.'

Kira was trying to remember, but her eyes and nose overflowed. Her mother handed her a handkerchief. 'Wipe your nose, and think!'

The elder girl Ada remembered that the case was in the cart when they were loading. 'I'm quite sure of that now, Mama.'

'Let's check the cart,' Katya ordered. Her short plump figure could have been Napoleon himself, ruthless and decisive.

The driver had also climbed down from his seat. If the luggage had to be unloaded, that was all right with him, he'd unload. His phlegmatic nature defied upheaval. As far as he was concerned, it was too hot to worry about little things. The roan mare was even more apathetic; she swished her tail and accurately swatted a fly on her dusty rump.

Everyone was out now, except Vera, who had slept through the noise of the battle. Generalissimo Katya was once again transformed into a motherly aunt. 'Verochka,' she murmured, 'wake up, little one . . .' But Vera was a dedicated sleeper; being woken up always brought on a flood of moaning. Vera was whimpering, Sofya was getting impatient with her. Katya tried to defend her niece. The poor child was exhausted. 'Let her be, Sofya. We'll look around her.'

'No.' Sofya was not about to relinquish her disciplinary rights to Katya. 'She's been told to get off the cart, and off she goes.' She yanked Vera's arm, and pulled the girl out on the road.

Vera moaned, standing beside the cart; her feelings were mortally hurt. And there in front of all the eyes was the music case. Vera had been sleeping on it, comfortably, all that time.

They all said they would remember the Ukrainian summer for the rest of their lives. And later, in the Leningrad famine, the cousins would talk about its abundance. 'Remember the wonderful soup we used to eat?' and they would recite the ingredients of the Ukraininan borsch, beetroot-scarlet, thick with vegetables and chunks of meat. And the apples! Those lovely apples. Golden globes they were, honey-scented, crisp and juicy. You picked them up in the long grass of the orchard, and watched out for wasps. You tied an apple to a string on the end of a stick, and bobbed it in the water as you crossed the little bridge. Nadya's apple dropped into the stream and the fast current carried it away. Remember the sour cream? Who could forget that amazing sour cream — white, thick, smooth. They used to spoon it over the potatoes, and sprinkled it with delicate fringes of dill, like bright-green eyelashes. And a plateful of huge knobbly tomatoes sliced, salted, sprinkled with sunflower oil. Giant sunflowers grew against the wooden fence; on the other side was a field of watermelons, green- and white-striped heads lolling in the sun. Even the sun in the Ukraine was different from the Leningrad sun. From dawn to sunset, it burnt the sky clear of clouds.

Nadya loved watching her mother and her aunt together. Sisters, she thought. Three sets of sisters here. Two mothers, each with her two daughters. Two aunts, each with two nieces. And then two pairs of cousins. Even their landlady had neither husband nor sons, only a daughter. A women's congress of our very own, Katya called it. 'No,' said Sofya, 'we're in a united kingdom of women.'

Summer. Day after leisurely day of summer. As you lay on your back in the long grass, dreaming into the blue curve of the sky, you could hear separate insect voices buzzing, clicking, whirring softly in the midday hush. Side by side, Sofya and Katya sheltered from the noon heat under the apple tree. Lazy. Too lazy to talk, even to think. Sofya lay on her stomach, quite naked, her sarafan within reach, just in case anyone intruded; no one ever did. More modest than her sister, Katya wore her panties and bra. Tessellated by sunlight and shadow, the sisters' bodies had become part of nature, part of the insect world in which colouring and design, all those spots and stripes, squares and variegations had been created for camouflage as well as decoration.

'You've got white stripes from your bra straps and a lily-white bottom.' Katya admired her sister's shapely back and buttocks. 'How do you keep that girlish figure of yours?'

'Worries,' Sofya mumbled through the haze of drowsiness. She brushed away a ladybird tickling her tanned arm, and turned to face her sister. Her breasts, inlaid with the criss-cross pattern of grass blades, had not been in the sun, and looked very white against the brown of the arms and shoulders. 'Sofya, you're shameless,' laughed Katya, admiring her sister's body. 'But then with a body like yours, perhaps one should walk about naked. You'd make a lovely model for a painter.' Katya looked down at her own soft stomach and sighed.

'Mmm,' Sofya guessed the cause of Katya's sigh. 'You eat too much, Katyusha. You're a glutton. I watched you at breakfast this morning, drinking milk as if you'd never seen it before. You spread half a kilo of butter on your bread, and then pour a litre of honey on top of it . . .'

'That's true, I just can't stop eating; everything here tastes so fresh,' Katya agreed. 'As a matter of fact, I'm storing up vitamins for the grey Leningrad winter.' The amiable jest did not conceal a pained note in her voice. Katya was hurt; well, a little hurt. Her sisterly compliment did not deserve such a thoughtless remark. As always, Sofya was oblivious of other people's feelings. 'She never stops to listen,' Katya thought.

'Oh, Katyusha, you've got a h-u-g-e blackhead on your cheek. Let me get it out for you.' With her deft fingertips Sofya squeezed her sister's skin. 'Am I hurting you? It's so-o deep.'

Katya forgave her sister. 'No, Sofya isn't mean. It's me — I'm too sensitive.' She sat up. 'Oh, heavens, we've promised the girls a swim.' The river was a good half-hour's walk and Kira had to be back for her evening practice before dark.

'Look at Nadyenka!' the girls screamed, pointing at the tiny figure clambering up the cliff. No one had seen her start out. Nadya was a dragonfly on the vertical slope; a dark head of hair, a pale smock, brown limbs flitting from rock to rock. Her face was a blur at that distance. Now she stood on the top of the bluff, and below was the river pool.

'Nadya,' the cousins shouted, 'be careful.'

'Nadyenka, come down immediately!' Sofya called out, and knew in that very instant Nadya could not possibly make her way down the cliff. 'No, don't do anything. I'm coming up to get you.' The little figure turned away from them and walked to the edge of the bluff.

Nadya was fed up with all of them — her cousins, her mother, her aunt. They had been swimming for ages and forgotten about her. Everyone had a swim, while she sat on the riverbank. First her mother demonstrated the backstroke and then taught the older girls how to do it. Then Katya and Sofya had a race to the opposite bank and back. Sofya won. Then they all watched the older girls diving from the rise. And so it went on. Well, Nadya was going to show them that she, too, could dive. She looked down into the green river pool. It was dark and deep. Even if she wanted to find her way back, she couldn't have done it. It was a long, long rock-studded slope, and she was terrified. Before she could change her mind, Nadya filled her lungs with air, instinctively, and jumped. A bundle of flailing limbs plummeted down, slicing through the layers of heat, swung on the faint current of the breeze and, with a short burst, broke the green glass of the water.

Sofya fished her out. Katya fussed. The cousins watched the shivering little girl with awe. 'Wasn't she brave?' Kira whispered. She couldn't imagine herself jumping off a cliff, could Vera and Ada? No, the others agreed, they couldn't. Never. Not in a hundred years.

'Nadyenka, you could've drowned. God, you gave us such a fright. Oh, you stubborn, stubborn child. You're a true Shubin child, aren't you?' Sofya crooned and rocked her baby, wrapped in a large bathing towel.

Nadya's teeth wouldn't stop chattering. She tried to say something to her mother and aunt, but her jaw and tongue would not obey. At last the shivering subsided into an occasional hiccup. Nadya wriggled out of the towel, a brown skinny child, with wet spiky hair and spiky eyelashes. 'Anyway,' she said, 'I've had my swim.'

At night there were stars. Nadya's side of the bed was by the open window, under the velvet drapery stuck with stars, like glow-worms on the bank of the creek at the bottom of the orchard. A diaphanous scarf trailed across the constellations. She recognised only the Great Mother Bear hibernating. If you watched the sky long enough, you began to see the darkness curving upwards into a cupola. What lay beyond the vast dome? she wondered. Are there other worlds with starry skies, like this one? And what lay beyond infinity? Years later Nadya saw a silkworm weaving a barely visible thread shaped like the symbol of infinity.

Outside, in the dark, Katya and Sofya watched the stars from a garden bench. Their voices were insect wings rustling and crackling, drifting into Nadya's dream.

'She's reckless like Alexei. A true Shubin, isn't she? God, she could have killed herself on a rock.' Sofya was reliving her earlier fright.

'Nadyenka is like you. Like mother, like daughter. Both of you are determined to have your own way!' Katya laughed into the darkness. Just then the pair sounded like twins, indistinguishable, inseparable.

When they laughed together, the melody of the sisters' laughter sang in two parts, blending into a duet. Lulled by their harmonious voices, Nadya slept.

Trains in Wartime

> Wasn't I there at the cross,
> Didn't I drown in the sea,
> Could my mouth forget
> Your taste, grief?

'Afterword', from *The Leningrad Cycle*, January 1944

On the third day of the war Anna Pavlovna was at the Nikolayevsky Station, queuing at the ticket office. She was going to book good sleeping berths for herself and her two granddaughters. Even at the best of times, the train journey to the Caucasus was arduous; now, with the war on, it was bound to take longer; and it would be more difficult as well. She intended to travel comfortably. Although for the past two decades the railway station had been the October Station, she still referred to it by its old name. Everyone should know, she maintained pedantically, that the station was not named after the last Romanov tsar, but after his great-grandfather, the first Nicholas. If there was no respect for history, she argued, neither was there any compulsion to use those absurd new names which, no doubt, would change again. But she kept these arguments to herself, especially since her son's ten-year sentence in a Siberian prison camp.

When she arrived at the station her courage sank. The large restless crowd in the concourse reminded her of the nightmare journeys in the days of the civil war. She had hoped never to see again the packed trains of those years. If you were lucky or forceful enough to board one, they still took forever. The trip from Moscow to Yaroslavl, with her sick husband, lasted two weeks. At the railway stations then there were just such crowds of desperate people, mobbing the carriages, screaming, pushing; lost children weeping. Alexandra was with her then, helping with the sick man. Irritable in his illness, Yevgeny Shubin loudly blamed the Bolsheviks for the chaos in Russia, while Anna Pavlovna and Alexandra tried to protect him from drunk sailors and Red commissars. They trembled for him. When he saw soldiers, he recalled that his youngest son had joined the Red Guard, and muttered bitter accusations. Her poor husband. That was his last journey. He died soon after they reached home.

Anna Pavlovna had since travelled the whole length of European Russia several times, but even the longest and the most trying journeys had seemed comfortable, even luxurious, after the horrors of the past. Setting out for the tickets in the morning, she declared haughtily that she was not decrepit and could manage alone. She told Alexandra that she could endure anything, but now she realised that she could not fight her way through this hysterical humanity. Standing on the edge of the crowd, she simply couldn't bring herself to plunge into the seething vortex. The noise distressed her. She felt so weak, she thought she might faint. She was too old, she had to admit, to be pushing and shoving with everyone else. To survive in this society, you had to be bold and tenacious; above all, you must not give up. Bozhe moi, hadn't she lived through enough disasters in her time. Why another so soon after the last blow? Still, even if the time of troubles was back and destruction was again sweeping Russia, nothing would stop her from taking the girls to the Caucasus. She straightened her back, took a deep breath to renew her courage and plunged into the crowd. She prayed as she pushed in, accepting curses from her fellow human beings and the punishment of sharp elbows. The river of humanity swirled around her, tugging and tossing her in a fast current. Her keen eyes, which had refused to submit to age and adversity, could pick out the ticket windows ahead. Like a strong swimmer amid the bobbing debris, she struck out for the shore.

She limped back to the house of the seven winds, taking the six flights of stairs to the Voskresensky apartment one step at a time. The doorbell — she had barely enough strength to press it. Voices. The lock clicked. Alexandra was on the doorstep, gaunt from sleepless nights. It was then that Anna Pavlovna's pride and legs gave way, and she slumped into her daughter's arms.

'Oh, Mother, I've been frantic with worry. I thought you'd been trampled to death. Dmitry tried to find you in that dreadful crowd. It was terrible.'

Nadya came running, 'Babushka is home! Babushka is home! I knew my Babushka would never get lost!'

Alexandra continued to moan. 'You could have been killed. You're the most stubborn person in the world. Sit down here. Rest. I'll make you a foot bath.'

'I did what had to be done,' the matriarch explained. She was sitting on a high-backed chair with her feet in a steaming basin. Alexandra had put mineral salts into it and was now adding hot water from a jug.

'A bit more, Alexandra.'

'I don't want to burn you, Mother.'

'Don't worry. I'm a seasoned old warrior.' Anna Pavlovna was not apologising for the worry she had caused the family, but she granted her anxious daughter the gift of a half-smile.

'Oh, you are a warrior indeed, Mother. Who else would have lasted all this time in the ticket queue? You're heroic!' A tentative stream of hot water spurted from the jug in Alexandra's reverential hands.

'Keep on pouring,' Anna Pavlovna ordered, rubbing her aching feet. 'You know what the most terrible thing was? A total lack of information.' She was telling the story of her ordeal to Alexandra and Nadya, who sat perched beside her. They heard how the authorities had commandeered all the trains to evacuate essential industrial machinery and personnel. 'Though some of the essential workers looked suspiciously like party officials and their families.' Anna Pavlovna was scornful.

'There were no porters, so the poor things had to carry their own luggage. And while this charade went on, thousands of us waited in the ticket queue, hoping that in the next hour, or the next day, there might be a few trains for people like us. No such luck. I've always known that ordinary citizens came last in this country,' Anna Pavlovna muttered bitterly. 'I wish, though, I had managed to get tickets to the Caucasus. Even a ticket to Moscow would have been a help. There are more trains going south from Moscow.'

Dmitry Voznesensky said from the doorway, 'You mightn't have got away from Moscow. I think we'll have to keep the children here in Leningrad. Until things settle a bit.' The Germans, he went on to explain, were pressing towards Moscow, and moving on a broad front into the Ukraine.

Dmitry's uniform made him an immediate authority on the war. He had been called up on the second day and attached to the city headquarters. He came home in the evenings to share the war bulletins with the family, and left early the next morning for the HQ. He had no idea how long this routine would last. Indeed, he suspected that quite soon he would be sent to the front, and did not want to alarm his wife, already burdened by many terrors. Alexandra, with her nervous intuition, had guessed what mobilisation meant: a forty-six-year-old lecturer, whose peacetime expertise had been in the deployment of military railstock, could only be called up to fight. Apart from fearing for Dmitry, Alexandra worried about her brother's children. She fretted about Nina and Slava, who had been conscripted with half the Leningrad population to build defences against the advancing Germans. They were now digging trenches and anti-tank ditches somewhere on the Luga Line.

'Oh, Mother,' she sighed. 'While you were away they took Nina's class straight from the medical school to dig the trenches.' On Wednesday, she said, the students were divided into work brigades, and taken off to build fortifications and tank traps. Alexandra's anxiety had aged her visibly: she now looked more like Anna Pavlovna's sister than her daughter. Except that, even in her exhausted state, Anna Pavlovna appeared determined, whereas Alexandra's features sagged in defeat.

'And you, Dmitry?' Anna Pavlovna asked her son-in-law.

'He'll be posted to the front any moment!' Alexandra answered for her husband and turned away to hide the return of tears.

Anna Pavlovna did not continue the questioning. She had no desire to hear what she had already concluded, that this war, which had burst into the summer landscape of Russia eight days ago, had irrevocably altered life in this family, as it had, no doubt, invaded every household in their vast and vulnerable country.

Nina came home from the trenches. 'You're one of the first casualties of war,' Dmitry joked, but the expression of tenderness he kept for his only child was laced with worry. 'Let's have a look at your wound.' He examined the curve of inflamed stitches across her palm. 'You could have lost your hand.'

'Who's the doctor in this family, and who is the engineer?'

'You're not a doctor yet.'

'Only one more year to go.'

'In any case, you look ridiculously young to be one. Who'll trust you?'

'You just wait, when you're sick, I'll refuse to treat you.' Nina and her father enjoyed their private combative exchanges. Dmitry spoke to his daughter with the kind of gruff affection he might have shown to a son. Sometimes he wondered if a son would have followed him into the Army Engineers.

Nina sniffed and tossed her cropped hair. 'Papa?' She was serious again. 'It doesn't look good out there. It's chaos. Panic. Our army is retreating. We can't stand up to the Germans. I'm right, aren't I?'

Dmitry lifted his daughter's injured hand and touched the angry scar very lightly with his fingertips, as if willing it to heal quickly.

'Yes, it's very bad out there, and it'll probably get much worse.'

Goodbye to the Statues

Dearest night,
In your star-studded cloak,
In funereal poppies, with your wakeful owl . . .
Dearest daughter,
We covered you
With fresh garden earth.
The cups of Dionysus are empty now.
The face of love is tearstained . . .
Hovering above our town
Are your terrible sisters.

'The Statue of Night in the Summer Garden', *The Wind of War*, 1942

Nadya thought that her cousin Nina was the loveliest creature in the entire universe. 'And she's the most fun!' Nina was decidedly prettier than the musical cousins, Ada and Kira. Much brighter than the four Moscow cousins Nadya had met earlier this summer. The Moscow team had interstellar names like Astra, Aliana, Dinara, Rheingold. Reflecting ungenerously on the flock of cousins, Nadya skipped alongside Nina the incomparable, down the central avenue of the Summer Garden. In her adoration, she squeezed her cousin's injured hand. Nina cried out.

'Let's say goodbye to the statues,' Nina had proposed that morning. 'They're being buried in sand until the end of the war.' The end of the war couldn't come soon enough for Nina. She missed Slava, still away on the fortification works, and felt depressed because her silly hand was mending too slowly. She still couldn't bend her fingers, and at night the pain kept her awake.

After breakfast, Nina and Nadya hopped on the tram and got off near the Engineers' Castle. They walked across the funny humped bridge with the bronze lanterns perched on bunches of lances, and entered the Summer Garden from the top, its narrow end, near the Carp Pond, which had no carp swimming in it. As they walked down the wide sandy avenue, the Summer Garden opened up before their eyes like a fan. The statues were still posing on their pedestals, but gardeners had already started digging graves for them on the side of the path.

'Sad, sad,' Nina murmured, staring ahead to the far end of the avenue, where they could catch the cold glint of the Neva through the spokes of the railing. The heavy gates stood open now and the granite parapet of the embankment stopped the garden from rolling into the river. Nina was pensive. The playfulness Nadya so loved in her grown-up cousin was half-hearted today. Nina started the old guessing game, but it didn't work because Nadya knew all the gods and goddesses; she had learnt to recognise their names on the plinth.

Nina's smile was slow on her lips and didn't spread as far as her eyes. She had Shubin eyes, but a mouth from the Voskresenskys. Nina's swollen lips suited her. It made Nadya think of a portrait of the young Pushkin in her poetry book. It was nice to have your favourite cousin resemble a famous poet.

'So you can read the names, Nadyenka, but it means that we've done ourselves out of a lovely game. Let's sit for a while?' Nina sat down on a green bench and patted the planks at her side. She didn't order Nadya about. Aunt Alexandra also checked for her preferences: she took Nadya every morning to choose one of her fine china cups for breakfast. But Nina offered her an equality that the child instinctively valued. There was no awkwardness between them. Nadya could ask her adult cousin any question and have it answered, gravely. When Nadya confided secrets, Nina listened seriously.

'Nadyenka, look at Night. See the stars on her drapery, and the garland of poppies on her head. From these poppies comes opium, a drug that induces oblivion. See the bat and the owl beside her? They're nocturnal creatures, symbols of sleep. And so our lovely Night is going into that hole for a long, long sleep. It's a burial service . . .

'Have I told you, when I was a little girl I went to a German school? There were two German schools on the Nevsky: Annenschule for girls and Peterschule for the boys. We had to speak German in class and in the interval. Then the school was closed down, and now I've forgotten all the German I'd learnt there. It might have come in handy now, who knows?'

Nadya clung to Nina's good hand possessively. Each was lost in her own thoughts. Nadya was thinking how lovely it was to have her cousin to herself, without Slava. She sensed that the rest of the household also resented him for taking Nina away from them, even if they didn't call him the Red Devil, as Babushka did. When Slava was about, Nina had eyes only for him. Even now, on the park bench, she must have been dreaming of him; her face had a sad and tender look.

Nina was wondering how long her silly injury was going to keep her from Slava, who was digging trenches under enemy fire and might be killed without her. She remembered how, on the eve of the war, they had walked along the canals, through the pallid June night; a landscape suspended between light and darkness, created for the dreams of lovers like themselves, and for the phantasmagoria of poets. She was going to marry him as soon as he came back. They had planned to wait until their finals, and then go to the ZAGS on their graduation day. But that was before the war. Now everything had changed, was changing every hour. It might already be too late, and he might be dying from a shell splinter this very minute. 'Oh, Slavka, come back, come back to me!' she wept inside. Her hand quivered in Nadya's warm palm.

Later, after the burial of the statues, they stopped going to the Summer Garden. The park was ruined, Nina said; no one went there any more. Now the Army grazed horses there in the meadows, and some of the old trees had been felled for some reason. Even Babushka didn't offer a view on the matter. Waiting for Slava to return, Nina was silent. Every morning she went to the institute to help with the blood bank, to roll bandages and to train first-aiders. She came home late, exhausted, and went to bed behind the screen, while the others were still at the table. No, thanks, she didn't want any tea with wild strawberry, Alexandra's last jar of home-made jam. It'd be a waste of precious jam, Nina explained; she suffered from indigestion just then. Must be the stress of her workload, sighed Alexandra. And she's missing Slava, naturally. Babushka only nodded to that and didn't offer one of her authoritative opinions.

Nina was pale and wretched in the mornings, and took off in a rush before breakfast. Not that breakfast was much at the Voznesenskys: it was bread and tea. The bread was now rationed. Aunt Alexandra wept a great deal, as if her husband and daughter had already died at the front, whereas they hadn't even been sent away. Soon, soon they'll all be gone, she moaned as she went about her household chores.

A Wartime Marriage

When Slava came back from the trenches, Nina took him out into the green square across the street from their apartment building. For a bit of privacy, she said; just to have a real talk. There were all kinds of practical things they had to decide, which couldn't be discussed upstairs. To start with, they had to work out where they were going to live. Nina watched the thinning tree-tops above them and listened to children's voices in the playground. She wanted to weep, to abandon herself to the tears she had held back all the lonely weeks without him. Whatever time was left to them must be spent together, but she couldn't move in with him. Slava's home was in the dormitory at the student hostel. And he couldn't live with her family, could he, unless they got married.

'All right,' he proposed, 'let's get registered.'

Late that evening, drifting in and out of sleep, Nadya heard the family debate around the table. A crack under the door let in a strip of apricot light and Aunt Alexandra's complaint: 'A church wedding may be against your Komsomol principles, Nina, but, in my opinion, a ZAGS registration is not a real marriage. It's a licence to live together, that's all.' For a while all was silence on the other side of the door. Then Alexandra asked, 'Have you been baptised, Slava?'

'I really can't remember,' he answered playfully. It sounded as if this lapse didn't worry him either.

'Oh, Slavka, do be serious. You're upsetting my mother.' Even Nina's reprimand was tender; she found no fault with him.

Now the young people were laughing, and Alexandra's agitation was growing. She was trying to enlist the support of the older generation. 'Why don't you say something, Dmitry? Or you, Mother? After all, a sin against God is a serious matter. Young people should get married in a church.'

Nadya could imagine Dmitry patting Alexandra's hand, calming her and all the others with his rumbling bass. Her uncle's bald head would be glistening in the lamplight, and his big lips would be folded in a kindly smile. Whatever the crisis, Babushka would be majestically pouring tea and keeping her own counsel until the end; then she would put forward her view in a casting vote.

'I think Nina and Slava should decide for themselves. They're old enough to know what they want,' Dmitry was saying, probably avoiding his wife's eyes.

Alexandra sounded dismayed, 'How can you say it!'

Anna Pavlovna, who had been against the Red Devil all along, now seemed to have changed sides, or changed her mind about his suitability. The war may have softened her view of him. 'The world the young live in is different from ours, Alexandra. We can't force them to observe our principles . . .'

Alexandra's protest died; she couldn't fight all of them.

'Of course, if they decided to have a church ceremony,' said Anna Pavlovna, 'we would make it simple and quiet, and no one would ever find out about it. It would be in the family.'

'We may as well tell you now, Mama, we're going to register at the ZAGS tomorrow.'

'Tomorrow? But nothing's been planned. There won't even be time to prepare anything.' Alexandra began to sob.

'Everything will be fine, Mama, please don't cry.' Nina must have moved to Alexandra's side and was now hugging her rounded shoulders. She spoke to her mother carefully, as though Alexandra might crack like one of her precious china cups. 'When I left Slava in the trenches, I thought I'd never see him again. We are so happy to be together again, and there may be so little time left.'

At the other end of the table Anna Pavlovna leaned toward Dmitry and asked softly, 'Do you think Slava has been called up?'

'Not yet,' Dmitry whispered back, 'but he might be any day now.'

'Bozhe moi,' sighed Anna Pavlovna, 'bozhe moi.'

Nina and Slava went to the ZAGS the next morning. In the afternoon he moved his suitcase into the Voskresensky apartment. They were to have the dining room to themselves at night and sleep on the large divan. A bed was made up for Babushka in Alexandra's bedroom, behind the Chinese screen. Nadya's cot was pushed farther from the window, for fear of shrapnel and broken glass. Everyone expected the Germans to start bombing Leningrad any day.

Slava was not called up. The medical institute, which both he and Nina attended, was ordered to continue with its fifth-year course and to send students directly to the front when they finished the year. And a few days later the newly-weds, as Alexandra now called Nina and Slava, went away for a weekend to the Karpov dacha in Murzinka.

Dmitry Goes to War

Now they've called you up, my friends.
My life has been spared to mourn you.
I won't droop like a willow tree over your memory;
I'll shout your names to the world . . .

Why worry about names?
Names don't matter, you are still with us.
We all must go down on our knees
Before the burst of crimson light!
The Leningrad ranks move through the smoke,
The living marching beside the dead.
All are carved on the roll of honour.

The Wind of War, 1942

In the night the guns boomed. Nadya dreamed of her mother shooting down German planes, and woke up terrified. Stay awake, stay awake, keep your eyes wide open! If she fell asleep again the dream would be back and her mother might be dead. Now that her heart had stopped pounding, she could hear movement next door and hushed voices. She peered through the darkness at Alexandra and Dmitry's bed, saw the empty white sheets. They were up, sitting in the dining room. Why, Nadya wondered. She lay still, pulled up the blanket with the pink carnations on it that used to be Nina's Guten-Abend-Gute-Nacht blanket when she was a little girl, and listened. The voices next door grew louder, more urgent.

Nadya knew exactly where her clothes were, draped on the back of a chair beside her bed, and the shoes stood just as neatly under the chair. This was one of the orphanage habits she had brought back with her; sometimes she climbed out of bed to check the symmetrical alignment of her shoes. If they were moved, however innocently, Nadya was upset. She got into her dress, put on her shoes and patted her socks. It was a mechanical gesture of which she was hardly aware, except that things always had to be just so for her to feel secure. And now, with those agitated whispers in the darkness, she needed proof that life was safe.

She tiptoed to the door of the dining room, opened it a crack and heard Dmitry comforting Aunt Alexandra: 'You'll wake up the child.' He heard the creaking door, and looked round. 'There she is. Good morning, Nadyusha. You're up early. And already dressed.' He came to the doorway to pick her up. His face smelt of shaving soap. The fresh cut on his upper lip was a war wound, probably; he must have been injured in a battle while she slept. He kissed Nadya on both cheeks, as if they were saying goodbye at the railway station, and he was setting out on a long journey from the Caucasus to Leningrad.

Aunt Alexandra was packing things into his Army bag. Perhaps not realising that Nadya was already awake, she kept her voice low. 'You'll need your warm underwear. The nights are getting cold. And the cross, where's your baptismal cross?' she cried in panic. 'Haven't I given it to you. Are you wearing it?'

Dmitry patted his chest, and then unbuttoned the khaki shirt to show her the cross hanging from a gold chain round his neck. He put on a happy smile, but it came out looking strained. He knew how to cope with his wife's superstitions, but his own burden was harder to bear. The irony of it, he thought, that on the eve of his departure to the front he had to appear at the NKVD.

'So, we're off to fight. Yes, it'll be good for you.' Dmitry was confused. Did the interrogator mean 'you' as a singular or plural? Did he mean just Dmitry or all his fellow officers arrested in 1937, who had survived the camps and now were given another chance to prove their patriotism? He waited for the usual admonition, the familiar reminders of what they expected from him. But the NKVDist didn't follow the old sinister routine. His face was weary; he looked human for the first time. 'Well, none of us may survive,' he muttered under his breath. With a sigh, he waved Dmitry out of the room, out of the building, away from the poison that had destroyed his life.

As Dmitry now pieced together all the details of that visit, he was certain it had been the last one ever. Here at last was liberation. It was surely the answer to Alexandra's prayers. Yet it was also a farewell. His heart was empty. He had no desire to stay alive, if survival meant a return to the lie he'd lived with for years. He wished his daughter was here; he wanted to hug her thin little shoulders, tell her something very tender, unforgettable — something she could keep forever in her heart.

Nadya snuggled up to Babushka. Both were witnessing the oldest of rites, the immemorial scene of a wife equipping her husband for war. Or for prison, as Sofya had packed Alexei's bag in 1938. Alexandra hadn't had time for a proper cry. She kept wiping her eyes and blowing her nose, as she went on with her task until the knapsack was ready. Then she said solemnly, 'Let's sit down,' and patted the chair beside her.

Silence. As if she had ordered all of them to stop breathing. Silence like a fuse about to ignite, to blow up the world they had lived in yesterday. Alexandra stood up and pulled her husband down by the shoulder. She made a sign of the cross over him: 'Christ keep you and save you.' Then she kissed him on the lips.

Dmitry came up to Babushka — 'Goodbye, Anna Pavlovna.' She, too, crossed him and kissed him on his bald head. Then it was Nadya's turn. Dmitry lifted the child and pressed her tightly to his chest. 'Be good.'

When he had gone, Alexandra lay on the bed and buried her face in the pillows. Babushka closed the door, and led Nadya towards the tall dresser. 'Let's look at the Napoleon cups, shall we? There's a new Napoleon now outside Moscow.'

A Wartime Honeymoon at Murzinka

> To the right, empty streets sprawl,
> Streaked with dawn, ancient as the earth.
> To the left, streetlamps like gallows
> One, two, three . . .
> High above, the cry of jackdaws
> And the irrelevant moon, cold with grief.
> That's from another lifetime.
> That's when the golden age will come.
> That's when the battle will end.
> That's when you and I will meet.

The Wind of War, 1942

'Ours will be the shortest honeymoon on record.' They were on the tram to Murzinka. Slava shook his head sternly: 'Comrade Nina, it's illegal to abandon duty.' 'And immoral,' agreed Nina, looking happy.

Alexandra had taken over Nina's Saturday fire-watch on the roof of the apartment block. At the institute fellow students covered up for Slava. On Monday morning they both had to be back at their lectures. Now, with their food ration packed in a rucksack, they were riding on the tram to the suburbs. As they travelled down familiar city streets, they counted the fresh marks of war around them.

'The Bronze Horseman's sandbagged.' Nina nodded in the direction of the wooden pyramid over Peter's statue. 'D'you think it's mined as well?' Everyone had heard about the order from Moscow not to abandon Leningrad and its monuments to the enemy. If the Germans captured the city, all the masterpieces must be destroyed. Leningrad was braced to do a house-to-house battle with the invader.

At some of the crossroads, they recognised camouflaged firing points. As the tram left the centre and rolled down neglected suburban streets, they saw anti-tank defences put up in one place, and a stopbank of barbed wire in another. It was a sombre landscape of a city at war.

Murzinka was the terminal on this suburban tram route. The village sat on the edge of a park, by the river. A holiday place in summer months, Murzinka looked sleepy now with the approach of autumn; untouched by the fever of wartime activity, except for the highway nearby, noisy with military traffic. They walked from the tram stop towards the park and the Neva, down a street of gardens that spread their branches above old-fashioned wooden footpaths which no longer existed in the city. The trees here were touched with gold, but the air still smelled of summer.

The wooden house badly needed a coat of paint; it reminded Nina of the old manor houses in Turgenev or in Chekhov. The Karpovs' apartment was the corner one, downstairs. Its door opened straight on to a creaking verandah and both the windows looked out on the park. Through the dense picket of tree trunks they caught sight of the river, a bronze sheen on the water. These days everything might turn out to be a mirage.

Nina sat down on the floor to unpack their rucksack. She had none of her mother's tidiness; the middle of the room was soon littered with their provisions and clothing. Slava wanted to go for a swim before dark, but he couldn't find his swimming trunks. 'Where can they be?' He found them, and stripped. She had never seen him naked in daylight. In the past they had always made love in dark places, in the attic, or under the stairs, or sometimes in the park thickets. He stood before her now, smiling, unashamed. A marble god from the Summer Garden, she thought. 'And his penis is quite small for his powerful build.' She dropped her eyes and went back to unpacking while he laughed aloud at her scrutiny, at her embarrassment. 'Come on,' he hurried her, pulling up the trunks, 'we'll miss the sunset on the Neva.'

They ran between rows of russet trees, through the waist-high grass, to the water's edge. The river before them was molten metal laced with fire, a flood pouring out of some hidden giant furnace.

'Like blood,' it occurred to Nina. 'Must be sticky as well.'

'Be careful,' she called after Slava, who was already taking a running leap into the water. He dived in, disappeared for an eternity, and bobbed up far from the shore. He was swimming now against the current with a lazy, confident crawl. His hair was dark red against the shining surface of the water. White shoulders flashed in the waves. The rhythmic stroke of his arms sent up a spray of tinted water drops. 'Be careful,' Nina said to the water, to her lover or to herself. The river was fast, dangerous even for a strong swimmer like Slava.

In the twilight later they sat on the verandah steps with their arms around each other, waiting for the last streak of light to fade on the opposite bank. The sounds of war made them cling more tightly. Gunfire was creeping closer. Nina shivered. 'German or ours?'

'Scared?' He stroked her head. She had cut her hair very short in the trenches. That and her flat-chested body made her look like a young boy. 'Not of the guns.' Nina burrowed into the shelter of his hard muscles: 'My shield and my buckler.' Like everyone else in the city, she was getting used to the guns, to the howling air-raid alarm and the drone of enemy bombers cruising over the city. 'You know what it is . . . I'm thinking about it all the time.'

To Slava her pregnancy was no longer a problem, not even an emotion; it was a clinical condition they had discussed and decided how to resolve. He genuinely forgot about it most of the time. To Nina it had been a disaster from the start, and her agonising went on. When she first missed her period in the trenches, she thought it had been due to stress and, of course, she did not mention the event to Slava. Bodily functions were an embarrassing topic with your lover. It was only when she returned home from the Luga Line, and missed the next period, that she realised its significance, and sank into a torment of indecision. She couldn't get in touch with Slava on the fortifications; it was impossible to contact anyone near the frontline. If she had, she probably wouldn't have known how to tell him that she was pregnant. She couldn't confide in her family, especially not to her anxious mother.

Now, two months into the war, their old hopes lay under the

rubble of a once orderly world. Plans, which had been so simple in the past, now seemed irrelevant. They had planned to get married on their graduation day, and take on a rural assignment, perhaps somewhere near Slava's home, in the Urals. She had had a vision of them as a dedicated team: two young doctors helping people in a rural clinic. Now, day and night, she tried to rein in her fears, not allow herself to imagine the countless terrible ways this war might further mangle their lives. They both knew for certain that doctors would be needed at the front, and both of them would be sent there as soon as they were qualified. This pregnancy was destroying their last chance of remaining together. If she had the child, Slava would leave for the front alone, while she would have to remain in Leningrad. If he were to be killed (the thought was unbearable), the child would be born fatherless. 'We can't bring a child into this terrible world,' she told Slava, as soon as he returned from the fortifications.

'All right, let's abort it.' He sounded so calm, as if he thought the baby wasn't theirs. Indifferent to what Nina might be feeling. She could see how exhausted he was. It must be his fatigue speaking. His apathy was a sickness he had brought back from the frontline. She had been there herself and experienced it all. In the trenches, they dug in long shifts under enemy fire, watching their neighbours being maimed or killed. Yet a poisonous resentment was flooding her mind. What about my feelings? she cried. What about my agony? She had changed her mind, she told him, she was going to have the child. But immediately after, she began to doubt, to question. Was she being rational, or hysterical? Her decision might have sprung from a deeper instinct to save life, not to destroy it. Could it be that, unlike her contemporaries, she simply couldn't bring herself to terminate her pregnancy?

'All right,' Slava was never easy with the feminine psyche, 'so you won't have an abortion. That's fine with me. Keep it!' But had she considered facts: he would be away at war, and she would be alone when the time came.

Now, on the steps of the Murzinka house, Nina clung to him, desolate, confused. The gunfire came in waves, approaching and receding. There was a direct hit at one of the industrial plants across the river. The explosion lit up the gaunt factory skeleton, and its force shook their house. Slava pulled both of them on to the verandah floor and sheltered her with his arm. When the shockwave passed, Nina pressed her wet face into his chest. 'No, it's not the right time to have a baby.' His shirt was damp with her tears.

'So what is it you want?' He didn't mean to be impatient, but that's how his exclamation affected her. She drew away from him.

'I want you to do it here at Murzinka,' she said after a pause, as if she'd taken a fresh breath of courage. Her voice was flat. 'Now!'

He could see it all now, how she must have tortured herself, and made her secret preparations. She showed him the syringe she had brought with her. The water in the kettle, she said, was sterilised and should be cool enough. All her trembling and yielding in his embrace were an icing on the real Nina, who was made of stone and steel. 'With a bit of luck, it'll all come away by the time we go back to town.' She was planning her abortion, unemotionally, as if for someone else. This cold-blooded strategy unnerved him. He watched her spread out the towels, testing the temperature of the water and filling the glass syringe. 'Scrub your hands,' she ordered calmly. And Slava, awed into speechless obedience, walked across the room to the washstand. When he had finished drying his hands, she gave him the syringe. 'Now, you can take over.'

She lay down on the bed, her naked hips resting on the towels, legs wide apart. 'Can you see in this light?' she asked in that detached voice. Her hardness frightened him. Why did she force him to kill her child? His child. For a terrible moment he saw himself, the killer of his own child, and felt a surge of sweat over his skin. Why couldn't they wait a little, talk it over again, he thought. Her silence paralysed his voice. The callousness of the act appalled him; even more shocking was their apparent detachment

'I hope it won't hurt you. I'll try to be careful.' He heard the calm voice of a medical professional. He realised that her nakedness did not arouse him; her limp submissiveness even repelled him. He was no longer her lover; he couldn't have dredged up the slightest bit of erotic feeling, if he tried. Worse still, he felt neither pity nor tenderness. Nothing. His competent fingers parted the folds of the labia and distended the rim. He inserted the syringe into the vagina until the needle rested against the firm muscle of the cervix, then he injected the sterile water into her uterus. This was not his wife, not the might-have-been mother of their child, this was a female vulva tensed around the glass bullet.

Nina

> Trenches have been dug in the garden,
> The city is blacked out.
> My little children,
> Orphans of Peter's city!
> It's hard to breathe under the earth,
> A pain drilling into the temple.
> Through the bombardment I can hear
> The voice of a child.
>
> 'Leningrad Children 1', *The Wind of War*, 1942

Sunday was a dull day. They left Alexandra alone and in tears. The walk with Babushka didn't cheer Nadya. She had not been to the Summer Garden since the day when the statues were buried. Without the marble gods and goddesses this was no longer the park she remembered or even liked. It was an ugly place, with rows of cabbages and potatoes growing on cleared patches of ground, amid fresh tree stumps. People were hoeing and weeding in those new vegetable gardens. Cut logs were piled on the sides of the walks, waiting to be carted away for fuel. It wasn't that the entire park had been destroyed — the ancient linden trees were still in place, and the most beautiful fence in the world was still guarding the park from the river — but the magic of the Summer Garden had vanished; its eighteenth-century elegance was gone. Peter's dream had reverted to the wilderness of the Finnish marshland.

When they returned home, Nina and Slava, who were not expected until Monday, were back from Murzinka. Alexandra was making tea, and pouring out a stream of complaints. Dmitry had been sent off while they were away. It was hard for him to leave without seeing Nina. She continued talking quickly, as if she didn't want to hear anyone's voice but her own. No one in the room was listening to her. Nina was unpacking the rucksack in the far corner. Slava on the sofa was pretending to read, the newspaper page a barrier between him and Alexandra's agitated voice.

Nina was getting up from the floor to greet Babushka and Nadya, when all at once she fell back clumsily into her earlier position. Kneeling, she bent her body forward until her forehead was touching the floorboards, as if she was praying, bowing before an icon. She clasped herself with her arms and rocked up and down. 'I'm all right.' Her voice was thin. 'It'll pass . . .' She tried to smile at the anxious faces surrounding her.

Slava jumped up from the sofa. 'I'm taking you to the hospital. Nina! Don't you understand? You've got to be in a hospital, as soon as possible,' he hissed, as if angry with her pain. But Nina went on protesting, 'No, no, I'll be all right.'

Anna Pavlovna led the child into the bedroom with a firm grip — 'This is not for us.' As the door was closing behind them, Nadya heard her aunt's anguished questioning and Nina's furious voice: 'Mama! Are you stupid or something! Can't you tell? It's an abortion gone wrong. Will you stop screaming? I can't bear it.'

Katya's Diary

The birds of death hover on high,
Who is coming to save Leningrad?

Hush, don't make a sound — he's breathing,
He's still alive, he hears everything.

He hears his sons cry in their sleep
In the damp Baltic depths.

From within his bowels comes the cry 'Bread!'
Reaching the seventh heaven.

Death looks out of every window
In this pitiless fortress.

The Wind of War, 1942

Leningrad, Saturday 23 August 1941

We've been cut off. The Germans have encircled us. The last train left the day before yesterday, and all of us here in Leningrad are caught in a trap. It's such a helpless feeling when there's no escape. I keep thinking that a few days ago I still could have written to my sister, and the letter might, just might, have reached her, in spite of the Germans. We are not told much about troop movements, but we have learnt how to read between the lines. It's been perfectly clear from the enigmatic news bulletins what 'fierce fighting' along the Luga Line was about; it really meant that we have again retreated and the Germans were just outside Leningrad. We can hear their artillery fire day and night, and although we haven't had any air raids yet, there have been almost daily alarms, and our repeated flight into the basement shelter. German planes drop leaflets warning us that unless we surrender, they'll bomb the city. Their deadline is the 9th of September.

Well, Leningrad has been preparing for the attack since the start of the war. The monuments are sandbagged, the statues in the Summer Garden buried in the ground. The Hermitage paintings and treasures have been evacuated or stored securely, we are told. The Winter Palace is covered with camouflage netting; the Alexandrine column in the middle of the square is boarded up against the air raid. St Isaac's dome has been painted over; and the gold spire of the Admiralty Needle, which has been such a dear landmark of our childhood, is now a wartime grey. It's as though our city has been stripped of all its rich clothing, and sent out begging. Even the facades seem to have lost that classical harmony.

I've decided to start this notebook, and write in it as though it were a letter to you, Sofya. There's no one else here I can talk to about my terrors. Misha is away at the Leningrad front. The girls are too young. Misha's sisters too old; panic-stricken, pessimistic, they rely on my 'sensible' shoulder to cry on. Besides, being superstitious, I feel that if I write down my worst fears, they may never materialise. Things might turn out better than I dread, we will survive the war, and live happily ever after, as they say at end of the fairy tales.

Sunday 24 August

The day is hot and blue. It's the end of summer. Leningrad streets should be rippling with excitement, with students arriving for the start of the first term. All those naval cadets, the artillerists, the engineers, taking over the pavements of the Nevsky in autumn. The smart navy, or grey, or brown uniforms. Their neat tunics, buttoned-up and belted tightly, and shiny badges on their caps. Polished boots creaking on the parquet of the Winter Palace, as they walk with their Leningrad girls past the bronze-framed masters. You could always see how blind they were to Rembrandt, even to Leonardo's Madonna; they kept their eyes on live northern faces.

No military cadets in Leningrad this August; all those boys have already started their new career at the front. And their fair-haired Leningrad girls were drafted back in July to dig trenches. Picked up at work or in the street, wearing their summer dresses and flimsy sandals, they were sent to the Luga Line. Not even allowed to go home for a change of clothes. I've heard that a million Leningrad civilians are building fortifications. Hard to imagine that a third of our population has been mobilised for defence work. Virtually all able-bodied people have been taken: students, teachers, scientists, factory workers, actors. Anyone in non-essential work. Nina and Slava went with other students, but were brought back to finish their course, because doctors are an essential occupation.

Most of the staff at the Conservatorium were sent out to dig. Even Shostakovich was digging trenches not far from Nina and Slava's brigade. Nina told me how she recognised him: there he was with his thick glasses and stooping back, looking bewildered. What a pity, she was too shy to go up to him. But then the Voskresenskys have no links with music, play no instrument . . . Nina was saying that they didn't have enough picks and spades to go round, so they dug with their hands. Makeshift camp kitchens. No shelter, and the weather since July has been changeable — weeks of heatwave broken by cold wet spells. They've all come back now. The Tomilin girls (remember the twins down the corridor, who looked like Matryoshka dolls when they were small) have returned with septic blisters, and bronchitis. They had to sleep in a haybarn or under the stars. And since they're veteran fortification workers now, they're building defences inside the city. On Ligovka we have an anti-tank barricade bristling like a hedgehog; there are firing points in the corner buildings. Oktyabrsky Station has been mined, and all the bridges. Every day we are reminded that Leningrad will not surrender to the Germans without a fight. But will there be anything left of Leningrad, if the 'scorched earth' order, which I understand operates in the countryside, is extended to our beautiful city? Will everything be flattened, burned?

Instead of summer holiday faces, there is a new wartime expression in the queues. Everyone is worried about the food situation. We've had ration cards already since mid-July, as in the rest of the country. The food coupons are quite generous if you can find goods in the shops. Bread is always available, that's 400 grams a day, but butter and cereals are getting scarce. You've got to queue for everything. And the queues are longer than they used to be in the hungry years of our youth.

Yesterday I waited for flour all morning, and it ran out just as my turn came. I was upset, as if my life depended on that miserly kilo; I almost cried. But at least you get all the latest rumours in a queue. I heard today that the Moscow railway line's been cut. Someone showed me a leaflet of enemy propaganda. I was nervous, in case the man was a provocateur, but since other people around me were reading it, I had a quick look. It was printed on good paper, and expressed in good Russian. There's the proverbial German thoroughness for you — Stolz vs Oblomov.

I struck a miracle the other day: I managed to buy 250 grams of chocolate. It hasn't been seen for weeks. About this time last year the girls and I were chocolate brown when we returned from the Ukraine. What a wonderful holiday that was. I'll ration the chocolate for the girls: a small square on Sundays. And I'll save a little for my sweet-tooth, Misha, for when he visits.

1 September

Another celebrity broadcast. Famous citizens have been speaking on the Leningrad radio, telling us about their work at this time of national calamity. Today it was Dmitry Shostakovich. I have never heard him before. His voice on the air was as I had imagined it, hesitant, ill at ease. It matched the mournful eyes behind the thick spectacles; the lost-in-a-world-of-his-own look I'd seen on posters at the Philharmonia.

He started: 'Just an hour ago, I completed the score of the second part of my new symphonic work . . . Notwithstanding war conditions, the dangers threatening Leningrad, I have been able to work quickly . . . I tell you this so that Leningraders who are now listening to me shall know that the life of our city is continuing as normal . . . Leningrad is my native city. My home and my heart are here . . .' When he finished, I felt that he was someone I had known and liked all my life. No wonder Misha and his football friends get on well with him. Not just because he's a football fanatic like them, but because he must be a decent human being. And a native Leningrader.

2 September

I went with Kira and Ada to the Conservatorium yesterday. That lovely facade guarded by the bronze Rimsky-Korsakov. Normally, the start of the new school year is such a starry day. After the long summer holidays, boys and girls are like chattering sparrows. Tutors are being assigned. Lists go up. But for us life is not normal, is it?

Yesterday everything was chaos: no one knew what teachers were still around and what classes would be available. Some musicians were evacuated in August with the Kirov Theatre, though all along heavy industry had first priority on the trains. Factory machinery and workers were moved out of the city as far back as July — most of the Kirov Works. Some of the specialist workshops have been evacuated. Papa's Nautical Instruments have gone, I think, though I can't be sure. Wartime secrecy is everywhere. It's when you meet someone who works in a place you know, or you hear talk in the food queue.

Well, in any case, at the Conservatorium we spent the morning making plans, for the absolutely immediate future, that is. Whatever happens next, the girls must continue their music classes, and practice. There have been so many interruptions already. Like the panic evacuation of children in July. That was awful. All three girls were snatched away from me and sent to safety. I almost went mad searching for them in the villages. When I tracked them down, they were closer to the frontline there than here in the city.

You wouldn't believe it! Thousands of Leningrad children were carted into the countryside, herded into makeshift camps. There weren't enough adult supervisors. Some younger children were so badly neglected, that they developed sores, got lice and had to have their hair shaved. It was a nightmare. Mothers, like me, were mobbing suburban trains or walking along country roads to locate their children and bring them back. And throughout this ordeal, you couldn't get any information! No one could or wanted to tell you where your children might be. Chaos and panic. Ours were in Bologoye. Right beside the children's camp, defence brigades were building fortifications, and the Germans were shelling them. When I found the girls, I couldn't stop weeping for joy. I snivelled all the way home, but the children were cheerful and thought it all had been a fine adventure. Ada especially missed the camp, because they didn't have to practise a single note there. So much for a sensible thirteen-year old! Today our bread ration has been cut down to 350 grams. It's a worry. Another worry is that the kommissionki have been closed down. True, they're free enterprisers, speculators charging astronomical prices for food, but still, life will be leaner without them. Even if I couldn't afford to pay 30 roubles for butter, at least I was comforted that it was still available, at a price. Now all the foodstuffs have vanished overnight. I must get out into the country. We've heard that there are potatoes left in the fields and people are allowed to harvest them. Neighbours brought back half a sack.

3 September

I invited Alexandra Voskresenskya to come with us on a potato hunt. We met at the station. So quiet now; only a couple of suburban lines still running, and the carriage was half empty. Alexandra, vague as ever, was telling me about a lovely dacha they once had in Ryabovo, how they used to pick poppies and cornflowers in the grain fields. Wheat or rye or oats, she can't tell the difference. I mustn't laugh. She's desperate. Hasn't heard from Dmitry since his move to the front. Doesn't see much of Nina and Slava; they come home only to sleep. Anna Pavlovna, as ever, is strong, a great support. Nina has been in hospital. Don't know what was wrong with her. Some female complaint. Alexandra is upset, and secretive about it.

The girls had a fine time together on our potato outing. Your Nadya is a bright little thing. At times an extrovert, but then again she can be as wise as any greybeard. She usually manages to startle the older girls with one of her performances. Once when she came to us with Anna Pavlovna, she knelt down and started to pray. Anna Pavlovna was not pleased. Yet she's the one who teaches the child all this nonsense: how there used to be an icon corner in every house, and anyone entering the house would pray. Imagine.

'Get up, Nadezhda,' she ordered. 'Praying is done in private!' Nadya ignored this command, and finished her performance. 'You shouldn't interrupt prayers,' she reprimanded her grandmother. 'Only God is allowed to do that!' And she looked just like Anna Pavlovna.

After being cooped up in the city with all the rumours and fears, our potato outing was liberation. We walked down the furrows, poked the mounds of dry earth with our sticks, and dug up a potato now and again. There weren't many left from the harvest and the field had been thoroughly gone over by other gleaners before us. The girls were much better pickers, than Alexandra and I. She stopped every few paces to admire the beauty of nature, and I had to listen politely. You know me. I can't bear to hurt Alexandra, she's like a moth rushing into lamplight. Besides, the day was lovely, still and warm. I wanted to enjoy it. Only late in the afternoon was there a real feel of autumn. That sudden bite in the air, and a veil of mist drifting over the fields.

On the platform, as we sat waiting for the train, Nadyenka started singing. She entertained us with some dozen songs; she carried the tune and knew all the words. Her pitch is really excellent. Alexandra is used to these musical performances, and barely listened, but my girls, and even your Vera, were open-mouthed. Ada and Kira remarked later how confident she was. Vera, who is a bit jealous of her sister, said Nadya was a show-off.

We saw a terrible thing. Not even a dogfight but a massacre. In the sky two Messerschmitts were chasing a solitary Soviet Chaika. They shot our poor little seagull; it nose-dived to the ground, trailing a black plume. Horrible, horrible war. You'd think that by now we should be hardened to such sights, but we all were upset.

4 September

Just as the girls settled down to their practice today, shelling started and, with it, a screaming panic in the apartment. We've been living with the sound of guns for weeks, mostly in the distance; this time the artillery shells were over our roof, exploding all round us. It was a real bombardment! You know what my husband's sisters are like in a crisis. But, for a change, Maneka kept her head, told us to take shelter in the corridor, in case of flying shrapnel and glass. That was sensible. We huddled in the dark passage, with the doors closed. There was a direct hit on the Old Nevsky; the first death of a house. But most of the damage was in the factory suburbs. The Germans are aiming to stop production.

7 September

It's Sunday. Misha is home for a few hours. He is attached to the transport unit at the HQ. I keep telling myself, I should be grateful that he's here in Leningrad, and not out in the frontline trenches, but I hardly ever see him. The transport lorries he drives are on the road day and night under bombs, shells and strafing. I can't sleep worrying about him. I wouldn't even have known about the strafing he had escaped, if it hadn't been for his bandaged shoulder, and the fact that he'd been transferred to desk duty for a few days. But you know my Misha, he made fun of it. He is the last person to be alarmist, but he did tell me that the military situation was serious. Complete chaos at the front. The Germans are in Uritsk, Chudovo and Mga, astride all the railway arteries. The left bank of the Neva, at Schlusselburg, is in German hands, and the south shore of Lake Ladoga. They're just outside Kolpino, a few kilometres from the Kirov Works. They've got us in a tight ring.

Misha is confident the Germans won't take Leningrad; he says the real problem will be this blockade. Apparently, we have just enough supplies to feed the city for a month. Misha was driving some officers from a meeting at the Leningrad Soviet, and heard them talking. With the German stranglehold on the city, and all our communication lines cut, there is no way for supplies to reach Leningrad. Did you know that three million people need 1000 tonnes of food a day. What will happen to us?

Locked in my heavy thoughts, I looked up and saw Misha, all hunched up, suddenly much older. The clumsy uniform didn't suit him back in July when he was drafted. Now with the tunic bulging over the bandage, he was even less soldierly. The shoulder must have been hurting badly, though he denied it. His face was so strained. I gave him a glass of strong tea with the last of the honey, and told him to get into bed. He slept like a child, and we tiptoed around him. No practice for the girls tonight!

Late that evening, when the girls were asleep, I crawled in beside him, with my clothes on. I'll be forty next year, I thought, and here we are, young again, making secret-sweet love. I would have stayed with him till morning, just to feel his skin against mine, his warm hands on my body, but his shoulder was throbbing. I moved over to the big bed beside the girls. Will we ever make love again? I remembered you, Sofya, on one of those dark Ukrainian nights, telling me how you couldn't forgive yourself for not making love once, while Alexei was with you. You kept putting it off, waiting until he was better. Then they took him away, and you hadn't even slept with him or kissed him, as though you'd been afraid of infection.

9 September
Leningrad bombed today. The Germans have carried out their threat. Ada and I were just walking into the gateway when the siren started. How I hate that wail, like a dog howling at the moon. Superstitions disgust me, but I kept remembering that a baying dog means death. We had been queuing all afternoon for potatoes, and our shopping bags weighed us down. We thought at first that it was a false alarm; we've had many over the past two months. Then we heard bombers overhead, their heavy drone. I looked up and there they were, raiders in formation, blocking out the sky. So much for the assurances that our air defences will keep the bombers away from Leningrad.

Then the bombing started. The whine of bombs and the explosions. The whine and then the bang. It seemed unreal that this was happening to us. The whole house shook. Glass was shattering somewhere. People were screaming on the stairs. And I was a spawning fish racing upstream to reach the apartment, to get to the girls. Kira and Vera came leaping down the stairs towards us, with the air-raid bag. I had packed a bag with documents, photographs, some food. I had our ration cards. It's vital not to lose them; getting new ones is a nightmare.

The raid went on and on. I couldn't judge how long it lasted. It was worse in the shelter than out in the open; the thought of being buried alive was more frightening than of the bombs. My chest was so tight, I couldn't breathe properly. Claustrophobia, I suppose. For the girls' sake, I tried to appear calm. They were so quiet. Even Vera didn't weep; she was heroic. Then the lights went out. A woman was reciting the Lord's Prayer, monotonously like a Gregorian chant. It was probably the only prayer she knew.

Misha's sisters sat opposite me. We haven't been on friendly terms lately. They've changed. This blockade and the threat of famine have turned us all into nervous wrecks. Especially Maneka. Sometimes she seems quite unhinged. She's been saying loudly that the sooner Leningrad is surrendered to the Germans, the better it'll be for everyone. I warned her that she is putting the whole family at risk. The NKVD is as vigilant as ever, and there must be plenty of informers still about. One hears of people being arrested on suspicion of collaborating with the Germans, spying or sabotage.

We came out of the shelter into a smoking rubble. The house across from us was burning, and already cordoned off. The fire brigade was there and the militia. My first thought was for the people buried in the shelter. Why are the Germans killing women, children and old people?

So much for Maneka and Lika's faith in the noble German culture. They had a German governess and Maneka studied singing in Germany. I say to her, 'Maneka, that was a different world. The Germans today have a new faith.' I wonder, though, who is more cruel, Hitler or Stalin? God, help me, the things I write! But I may as well be honest. Most of the time I feel that we are doomed here anyway.

13 September

The Badayev warehouses are burning. Since yesterday the smell of burnt sugar has been choking Leningrad. They say all the food supplies have perished in the blaze. A terrible disaster, or negligence. Anyone could see that the Germans were targeting warehouses and factories all over the city. They would have prevented such large-scale destruction if they had moved the supplies to several locations, instead of storing them in one place. Why couldn't they have shared out the food? We would have kept our own rations safe. What's left to feed our children? How shall we survive? Late night terror.

An obscene rumour is filtering through the queues: that this is all part of the scorched earth order from Moscow, that our own city administrators had set fire to the warehouses to keep them out of German hands. The idea is just too monstrous. To save my children, I would surrender to Genghis Khan.

17 September

Bombing every night now. Exhausted. Barely enough energy to climb the stairs and fall into bed. The Germans are now dropping time bombs as well as incendiaries, and thirteen-year-olds like my Ada have been appointed fire wardens on the roof. Adults, you see, are needed for tougher tasks, like digging out people from collapsed shelters. So Ada is on duty every second night. She can't come with us down to the shelter, and has to stay in the attic during the air raids, to put out fires. I am petrified for her but can't do anything about it. I'm not allowed to take it over from her. She's been mobilised to do a job and must do it. Ada comforts me with an old-woman wisdom: 'Well, Mama, if there's a direct, I'll die a few seconds earlier than everyone else.' A realism (or cynicism) that chills my heart.

As a result of the Badayev fire, our bread ration has been cut again. That's the second cut in a fortnight. Now we'll be getting 250 grams of bread per day. That is we, the dependants. Industrial workers are still entitled to 450 grams. Our soldiers get their full ration, Misha tells me; and so they should, poor boys. My heart breaks when I think of all those teenagers in our house, on our block. I watched them playing games in the yard, starting school, growing up, walking out with their girls on Sundays. Then, on the last day of June, all those youngsters were in uniform. Hugging mother. Walking out of the gate, and turning round at the Ligovka corner to wave a last goodbye. The war has swallowed up all our boys. And to think that I used to grumble at the noise they made in the yard. Bozhe moi, bozhe moi.

24 September

We listen to the radio bulletins every day but the news is so vague it needs a military expert to interpret the wording. We hear that battles are fought across Russia, from the Finnish Gulf to the Black Sea. These battles are described as 'heavy' or 'fierce' or 'stubborn', and we are getting used to these euphemisms for continuing disasters in the battle zones. But it's beyond my understanding how a country as huge and strong as ours could have been overrun by the Germans in just three months. To think that only last year you and I were enjoying our summer holiday in peaceful Ukrainian fields, and now Kiev is in German hands! Here in Leningrad, they arrive punctually at seven. Night after night. The all-clear sounds at midnight. When we came out of the shelter last night we saw a huge fire in the direction of Peski. Through smoke cloud, the sky appeared furiously red. No stars. My immediate terror thought was: Nadyenka! Had the house of the Voskresenskys been hit? But there wasn't much I could do. Even if we had a telephone in the house, it would have been of no use; all private telephones were cut off early in the war.

An orphanage near us has been bombed. The children's homes were meant to have been evacuated in August, but since transport was short some didn't make it. When I think of the kind of people who got the train seats! It was logical that the heavy industry had priority — the country couldn't lose key workers and valuable plant, desperately needed for war production — but it was the party élite and their families, with mountains of luggage, who got out in the civilian trains, while your poor mother-in-law queued for a week and couldn't get on a train to the Caucasus.

27 September

It's Saturday. I took the girls to the baths. Our flat is so overcrowded now that it's almost impossible to get into the bathroom. I've already cut the girls' hair short, because it's been difficult to keep them clean in these conditions. Tears from your Vera, who was proud of her tresses.

Some neighbours have taken in relatives who had been bombed out. Maneka and Lika agreed to move in together. We are still in our room, but heating is going to be a problem. I've already arranged to install a burzhuika stove. Remember the little iron god that kept us warm in our orphan years?

We went to the lovely old Banya where we used to go with Mother. Remember the blue and white tiles and the brass faucets? The same old aluminium shaiiki. My girls wanted to act like adults. Each collected two basins, one for standing in and the other for sluicing themselves down. In no time they were splashing each other cheerfully, forgetting their adult intentions. Not Ada. She is so shy that I regretted having brought her. She undressed with her back to us, then insisted that we walk ahead of her. She kept shielding herself with the loofah. She has hardly anything to show, she is so thin! But then all the women in the Banya were thin. A new type of woman is emerging. What you see now are slender limbs like the Lucas Cranachs at the Hermitage. The big-bottomed, ample-breasted Russia has vanished.

When we were dried and dressed, I kissed each of my little birds in turn, as Mama used to kiss us: 'Slyokhkim parom!' I said. When we got back from the banya, there was a crisis at home. Our supply of rice was gone, stolen from our padlocked kitchen cupboard. It had never happened before in the Karpov apartment. Other tenants might have had light-fingered neighbours, but never here. What's happening to us all in Leningrad?

Sunday
Another broadcast: it was Anna Andreevna Akhmatova addressing the women of Leningrad. I can't tell you how moved I was. I felt she was talking to me personally. I've taken her broadcast down in shorthand and transcribed it verbatim for you, Sofya. For the girls also. When they grow up they'll be proud to have lived through the siege of Leningrad alongside this wise and wonderful poet. Her words, more than any statistics or propaganda, will help them to understand the horror of this war and the heroism of Leningrad women. Here is what she said:

'My dear fellow citizens, mothers, wives and sisters of Leningrad. It's more than a month now since the enemy has been inflicting wounds on our city, threatening to capture it. The enemy threatens the city of Peter, the city of Lenin, the city of Pushkin, Dostoyevsky and Blok, a city of great culture and endeavour, with death and disgrace. Like all Leningraders, I can't bear to think of the enemy trampling my city under foot. My entire life has been bound up with Leningrad — in Leningrad I became a poet. Leningrad has been the breath of my poems.

'Like all of you today, I firmly believe that Leningrad will never belong to the Fascists. This belief grows even stronger when I see how simply and courageously Leningrad women defend the city and maintain its everyday human existence.

'Our descendants will honour all the mothers of this war, but especially the Leningrad woman, who kept watch on the roof during bombardments, ready to protect the city from incendiaries with a boathook and tongs; the volunteer giving first aid to the wounded amidst the debris of burning buildings.

'No, a city that has raised such women can't be defeated. And we, the citizens of Leningrad, enduring these desperate days, know that this land of ours and all its people support us. We feel their concern, care and affection. We are grateful to them, and promise that our courage will not fail . . .'

When I finished transcribing my shorthand notes, I started to weep. The words on the page may not be as powerful as the emotion in her voice. There is propaganda in her text, some bombastic phrases you hear in party speeches. But her feeling was genuine, deep, passionate. Oh, Sofya, Sofya, how many tears are we destined to shed, before this war is over?

2 October

Another bread ration cut: 200 grams for adults and 170 for the children. It's insane, because Ada, Kira and Vera need more food than I do. I don't grudge the factory workers and soldiers their larger ration, but I can't bear to see my children starving. Kira and Ada are going to have only one music lesson a week from now on.

4 October

'Give us this day our daily bread . . .' Maneka was praying in the shelter last night. She is as large as ever, and even prays in that big operatic voice of hers! The Lord's Prayer is our signature tune; everyone says it. Now that the Great Father in the Kremlin has abandoned us, all that's left, it seems, is to implore our Father in Heaven to give us our daily bread and to deliver us from evil . . .

You can't imagine the quality of 'our daily bread'. It's a mixture of rye, flax cake, bran, cellulose and mouldy flour; the wheat has been rescued by the divers from a sunk barge in Lake Ladoga. The bread has a brackish flavour (remember Akhmatova's bitter bread of exile) and because it's so full of moisture, the 200 grams amounts to three slices. Three thin, thin slices of bread a day is all the food we receive, now that there's nothing left on the shop shelves.

Early in the morning I join the queue at the bulochnaya for the family bread ration and if the supply runs out, as it did yesterday, you rush to the next bread shop. I queued on the Nevsky corner till midday. My only thought these days is how to find some extra food for the children. Our daily ration allows us 10 grams of fat, 15 grams of meat, 20 grams of cereals and 30 grams of sugar, which doesn't sound too bad, if we could actually receive the ration — even some of it. But the shops are bare and the coupons are not honoured any more. Quite an event to get anything at all. The other day I managed to get a little jelly made out of sheep gut on our meat coupons. It tasted like wallpaper glue, and the smell was revolting, but at least it had some calorie value, whereas the yeast we get to make soup has no goodness in it at all; it just blows you up.

A little while ago we could still barter some of our valuables for potatoes or a handful of grain. But as the food supplies ran out, barter has been getting harder. The peasants at the market have had such rich pickings since the start of the blockade that they are very choosy now. Maneka traded her silver-fox stole for a cup of barley and a bit of salt pork. But, would you believe it, the sisters didn't offer to share it with us. I'm so appalled that I don't even want to think about this!

Kira was in the kitchen stirring our yeast soup on the stove, while Maneka cooked barley kasha with pork in it. Kira ran crying to our room: 'Mama, why didn't Aunt Maneka offer us just a tiny taste of pork?'

'Hush, my love, Aunt Maneka hasn't any children of her own, and she doesn't know how hurt you feel.' No, she doesn't realise that children suffer from hunger as much as adults; perhaps, even more so. I hugged my daughter. 'Aunt Maneka is getting old. Forgive her.' Inside I was boiling. How dare she be so callous! I've shared everything with Misha's sisters, everything I ever got in the shops or on the market. I'm the one who's queuing for bread every day. I've been going to the villages to barter for food. All the sisters do is rummage in their trunk for some priceless possession they can bear to part with. That sunduk of theirs is bulging with furs and jewellery; there are antique silver pocket watches from their father's collection, exquisite Dresden figurines, some rare books — first editions, no less! They also have some valuable paintings; canvases taken out of their frames, rolled up, stored in that Aladdin's Cave of theirs. Maneka actually owns a sketch of Akhmatova by Modigliani; there's also a Malevich and a Picasso drawing. These days people give away entire collections for a meal. Anything to survive. If one could just survive until the blockade is lifted.

Do you remember Tolstoy's argument that, for a peasant, a pair of boots was more important than Shakespeare's plays? How we debated the value of art for a socialist society. Didn't we both agree that art surpassed basic human needs? What idealistic creatures we were in our youth. Now I know the truth, that bread for my children is infinitely more precious than the works of all the artists of all times. But Maneka, I know, will cling to the Modigliani sketch and to Scriabin's autograph until she dies. She gave me her Chinese silk shawl to trade.

8 October

It's the autumn of 1918 all over again. Remember the cold, wet days our father spent in the cemetery, talking to Mama's grave? We took turns to bring him home, and he followed us like a child, so numbed with tears that he was too tired to protest. Yesterday I walked past our childhood home, with Maneka's silk shawl and silver spoons stuffed inside my coat. Eternal fear of muggers. There's a village past Malaya Okhta where one can still trade for some food.

A peasant woman, glossy like a freshly baked bun, gave me some flour for the spoons, and a chunk of lard for the shawl. I could tell she coveted the Chinese shawl. She eyed the silky birds as greedily as I the lard. Well, at least we both were getting what we wanted. I had to wait a long time for a tram to take me back into Leningrad late in the afternoon. Trams are unreliable these days. It was getting dark and it was lonely in the suburbs. I was suddenly terrified that someone might take my precious flour and lard away from me. So I stuffed the bag inside my winter coat, and looked like a pregnant woman. You hardly ever see a pregnant woman these days. I wonder if any children are born in Leningrad?

9 October

Maneka shared the flour and the lard with us. God forgive me for thinking so badly of her last week. I was also glad that the girls' faith in their aunts has been restored. The most terrible thing in all this anxiety about food is the change in our humanity. In the bread queue, people are animals. I suppose that's inevitable, when the only thing that matters is personal survival. It's devastating, though, when people you know change.

Lyova Tomilin, our neighbour, hasn't been at work for weeks; he's a physicist in a research institute. He's been walking round the apartment like a shadow, looking for food. I saw him peeling off wallpaper in the corridor and licking the old glue on the seams. Olga used to be a loyal wife, defensive about Lyova's absent-mindedness. Lyova is the kind of dreamer who doesn't remember street names; still calls some streets by their pre-revolutionary names! Anyway, Olga told me that Lyova has acute dystrophy. She said it so indifferently, as if she was talking about a stranger and not her own husband. I know they've suffered a lot. Tamara, one of their twins, was arrested, and there hasn't been a word from the poor girl. But for Olga not to care that Lyova is dying . . . I simply can't understand it.

Sunday 12 October

Today Lyova T. died. The first famine death in our apartment. My girls cried, but Olga T. was calm. You can see people dying in the street now. I saw a man resting on a bench, and when I was coming back from the bread queue he was lying there dead. I'm ashamed to say I just walked past. My feeble excuse to myself was that, since I was carrying the precious bread ration for the whole family, this was my priority. The truth is that I have neither strength nor compassion left for strangers.

All at once there are many deaths around: every time you meet a friend, you hear that some other friend has died.

15 October

Joy! Misha has arrived out of the blue. We had not seen him for weeks. Like all of us, he's very thin, but still the same dear cheerful

Misha. At least he doesn't have the puffy look that many Leningraders get these days. The men, especially, seem to give up more easily than women. All of us have dark rings under the eyes, we've all shrunk and shrivelled up. And that awful apathy. I don't think I've seen anyone smile for days. Except the children.

My three lovely girls, with their cropped hair, wearing extra layers of wool, still find some fun or purpose in life. Kira and Ada practise their music, while your sweet Vera plays with her dolls under the piano . . . Ah, yes, the piano. We wrap it up at night, when the stove is out and the room gets very cold.

Misha brought us some food — his own bread ration, a handful of lentils — and news from the outside world. He's been driving lorries on both sides of Lake Ladoga. Ammunition, fuel, food (in that order) are transported now from the Urals to the Tikhvin railhead, by rail to Volkhov and from there, on lorries to Novaya Ladoga. Then the supplies are shipped across the lake to Osinovets, and from there by lorry again to Leningrad. This Ladoga lifeline has been operating since early September; but the whole route is under gunfire and air attacks. I can't bear to think about all the dangers along Misha's route.

The Germans are shelling the lake continuously from the south shore where their batteries are. Even without the constant shelling, October on the lake has been stormy and dangerous for shipping. Transports are sunk frequently. Airlifts are more suicidal still; our planes are torn apart by the Luftwaffe. Misha tells me that the airport on the other side of the lake is bombed all the time. We have watched several air battles; mostly it's the Messerschmitts destroying our Chaikas. Black ravens hunt down the white seagulls.

The Panzers are pressing towards Moscow. We may not hold it, Misha says. He is more pessimistic than he was in September, but in the few hours he spent at home, he managed to cheer us all up; even his older sister, who is ill and depressed. Maneka still looks like a boyar lady in a Moussorgsky opera, tall and buxom. But, if you look closely, her bulk is unhealthy puffiness. Her face and body are swollen, the eyes dull. I find her often sitting in front of her treasure chest, leafing through a first edition of poetry that she so loved before this famine snuffed out her bright enthusiasms.

25 October

These days I walk carefully from the bulochnaya, and hide the bread inside my coat. At the shop today a young woman pushed aside a sick man and took his place in the queue. And no one said a word. I didn't stand up for him either. Sofya, my dearest, we have become animals here! This is not Leningrad, this is the taiga forest where the Siberian tiger hunts in the midnight snows. I'm probably just like the rest, only I can't see myself, and harbour a comforting illusion that I am still a human being. The other day, I saw a hooligan grab the bread ration from an old woman, and run away with it. Loss of bread is a death sentence. The woman was crying as she walked away slowly. We all walk slowly now.

3 November

The queue at our bulochnaya was enormous and it was icy cold. Since we are registered here, we can't go to another bread shop. The shop assistants behind the counter are sluggish, not much different from us. The woman behind me muttered, 'At least they've got a good job. I bet they won't be going hungry.' But my neighbour Olga Tomilina works in a bread shop on the Nevsky, and she had to give up her own bread coupon because there was a deficit at the end of her first morning. No idea what had gone wrong, she said. Most likely, she had given someone an extra ration by mistake. So she had no bread that day. That's a terrible punishment! Not as terrible, though, as losing your coupons, because they don't replace lost ration cards any more. There have been too many abuses: people concealing the death of relatives, forging cards, stealing them, making false declarations. You have to wait for the next issue. By then you'll probably be dead.

    I finally got home at midday. Four hours queuing for bread! I don't know how I have the strength to queue every day. Though I must be fair, this was an exceptionally long wait. There had been an accident with our delivery truck: it was hit by a shell and the driver was killed. People in the street called a militia man, who drove the truck to the bulochnaya. (Now there's a good job! Militia men have chubby cheeks and bright eyes.) While people waited for the law, no one touched a single loaf of bread! Amazing, isn't it, that starving people should be honest!

I walked into our apartment and everyone was waiting for me with that worried look: Has Katya eloped with our bread? I started sharing it out on the table, where I keep the kitchen scales: 200 grams for Lika, for Maneka, for Lika's ex-husband and for myself. For Ada it's 175 grams, the same as for Kira and your Vera. Oh, my God, even the children now watch my hands and the scales, as though I would short-change them, deprive them of their share.

The adults decide themselves how to make their bread ration last through the day. Maneka takes her bread to her treasure chest, and eats it all at once. Lika divides hers into three portions, and even gives small bits of it to her ex-husband, Maksim Ivanovich, who is very ill. He simply appeared on our doorstep one evening, after his second wife was killed in an air raid, and Lika took him in. Many years ago he left her for that other woman. She still refuses to speak to him, but she cares for him like a mother.

When the bread has been distributed, I make a big pot of coffee. It's the only thing we still have in the cupboard, apart from the oatmeal I managed to trade on the market for Maneka's gold brooch. The barley is guarded communally, and no one, but no one, is allowed to touch it. At five o'clock, we all get together to make our evening meal: oatmeal soup. A large pot of water, a small cupful of oatmeal, salt, perhaps a bayleaf. When it's dished up and eaten, it's time to get our things together and go down to the shelter. The siren starts howling punctually at seven. Maneka locks up her treasure chest with a double padlock before she leaves.

Revolution Day

Today when I got back from the bulochnaya, Moscow was speaking. As you can imagine, we had no October Day parade in Leningrad. No one here would be strong enough to march. I had just finished sharing out the bread, given my girls their breakfast ration, and sat down with my cup of coffee and morning slice, when Stalin came on. I almost choked on my precious bread. We had not heard him since the 3rd of July. Remember, he spoke then to the nation, called us his 'brothers' and 'sisters'. What irony, after years of terror, arrests and executions. Now his Georgian voice was back on the air. It wasn't only the thick accent that revolted me, but the whole desolate picture of our poor Russia trampled on first by the boots of Stalin's NKVD and now by the Germans.

'Comrades! We are celebrating the twenty-fourth anniversary of the October Revolution in very hard conditions . . . The enemy is at the gates of Moscow and Leningrad . . . Yet despite temporary failures, our Army and Navy are heroically repelling the enemy attacks along the whole front . . . And it is these people without honour or conscience, these people with the morality of animals, who have the effrontery to call for the extermination of the great Russian nation — the nation of Plekhanov and Lenin, of Belinsky and Chernyshevsky, of Pushkin and Tolstoy, of Gorky and Chekhov, of Glinka and Tchaikovsky, of Sechenov and Pavlov, of Suvorov and Kutuzov. The German invaders want a war of extermination against the peoples of the Soviet Union. Very well then, if they want a war of extermination they shall have it! . . . No mercy to the German invaders! Death to the German invaders!'

A few years ago, it was death to enemies of the people, saboteurs, counter-revolutionaries, industrial wreckers, their wives, their neighbours, all of Russia, and now he was appealing to our Russian patriotism. I couldn't listen any longer. But before I could get to the switch, Lika darted to the corner where the loudspeaker was hanging, lifted her arms to the black canvas disc and shouted: 'Stop him! That's enough! He's abandoned us here in Leningrad. He's left us here to starve to death.' She was so agitated that she choked on her words. Coughing, she ran back to her room, threw herself on the bed and clawed at her breast as if to unlock all the pent-up grief.

'Lika, my dear, please, calm yourself.' Her shoulders felt balsa-wood thin when I held her. To comfort her I offered a bit of bread from my slice, instantly regretting my crazy impulse, but Lika had already crammed the bread into her mouth. Then, with a heave, she fell on my neck and sobbed and sobbed. I suppose she understood my 'sacrifice'. Sensible Ada climbed on a chair and turned off the speaker.

That afternoon the Germans arrived with a massive air raid; they pounded Leningrad for hours. The frightened children clung to me. Vera hid her head in my lap. I started telling them how my head was shaven when I had typhus, and how my sister Sofya cut off her pretty hair to keep me company. It was very late when the all-clear sounded, and we left the shelter. Outside the sky was crimson with fires, and all around was the stench of burning. Our house was still standing; even the glass in the windows was intact.

13 November

They've cut our bread ration again today, the fourth time since early September. We'll be getting 125 grams. The slice of daily bread gets smaller and thinner. Famine rations now.

On this dark and bitter morning I suddenly remembered, it's the 13th, your birthday, Sofya. In the old calendar it would have been 30 October. The revolution robbed us of all past landmarks, even the dates of our family anniversaries. Strange that the constant pangs of hunger haven't driven out emotions, that I can still feel tenderness for my sister, gratitude for our childhood, which seems happier each time I think of it. My love for Leningrad, now dying around me. And we, the inhabitants, are dying with the city. Soon there will be no native Leningraders left. Nor any adopted ones either.

My dearest Sofya, if you could see our proud city now! We thought it was a sad place in the days of the civil war, but this is much much worse. Our city has been abandoned to a slow painful death. Leningrad is blind: gaping sockets of former windows have been nailed down with plywood. Most of the houses around us have been gouged by bombs, damaged by shrapnel or gutted by incendiaries. Some buildings look sound from the distance, but close up they are facades with rubble behind them. Ghost houses in a ghost city. Only workplaces get electricity in Leningrad, and even there it's rationed. Our streets and houses are dark, but after air raids the city is usually lit up by fierce fires. Like a foundry oven, or like the gates of hell.

Every morning skeletons rattle their way out of the rubble to queue for their bread ration. Wrapped up against the cold, all hunched up, they creep along the street. You can't tell whether they are women or men, adults or children. When you see one of their faces, you know them all: it's the face of famine.

16 November

Misha has come and, as before, he's brought us food. His own bread ration to share with us, of course. A chunk of frozen horse skin, the size of a saucer but quite thick, with some fat on it, and four frozen potatoes. He helped me to singe the fur off the skin, to make a stew out of it, and he stopped to eat with us. What a feast! We ate in our room, and invited Maneka and Lika. Maksim Ivanovich (Lika's ex) has disappeared. Lika said simply, 'He's gone away to die.'

Misha tried to cheer us up. He sang some funny Army ditties, but no one laughed, not even the girls. So he told us about the Road of Life. You see, Lake Ladoga has frozen over, much earlier than usual, and as soon as the ice is thick enough to hold the laden lorries (you need a thickness of 2 metres, he said), the winter road across the lake will be operating. Then there will be more food; more people will be evacuated. The frosts we are having just now are exceptionally hard for this time of the year: minus 30 degrees.

He asked Kira and Ada to play for him. They protested that it was too dark to see the music, and anyway the air raid would start soon. I warned them quietly, 'You must play for your father! Play any piece you know by heart.' And they played. But before they came to the end of the first movement, it was time for Misha to rush away. He is on night duty now. Oh, God, I worry for him!

20 November

We've found Maksim Ivanovich, in the yard behind the woodshed, eternal peace frozen on his face. I asked the girls not to tell Lika, not to upset her. Why such sensibility, I thought later, why secrets? There is so much death around; you can't weep for them all. You see someone on the street, and the next moment he has fallen down and died. And you just keep on walking . . . Bodies are everywhere. Stacked up like logs, curled up by the kerb or, like Maksim Ivanovich, sitting against the wall. Eyes open. Skin blackened by frost. The yard of the bombed-out house next door is now a morgue. A large plywood board nailed in the gateway says BODIES HERE, with an arrow directing the collectors.

Student brigades pick up the dead and cart them off to the nearest cemetery. I saw two girls sitting on a pile of frozen corpses, eating their bread ration, and this didn't even surprise me. Later, thinking about it at home, I realised the horror of it.

22 November
Snow! How I used to love the first snow of the winter, the silent stealth of it. How we waited for it; the earth, the trees, the air itself ached for that first snowfall. Yet it was always a surprise; it always came at night. You woke up in the morning to the great hush, as if your ears had been plugged with cotton wool. Even before you opened your eyes and drew the curtains you could tell that the miracle had occurred again. You dropped your feet on the floor, freezing cold. You ran to the window, and there was the glory of winter, the immaculate white. A tidy layer of snow on the windowsill, on the roofs; trees tortured black limbs against the white; a spotless cover on the path below. New snow — a promise of peace, joy of warm rooms, steaming food, stories by the fire . . .

The snow will make it easier to carry the dead to the cemetery on the toboggan. Before the frosts came, and the ground froze, they dug some common graves, huge trenches, and this is where the girls and I took Maneka. Lika was too weak to come; she doesn't leave her bed any more. I wasn't sure that she understood that her sister had died.

I didn't try to find a coffin for Maneka. I must keep my strength for things that matter. We wrapped her in a blanket, Ada and I, and tied her like a bundle with a rope. She was so thin and light before she died that no one would have recognised the plump Russian beauty, who played four hands with the great Scriabin at her father's musical evenings, turned the heads of the Symbolist poets and modelled (nude, they said) for Goncharova and Larionov.

There was a shimmery gown in her treasure chest so we dressed her in that, and put her feet in the finest shoes we could find. In the end all that finery was hidden inside the blanket. So small, she fitted easily on the children's toboggan. We took this little hearse to the Alexander-Nevsky Lavra, to a common grave, where nobody keeps a tally of the dead. And left her at the gate with other corpses. Goodbye Maneka . . .

28 November

Misha seemed calm when he heard about Maneka's death, but I found him later in the corridor, crying, his forehead pressed against the wall. We stood there in the gloom of the unlit cold passage, holding each other, and wept together. Later he went to Lika and sat with her until it was time for him to leave on duty, just before the air raid. I knew he was thinking that he would not see her again either.

'Mamochka, I'll stay with Aunt Lika,' Ada offered, when the siren started to wail. I wavered but in the end I couldn't allow it. In the shelter I kept thinking of Lika, sick and alone. The all-clear sounded in about an hour, and when we climbed upstairs, Lika was dead.

I pushed the girls out of the room. 'Go to bed. Try and get some sleep. You never know, there may be another air raid.' The things you say to comfort yourself more than the children. 'Poor Aunt Lika's suffering is over. It really is better this way.' I sometimes think the girls are hardier than I am. They have accepted death. Then I went back to Lika's deathbed. She was lying slumped against the pillows, her eyes open, staring, and on her kindly face there was an expression I had never seen before and couldn't interpret. Was she blaming me for leaving her alone? I closed her eyes, smoothed her hair and folded her hands. I sat down beside the bed to wait with her till morning, when we must take her to her common grave, like Maneka before her.

It was silent in the room. Huddled inside my coat and boots, hat and mittens, I felt chilled. Lika's face seemed to change as I looked at her. The black shadow under the eyes faded, her wrinkles smoothed out and the agitation gave way to a surprised look, as if she had just met someone she knew, and couldn't recollect the name.

I tried to find a comfortable position in the armchair and at last, with my knees drawn up I huddled into a blanket and dropped off. It must have been in a dream that I sensed a presence in the room. I wanted to see who it was, but my body was set in granite, up to my chin; even the voice was petrified. Then I must have woken up, because I could move again. In front of me, Lika rested. All was quiet. I looked around and caught sight of a shape, rather the absence of a shape, on the right against the wall. Maneka's treasure trunk had gone. Again my body turned to stone, only this time it wasn't a dream, but fear, which wouldn't let go. I realised that someone had been to our rooms during the air raid to steal the trunk. Or, worse still, while I was drowsing.

We've heard about thefts and robberies, especially in abandoned houses, where all the tenants had left or died. But not in our house. We never used to lock the doors to our rooms, only padlocked our food if we had any. Someone who knew about Maneka's collection, had a key to the apartment, must have come and scared poor Lika to death. Literally. I sat there waiting for the morning, and didn't have the courage to check if the girls were unharmed. The night was full of unfamiliar creaks and rustles, and such terrifying thoughts: the girls alone in this wasteland.

By the time it got light, I had decided either to walk out of Leningrad with the children across the Ladoga ice or to move to Murzinka. Walking the Ladoga was only a dream, a madwoman's dream. The ice road is shelled by the Germans. Army patrols are everywhere; civilians can't just run around in wartime. Besides, starving people haven't got the kind of stamina it takes to walk across a frozen lake.

In any case, Misha told me that the ice was still thin in places and collapsed under the weight of laden vehicles. Some lorries had sunk. To make transports safer, they distribute the weight: load the lorries more lightly, and put the rest of the supplies on attached sleighs, so that each transport is a small self-contained caravan.

I thought of Murzinka as a refuge from Leningrad horror. Murzinka is on the highway, where Misha's lorry passes daily. He had been urging me to move there for some time, but I couldn't leave his sisters, and the grand piano. But now both Maneka and Lika were dead, and the piano didn't seem to matter any longer. We were going to Murzinka as soon as I could get Nadya from the Voskresenskys. I decided that at a time like this your girls must be together.

The Trees are Gone

They almost did not make it to Murzinka. It used to be an hour's ride from their Ligovka apartment, but now there were no suburban trams. Packing up for the move, Katya began to doubt that she would have the strength to walk the distance, with four children and a toboggan laden with household gear. Just then Misha arrived on one of his fleeting visits. Katya crossed herself: 'You've turned up like a guardian angel.' Wartime might not have changed her sceptical view of religion, but it had released from the catacombs the ancient Russian idiom of spirituality and pious gestures. The reverent sign of the cross also helped Katya to feel more patriotic.

'At last.' Misha still had the strength to laugh and to hug his family. For the past weeks, he had been in a state of constant worry about Katya and the girls. Since late October famine had been claiming countless lives, and now in December, they said, some ten thousand were dying every day in Leningrad. Wherever you looked there were corpses. The city was a battlefield, with the dead abandoned in the snow. No, it was a morgue, with frozen corpses stacked up in high piles in the squares and on intersections. Misha was sure that he would be able to keep an eye on his family more easily at Murzinka. It was on the highway which he travelled at least once a week with supplies from Lake Ladoga. And although it was closer to the enemy line, that part of the river was shelled less intensely than the centre of Leningrad. The main thing was that she had decided to move away from the Ligovka, where the deaths of Maneka and Lika and the sinister burglary hung over the living.

He was taking Katya and the girls to Murzinka himself, whatever the punishment he might have to face should he be found out. And although Katya knew that Army drivers were forbidden to carry civilians, and in the past wouldn't have accepted his offer, she was too tired to care about the danger.

'Keep low in the tray,' Misha reminded his illegal passengers as he covered them up with the tarpaulin. 'And huddle up close together. The wind up here is bitter.' He could not risk seating his wife in the cab beside him.

Katya had not been beyond the Ligovka neighbourhood for many weeks. Her bread queue was a block away from home and the only other long walks she had made were to the cemetery at the Lavra. Misha's lorry drove through an alien city. Locked in an arctic embrace, Leningrad was frozen to death. It was a city without electric power, without transport, water, or sewerage. Peeping from under the edge of the canvas Katya saw strange landmarks which faintly resembled those she once knew. The lines of dark and deserted buildings still followed the contours of what once used to be busy thoroughfares, with tramlines and footpaths and street lights; now they had become narrow rutted tracks. Even the Nevsky was a country lane running between tall pristine snowdrifts. There was nothing about this ghost to remind you of the Northern Venice.

'Well, my dears, here we are,' Misha called out cheerfully, setting down their bundles in the pockmarked roadside snow. He would have liked to help Katya open up the house, to check that the supply of wood he had laid in last autumn was still there, and had not been stolen. But he could not delay any longer; if he missed his convoy, he risked a court martial for desertion. He knew that men had been shot for less than that.

'Goodbye, Papa . . . Goodbye Uncle Misha,' the girls waved, while Katya, the ever-anxious Katya, watched the lorry pull out, sliding on the hard snow, accelerate and disappear round the bend of the highway. Then she began to load up the toboggan. The girls were helping to push it towards the dacha. 'There it is!' Kira and Ada pointed to a house in a field of snow. They had last seen it in spring, and since then the landscape had altered. 'What's happened to the park, where are the trees?' they clamoured, but Katya realised instantly that the trees had been logged for winter fuel.

Nadya, who was at the Murzinka dacha for the first time in her life, saw a fairy-tale house. Sunk in snowdrifts, streaked with purple shadows, this was the palace of the Snow Queen. Its gabled roof, carved lintels and window frames wore crisp white cuffs. Stalactite earrings drooped from the eaves. Around the house was a white field dotted with snowclad tree stumps that used to be the park. Beyond stretched a parallel highway of the frozen Neva. Above the river the predatory eye of the winter sun gazed red and unblinking.

Leningrad Children

Knock with your fist — my door will open.
It has always opened for you.
Now I live beyond a high mountain,
Across a desert, through wind and heat.
But I'll never forsake you.
I didn't hear your cries,
You didn't ask me for bread.
Bring me a maple branch
Or just some green grass
As you did last spring.
Bring me a handful of our clean,
Clear water from the Neva,
And I'll wash the blood
From your fair hair.

'Leningrad Children 2', *The Wind of War*, 1942

Nadya woke up to the rustle of paper and kindling. She snuggled up inside her warm blankets, and followed the sounds of the morning ritual of stove lighting. Aunt Katya's felt boot steps padded about, soft and stealthy. Wrapped up in every warm thing she possessed, she was clumsy and kept bumping into chairs. Her chapped hands dropped the matchbox twice. At last the match scraped, hissed. The twigs caught alight, began to crackle. The fire murmured and then, with a sudden roar, the flames rushed up the flue. A red glow rose from the open crown of the burzhuika; it lit up Aunt Katya, bulky in her wintercoat and scarves.

She was now ladling water from a bucket into the large black kettle. She closed the ring and put the kettle to heat on top of the iron plate. At last she stood in the doorway of the room where the four girls slept in their eiderdown cocoons and layers of warm clothing, and whispered into the darkness, 'Ada, will you watch the stove? Don't let it go out. I'm off for the bread.'

Ada wriggled her nose out of the warm covers and replied in a voice that was thoroughly awake, 'Yes, Mama.' Katya would be gone for hours. The blackout curtains would remain drawn while the warmth from the stove thawed the iciness that had invaded the room overnight. Until then you stayed in your warm hollow and listened to your cousins. All of them were reluctantly awake now, wishing they were still asleep. In the morning, pangs of hunger were sharp, almost unbearable. As they waited for Katya to return with the bread, they imagined all kinds of terrible disasters: the queue might be too long, the shop assistant too slow or the bread delivery delayed. There might even have been a cut in the bread ration while they slept. Or a shell might have hit the bulochnaya and destroyed all the bread. Vera, the first to voice her fears, stirred in her dark corner. 'What if they run out of bread just as it's Aunt Katya's turn?'

All this was still new to Nadya. Since her move from the Voskresenskys into Aunt Katya's family, Nadya's relationship with her cousins had been more complex. Ada and Kira, and even her sister Vera, seemed infinitely older somehow, more experienced, confident in the ways of their own world. Their conversations were conspiracies. They played games she had never heard of. Just now they were starting the food game.

'Today I'm going to have . . .' Kira tantalised them, 'some lovely half-white bread, spread thickly with butter and on it . . .' she held them on the line of suspense, dangling, 'and on it, I'm going to have Dutch cheese with holes . . . and salami . . . and some pink ham with a white rim of fat, and then . . .' Kira was about to go on, when Ada cut into her meal.

'Leave some for us, Kirka!'

'Oh, all right. So what are you having, Ada?'

'White vienna loaf.' Ada jumped in quickly, as if the cupboard of imaginary delicacies was about to be locked up and she would remain empty-handed. Like her sister, she went on to concoct a mouth-watering butterbrot topped with remembered sausages and cheeses.

Vera, a seasoned shopper who, in the days before the famine, used to accompany Aunt Katya on her errands, waited her turn. 'Crusty bulochki,' she declared, 'large ones, straight from the oven, with lots and lots of ham.'

'And you, Nadyenka?' Ada's kind tone warned the others they must be fair to the youngest; certainly not ignore her presence. Vera sighed wearily, audibly, as they waited for the younger sibling to catch up.

Nadya was hurt by their condescending airs. In the Voskresensky household she could do no wrong. Several adults stood ready to gratify her wishes. Even in the hungry months, Aunt Alexandra would save an extra crust of bread for the child. Nadya knew, of course, that the bread came from her aunt's own ration, but she wanted that crust desperately; its wonderful taste obliterated the aunt's sacrifice in seconds. Like all the starvelings in the city, her instinct for survival was fierce. The Leningrad young were fledglings in a nest: they opened their beaks and clamoured for food. A maternal heart could not refuse them.

Nadya was homesick for Aunt Alexandra and Babushka, but most of all for Nina. She had not even said goodbye to her flawless cousin. Nina was at the institute when Aunt Katya came to collect the child. Alexandra had packed Nadya's clothes into a soft bag. 'Your favourite toys, your ration card.' And then the farewells. Nadya's face was wet from Alexandra's tearful kisses.

'I won't stay away too long,' Nadya comforted in the soothing tones of an adult. She knew not to betray how excited she was to see her sister again, and the musical cousins. The Karpov home, she imagined, must be as noisy with talk and laughter as before. Life at the Voskresenskys had been gloomy. Aunt Alexandra, like a frightened mouse, waited for the next air raid. And there was Nadya's empress, shrunk and helpless. Her storytelling voice was gone, and often she didn't recognise Nadya.

'I don't want to leave you, Babushka.' Nadya wound her arms around her. 'I'll visit you often,' she whispered into the steel wool of grandmother's hair.

'Don't forget, Nadezhda,' the voice was muffled, 'you are a Shubina.' The empress's eyes vaguely searched the space above Nadya's head.

Aunt Katya was in a hurry to get on the road. 'We must go. It's a long walk. Soon it'll be getting dark.'

Nadya imagined the Voskresensky apartment as it was when she left. Babushka lying on the divan. She did not get up any more, not even for the air-raid shelter. It was dark and cold in the mornings, when Alexandra went out for the bread. Loneliness and the silence. Even the Napoleon cups were no longer comforting. Aunt Alexandra still lifted her up every morning for the habitual inspection, but Nadya could feel her aunt's waning strength, as if day by day the child grew heavier and the aunt weaker. Then Alexandra packed the precious set into a box and stored it in a safe corner. Yes, it was better living with Aunt Katya, and the girls. Here in Murzinka it was not so frightening.

'Nadka!' Whenever she plotted against her younger sister, Vera's voice would rise to a peremptory pitch. 'Hurry up, we haven't got all day.'

Oh, but they did have all day, didn't Vera see that! As well as a long, long evening. Sometimes pangs of hunger kept them awake in the night. When they slept their dreams were about food. They dreamt of gargantuan meals: cakes rich with raisins and icing, Kiev cutlets dripping butter on the plate, pitchers full of creamy milk.

Nadya hesitated. It was not that she had forgotten about food, simply that for a second she had been distracted by thoughts of her grandmother. 'Doktorsky,' she said hurriedly. She liked the name, but couldn't remember exactly what that special doctor's loaf was like. As for its taste, she didn't have the tiniest recollection how it tasted or smelled.

'And . . .?' Vera looked severe, meaning to make her sister feel guilty for not producing a snack acceptable to the tastebuds of the other players.

'And . . . nothing.' Nadya hid under the blanket. In her confusion she had forgotten about fillings and toppings; her mind was only on the palpable luxury of fresh bread.

Ali Baba couldn't have been as stunned by the gold and jewels in the cave, as the four children were by each remembered delicacy. Like the Covetous Knight, they gloated over their gastronomic treasure and hoarded it in the chambers of imagination. As the fantasy menu expanded, they salivated more profusely than Pavlov's dogs.

Water from the Neva

In Murzinka they fetched water from the Neva, but Katya did not allow the girls to go down to the ice hole on their own. For safety, she accompanied them wherever they went. Swinging their buckets, they walked Indian file along the path, down the sloping bank, on to the river ice and made their way to the water hole marked with a stick. The piece of cloth tied to it had frozen into a red arrow. Katya carried an axe with her to chip at the overnight ice if it got too thick, or to chop up any bit of wood or tree branch they might spot in the snow. The girls believed that the axe was brought along to protect them from cannibals. Before they came to Murzinka, the cannibal scare had swept Leningrad, and they continued to talk about it. Katya disapproved of gossip and, since she was often impatient with the girls these days, they kept these frightening stories a secret from her; they took turns whispering them at night when hunger kept them awake.

Vera would whisper to Kira, her bedfellow, 'Do you think they cut people up for sausage? What if that tiny bit of sausage which Uncle Misha brought last time . . . What if . . .?'

'Made of human meat? Quite likely,' said Kira, even though she was certain her father could never have done such a thing. Anyway, she was not going to confess to panicky Vera that the thought of eating human flesh nauseated her as well.

'They kidnap and kill children, because children are fatter than adults,' mused Nadya aloud. 'That's why Aunt Katya won't let us out of her sight.'

'We can't go anywhere on our own, not even to the ice hole,' Vera complained.

'Rubbish.' Ada tried to inject a note of sense into a conversation that was bound to wind the younger girls into a state of such terror that they would all be jumping into bed with her. It had happened in the past. 'Mama is afraid we may slip and fall into the river. You can't be rescued from an ice hole. If you float under the ice, you drown. Besides, the frosts are so bad now that you wouldn't survive in the water for long. And even if we grabbed you quickly, and managed to pull you out, you'd die in any case. It takes only a few seconds for a person in wet clothes to turn into a block of ice.'

'Well, we had no ice hole on the Ligovka,' Kira stated firmly. 'But after the human-meat scare on the market Mama didn't let us out of her sight, did she?' And the defeated Ada had to agree that to have kept such a close watch on them, Katya must have been pretty frightened by the cannibal rumours.

Going down to the river, Nadya walked at the tail of the procession, but on the way back she helped Aunt Katya with her full bucket. Ada carried a smaller bucket of her own, and Kira shared hers with Vera, who moaned all the way, as was her wont. Water, spilled on the path every day, turned to ice. Some parts of the path had become as shiny as a skating rink; even their felt boots could not stop them from sliding. They walked with their eyes half shut, because the snow blinded them. The few remaining trees, in what used to be the park, were black skeletons against that unbearable whiteness; they were like the bombed-out factories on the opposite bank of the Neva.

At least the Germans had now stopped bombing, sighed Aunt Katya. She heard it explained in the bread queue that aviation fuel froze solid in such severe frosts, and the planes could not take off. Whatever the reason, it was peaceful now in the evenings. But even if the Germans had started their air raids again, Katya couldn't have taken her brood to a shelter; there was no proper cellar in the Murzinka house.

They brought the water carefully up the verandah steps. A spill here would make the steps too dangerous. Some of Uncle Misha's wood supply stacked under the verandah was still there, though the neighbours pinched a few logs every night.

'Let them. It doesn't matter,' Katya pacified her indignant girls.

'We're all perishing.' She would not embroider her sad thoughts. There was so much to do, and so little daylight for all the tasks. On a winter day it grew dark mid-afternoon. Wood had to be chopped for kindling and that was a slow, exhausting job. Ada tried to help, but Katya was afraid for the girl's hands. What if the girls damaged their fingers and could not play? There was always the danger of frostbite too. Inside, the stove was kept going all day and evening. They worshipped their burzhuika; they brought the pot-bellied idol frequent offerings of wood, and waited for it to start roaring in a red-hot rage. It seemed at times that the metal itself would melt and flow like lava.

There was always hot water on the stove for tea and for washing. Katya was fanatical about keeping the girls clean. She checked their hair and clothes for lice. Some days she ordered an inspection; she spread a sheet of white paper on the table and combed their hair over it, looking for nits and lice. At bedtime, she made them wash their faces and hands, and on Saturdays she filled the tin bath with hot water and bathed them in front of the roaring burzhuika stove. Then she washed their underwear and hung it above the stove to dry. Saturday was their kasha night, when they had a plate of filling millet porridge for supper, instead of the weekday fare of watery soup.

The temptation to use up the tiny store of millet at one go was hard to resist. Sometimes, she thought wearily, why not have one really satisfying meal, and to hell with tomorrow. But prudent as always, she couldn't bring herself to do it. She constantly searched the children's faces for signs of dystrophy: for listlessness, puffiness, sores on the body, darkening of the skin and that tell-tale bruising around the eyes she had seen on people who were on the brink of death. She knew it was only her willpower, and Misha's occasional meagre contributions, that had kept them alive and looking healthier than many others. And so she continued her careful management, thinking wryly that she had inherited this iron discipline from her German father, and now all Germans were monstrous. Strange, she thought, that no one had ever accused her of being a German, with a maiden name of Meier, with a father who came from Baltic German stock.

It was even harder to make the girls keep up music practice. By the time she came home with the bread it was already nine or ten o'clock and getting light. She gave them their breakfast slice of bread with a cup of bayleaf tea. Next it was time for the wood and the water, and some snow clearing if there had been a blizzard in the night. After that, she made sure her nieces were occupied with a game or a chore, like stacking the kindling in the corner behind the stove. If it was not too cold, she sent them outside to make a snow baba below the steps, where she could see them. Then Katya, the human metronome, would settle down to music with Kira and Ada.

Happy New Year

On New Year's Eve they had a celebration. They sat up by the fire, with a bottle of sweet red wine and a tiny bag of sweets on the table, waiting to be shared out at midnight. The wine and the sweets were a special holiday issue. The bread ration for the New Year had also been increased by 100 grams. To celebrate the advent of 1942, they had already eaten the extra slice of bread.

The primitive wick in their koptilka was smoking and needed frequent trimming. Now it was again streaking the glass black. In the dim light of the paraffin lamp, Katya's face looked immensely sad. Perhaps she had been hoping that Misha would knock on the door. He had not been near them since the day he dropped them off in the snowbank beside the highway. Katya sat half-hidden behind the iron flue; swollen feet propped up on the wood basket; chilblained fingers casting stitches, on and off, off and on. If you were occupied, it was easier to forget about hunger. Her hands were never idle.

Kira watched the ball of wool rolling softly around in the blue enamel bowl on the floor. 'Remember Murochka? Aunt Maneka's cat? Such a sweet creature, she always played with your wool.'

'Poor Murochka was stolen and eaten,' Ada muttered to herself and sighed. Everyone knew that there was not a pet left in Leningrad, nor any birds. Even all the rats and mice had disappeared. Every living creature had been eaten; except human beings, who died unassisted.

Quietly, pensively, the four girls sat in a circle around the humming stove. Devoted to early bedtime, Vera yawned. If anything, war had increased her need for sleep. When they were still in town, they were waking up to the sound of the air-raid alarm every night, and running to the shelter. Nadya sat closest to her aunt. She missed the Voskresensky adult household. She had not seen her grandmother, or Aunt Alexandra and cousin Nina, for weeks. What were they doing tonight, she wondered? Was Slava pouring out the red wine to toast the New Year? She remembered her parting from Babushka; how listless she was, as if she no longer cared about anything. Nadya's desire to see them was the powerless longing of a child. The frustration of a human being in wartime, who had no control over anything in life. She looked up at Katya, her new anchor, and felt frightened for her. How tired she looked. 'What if Aunt Katya dies?' Her fears, however, were mostly for herself and for the cousins. 'What if she leaves us alone?'

'Tell us about the Christmas play,' Ada begged. Being the eldest, her preferences counted. Often, Katya told them stories from her own childhood, which had been orderly and secure, never mind what came after. When the children asked about an event with a sad ending, Katya parried their request, and offered a happier subject. The Christmas play was a happy story.

'We don't have Christmas any more, we have a New Year tree instead.' Kira tossed her cropped head, as if she still had her braids, to be swung, pulled, bitten and brushed. 'Even Nadyenka no longer believes in Father Frost and the Snow Maiden, do you, Nadyenka?' Nadya shook her head sagely, enjoying her promotion into the superior rank of unbelievers.

Katya may have been disappointed with this rejection of magic, but she didn't show it. Perhaps she even agreed with the girls' realism. These children, after all, were the product of the Soviet era. They had only heard tales of old Christmas festivities, never seen them. With the canon of religious superstitions, she thought, Soviet Russia had discarded the beautiful traditions of her childhood. No more Christmas. No more Easter. No carrying of candles through the frosty night. If she asked the girls what Christmas symbolised, they would not be able to explain. Perhaps only Nadya, the youngest, might have learnt something about the meaning of Christian church feasts, because she had spent so much time with her religious grandmother. As for Katya herself, she was a heathen. Even while the churches were still open, she had never taken her daughters to liturgy or vespers. And now as she retrieved from the past all the warm, rich clutter that had once filled her own childhood to the brim, she felt sad at the loss of tradition; desolate that an entire world with all its colour and magic had been destroyed, and such an arid cult had replaced it.

'What about Christmas presents?' Vera sat up, alert like the others. If Katya was going to start one of her spell-binding stories, Vera would be prepared to stay awake with the other girls.

'On Christmas Eve, our friends, the Vasilyevs always put on a play for the children.' Mr Vasilyev, she went on, engaged a professional actor to direct the play. He spared no expense on the Christmas production. One year the play was called *Prince Almaz* and Sofya, the best actress of them all, was given the part of the prince. They rehearsed at weekends, all through December. Katya described the elaborate costumes that were specially made for the play. The important guests who were invited to the performance. How the curtain went up on a marvellous set painted by a real artist. And how the star of the evening was her sister Sofya.

The story of Sofya's theatrical success thrilled Katya's nieces; Vera and Nadya stared into the fire, wide-eyed, dreaming of their mother, who appeared to them even more remarkable because she was unreachable, so far away.

'A theatre director, who came to the performance as a guest, enjoyed Sofya's performance so much that he offered her a part in a real production, at a professional theatre. A real part. Such a triumph! Can you imagine the excitement? But there was a moral hitch. Sofya was to play a child whose parents were unhappy together. And so in the last act the mother takes poison. Divorce was a shameful thing when I was a child.'

'And what happened? Did your parents forbid Sofya to play the little girl?' The girls wanted to be reassured quickly that the story would repeat its previously happy ending.

'No one could resist Sofya's pleading. My mother begged. My father relented. And Sofya had her part.' Katya smiled to herself, remembering Sofya's tragic sobbing: if she didn't get the part, she would die.

'Go on, please, go on.' The girls wanted the radiant ending.

'Sofya played the part,' Katya continued. 'She ran on the stage with flowers she had picked for her mother: "Mama, Mama, look what I've brought you!" She tries to wake her up, talks to her, shakes her by the shoulder. And then she begins to understand that something is terribly wrong, that her mother is dead. Everyone in the theatre sobbed.' The play,' Katya concluded, 'ran for a week, and every night the theatre sent a cab for Sofya and their mother, who was the chaperone.'

The girls had such trusting faces; they expected her to provide food, shelter them from harm and even to entertain them. And wasn't this what childhood was about? This acceptance of comfort and loving. If you think of it, these were quite astonishing riches. And then one day, childhood was over, as her own vanished overnight with the death of her parents, and the hungry years began. Was it possible that the childhood of her own daughters had already ended? No, she had to believe that not everything had been destroyed by this war, the German blockade, the famine. Her daughters still had both parents. Yet all this might disappear in a flash, she thought, and felt the needles of terror. If Misha's lorry were to fall through the Ladoga ice, if it were hit by a shell. If she gave up struggling as so many around her had already done. No, she must not give up; must keep on going; must not die.

To cheer herself even more than the children, Katya began to tell them about the Finnish sleigh rides, which used to be another treat of the festive season. How at Christmas time the Finns brought their shaggy ponies into town. Their manes plaited with bright ribbons, they trotted cheerfully in the snow, snorting and tossing their heads, like Kira. Little bells rang on the shafts as you rode in a low sleigh, snug under a fur blanket. The frost nipped your cheeks, and your breath turned to ice crystals on your fur muff.

Kira liked being compared to a shaggy pony from Finland. 'And the skating parties,' she demanded, 'I want the skating and the dancing.'

'Yes, of course.' Katya's cheeks were flushed with the joy of revived emotions. 'That was wonderful! We spent Sunday afternoon on the skating rink, and then we gathered at the Vasilyevs. They had a large drawing room. Their mother played the piano and we, the children, danced till it was time to go home.' Her fingers felt again the luxury of the silk and brocade in those rooms. She saw the lights reflected in the mirrors, in the children's eyes, in their laughter.

Vera wanted to know, 'What did you have for dinner?' She was the most practical of all, thought Katya, but she would not be drawn on the subject of food. It was almost midnight. Katya uncorked the wine and poured it out to the last drop, evenly into five glasses. Everything in Leningrad had to be divided into exactly equal portions.

'Well, my little little chicks, Happy New Year to all of us! Let's drink to it! Let's hope it brings us better luck than last year.'

'Happy New Year, Mama! Happy New Year, Aunt Katya! Happy, happy New Year . . .' the girls chirped, full of wonder that a brand-new year had been born a minute ago and they were witnesses of its advent. The wine tasted sweet and, on an empty stomach, the alcohol quickly went to their heads. The girls clinked the glasses. Yet even this rare excitement was subdued, almost sedate. In the past there would have been wild hilarity, of the kind that usually ends in tears and remonstrations, but tonight, four little wise old women (well, five, really, if Katya included her own ancient self) sat hunched round the puffing stove and giggled tipsily in the shadows. She saw the youngest quietly slip away towards the window and dive under the blackout curtain. Nadya — sliding off the planet into her own unfathomable space.

Nadya stood at the frosted windowpane and, with an icicle finger, traced magic etched on the glass. She breathed on it to open a peephole into the night. Moonshine was bright on the snow. The moon itself hung above like a Leningrad street lamp. No! the street lamps used to glow in a warm amber, whereas this moon was anaemic, had bled white. It radiated its glacial light over the icebound river, the blacked-out city and all the dead stacked up like logs in the Leningrad streets. It was already the 1st of January, but no one in the room behind had remembered that it was Nadya's birthday.

The Road of Life

In the middle of March a tantalising taste of spring weather came and disappeared. A few days of sunshine thawed the footpath and melted a few icicles to drip and crash down from the roof. On the third night a late blizzard swept in mountainous snowdrifts. The piled up corpses in the streets of Leningrad were once again decently shrouded, to rest in peace a little longer.

Since the Road of Life across the lake opened late in January, Katya had hardly seen her husband. Misha came on a fleeting visit with 5 kilos of frozen potatoes. Shrivelled and sickly sweet, the potatoes were an unimaginable luxury. She had been feeding the girls potato soup for a month. Another time he brought a chunk of horse meat. They had a fine stew, and a nutritious jelly was made out of skin and bones. Keeping the food refrigerated between the double panes of the windows, Katya fed her family a morsel of meat every day for a week. It was all gone now, and she was again trying to spin out their bread ration.

The extra food and the hope of spring had kept them alive, but Katya felt increasingly tired. Waking up and starting the day was hard. She knew that the famine epidemic was continuing, that people still collapsed in the bread line. Even here in rural Murzinka, fresh corpses were laid out in the street every morning. Katya had not looked at herself in the mirror for weeks. She had learnt to recognise death on human faces and was afraid to discover signs of death in her own. Sometimes, she had a spell of vertigo in the bread line, or as they trekked down to the river. In such moments of weakness, she focused her mind on the girls, and dizziness passed. She was not afraid of dying, but the thought of the girls trying to survive alone in the Murzinka house forced Katya to keep on going.

On a cold morning Katya was bringing her little flock from the river, with Nadya leading the procession. The child was not helping the aunt with the water pail today. She bounded ahead up the slippery path and stopped at the last corner, from where she could see the house and a stranger at their door. There was a bicycle leaning against the verandah post. Nadya beckoned her aunt, who was coming up slowly with a full pail, trying not to spill water on the path.

'Aunt Katya, there's a man on a bicycle at our door!' she whispered. Katya frowned. Her brows and the dark moustache on her top lip had turned white in the frost and she sniffed like a fur seal.

'I wonder who it might be?' She knew it could not be Misha; he would have followed them down to the Neva. But who in his right mind would be riding a bicycle on these roads? At that moment, she recognised Nina's husband, Slava.

'We've got a visitor. Ada, hurry up. Quick, Vera. Kira, come along, but whatever you do, don't spill the water! Oh, clever Nadyenka, you were the first to spot him.'

Slava Lukyanov had been on the road since early morning. He came on his bicycle because he thought it would be quicker than walking, and less tiring. The main highway was not as slippery as he had feared. Parts of it had a layer of sand and gravel. He was aware, however, that cycling required an athletic skill he no longer possessed. He reached Murzinka, breathless and in a sweat. At least the effort had kept him warm, he thought, as he approached the house, pushing his bicycle along a narrow track. Smoke was rising from the chimney into the frosty air. He also noticed how the stack of wood under the verandah had shrunk since autumn; he doubted it would last Katya till summer.

He carried the bicycle with him up the steps, a precaution he would not neglect even here in the empty countryside, and knocked on Katya's door. No answer. He tried the handle; the door was locked. Well, at least Katya was not taking any risks. But what if she and the girls were not here, perhaps no longer alive, and the house had been taken over by someone else? 'Now, Slavka, don't anticipate.' He checked his panic with a firm reprimand. 'Wait and find out.' He stood on the verandah, stamping the snow off his boots, and sadly contemplated the vanished park. All the trees had been cut down since last August, when he and Nina came here for their unhappy wedding night. Here they sat on these steps in the dusk and the German guns boomed across the river. As so often these days, he was overwhelmed by regrets.

Whose fault, whose guilt? 'She made me do it,' he sighed wearily, peering into the window of Katya's room, and going over his own past. 'Yes, but you did it without protest. Good old Slavka! No trouble. All in a day's work.' Until that evening in August, he had not thought about the ethics of abortion, the emotions or the resulting guilt. Abortion was far from that carefree Slava's mind. It was a safe method to terminate pregnancy. Safe for most, but not for Nina; hers was botched. Why should her abortion have been an exception to the rule, one of those miserable mishaps? He tormented himself, alone, in the Voskresensky family. There was no one he could talk to about his pain. The Voskresensky women ignored him; occasionally he would catch a look of disgust.

He wanted to explain that he had been careful, professional, had handled the injection efficiently. Nina's sepsis was a calamity, as terrible as war or famine. Had she not herself seen that the water was sterile, checked the syringe. Poor Nina, he grieved, poor Slavka Lukyanov.

He pictured Nina as she was when they first met and fell in love. A fragile figure balancing on the edge of the diving board, in a black swimsuit, her hair hidden in a white rubber cap. In his home town in the Urals he had fucked large, lusty factory girls; in Leningrad he was smitten with this boy-girl creature. He had already singled her out at lectures; now she turned up at his sports club and he, Slavka the coach, was caught. Slavka, the champion swimmer, who could bed any girl he chose any night of the week, wanted this puny girl. 'No tits, no bum and no octane,' he mocked her, and more so himself for an idiotic infatuation. He was gripped by an obsession he could not control; crazy about a girl, who declined his advances in that cool accent of her superior Leningrad voice. That's how it began. And then the pregnancy, the hospital, and . . . the silence. Nina, that skin and bones girl, had ruined his life more than any German blockade could. All he wanted now was to be sent into action, to drown himself in the cauldron of the war.

Now all the women in Leningrad were skin and bone, thinner than Nina. In famine, mammaries ceased up, and so did ovulation. The human image itself was vanishing. He had watched Nina day by day growing more transparent. A pale blue glass woman, she would come out of Alexandra's room, and walk past the divan, where he slept alone. 'Good morning, Slavka,' she would whisper, and give him her once-a-day smile. She did not touch him, nor he her. Since her return from hospital, they cruised past each other in their separate orbits, distant planets in alien space.

When he took her to the hospital, he thought she was dying. He was so certain she would die that when the crisis passed and he was told she would recover, he didn't believe the nurse. There was no joy, nothing. His earlier emotions had been flushed out with the fear and guilt he had lived with during the crisis. The only feeling left was relief that he, a medical student, had not killed a woman. The fact that the woman happened to be his wife Nina seemed unimportant at that time.

The child, if it had lived, would have been born this month. These might-have-beens were absurd, a self-inflicted agony, but he could not stop tormenting himself. Sometimes, his conscience craved anodyne arguments. Nina was unstable, neurotic like her mother; like other famine victims, she would have miscarried the baby or died with it. In the winter months of the blockade there were hardly any live births in Leningrad. But in the face of the Voskresensky reproach, such palliatives failed him. The three women had closed ranks against him, and their condemnation was more expressive because it was wordless. Their silence was a constant reminder that his marriage to Nina was over, that he was an unwelcome lodger here in the family apartment. Yet he stayed on. (As her husband, I'm entitled to live in this apartment. I've a permit with an official stamp.) Hoping that Nina would change her mind, he could not bring himself to leave. Didn't she see that they were both responsible? That guilt must be shared. He also sensed a need, so vague that he couldn't put it into words, to make amends for the misery he had brought her. An emotion more generous than guilt, it was an impulse he had not expected to possess. Yet there it was a stubborn imperative, urging him to stay on against the will of three women: the old deranged one, the hysterical one and beloved Nina.

Slava turned towards the sound of voices and saw a group of padded figures trundling up the path. Five small creatures carrying pails of water from the river. He recognised the leader straightaway. 'Katya!' he cried and sprang down the steps towards her, his boots clogged up again with heavy clumps of snow. The first thing he noticed was how deeply Katya's eyes had sunk into their sockets. Then he saw that there was still some of the former sparkle left in them, and was grateful. Her smile was as warm as before. The girls, who were shuffling behind her, looked sturdier than Katya but on their faces too he could see the unmistakable marks of famine.

'You're alive!' He blurted out in his relief, heedless how these words might affect Katya. It occurred to him then that surely this woman, or someone like Katya, must be the embodiment of compassion, of selfless love.

Katya understood that, in his pessimism, Slava must have thought he wouldn't find them here. Her eyes swelled with tears, her arms opened out to him. 'Slava Lukyanov!' she cried. 'Bozhe moi! It's Slava, dear Slava!' Clasping both his hands in her own mitten-clad ones, she peered up into his face. 'Let me look at you.' She almost said, 'Oh, how you have changed,' but checked herself. The former Slava had the broad shoulders of a swimmer; this one was not the powerful sportsman she once knew. In the hard winter light she saw a young man with a prematurely aged face and a stooping posture. The red hair was dull; the face was blotchy. This new Slava was all skin and bone, but he seemed to have some energy. His pale eyes observed everything around him with a sharp keenness.

Katya clung to his hands a little longer. Then she let go, and led him, like a child, up the verandah steps. 'Come inside. You must be cold,' and held the door open for him, motioning him ahead. 'Never mind about the boots. You must tell me about Nina and Alexandra. About Anna . . .' She cancelled the name. 'About all in the Voskresensky household. I haven't heard from them since last November.'

'Katya . . . Yekaterina Nikolayevna . . .' He was confused, and for a moment couldn't remember how he used to address her in the past. In that golden past, a time of peace and plenty, did he call her by the full name and patronymic? Nina certainly called her Katya, while he, a newcomer to the family, was expected to be more formal.

'Wait, I can't walk inside with those clogged boots.' He stopped to stamp his feet on the verandah boards and sent clumps of snow flying in all directions. He caught a glimpse of the four girls. Gathered below the steps, they watched him and his snow missiles solemnly. Their unsmiling faces reminded him of wild creatures behind the bars of a zoo cage.

'That'll do. Quickly, come to the fire.' Her voice sounded as unsteady to her, as her slackened body felt. Too much joy, she realised; emotions are exhausting.

Inside, was a real human dwelling. Warm. Cosy. Slava was not used to comfort. From an orphaned home, he moved to a factory hostel; from there to the student dormitory at the institute. His brief marriage to Nina had been chilled by her family's disapproval — lonely nights on the dining-room divan. But here at Katya's, he felt the warmth of family life. One of the girls added more wood to the banked fire in the burzhuika. The large black kettle on top of it began to hum. He saw knitting on the seat of a chair and sheet music on the open piano. Could all this be a remnant of a dead civilisation? Were Katya and the girls the only survivors? Whatever it was, he was deeply moved. He felt his blood pulsing through the body; a spring thaw was melting his refrigerated heart.

Katya lifted the knitting off her chair. 'Come and sit here.' She patted the seat. 'This is a wonderful surprise.' She helped him to settle close to the stove. 'Let's have some tea,' she called out to the girls, who were taking their time, unwinding scarves, pulling off their coats and felt boots. Behind them, the front door was draped with a woollen blanket, to keep out the cold. The blackout curtains drawn back from the windows were also made of heavy stuff. Slava felt drowsy. If only his body were not so large, he thought, he would curl up in the armchair and go to sleep in this cosy room. He stifled a yawn, and reminded himself that he had to be back in the city before dark. Katya was making tea. The teapot was balanced on the edge of the hot plate, next to the purring kettle. 'Put out the saucers,' she reminded Ada, who was setting out the cups on the table.

Slava was surprised that anyone in starving Leningrad should bother with saucers. It did not occur to him that these formalities celebrated his arrival. He remembered how, when the air raids began, Alexandra packed her precious Napoleon tea set into a sturdy chest. Or was it a coffee set? He couldn't tell the difference, and was embarrassed to ask. He offered to help, laughing, showed her his hands of a surgeon-to-be. See how steady they are. Alexandra held his hands and examined them seriously. Her own were trembling badly. 'Sensitive fingers,' she said, 'like those of an artist,' but she didn't look him in the face. He realised that the rest of him did not please her. As he wrapped those delicate cups in cotton wool, he wondered about the artist who painted these miniature scenes of 1812; even after a century the colours glowed like jewels. 'How astonishing,' he thought, studying Napoleon in burning Moscow. 'Now Hitler's panzers are outside Moscow. Why is this country of ours such an irresistible, perpetual lure to foreign megalomaniacs?'

Are They Still Alive?

Slava had a silent audience. Sitting in a circle around the burzhuika stove, the watchful girls had still not said a word. Even Nadya remained locked in the solidarity of the group, and made no sign of recognition. He realised how much that child reminded him of Nina. Those serious eyes and the olive skin. Katya poured him the first cup of tea, handed the girls theirs in order of seniority, then she sat down with her own cup and saucer.

'Here we are, sitting together.' She relished this unplanned respite from her usual arduous chores. 'Now tell me about Nina, and the others. Are they . . .' The word 'alive' was on her lips but she stopped in time, 'Are they well?'

He understood what she meant, and was quick to reassure her, 'Nina and Alexandra have left Leningrad with a student transport on the ice road. The institute has been evacuating students since February. That's when Nina left. She was allowed one dependant and took Alexandra with her.' He paused. He couldn't tell Katya and the girls the brutal truth of that departure. How Nina and Alexandra went away, abandoned Anna Pavlovna, left her to Slava's conscience. They didn't ask if he would care for her, watch over her dying. When he came home that evening, he found the old woman alone in the cold darkness. Their bread coupons were on the table. And a note from Nina. 'Dear Slavka, If you have any feeling left for me, take care of Babushka. I don't think we'll ever see each other again. Forgive me.' It was signed 'Nina'. Without love or kisses. Across the room, senile and incontinent, Anna Pavlovna slept in her armchair.

Katya intruded into his brooding with a sigh: 'Thank God, they're safe.' She longed for detail that would glue together some fragments of her shattered world, strengthen the illusion that at least some members of the family were out of danger. Had he any idea where they were heading?

'Nina must have got through to the Urals.' That's where they were being directed in February. At present the transports were headed south, to the Caucasus. Everything depended on the shifting frontline, he said, and which railway routes happened to be safest at the time.

'But what about you, Slava, why haven't you gone?' Katya asked. 'Surely, the country needs all the doctors it can get at the front.'

'Well, I'm ready to serve,' his smile was teasing her, 'I'm ready to leave.' He left her uncertain whether he was joking, whether she had exhausted him with her questioning, as she had herself.

'And Dmitry?' Bleached by the hopelessness she felt, Katya's voice lost its colour. Had the family heard from him? Was he somewhere safe? Though who was safe from danger these days?

But there had been no news from Dmitry. He was probably fighting farther south, Slava said. If he had been with the defence force outside Leningrad he would have managed to send word to Alexandra; surely, he knew better than anyone how anxious she was. Her hair had turned completely grey, he said, giving Katya a clue how desperate things had been. Yet again Slava reined in the truth. He held back from Katya how Alexandra wept and prayed noisily at night; how she refused to go down to the shelter, in case a message came from Dmitry and she wasn't there to receive it. He remembered that Nina had also gone grey. When he last saw her, Nina's face was an icon, dark and ancient, framed in the metallic corrugations of her hair; solemn eyes contemplating mortality.

Katya sat opposite him, waiting. He had still not said anything about Anna Pavlovna. Sensing his reluctance, Katya could not risk asking. In her heart, she was certain that Anna Pavlovna had died. 'All that fine intelligence and that proud bearing,' she thought sadly. How could a frail old woman have survived, when thousands of stronger, younger people died every day?

As if reading her thoughts, Slava decided on a gentler version of Nina's and Alexandra's departure. 'Anna Pavlovna was too weak to be moved. She had dementia, couldn't grasp what was happening around her. Finally Dmitry's sister agreed to move in. They left her their ration cards,' he trailed off. His inventiveness was evaporating.

'Is my Babushka dead?' cut in Nadya's hysterical, high-pitched voice. Browsing through the sad catalogue of events, Katya had for a moment forgotten the vigilant presence of the children. Caught out, she scolded herself silently for having acted so thoughtlessly. Nadya's pain reminded Katya how she and Sofya felt when their parents died in the revolution.

'Oh, Nadyenka.' She knelt beside the child's chair and tightened loving arms around her. She could not lie, she could only try to comfort. Rocked in her embrace, Nadya was weeping helpless tears.

'Nadyenka,' Katya spoke to the child gravely as to another adult, 'I'd like you to go with the other girls and get some wood. Slava and I haven't finished talking, and I don't want you to be distressed. If there's anything important, we'll let you know, I promise.' But just as the girls were about to put on their felt boots, Katya changed her mind, 'No, stay here,' she called out to the girls. 'Slava, I know there's something urgent you want to talk to me about. But whatever it is, tell it to all of us.' She regarded him sternly. 'I have no secrets from the girls.' And, with a firm gesture, Katya beckoned the children back.

Yes, it was urgent, Slava nodded, as Katya had guessed when he arrived at such a speed out of nowhere. He waited for the girls to settle in their chairs round the pot-belly stove.

'All right,' he said, 'you asked me why I'm still in Leningrad. Well, my class was held back for hospital duties, looking after people with dystrophy who were brought in to die. There was nothing we could do to help them. In its final stage, dystrophy destroys the whole metabolism. We might have saved less acute cases if we had had food and medication. But even hospitals didn't have any extra rations. And in February, the typhoid epidemic struck us, and our patients just died. They were too weak to fight any illness.' He spoke in a cold, clinical voice, indifferent to the human suffering he described, as if the winter they all had just survived, the coldest in a century, had frozen all human compassion. And he was well aware that death was still on the prowl; any one of them in this room could succumb to it.

'I've just received the evacuation order,' he said. 'I thought at first that the transport was heading east to Central Asia. But yesterday I heard that we were going to the Caucasus. That's when I decided to collect Nadya, and take her to her mother in Pyatigorsk.'

Around the stove everyone had stopped breathing. Surely it's a dream, the girls' faces said. Katya turned to Slava, as if to verify his proposal. 'Nadya? You're offering to take Nadya?' She shook her head in disbelief. 'But what about Vera? How will my sister feel if her older child is left behind in Leningrad?'

'But I can't take two children with me.' He had not even considered taking both girls. When they told him about the Caucasus, he only remembered Nadya; he didn't think of the other child, didn't really know Vera. And his motives were a mystery to him: one moment he hoped that Nina would hear about this heroic deed but, the next moment, his decision to save the child appeared to him as a quixotic mission, a burden he didn't need. As he cycled to Murzinka, he had wondered if he should turn back before it was too late. He looked nervously into Katya's reproachful eyes, wondering if she had detected his vacillation. A few minutes ago he was still scheming to abandon his plan altogether. All at once he realised what he should have done from the start. The answer was so simple.

'Yekaterina Nikolayevna, I'm going to take both girls,' he said and saw tears welling up in Katya's eyes. The girls' faces lit up with surprise.

'Will you . . .?' she gulped and for a second was speechless. 'Will you really take both of them to Sofya? This is a miracle, and you, Slava, are a saint.'

'Please, Yekaterina Nikolayevna.' He felt relieved and elated, although her gratitude embarrassed him. 'Let me give you the details. The transport is leaving from Finland Station on the 31st. That's the day after tomorrow. The girls can come with me this afternoon, or you could bring them into the city. As long as they're there on Tuesday morning.'

Looking at the girls and waiting for their decision, Katya hesitated. Ada, the eldest said, 'We'd better take Vera and Nadyenka ourselves. If they go with Slava now, we'll have no time to say goodbye.'

'Yes, we can have one more day together,' Kira said in a brave voice. And the two Shubin girls nodded in silent consent.

'What about my girls? Who will save them?' Katya thought. She felt a heavy rage choking her, and made an effort to extinguished the burning protest about to spoil her joy.

'We'll be with you early on Tuesday morning,' she said to Slava.

Letter to Sofya

Katya's thoughts were in a muddle. There was just enough daylight left to finish the chores, then to hear the girls play. Yes, the Sonata in B Flat Major, piano and violin. Amazing that the upright was still in tune. Katya wondered what they would do in the future. Like most Leningraders, their piano tuner had died. And tomorrow will be the last day with Vera and Nadya. Was she happy for her nieces? she asked herself, and again felt the oppressive weight of resentment. Why should her own children be left to die in Leningrad? She had not allowed herself before to think about their fate; now, with no relief in sight, she no longer had the strength for optimism. The light of the afternoon was fading fast, when Katya sat down to write to Sofya. She knew it was the last letter she would write to her sister.

Dearest Sofya,

Your girls are leaving with Slava the day after tomorrow. They'll be with you soon, and your anguish will be over. I have felt your pain as if it was my own. My heart aches for you still, though I know that you'll soon be comforted. How have you managed to survive so much loss, Alexei and then your children?

I want to think only of you at this moment, but my mind is confused, worrying whether I'll have the strength to make the long walk from Murzinka into the city. The main thing, surely, is to reach out and touch you, after all these months of silence. Sofya, my sister, my friend, you are the only witness of my childhood and youth. We two are the only survivors of the Meier family. I used to think we had suffered enough being orphans in the midst of war and revolution, but now that I have seen what famine has done to Leningrad, how it has wiped out entire families here, I no longer see our own misfortunes as unique. At least you and I survived the first act of the Russian tragedy.

I often think that our generation has been the unluckiest of all time. True, we did have a real childhood, before the first war struck us. Then the revolution took away our parents, our home; and there were the years of hunger and homelessness. Except that all these hardships were later overshadowed by the horror of the purges. You, Sofya, stopped at each station of that journey: the Black Maria at the door, the midnight knock, outside prisons, inside prison, child in an orphanage.

And now we have to suffer through another calamity — war. We, the silent ones, have been sacrificed again. How criminal to have Leningrad abandoned to famine. Criminal, because there was no effort to stock the city with supplies, even though it had been obvious to all that the Germans were closing in and a blockade was imminent. Worse than that, our leaders panicked and burnt down the Badayev food warehouses. Convinced that the Germans would take the city, the powerful and the privileged evacuated their own families, and left us to starve here. And we heard rumours how our leaders in the Smolny 'mobilised' schoolgirls to their orgies: caviar, champagne and virgins for them as we died.

Death! I had no idea what mortality meant, until last November when Leningraders began to die in thousands every day; when the still-living grew indifferent to corpses in the street, in the yard, on the stairs; when wives no longer grieved over dead husbands, and children were left alone in silent apartments with unburied bodies of parents and grandparents. Nobody wept any more in Leningrad. Death became a member of the family. Even our children wouldn't share their daily slice of bread with you or me.

We've been in Murzinka since December, throughout the coldest months of this coldest winter. Yet it has been the most beautiful winter I've known. A fairy-tale winter of crackling frosts, bright days and night skies sparkling with stars. We were living on the outskirts of a silent city, where most of the people I used to know had died. I wonder sometimes if there will be any native Leningraders left alive. Our Leningrad voices will disappear, and when this war is over true natives will be a historical memory.

This is a terrible letter, Sofya dear. It's cruel to tell you all this. But when and who will be left to tell the truth? But who will know about us, if mothers like me don't cry out against those who have inflicted this suffering on our children?

I'm sending you my diary, which I've kept through the famine; I'm sending back your daughters, whom I have loved and protected as my own. May God grant you a happier future. Don't forget us — the hungry Leningraders.

Your Katya

A Letter from Kansk

'Sofya Nikolayevna . . . Comrade Shubina.' They called her to the telephone. That could only mean an urgent message: the telephones were not for frivolous use. Sofya's heart was beating violently as she ran to the gatehouse where the call was waiting for her. What if, what if it was news of the children in Leningrad?

'Sofya Nikolayevna?' It was Raissa, her only friendly neighbour. Raissa with her kindly peasant face and folksy proverbs.

'News from the children?' cried Sofya. They had agreed that Raissa would let her know immediately if any news came from Leningrad.

No, it was not from Leningrad, Raissa apologised, 'It's a letter for you from . . .' Her voice was barely audible on the crackling line.

'A letter from where?' The thumping of her heart made it impossible to understand a single word. She couldn't connect the lurching syllables in the static: 'From whom? Where from?' she shouted in a demented voice, not her own.

Raissa's voice surfaced. 'From Siberia, from Kansk.' — a faint whisper.

'Read it to me, please read it,' Sofya begged. 'It's a letter from Alexei!' She had not heard from her husband since the outbreak of war. And here at last was his letter, a desperately needed, hoped for message from Alexei. 'Quickly, Raissa!' She was shivering and sweating all over her back, her shoulders, then her hands, while Raissa fumbled with the envelope. My God, so slow.

The small, hesitant voice came again. 'Sofya Nikolayevna, I'd rather not read it on the telephone.'

'Please, please, read it!' Good heavens, there were still people about too decent to spy on their neighbour's personal correspondence. If Raissa only knew how unprivate a prisoner's letters were. Alexei's letter would have been inspected by warders, camp administrators, anyone who could be bothered to put an extra fingerprint on that scrap of cheap paper bearing a few scrawls scratched with a blunt pencil. Withered words that only Sofya's imagination could transmute into lyrics of love.

'Please, Sofya Nikolayevna, I'd rather not.'

'Oh, for pity's sake, stop tormenting me. I must hear it.'

Under this pressure Raissa's reluctance was folding. 'Well . . . it's up to you,' she muttered and, hesitating between the words, she began to read:

'Dear Sofya Nikolayevna, Babushka and children . . .' This was not Alexei writing. He wouldn't address her with a formal patronymic; wouldn't call his mother Babushka; his children were his little ones, his girls. This letter was from someone else, who knew the family by their names. Sofya's heart stopped beating altogether; it was a dead weight inside the ribcage. She pressed her palm against her mouth to stifle a sob. She must not interrupt the reader.

'Dear Sofya Nikolayevna, Babushka and children, I am sending you greetings and at the same time must inform you that Alexei died on 19 November. Please don't take it too hard. This had to be expected because he had been very ill for a long time. I was his friend and I have a request: can I keep Alexei's padded jacket that you made for him, also his boots (mine are very worn and leak) and his quilt? If you agree, please write to the Camp Admin. I'm waiting for your reply.

Yours respectfully, A. Novikov'

Sofya heard it out to the end, in silence, dimly realising that Alexei was dead. Someone called Novikov was begging her to give him Alexei's jacket and boots. But Alexei needs all these things himself, she thought. Siberian winters are bitterly cold. Kansk is in Siberia. Her mind was sluggishly churning over the dilemma of the boots Novikov wanted, and Alexei couldn't possibly do without. And the jacket, and the quilt, Alexei needed those himself. How could she then help his friend Novikov to keep warm? What can be done about his leaking boots?

'Sofya Nikolayevna!' someone was calling in the distance.

'Sofya Nikolayevna . . .' Another anxious voice crooned much closer.

She didn't want to respond; she was floating, falling, and at last sinking softly into padded deepest darkness.

She was awake, weightless, a cloud drifting, passing. Her skin felt smooth and cool against the sheet. I'm in bed, she thought, I must be in a bed. She didn't want to find out where she was, and pressed her eyelids tighter together. She lay listening to the voices murmuring on the edge of memory, 'Sofya Nikolayevna . . . Sofya Nikolayevna . . .'

'Let me sleep,' she begged.

'Yes, my dear, it's best to sleep,' the cloud whispered.

And Sofya slept. When she opened her eyes again, everything around her was different, the place and the season. The room was familiar, though. (It's home, she realised.) The window was filled with a hard white light. The stove in the corner was lit. A woman sat at her bedside sewing.

'Has the snow come?' Sofya couldn't work out the season.

'Yes, winter's come and brought the snow.' Raissa chanted the words like a rhyme and bit off the thread with her strong teeth. She spread the sewing on her knee, smoothing it out with her hands. 'It's been snowing since Sunday.'

'I must have been lying here for days,' Sofya puzzled, but her lazy brain didn't want to question how long it had been. Her body was warm and her mind comfortably blank. She watched Raissa's bent head, and understood. 'I've been ill,' she said, 'and you've been nursing me.' Such a kind woman. Could one ever repay such kindness? With a detached clarity she studied Raissa's face, as if she had never seen it before. Coarse features. Short brown hair combed behind the ears. Small bright eyes. 'It's a Russian face.' Her mind struggled for a moment with the concept of Russia. If there was such a thing as Russia, would she look like Raissa?

Raissa shook her head mournfully. 'Ai-ai-ai.' Didn't the peasants lament just like this? Ai-ai-ai. Russian compassion. 'It was the shock that made you ill. Now you must get your strength back, to take care of your children when they get home.' Raissa sighed again. 'I wrote to the camp and told them to give your husband's things to that friend of his. You know, the boots and the jacket. You kept worrying about it, while you were ill. And that poor man Novikov needed them badly.'

'Thank you.' Sofya closed her eyes because the glare from the window burnt her eyelids like tears.

Later, when she recovered, she put the letter from Kansk on the desk, under the lighthouse lamp, which her father had made. Katya had the twin lamp. She was not going to think about her husband's death until she had her children with her. When the girls were back from Leningrad, she could start grieving for Alexei.

Days and Nights

Sofya's first thought each morning went to her children. They were trapped in the German blockade, dying, perhaps already dead in the famine. It struck her like a body blow. The pain was deep and visceral; it winded her. As she regained her breath, she would be left with an ache in all the muscles of her body. She felt shaken and broken, until the cares of the day claimed her, and activity recharged her spirit. Her anxiety about the children would be stored for the next morning's awakening.

Daylight was for the living. She believed fiercely that her children were alive and would be returned to her. Nights were for the dead; she mourned only one, Alexei. In her dreams she retraced their meetings and their partings. The letter from Kansk, which she knew by heart, was thrust at her nightly to confirm his death, to deny any hope which might have sprung up in her waking hours.

Her day at the office was long and in the evening, when she reached home, she was limp with exhaustion. Yet she willed herself to do the chores. She washed her hair, mended a run in her stocking and even pasted in photographs, proving to herself that she could look at the faces of those she loved. All of them had slid out of her life, and came back to her on the pages of the album or in dreams. She even started making a summer dress from a silk kimono she had found in her mother-in-law's box. 'Anna Pavlovna won't mind my going through her things. When she comes back, she'll understand that I had to keep myself busy.' She didn't expect to see Anna Pavlovna again.

She listened to the evening news bulletin, invariably obscure. Battles were raging along a wide frontline: from north to south, from Leningrad to the Crimea. Some were described as 'heavy', others were 'persistent'. One could only guess what was going on when cities fell to the Germans and the enemy pressed deeper and deeper into the Russian heartland.

She stayed up as long as her determination lasted; until the second wind, which helped her to become engrossed in detailed domesticity, was spent. Then she could barely drag herself to the bathroom down the hall, which would be mercifully vacant at that late hour. She went to the toilet, gave herself a sponge wash, brushed her teeth. All the while delaying the moment when she put out the light and was joined by the nightmare. It came to her as soon as she touched the pillow. Alexei sat on the edge of her bed, tearing at his pyjama collar, choking: 'I can't breathe, Sofya. Air . . .' 'Hurry, please hurry,' she begged the butcher and brought her childhood pets for him to slaughter. The little terrier watched her with his clever eyes: 'Why are you doing this to me?' Boulle, the Dobermann, fought for his life, bit Sofya's hands, snarled. 'Darling Boulle, please, forgive me, but you must die.' And she poured large spoonfuls of dripping yellow dog fat into a man dying from TB.

Alexei is going to live! The pores in her body opened like night flowers to inhale joy. But why did they take him back to prison? 'No . . . no,' she screamed at Kozlov, who now stood between them. 'Just a formality . . . No need to say goodbye,' said the interrogator. And then, a voice began to read the letter from Kansk. 'Why it's Raissa, my neighbour!' She knew each word in advance, but was still surprised: 'Why is she telling me these lies?' And woke up crying because she had bitten her hands in her sleep.

Sofya worked at the Myasokombinat, the centralised industrial complex that combined all branches of the meat industry in the Northern Caucasus. Cattle were slaughtered, fresh meat was distributed from here throughout the region and all manner of small goods were manufactured in specialised workshops. The famous Pyatigorsk sausages, hams and smoked brisket were dispatched all over Southern Russia.

In wartime the Myasokombinat was charged with a special production schedule which meant extra shifts for the workers and even longer hours for the office staff. Sofya was an accountant in the planning section, where production targets were set, progress monitored and monthly accounts compiled. At the end of the year, nerve-wracking days and nights were devoted to the writing of the annual report, which was duly dispatched to the ministry in Moscow.

Everything was confused now. The ministries had been evacuated from Moscow, and the 1942 industrial plan came from Kuibyshev. Wartime production targets were aimed at ideological as well as practical goals. They demanded from the workers maximum effort and increased productivity as a mandatory contribution towards victory over the Germans. There was, however, no suggestion how these goals might be achieved. Since the country's production was in chaos, each industry was left to its own devices, to do the best it could.

For the planning department staff it was a precarious reversal from total control to temporary autonomy. 'Who's going to accept the responsibility for this and put his head on the block?' they muttered. Sofya, too nervous to voice an opinion, nodded cautious agreement. She had never ceased to be grateful to the director of the Meat Works for employing her, an ex-prisoner. She felt indebted to her colleagues for their acceptance of a pariah like herself. Other wives had not been so fortunate. Her friend Shaiira, who had stood pressed against the cell door with her on their first night in prison, now supported her three children by taking in sewing. Her eyes were always red from working through the nights. Ration coupons were meagre, there was rarely meat in the shops and Shaiira couldn't afford to buy at the market for her hungry teenagers. Sofya invented tactful reasons for the bulging basket she brought along when she visited. 'Oh, these were offcuts, and those were rejects, or specials,' she would explain to her destitute friend, who could not have paid even the staff-discount prices. Sofya could afford it; she had no family to feed.

Watching Trains

Sofya went to the station to meet the first evacuees from Leningrad. She hoped for a miracle; she imagined how the doors of the carriage would fly open and out would tumble Vera and Nadyenka. Yet she knew the dangers of hope and comforted herself with the thought of more transports following this one, now that the evacuation was once again under way. The welcoming crowd on the platform was large and mixed. In the front row members of the city Soviet waved bunches of flowers. Sofya gazed at the vulnerable blooms, so beautiful, so strange in this wartime winter, and wondered absently where they had come from. Inside her an icy bitterness was thawing. She was grateful to these representatives of the state for their compassion for the Leningraders. Faith in fellow human beings was such a rare and happy feeling. Sofya stood smiling as the refugee train pulled into the station and came to a halt with a screech of metal and a warning hiss of steam. Through the smoky cloud Sofya saw at last the famine victims appear in the open carriage doors.

What had she expected, she asked herself a little later, disappointment dry in her mouth. The brief happiness she had felt before the train arrived died under an icy crust. For months she had hidden from herself images of human beings, barely alive, of sunken eyes, emaciated bodies and desperate voices begging for bread. An unbearable vision, because she imagined the children and her sister among these skeletal shapes. And here came the train with the heroic Leningraders who had endured daily shelling and bombs in a dark and icebound city, who had survived famine. A welcome committee was applauding. Men, women and children began to disembark. Embraces exchanged for flowers. Laughter mingling with weeping. Exclamations of alarm for children lost in the crowd. And a mountain of suitcases, boxes and trunks rising on the platform.

'These are not Leningraders,' Sofya muttered to another incredulous bystander. These people had not been starving, nor were they destitute. How dared they come here as the victims of the Leningrad blockade. With the poison of bitterness spreading, numbing every trace of pity in her heart, a cynical Sofya watched the new arrivals strolling along the platform, collecting their children and their luggage, as if they had come to the Caucasus for a holiday. She heard later that those families from the first transport were housed in the white palaces on the slope of Mount Mashuk. They were all recuperating from the horrors of the blockade at the mineral springs.

More transports were arriving in the Caucasus. Ladoga, Sofya read in the papers, already had its two metres of ice, and the Road of Life across the frozen lake was now used daily. Trains from the north stopped at Mineralnye Vody, and from there the evacuees travelled on the local line to the spa towns, Kislovodsk, Yessentuki, Pyatygorsk. Some were taken deeper into Transcaucasia. Sofya met each train and searched for her children. She could no longer rely on official information; chaos ruled all of Soviet officialdom; nor did she expect to receive a message from her family. She trusted only her own eyes and what news she could glean from the refugees. These more recent arrivals were staff and students of institutes and academies, and what was left of their families. There were orphans too: an entire transport of children. But hers were not among them. None of the people she questioned had heard of the Karpovs or the Voskresenskys. She had not met anyone yet who had lived on or near Ligovka, or had a link with the Rimsky-Korsakov Conservatorium. Her children were never among the evacuees.

The more often Sofya went to the railway station, the deeper her worry wormed in. Now she could see what real famine victims were like, she understood what they had suffered in Leningrad. The evacuees on these later transports were smelly skeletons bundled in ragged winter clothes. They scratched themselves. Their blotchy faces had a haunted look. Their greedy eyes searched for the next meal. Sometimes she thought that those who had escaped famine had been damaged by the blockade, were perhaps even demented.

Pyatigorsk was congested now. Leningraders were looking for rooms, for work, and always for more food. They could never eat their fill. Their special rations were not enough for them. What money they had, they immediately spent at the market buying additional food.

Sofya continued her watch at the station. Despair drove her to the distribution points, to the markets, questioning the refugees as if she was collecting a dossier on the Leningrad siege. Whenever she browsed through these mental pages, she was crushed by pain and fear for her children, but she refused to give up hope of their return. 'They're alive,' she insisted to her friend Shaiira. 'I know my sister. Katya will get the children to me, whatever the difficulties.'

Shaiira did not share in Sofya's optimism; her own experience of life had been travail and tears. Although their circumstances differed, she too was in agony about her three children. As her cancer spread, she worried constantly who would take care of them when she died. She had kept her illness a secret, even from Sofya, her closest friend and support. There was no one else she could rely on; some of her family were in Armenia or, like her husband, had perished in the recent purges.

The month of May returned to the Caucasus. On her way home, Sofya walked on a carpet of chestnut blossom. She stepped lightly, dancing on the creamy froth, not to crush the pale petals which gave her so much pleasure. After a long day at the office, she filled her lungs with the spring air and, feeling light-headed, she kept making little bows of playful reverence to the five giants of the Great Caucasus range. This place of many sorrows was her home. Not that she could love it as she loved Leningrad, but Pyatigorsk had been part of her life, a place of past joys as well as loss. Whenever she forgot her pain, she reached out to the mountains, felt the breath of spring and for a moment her spirit lifted.

The wide wooden gates into the yard were kept locked, and the tenants used the small side gate. Sofia took one last look at the chestnuts weighed down with blossom and stepped on to the cobblestones of the yard. Washing on the line all day long was another signal of approaching summer. Under the old pear tree children were playing. On the bench sat a pair of babushkas knitting and chatting; they scrutinised her silently as she passed. Although Sofya was used to suspicion, she wondered what new crime she was supposed to have committed, and even smiled at the absurdity of it. At least the war had brought some relief from the terror of the past years; the Black Marias were no longer on the prowl. As she walked into the annexe, Sofya saw that her door at the end of the corridor was wide open. It was sinister; she could think of no reason why the neighbours should be crowding at her door. Why in my room? she thought. Had someone died? But she had no one left here to bury. She began to run. And then she saw them. Neither her peaceful walk under the chestnuts nor the fear of a moment ago had prepared Sofya for the shock of her children's return.

Let Me Touch Them

Two little girls with shaven heads. Solemn faces. Purple shadows under those accusing Leningrad eyes. She had looked into such eyes many times as the transports came into the station. Their arms were twigs poking out from woollen sleeves. They must be cold, was her first thought. Their skin is transparent, they must be freezing. She knelt beside them and, because they were so fragile, so tormented, she kissed them like a holy icon, reverently; touched them gently like a precious gift. Let me be sure, she prayed, quite sure that they are real before I start thanking you for the miracle of their survival.

'Mama,' said her elder daughter Vera, 'when we crossed Lake Ladoga, the bus was full of water. We had to stand on the benches. I was afraid. But Nadya was very brave. She said we'd never drown because she was born with a cowl . . .'

'Oh, my love, my love!' The girl's voice was the most beautiful sound imaginable and Sofya was embracing a real live child.

'Mama, you're strangling me.' Vera wriggled out of her mother's tight embrace, and didn't finish the story of Nadya's heroism.

Sofya released the older girl and turned to the younger. 'Nadyenka,' she whispered with infinite gentleness, because even touching the child she could feel her breakable bird bones. There was so little of her. 'Nadyenka, my little sparrow, you're home.'

Nadya wound her twig-arms around her mother's neck, and slid into her lap. Weightless. She did not speak, just clung possessively to Sofya. She kept her eyes wide open, afraid that if she blinked her restored mother would vanish, as all those she had loved vanished in Leningrad.

Minutes passed, or perhaps hours. Sofya did not notice her

neighbours tiptoeing out. She heard someone moving round the room, and saw a gaunt young man unpacking his rucksack near the door. He squatted over a grey heap of dirty clothes. Her children's clothes? So this was the person who brought her children. She wondered who he might be, and was about to ask, when she recognised him. Of course, it must be Slava Lukyanov. Nina sent her a snapshot just before the war. A group of laughing students on the Neva embankment. She had written on the back: 'Slava is second on the right. You can tell he's a sportsman. He's got red hair and Babushka calls him the Red Devil.'

'Slava,' she whispered. She couldn't stand up to embrace him, because the limpet-child clinging to her had fallen asleep; she reached out for his hand and pressed it to her wet cheek. 'Slava, dear Slava!' And he heard her say, in Katya's voice and words, 'You're a saint.' She let go of him. The children were sleeping. Nadya still clutching her mother. It was getting dark, but Sofya did not ask him to turn on the light. Through the gaping door a shaft of light from the corridor beamed into Sofya's room. In the caves beyond rustled voices of unbelievers, awed by the miracle of resurrection.

For a second, Slava imagined another twilight, so long ago that it might never have happened. Guns across the river like flashes of summer lightning. Nina's face a bleached white, her voice toneless, 'I want you to do it . . .' He went to the light switch — 'Do you mind?' He turned on the light and closed the door into the corridor.

They regarded one another furtively in the glare of the electric bulb. As was bound to happen with relations who had never met, these two made awkward company. Instead of bringing them closer, Sofya's earlier impetuous gesture seemed to have embarrassed both of them. There was so much to tell, yet neither was ready to begin. They fell silent. Sofya thought that this was the moment she had been longing for, that here was the person who had saved her children, and she couldn't think of anything to say to him. 'It's a miracle,' she kept repeating to herself. 'The children are back, it's a miracle.' Her mind cleared at last and reality unfolded: the man in front of her was a messenger from her sister in Leningrad. He was a living link with Katya. He would have seen her not all that long ago, shaken her hand, spoken with her, heard the voice that Sofya hadn't heard since the Ukrainian holiday a year before war broke out. All she had longed to find out, all the things over which she despaired were now possible. With the vigour of impatience, Sofya began to question Slava, interrupting his answers with exclamations of dismay and delight.

'I must know one thing, first of all,' she implored. 'You did see my Katya before you left, didn't you?' He nodded. 'How stupid of me. Of course you must have seen her. How else would you have collected Vera. When did you last speak to my sister? How is she, and her girls? Tell me everything . . . I suppose Misha is at the front . . . Has Katya heard from him? And how, tell me how, you managed to bring my girls?'

Slava was only partially truthful in his reply: he was allowed one dependant and one suitcase, he said, and he took the second child instead of the suitcase.

Sofya pressed her hands to her chest, perhaps, to contain her leaping heart. 'But that was heroic.' Then she frowned at the thought of the choices he might have had to make, and asked cautiously, 'And what about Nina?' Surely, he couldn't have taken her children instead of Nina, and left her in Leningrad? She had not yet asked about Alexandra and Dmitry. Nor the saddest question of all. She couldn't have spoken it aloud just then. She prayed silently, 'Please, let him tell me that Anna Pavlovna is alive.'

Sofya's questions were like her sister's in Leningrad last March, and inhibited Slava just as much. When she realised that she had not given him a chance to answer, she bit her lip. 'I'm sorry. You better tell me everything at your own pace.' She rocked the child in her lap and waited for him to tell her the story of his escape from Leningrad.

How is My Katya?

Slava's story was disjointed. He started with his bicycle sliding all over the road to Murzinka, he backtracked to Nina's evacuation, and then he was telling Sofya how Katya walked through the night to deliver the girls to him. The sentries on the bridges didn't allow anyone through, but when she told them that the children were going to their mother in the Caucasus, they let them pass; they even gave her a piece of bread to divide among the four children. Until that moment Slava himself had not appreciated Katya's sacrifice, not even thought about. It was only in telling the story that he understood it. As though overcome by a sudden weakness, he lowered himself to the floor opposite Sofya. 'Imagine the courage it must have taken to walk through the deserted streets, in the darkness, in the icy March wind.' His whisper was as harsh as that wind. He described how he was waiting for them in the doorway of the Voskresensky apartment house and how, as soon as they arrived, he and the girls had another long walk to the Finland Station for the transport.

'And Katya? Did she go to the station with you?'

'No, Katya and her girls went back to Murzinka,' he muttered absently, remembering how sick Katya was that morning. Eyes sunk into dark caverns, lethargic walk, sluggish speech. Looking back on it now, he knew that she would not have survived the Leningrad spring. Should he warn Sofya with a clinical explanation, he wondered: that a metabolism, undermined by months of famine, had little or no immunity. Once the weather got warmer, epidemics would have inevitably swept through the city. With all the broken sewers and rotting corpses, there would have been typhoid, dysentery. And people who had willed themselves to stay alive through the worst of the famine would have abandoned their struggle, even if the bread ration might have improved.

He once found a study on suicides in the institute library. It was a most un-Soviet subject, but the title was deceptively optimistic: it was *The Call of Spring*. He read it secretly, intrigued and surprised that it had been overlooked in the successive library purges of the thirties. It described how, in Scandinavian countries, suicides tended to occur in early spring. The incubus of depression might remain quiescent through the dark winter months, but with the first warmth of spring it revived, and drove the victim to suicide. This illustrated a tension between opposing forces: light flooding back into nature clashed with the darkness in a human psyche. At the time, Slava had decided that the Swedish thesis was unscientific, but not any longer. He had observed how strong the self-destructive urge was; how lack of energy prevents a depressed mind from taking that ultimate life-affirming leap from despair to hope.

Slava had not planned how he would tell the truth about Leningrad to Sofya. What he would conceal from her about the Voskresenskys. When he was leaving Leningrad, with the children, he had no strength for reflection. In that city of death, truth, pity or guilt were obsolete values; coins in a currency of a forgotten age. The scent of survival obliterated all other concern. It did not even occur to him in that selfish hour how Katya and her hungry children would find their way back home. All he knew was that he was empty then; he had just spent the last of his human emotion in the apartment upstairs.

'I've got a letter for you,' he remembered, and moved to his bundle by the door. He settled on his haunches and began a search through the pile of belongings. 'Ah, here it is,' he called out softly, 'Katya's letter.' He gave it to Sofya and, tactfully, returned to sorting his grubby clothes.

Sofya forgot about Slava. Her hands shook as she unfolded and smoothed out the crumpled pages. Reading the first lines, she dug into her pocket for a handkerchief, dried her eyes and blew her nose. 'I mustn't cry,' she cautioned herself. Then she untangled the twiggy limbs of the child in her lap, put her down tenderly on the bed, beside the older girl, and covered both with a blanket. 'There,' she whispered, 'you're home, my darlings. Home.' She walked past

Slava to the desk, moving like a sleepwalker, yet every movement was deliberate. She switched on the lighthouse lamp and sat down at the desk. 'That's better,' she said, again not to him but to herself or, perhaps, for the benefit of her sleeping children. The warm glow encircled her head with a peaceful halo, as she sat lost in Katya's letter. Time passed; she must have read her sister's message several times over. Dry-eyed, she had the stern look of an examiner assessing a student's essay. Then she turned to Slava, severely, 'The diary Katya mentions here. Where is it?'

'Yes, yes, I've got it.' He dug deeper into the heap of smelly clothes and found the exercise book wrapped in a piece of fabric, which Sofya recognised as her sister's summer dress, the one she had worn on their last holiday together. Now the Ukraine of that holiday was in German hands.

'She gave me the diary in Murzinka. And the letter, when she brought the girls. I'm sorry, I should have given it to you straightaway.'

In the Voskresensky Apartment

The Voskresensky apartment was a short walk from the hospital where Slava had been living since Nina's departure. It was warmer in the hospital, and occasionally there was some extra food. Five silent figures were waiting for him in the secretive dark of the street corner. Swaddled in their coats and scarves, they did not resemble Katya and the girls. Slava couldn't have told them apart.

'Hello, Slava, hello.' Even their voices were muted, sexless. They whispered like conspirators. Then he distinguished Katya's voice: 'We were saying goodbye.' All four girls clung to her. Their muffled exclamations in the dark made him nervous.

'Yes, hello,' he whispered back. 'I'll just go upstairs quickly and check things. Would you mind waiting down here for me?' Slava vanished into the black doorway, and up the stairs to the Voskresensky apartment.

'Slava, will you please say goodbye from us all?' Katya called out softly after him.

'I will,' he echoed back from somewhere up the invisible stairwell.

'And Slava . . .'

'Yes?'

'Could you, please, find a pair of mittens for Vera? We can't find hers. She's probably lost them on our walk from Murzinka.'

The smallest figure slid away from the group and darted towards the gaping doorway, to follow Slava upstairs. 'I want to see my Babushka . . . say goodbye to her!' Nadya demanded.

'No, it's best if we all wait down here.' Katya wouldn't let her go up alone, and she herself didn't have the strength these days to walk up the six flights of stairs to Alexandra's. 'There's another person . . . Dmitry's sister is with Anna Pavlovna . . . We can't disturb old people at this hour.'

The stairs were empty, colder than the hospital morgue. He felt for the keyhole and unlocked the apartment door. The black space he entered was familiar, closer to being home than all the dormitories he had squatted in since his teens. Nina knew every hiding nook here. He touched the side of a grand wardrobe, and stroked the smooth oak. They had made love in here and in the storeroom at the end of the corridor. Silent perfection. Not a sound. Never detected.

He walked into Alexandra's rooms. Even in the cauterising chill, the stench of urine stung his nostrils. With the blackout curtains tightly drawn, the room was pitch black. Careful, mustn't frighten her: 'Anna Pavlovna? It's me, Slava!' There was no reply. The sound of agitated breathing was his own. He pulled back the curtain to let in the grey murk of dawn.

Her face was turned towards him in greeting, a pale patch in the gloom, her features blurred. The burner must be on the dressing table; he reached out for it, lit the wick and carried it towards Anna Pavlovna. Wrapped up to her waist in blankets, she stared up at him from her pillows. She wore her overcoat and a fur hat, with the earflaps tied under her chin. Inside that furry frame, her face was a moonscape pitted with deep hollows; from their cavernous sockets her eyes accused him. He touched her skin. Glacial. How long has she been dead? Hours, days? Peeping out of the fur cuffs, her hands were convulsed like animal claws, the fingers stained with faeces. He backed away in revulsion.

There were no other signs of human habitation in the Voskresensky apartment, only of chaos and flight. Someone had been through the place, searching, looting perhaps? The mirrored doors and the drawers of the mahogany wardrobe were open, and the contents dumped on the floor. In the other room, the china cabinet gaped. The box with the Napoleon cups and saucers that he and Alexandra had packed so carefully had been emptied into a heap of broken china on the floor. The hand-painted medallions lay in shattered fragments, blue, white, gold. He caught himself reflecting calmly that these bright slivers should be fashioned into a grotesque kaleidoscope; with each twist these porcelain pieces would shape abstractions of beauty and violence. One cup had survived the carnage. He picked it up and held it up against the jittery light of the wick. The jewelled colours of the miniature glowed on the deep midnight blue. Clutching the bridle of his live horse, a French soldier lay dead in a snowdrift.

By the time Slava came down, it had grown a little lighter. Katya's swaddled shape met him in the doorway, and whispered anxiously, 'How's Anna Pavlovna? Is Dmitry's sister coping?' She was still trying to protect the girls from death.

   He wasn't going to tell her what he had just seen in the Voskresensky apartment. He lied cheerfully, 'They're managing. They're coping.' And louder, for the benefit of the girls, 'No gloves. I couldn't find any gloves.'

   Men, Katya thought, helpless, unobservant and no common sense. Not that she would say such a thing to Slava. She peeled off her own woollen mittens. 'Take these, Verochka. I've got another pair at home.'

   'But, Mama,' cried Kira, 'you'll freeze on the road.'

   'Take mine, take mine, Mama. My hands will be beautifully warm in the muff,' said Ada, forcing her gloves on Katya.

   'Yekaterina Nikolayevna, it's time. I must get going,' Slava reminded her. It was a long walk to the Finland Station, he said, where they would be boarding the buses for the long slow drive across the lake ice.

   'Yes, yes, of course, you must be on your way.' As Katya helped the girls with their small packs, her hands shook. 'They're very light,' she assured Slava. 'Even Nadyenka can manage hers quite easily.' Katya was holding back her tears. 'Goodbye, my darlings,' she whispered and embraced first the older niece, then the younger Nadya. 'Give your Mama all my love, and lots of kisses.' She made the sign of the cross over them both: 'God keep and protect you.'

   The four cousins were now hugging one another goodbye, the older girls were crying. Katya embraced Slava. 'Don't lose the girls . . .' Her teasing sounded forced; the smile was awash with tears. 'And Slava, take care of the letter and the diary. Please make sure they get to my sister.' After all, men were absent-minded, and needed reminders.

As the evacuees turned the corner, they had a last glimpse of Katya and her diminished flock standing by the house of the seven winds, still waving goodbye. Ahead of them was the road to Murzinka; and another long bread queue awaited Katya.

Sofya turned away. She cried silently, not to wake up the girls. Looking at Katya's diary in her hands, she felt no urgency to read it. This was not a message of hope from Leningrad. In her heart tolled the final tocsin. 'Don't forget us — the hungry Leningraders,' Katya wrote in her letter. And that other ominous line: 'True Leningrad natives will soon be a historical memory.' That 'soon' was now; it had already happened. It was early April when Slava and the girls left Leningrad, and now was late May. There might not be anyone left for her to mourn in Leningrad, but here, at the other extreme of Russia, a woman could weep for her sister, and for an extinguished past that even in recollection seemed dreamlike.

The Journey

For the little girls, the journey from Leningrad to the Caucasus was an adventure, and the sadness they felt at parting from their aunt and cousins was soon forgotten. Once they were inside the gates of the station they were each given a large slice of bread. Real white bread.

Neither could bring herself to take a bite of this astonishing gift; this soft, fine-textured bread smelling of warm goodness. Vera gave in to the temptation first and bit into the crust, crisp and delicious. 'Go on, Nadya, your turn now!' she commanded. 'You take a bite, and then I'll have another one.' It was a good game, as long as you remembered how very precious, how unbelievably amazing that piece of white bread was. They weren't sure they had ever seen such bread, let alone tasted it.

Nadya plucked a crumb from her slice and put it reverently on her tongue. It tasted wonderful. She couldn't bear it any longer: game or no game, she wanted to eat, devour, that bread here, this minute. She took a huge hungry bite and closed her eyes, savouring the sensation. It was bliss. It was the happiest moment of her entire life.

'Look,' Vera nudged her to open her eyes, 'see that woman across the street . . . She's coming over to talk to us.' The sisters turned watchful faces towards the stranger.

The woman came up to the grille. Bundled up in her winter coat and scarves, she resembled their aunt. She even sounded a bit like Katya: a Leningrad voice. 'How does it taste, girls, the white bread? Is it nice?' The girls nodded politely, without words. They were too busy stuffing the bread in their pockets. In Leningrad you did not share bread with anyone. They resumed their breakfast only when the woman had gone.

'What if she were Aunt Katya, would you've shared with her?' Nadya asked her sister. Vera considered the problem for a moment, and shook her head. On the question of food, you had to be honest. 'I wouldn't share it even with Kira,' she said. And cousin Kira, they both knew, was Vera's best friend.

When they talked about the journey from Leningrad to the Caucasus, parting from their aunt and being reunited with their mother, the sisters were wide-eyed with hindsight. They revived dangers they had escaped: such as the crossing of the lake, just after the flash of a false spring had melted sections of the ice road. The thick crust of ice was cracking, thawing, thinning and, in places, threatening to collapse. The bus behind them sank, didn't it? And the children were drowned. The girls rolled their eyes, rounded their mouths into an O, and shook their shaven heads, acting out a horror they could not feel.

'We had to stand on the seats in our bus . . .' Vera told her mother. They saw the water wash over the floorboards, rising higher and lapping against the seats. The driver shouted 'Keep calm!' in a panicky voice. The motor strained and roared; the spinning wheels kept missing the firm edge of the road; finally they gripped, and the bus rolled out of danger.

'Look what's happening behind,' the adults cried, turning their heads, but holding their bodies still, so they would not unbalance their bus.

'It's the October orphanage,' someone said. And then silence fell over the fate of the orphans. The driver, who had eyes only for the road, just then crowed noisily with relief. 'We've made it. Relax everyone. You can sit now.' The water was draining fast. Rivulets of sweat poured down the driver's face; his hands were still locked on the steering wheel, glued to it forever.

On the other side of the lake there was a station and a goods train ready to depart. Somewhere ahead an engine chuffed in spumes of steam. Freight cars, identically drab and sequentially numbered, were coupled together into a long echelon stretching into the distance past both ends of the platform. They had been loading through the night, someone said, and were waiting to collect just these last transports before pulling out of the station. An air raid was expected any moment. The new arrivals were hurried along to embark. Slava and his charges were directed to one of the cars far up the track.

'Look for No. 7 . . . Not a minute to be lost! Hurry, hurry, or you'll be left behind. There won't be another train until the day after tomorrow, or later, or never . . .' They ran along the platform, down the end ramp and followed the line of the train. Slava lifted the children and their bundles into the open door of No. 7. Then he tried to push himself up with his arms. Push-ups were once the simplest thing in the world, but his swimmer's muscles no longer obeyed him. He paused for a moment on the clumpy snow of the embankment, undecided. The train gave a sudden lurch, and he accepted a hand from the men leaning out of the doors.

'You think all's back to normal just because you're out of Leningrad. We're all cripples here, Lukyanov, even sports heroes like you!' nodded one of the rescuers. Slava recognised a faculty member from the institute and rewarded his fellow traveller with a mirthless grin.

The car was full of human freight. Layers of wooden bunks rising up to the roof were crowded. The floor space below was packed tight with bodies, bundles and violin cases. Having left some of their dead cellists, violinists and double bass players behind in the common graves, these living members of a chamber orchestra were off on a tour. How could hollowed out people like this lift a fiddle or strike a bow, Slava asked himself, imagining that he was still tough and vigorous, until he remembered his own failed attempt at a push-up just a few minutes ago.

Hugging their instrument cases, the violinists shifted closer to the wall and cleared a small patch of floor for the newcomers. Slava and the girls settled close to the pot-belly stove anchored in the centre of the car, and joined other families of human beings, related by blood or professional bonds. All of them were Leningraders who had survived the first winter of famine. All of them on the train and on the great Russian plain beyond were casualties of this war. Gathering speed, the engine strained and puffed, while the freight cars rattled and rocked behind it. A caravan was crossing the vast white desert.

Food. All three of them could smell food. The train was barely under way, and already around them people were eating bread and sausage; they were even passing food to one another. Where did they get all this? Slava wondered.

'Can't we have some too?' As always, Vera was practical.

'No we can't.' Slava's irritation was prompted by hunger pangs, particularly severe in such intolerable proximity, as well as Vera's reminder that he must have missed out on an important distribution.

'Aunt Katya said that when you're across Lake Ladoga, you can have all the food you can eat,' insisted Vera, not very sensitive to vocal intonations. 'Couldn't we ask them where they got it?'

The child was being tedious, and Slava was about to snarl at her, when his neighbour explained, 'They've given us some provisions to last to the next distribution place.' It was the same faculty member who had given him a hand up into the car. 'I can spare some for the children.' He gave the girls a few slices of bread and sausage. Before Slava could thank the good Samaritan, other offers came from fellow evacuees. One had dry biscuits to spare, another had a couple of sugar cubes. A resourceful owner of the saucepan bubbling on the stove announced that everyone was free to use his hot water for tea.

Eating Can Be Fatal

On the first night there was commotion in the dark. People groped their way to the waste bucket at the door. Dysentery had started, Slava thought, on top of dystrophy. At the next station a dying woman was taken off the train. 'In Leningrad we died from famine, now we'll be dying from food,' said Slava's new friend, whose name was Ilya Ilyich. At each stop now sanitary orderlies knocked on the doors. 'Any dead?' they shouted. For a long time, Vera and Nadya were puzzled why people should be begging for bread, when their job was to collect corpses.

In the first days people died from overeating; the sick groaned and rolled about in pain. Later the most frequent killer became dystrophy, when a wasted metabolism could no longer respond to nourishment. With each death, a little more floor and bunk space was left for the living. The girls now had a sleeping hutch under the roof. They spent most of the day up there as well, peering down at the activity in the carriage.

Washing and laundry was performed in the middle beside the pot-belly stove. That was where Slava scrubbed the girls, and then he laundered their pants and singlets in the kerosene tin. (The other clothes they wore remained unwashed.) And while they waited for their underwear to dry, Vera and Nadya sat wrapped up in the one blanket they had among them. At night Slava slept on the floor, wrapped up in his winter coat.

'Are they yours?' the evacuees asked Slava at the start of the journey.

'No, they're my sister's.' A lie was easier than explaining complicated relationships.

They had stopped in Stalingrad. It was on May Day, Vera insisted, because all the children were given a present — small jars of honey from America — and all the adults were talking about the Lend-Lease help to the USSR. Slava wasn't sure. After the Leningrad famine, his memory was full of holes.

'To think that a week or so later, and they mightn't have got through to the Caucasus.' Sofya shuddered at the thought of the repeat horror her children had escaped. 'They could have been caught in a second German siege,' she was saying to Dr Nikolsky, who had been called out to see a very sick Nadya. He diagnosed the illness as dysentery. There was an epidemic among the Leningrad evacuees, he explained. 'Don't worry, it's not life-threatening.' A large avuncular man, the doctor patted the child's head and the mother's hand. A normal diet, exercise, lots of fresh air would clear up the problem in no time, and put roses back in Nadya's cheeks. Slava did not accept this diagnosis. He suspected advanced dystrophy. He had seen a lot of dystrophy in the hospital wards during the famine; and was unhappy that he had not picked Nadya's condition sooner. For six weeks, while the train wound a circuitous wartime route from Ladoga to the Caucasus, the children were in his care. Why, then, had he missed the symptoms?

Nadya was now in bed all day. Her legs were useless; she could no longer stand up. She had no strength at all and could barely hold the orange her mother brought her. To hold — not to eat! Runny semolina and clear soup were the only things she could keep down, but even this rigid regimen did not stop her diarrhoea. The long and frustrating illness was one of the few clear memories of that period, perhaps because images of the famine were still indelible in her mind at that time. At night she was haunted by stacks of dead bodies and was sure that she, too, was going to die. Nothing had changed for her: all day and night, her pangs of hunger were as fierce as they had been in Leningrad. She watched her sister eating sausage and white bread, all that food they used to imagine and describe with delectable detail in the nights.

'Mama, keep my share for me!' Nadya ordered. 'Lock it away, safely. I'm going to eat it all later.' The child's face was as angry as her voice. Sofya divided the food evenly, in front of Nadya, and locked her portion in the safe. But secretly Nadya didn't believe that she would ever eat again or run in the yard with the other children, who had become Vera's friends in a matter of days. She watched them enviously when Slava, still the child-minder in the household, carried her outside into the sun. She was so light, he said, like a feather. And, he thought, too light to live.

Sofya, too, worried about Nadya's illness. She fretted even more about the hours of separation from her daughters, although she believed herself to be the most fortunate of women. She stayed up late every night doing all those mundane family chores she had been denied for a whole tortured year. Wonderful, marvellous chores. Cooking for her children, changing their sheets, mending their clothes. The sensuous delight of bathing them in the old tin tub, touching the soft skin, drying their poor little shaved heads, kissing, hugging them. Sometimes she caught a glimpse of herself from the outside, as she must appear to others, and saw a grown woman playing with dolls. Not that she cared what anyone thought. Her nightmares had ceased; she was learning to laugh again.

Early in the morning Sofya left for work. She ran down Gogol Street like a schoolgirl, jumped on the moving tram and forgot to shudder at the prison building as the tram took her past it. At the Myasokombinat her colleagues returned her smiles: 'Sofya Nikolayevna, you look ten years younger.' The people from smallgoods sent up samples of sausages: for the children. Everyone she met in the course of the day wanted to hear how her little girls were and when her colleagues found out about Nadya's illness, they demanded a daily bulletin on the child's condition.

Yes, Sofya thought, happiness was contagious, and she raced through the working day, counting the hours until she was back with her children in the evening. She had not felt such a passionate yearning to be with another human being since she was first in love with Alexei and they couldn't live apart. Now she couldn't bear to be away for long from her daughters. On rare occasions, she remembered her neglected friends, who had been her mainstay in the year of her agony, but she felt no guilt. In those inspired weeks of summer, Sofya had no thought for anyone but her children. And Slava! Of course, she cared for Slava too, and didn't want him to leave.

Man and Woman

Slava would soon be leaving for Central Asia. He had not heard from Nina, but at least he knew where she was now. He found out that her echelon had gone through to Tashkent. From other refugees he heard that life was not easy there, and food not as abundant as in the Caucasus. He planned to take along with him plenty of stock supplies which would not perish on a long journey in summer heat, in overcrowded trains. He now spent all his time bartering and buying, and already had a sack of flour and smoked smallgoods from Sofya's Myasokombinat.

Sofya didn't want to think about his departure. He was her children's saviour, and very dear to her, but there was a deeper need as well. She had grown used to his presence; he was her friend, a member of her restored family. To have a man in the house who loved her children and helped to care for them was another luxury. She didn't question his feelings for her; but a few times she caught his approving glance, and blushed. She, too, had looked at his still powerful body and wondered how he and Nina would have made love. How did she feel being kissed by that smiling mouth? She liked his hands with their fine and long fingers. The only sensitive thing about him, she silently mocked. There were times when she was repelled by this man from a different sphere; tactless in his conversation, with features crudely hewn and a mat of red hair all over his arms, legs and chest. His thickset body, with its short neck and burly shoulders, made her nervous. He was a Red Devil, as Anna Pavlovna had nicknamed him. She could understand his attraction, and why Nina had married him; when he was near her, she was also increasingly aware of her own need. Living in a crowded room, she could hear his breathing at night; she watched his expanding muscles as he practised callisthenics and weight-lifting. 'God forgive me, and keep me from temptation,' she thought. He was Nina's husband, had saved her children from famine, and here she was making love to him in her imagination. At times she was convinced that he had already guessed her erotic secret, and turned away in shame, but then she would be reminded how unobservant he was, and hoped he hadn't noticed her longing. In rational moments Sofya urged him to leave. (Before I make a fool of myself.)

'You must go, Slava. You can't wait for Nadya to recover.' She hurried his departure for Tashkent.

Yes, it was time to leave, he agreed. But Nina's silence concerned him. It could be that she had not received his letters from the Caucasus. He had not mentioned his wife's desertion to Sofya. And it was true that he was still uneasy about Nadyenka as well. Not so much her present condition — he could see that she was getting stronger — but he worried about how her experiences would shape her growth, her emotions. 'This child has been affected by the famine and deaths around her much more deeply than Vera or her cousins. Nadyenka will probably carry the scars of Leningrad for the rest of her life, physical and psychological,' he warned Sofya.

Sofya didn't want to think about the influence of famine on her children's future; she wanted the girls to forget Leningrad, and to clear her own mind of the nightmare she had lived through. She had suffered her own torment, the girls theirs. She realised that, as a doctor, Slava considered his analysis important, and was trying to impress its seriousness on her, perhaps to warn her because they might not have another opportunity to talk. Yet she thought irritably, 'These are theories, theories. This war will probably keep us apart forever,' and she didn't want to think about separation. From Tashkent Slava would be going straight into the fighting forces; he mightn't be alive by the end of the war. But she wasn't going to think about the future.

Slava was leaving on Monday morning. His first stop was Kislovodsk, where he would be joining other members of his institute. From there, all together, they would make their way to Grozny, then to Makhach Kala, and from there across the Caspian into Central Asia.

'All those places with strange names we used to memorise at school: the deserts, Kara Kum and Kyzyl Kum. The slit-eyed dwellers of Kirgizia. A glimpse of the Aral Sea. South towards Afganistan there'll be the peaks of the Hindu Kush, the Pamir, and the Tien Shan Mountains of China . . . I've grown fond of the mountains here in Pyatigorsk.' Slava was packing the provisions he had bought into one of the old Shubin suitcases, which they had discovered in the communal attic. Sofya wrapped the smoked meats and sausages in layers of paper and sewed the package into muslin. The flour, too, received several layers of protective cover. 'There,' she said biting off the thread, 'it won't burst open.' She was rather uneasy about the telltale smell of smoked ham, 'As long as people around you aren't too hungry . . .'

The day behind them had been busy and stiflingly hot; now, in the cool of late evening, they sat down with a glass of tea. The window was open into the wild patch of garden where white nicotianas had grown again, and glowed in the dark. Their heavy scent was stupefying. 'And so you'll be on your way to Central Asia,' Sofya sighed. 'Another journey . . . Where will it end, Slava?' Even imagining the ravelled journey that lay ahead of him, with all kinds of possible dangers, Sofya felt weary. Alone again. The girls were with her, thank God, but nevertheless she was alone in a world that was menacing her from all sides. The war was creeping closer and closer. A battle to the death was now going on in Stalingrad, and the Germans had started their advance into the southern steppes. What if they came to the Caucasus?

Slava put his arm around her shoulders. 'You mustn't be sad.'

Feeling desolate, Sofya grasped both his hands and pressed them to her heart. Here was a man who had so recently seen her sister Katya, brought her children back to her. No, he was not a saint, but a human being who had survived the Leningrad ordeal; had endured a long, long train journey to the Caucasus with two children. 'Thank you, my dear.' Her smile was tearful and tender.

He sensed her helplessness; the loneliness of a woman too long on her own. Her face was flushed, the waves in her hair reflected the lamplight and her heart was beating fast under his hand. Inside the loose neckline of a summer dress, her breasts rose and subsided with emotion. He saw a new Sofya, mysterious, deeply desirable. He freed his hand from her grasp and touched the tears on her cheek. 'Don't be sad,' he murmured, 'don't be sad.'

In the dark, cold months of famine, Slava had forgotten how quickly desire could rise, how urgent the need could grow. He sensed that if Nina had reached out to him at the time, he would have taken her without appetite, simply comforting another human being. Now, as he viewed a theoretical coupling from this unfeeling distance, it seemed to him a counterfeit of compassion. What he was feeling now was different and real: it was a hunger for Sofya that matched, or almost matched, the pain of famine. 'If I don't . . . If she won't let me . . .' but he didn't finish the thought. The need to enter, to possess, to find release from this ache, flooded his mind; reason was drowning in a tide of inarticulate sensations. He pushed her down on the sofa, pinning her with his hands and knees. In the light of the green lampshade, Sofya's face was a pale green, her eyes wide with understanding.

'No, Slava, please, don't,' she whispered, trying to push him off, to free herself from the weight of his chest on hers, from the heavy breath on her face. It crossed her mind that her tears might have invited this attack, but she couldn't cry out for fear of waking the girls and alerting the neighbours. 'The children,' she whispered, 'please, Slava, please don't wake the children.'

For a moment, he let go of her, but only long enough to turn off the handiwork of Nikolai Meier. Bony and strong, his body pinioned her down on the cushions. His hands took possession of her breasts, kneaded them painfully. 'Don't,' she pleaded, but his mouth silenced her, the tongue rammed deep into her throat, gagging her. He forced a knee between her thighs, and reached her with his fingers. 'You need me, you want me too,' he gasped.

'No,' Sofya cried out, but his mouth clamped down on hers again, and cut off her cry.

'Mama!' she heard one of the girls call out in her sleep. Which one of them? she wondered, and a sudden fear that her children would see her like this, unnerved her. Resistance was draining out of her, she couldn't fight his strength; she gave up her struggling.

He pushed himself into that compliant centre, his ravening need plunging deeper, deeper still, until he felt his thrashing, sweating, moaning being carried away on a warm wave of relief.

She lay so still under him that, for an uncomfortable moment, he imagined he had crushed her. She had suffocated under him. 'Sofya?' He pressed his cheek on her face, and felt her tears. 'Have I hurt you?' he whispered. She turned her face away sharply, and silently eased her body from under his. Still lost in the humid mist, he rolled on his back and released her. She slid on to the floor.

Moving softly in the darkness, Sofya found the soap and a towel, fumbled for the small enamel basin, and let herself out of the door. All was quiet. The corridor was dimly lit and empty. The bathroom door stood ajar. Sofya locked herself in and, with her back against the door, began to weep. Her tears wouldn't stop. Tears flowed and water flowed, as she scrubbed herself unsparingly, painfully, washing away her shame and punishing her guilt.

A Present from Alexandra

Nadya read the letter just before the Germans came to Pyatigorsk. It was wedged under the brass lighthouse with the green glass shade. She pulled it out, spread it on the table, smoothing out the creases, and began to decipher the purple words.

'Alexei died on 19 November . . .' The purple worms squirmed off the lines. Who was it writing that her father was dead? Nadya's face was freezing just seeing him in that pile of bodies stacked under a thick crust of snow.

'Nadyenka, what's wrong?' Sofya heard the silence, and then she recognised the letter in the child's hands 'Oh, my dearest, my love.' Tears of pity and of remorse dropped on the head of the child in her embrace. A blessing of tears. Her joy in the children's homecoming had been her own dispensation from grieving for Alexei. Just as she had put away Katya's diary, unread. Just as she had been telling the children to forget about Leningrad. For weeks nothing existed for her outside the walls of this room where her daughters smiled on her pillow every morning. She missed them at work. When she came home, all her senses were centred on the girls: their needs, their quarrels. And all that time she had put out of her mind that Alexei's winter jacket and boots warmed another prisoner. The child's face glistened with the salt of tears.

Sofya reached into the desk drawer. 'Here, Slava left this for you.' She had hidden it away, as she had quietly removed all traces of his stay in this room, and when the girls talked about him she ran to stir the soup in the kitchen. In the palm of her hand lay a cup from the 1812 coffee set. Small. Flawless. On the curved medallion the dead cuirassier was a sapphire on the snow.

'Oh,' Nadya whispered, 'it's a present from Aunt Alexandra,' and she traced the gold rim of the Napoleon cup with a reverent finger.

Epilogue

Another Country

> One day we realise we could not even find
> The path leading to that isolated house.
> Choking with shame and anger,
> We run there, but (as it happens in dreams)
> Everything has changed: people, possessions, walls.
> We are strangers knocking on the wrong door,
> And no one knows who we are. God help us!
> It's the moment of a most bitter truth,
> We realise we cannot cram our past
> Inside the borders of our present.
> That past is just as alien to us
> As to our next-door neighbour.
> We couldn't have recognised the dead,
> And the living, whom God has kept from us,
> Have managed splendidly without us.
> Perhaps, all this is for the best . . .
>
> From 'The Sixth Elegy', *Northern Elegies*, 1945

On her return from Russia, Nadezhda went to the bay. She would stay at the beach for a while, and gather her thoughts, she said. While she was in Russia she had almost lost the sense of who she was.

Her jest sounded like a plea, Andrew thought. She looked troubled and he did not try to dissuade her. He knew she was not deserting him; he could feel how important it was for her that he should understand her need for solitude, and accept it. She had to think things through, sort out the muddle in her head, before she could talk about the Russian experience to him. Perhaps if she wrote it all down, he thought, she might get it out of her system. But he read uncertainty in her eyes, and realised that she might not be able to put this story on paper.

She talked, as if she had found all there was to discover. The jigsaw of her childhood was complete, she said. Although a few pieces were still missing, and always would be, their loss did not seem to matter, or to distort the image. But from the shore of another country, much of the detail, resurrected at such cost, seemed trivial; the discoveries she had made had not given her a sense of absolution, or the peace she craved. While she was in Russia, a live current linked her with the past. It lit up the likenesses on the old photographs and the rusty ink of her mother's letters; it connected Sofya's stories with Katya's diary. Now the light had suddenly gone out, and she felt as though she had never searched, nor found all those rich memories. Akhmatova was right, she thought,

> We run there, but (as it happens in dreams)
> Everything has changed: people, possessions, walls.
> We are strangers knocking on the wrong door,
> And no one knows who we are . . .

Was the moment of their flight from Russia final? Was the moment, when Sofya picked up her bundle and her children and plunged into the river of refugees, a farewell? As they attached themselves to the retreating Germans, followed the Wehrmacht out of Pyatigorsk, out of Russia, the door behind them slammed shut. Just then she could see the three of them distinctly: Sofya, Vera and Nadya, in their winter coats and boots struggling through the slushy January snow of 1943. A mother and two little girls caught up in a dark current of fear. A stream of German lorries splashed alongside. Behind them barked the gaining Soviet guns. And with that same anaesthetised clarity her mind focused on the map of their flight, illuminating the forgotten names of towns where they stopped and rested, before the guns drove them out and on. A slow journey, she thought, it went on for months, for years before they reached this country. A journey which she had completed, again, in just two days. The immensity of the distance between the two worlds, between the past and the present, stretched to its elastic limit, and snapped.

'But you finished the book.' he could feel her distress and broke into the silence. 'That's excellent news.'

'Yes, yes.' She pushed the dark thoughts aside, hid them deep for later. 'How stupid of me, I was going to tell you about it straightaway. After all, Akhmatova was the real purpose of my visit. Except that, once I was over there, everything turned out differently from what I'd expected. Not Akhmatova! No, she became my saviour, my excuse for being there. You know, work on the book was the simplest part of my Leningrad stay. There were no unexpected discoveries. I made hardly any changes in the text. The final chapter fell into place without a hitch. As I told you on the phone, I left Akhmatova, finished and ready to go, with the publishers in London on my way through.'

Next day Andrew saw her off at the ferry. She stood on the deck, waving, as the boat tugged away from its moorings and sliced a path across the harbour towards the strait.

Here at the bay, winter was at an end, though the tracks in the bush were still mired in mud and the nights were cold. Spring, real spring with its westerlies and capricious weather, had not yet arrived. Nadezhda opened up the cottage on a bright, windless afternoon. The place had been locked up too long. It smelled of mildew. She threw open all windows and doors, to get rid of the damp, and pulled the mattress out on the porch for a good airing.

She had bought all her supplies and provisions on her drive through the township. As usual, too much. This food panic, she now realised, was her Leningrad legacy.

'Haven't seen you for a while,' said the owner of the supermarket. The locals always had to be put in the picture. Would she be staying long? Was 'hubby' down for a break too?

No, her husband hadn't come this time. She would be stopping only for a week, at the most.

'Well, I hope you'll enjoy nicer weather than we've had up till now. The past winter's been the wettest I can remember. And I was born and bred here. Must be the global warming they're on about.'

Stacking the tins of food, packets of pasta and lentils in the pantry, she kept an eye on the shadows of late afternoon. As soon as the sun set, a damp chill would breathe from the bush, and all her hard work of airing the place would be undone. She went out to fetch the mattress and stopped to watch the sunset. A red-hot ball was balancing on the nose of the mountain ridge. It slid behind the peak and began to sink. The western bank of cumuli ignited violently like a furnace, and tinted the sea below. The tide was drawing a veil of golden gossamer over the sand, washing away the footprints of seagulls and the hesitant signatures of snails.

It's the colour of precious metal, she thought. That's how the bay got its name. There are abandoned goldmines in the mountains, where men had dreamed of nuggets and died of greed. Until now, her bay had been a tranquil place, rimmed with the deep green of the bush, awakened by birdsong at dawn, with the tides breathing on the beach. Where she had just come from, she thought, the earth had been saturated with blood, for so many centuries, that it cried in pain.

As she watched, her bay was filling up with ghosts. She knew most of its legends, of course, but she had never before seen them reflected in the tide. Perhaps, on her past visits here, she had been careful not to disturb the peace with imaginings. Now she could see the violence in the bleeding tide, in the sinister shapes of the rocks, and in the burning sky.

She could hear the cries of the invaders, as the prows of their war canoes headed for the beach. And the people of the land, who had trapped birds in this quiet bush and fished in these waters, must stand and defend themselves. She knew the story. All the warriors on the shore would be killed. All the women and children, hidden in a cave behind an unmovable boulder, would die in their tomb, because there would be no one left to release them.